# The Boy That Comes From Nothing

"Came From the Struggle, had no choice but to be a Hustler."

Jukwan Brooks

Published by Bossman Kwan LLC

Cover Art by

Joshua Allen

Edited by

Isabella J.

# Table of Contents

# Foreword

## by

## Frederick Douglas Griffin

To The Reader,

You're about to dive into a book that's a lot more than just stories on paper—it's a beacon of hope, a survival kit, and a straight-up chat from me to you. "The Boy That Comes From Nothing," penned by Jukwan Brooks, isn't just any story; it's a personal recount from someone who has truly transformed his life in ways that many can only imagine.

Jukwan's journey is a testament to overcoming real-world struggles that many of us face—challenges like growing up in tough neighborhoods, dealing with family issues, and navigating life's unexpected turns. His story, which I've had the privilege to witness and support, echoes the resilience and determination needed to change one's stars.

Just like legends such as Kendrick Lamar, who spun poetic gold out of the threads of Compton's streets, Jukwan has crafted a narrative that speaks directly to the heart of every young person trying to make sense of their tough world. Jukwan and I have shared many pivotal moments together. We met after he grappled with the loss of his Granddaddy—the first real mentor he ever had. Watching him channel his grief into building a relationship with Christ and healing his relationships with his family was nothing short of inspiring. His journey from mourning to reconciliation, and from high school dropout to college graduate, spoken word artist, author, and media producer illustrates just how much one can achieve with the right mindset and support.

Here's how to make the most out of Jukwan's narrative:

- Build Your Tribe: Look around and find those who bring out the best in you. For Jukwan, it was initially his granddaddy, and later, others stepped in. These relationships are crucial; they're your rock.

- Knowledge is Your Armor: Jukwan turned his life around through education. Remember, every book you read and every class you attend builds you up. It's your armor against the world's challenges.

- Redefine Hustle: Keep your moves clean. Jukwan learned, and so should you, that the right kind of hustle—the one that builds, not destroys—is the only kind worth your energy.

- Give Back: As you find your way, don't forget to lift others. Jukwan's journey is not just about personal success; it's about setting a stage for others to follow. Volunteer, mentor, and share your story.

As you read this book, engage deeply. Reflect on your own story. How does it echo what you read? What moves will you make next? I encourage you to not just passively absorb but to actively participate. Discuss it with your circle, jot down your thoughts, and let this book serve as a catalyst for your own path forward.

Having walked with the author through many of the experiences shared in these pages, I've seen the power of a changed narrative. Now, it's your turn to grab the pen. Whether you're a young man or woman, your journey matters. What will you write in the next chapters of your life?

Jukwan's story is here to show you that no matter how tough things get, there's always a pathway to a better life. This narrative is a powerful reminder that your current circumstances don't define your future—they only set the stage for the greatness you can achieve.

My deepest gratitude to Jukwan. Being part of your journey has been an incredible privilege—one that I don't take lightly. Your resilience, determination, and unwavering faith have not only inspired countless others but have also reminded me of what truly matters in life. Walking alongside you through the highs and lows has been a profound experience, and I am humbled by the opportunity to witness your growth and transformation. Thank you for allowing me to be a small part of your story, and for continuously reminding me of the power of hope, perseverance, and the unwavering belief in something greater than ourselves.

And lastly, for those of you who share Jukwan's journey, remember that faith can be a guiding light in the darkest times. Keep your trust in God, and let His wisdom and strength carry you forward.

Stay strong, stay inspired, and remember: your story isn't written yet. Make it one worth reading

Best,

Frederick

# Acknowledgment

First and foremost, I have to thank my Father, the controller of everything in my life: The Most High My GOD, as he is the main reason I am the Great man I am today.

To my grandmother, the One and Only Arlene Brooks, I love you with all of my heart. You have been there by my side through the good and bad. You saw greatness in me, and you have done everything in your power to ensure I succeed in life. I love you always and forever.

To the man who taught me how to be a man, my grandfather Willie Terry Dorsey, I know you're smiling down from Heaven as you see the man I have become. You were my best friend, and you saw greatness in me before a lot of people did. You sacrificed a lot for me to win and succeed in life. I will never forget what you always used to tell me when I was a kid: "Never forget the bridge that got you across." Meaning, never forget where you're from and the people who helped you get there. I will forever make you proud, pops; I love you!

To my other grandad, my OG, as I would call him, Vincent Andre Lupoe Sr., I'm glad we reconnected with one another before GOD called you home. Not only were you a great mentor, but a great friend of mine. I remember when I first told you I was writing this book, you were so excited for me. As you told me, keep everything authentic with the book. You told me, "Motherfuckers don't know who you are; show them who you are." I know you are smiling from Heaven with Grandma Weaver, as these people know your grandson is a star.

Rest in peace to Cuater B. Weaver(My Great-grandmother) and Celeste Dorsey(My Aunt); both of these amazing women did their best to help me grow into a powerful man. I love you, and I will forever make you proud.

To my parents, Vincent Andre Lupoe Jr. and Jennie Brooks, I love you both. I forgive both of you for not fully being there for me. Even though we might not see eye to eye at times, just know I love the both of you.

To my four brothers, Damarion Hill, Markel Hill, Chase Hill, and Demarquez Howard, I love all four of you. All four of you are powerful kings who are destined to do great things. Remember to believe in yourself, be around the right people, and believe in GOD.

To my cousin, but also to someone who I consider a big brother, Cameron Brown. I love you, big homie. We're doing big things in a big way, and we're just getting started. Stay pushing, Big Things Popping, Little Things Stopping.

A special shoutout to the mentors GOD has brought into my life who saw something in me when most didn't: Frances and Wayne Cooper, Johnnie Clark, Kimberly Wilson, Mary Booth, Kenneth

Lane, John Benning (Rip), Dazzmo Hill aka Dee Dee, John Roy, Anthony Tutt aka Unc, Frederick and Anna Griffin, Jr. King and Natasha Jonelle, Steve Steward, and Paul Sanders Jr.

To the rest of my family, friends, and supporters, I love each and every one of you. Thank you for your love and support, as we are just getting started.

To my brother, the amazing person who designed the cover of this book, Mr. Joshua Allen. Thank you for your contribution to this book, but most of all, thank you for being a great friend.

To my editor, Isabella, thank you so much for your support and contribution to this book; you did an amazing job.

To my fans and supporters, thank you for reading this book. I hope this book entertains you and that you gain something life-changing from it. Stay tuned, as Jukwan Brooks and Bossman Kwan have a lot in store for you guys. Peace and blessings to you all, and remember you are a star destined to shine bright.

# Testimony

First off, I have to thank GOD for giving me the gift and guiding me into the man I needed to be to tell this story. The Boy That Comes From Nothing is a story dear to my heart as I am a boy who comes from nothing. As a kid, I grew up in the Thomson New Projects in Thomson, GA. My Dad been in prison since I was two years old. I didn't have the best relationship with my mother growing up. My grandparents raised me as they taught me about life and showed me the true meaning of love. Sadly, at the age of 14, I lost my grandfather, the only father figure I had in my life up until that point. Then, at the age of 15, I became a High School dropout. The odds were against me: I had no father figure or education and lived in a neighborhood where you are automatically considered a statistic. The only person that I felt that had my back in my life during that time was my grandmother. It seemed like I wouldn't amount to anything as the odds were against me.

People counted me out, as many people thought I would be nothing in life. But at the age of 16, I decided to accept Jesus Christ as my Lord and Savior. I told myself all I had to do was believe in myself and GOD and that great things would happen in life. Eventually, they did, as I got my GED at 17, and I graduated from college at the age of 20. Now, at the age of 23, I have a prominent job in the IT Field, a Spoken Word Artist, author, and media producer, and having my own business. I'm living proof that a boy that comes from nothing can make something of himself in life. It doesn't matter where you are from or what you have been through; you can be somebody in life.

# Introduction

The Boy That Comes From Nothing is a story dedicated to any individual that had to find success through hard circumstances. We have so many young people who get caught up in a street lifestyle. Which sometimes results in incarceration or even death. As a person who grew up in the hood, I have seen firsthand how being on the streets can negatively impact someone. This book is going to take you on a journey of how a young man tries to find his way in life and tries his best to find his purpose in life. This book is going to show you some of the things kids and teenagers in the hood go through. Just know it doesn't matter your circumstances or where you from you can be someone in life. This is for all my people that comes from Nothing.

15

# Chapter 1: The Street Hustler

Steven is an 18-year-old kid caught up in his environment and trying to make it out. He stays in the Harmony Projects with his Mom in Thomson, GA. His father has been in prison since he was a kid. Steven is a smart young man; he had the highest IQ out of everybody in his high school, and he was captain of the debate team at his high school. Unfortunately, due to his mother getting diagnosed with breast cancer, he dropped out of school at the age of 15. He has been selling drugs with his friend Darius ever since. Even though his mother has been in remission for two years, he still is addicted to the street lifestyle. This story will show you the hardships that a lot of young people and people in general deal with.

It's a Friday morning, and Steven is sleeping in his bed when his Mom wakes him up. "Mom, what do you want?" asked Steven, and his Mom said, "Boy, wake up; I'm about to go to work. Breakfast is on the stove, and instead of laying down all day, look for a job." Steven's Mom is well aware of her son's street activities; she hopes and prays that her son changes his ways, as she doesn't want him to be like his father.

"Alright, momma dang, I will." As she was departing, his Mom came to hug him and said, "Love you, Steven." He returned her hug and said, "I love you too."

Steven gets up to eat breakfast, turns on the TV to see a pastor preaching, and says, "I'm not trying to hear this old man speak." He turns the station to start watching one of his favorite TV shows, Martin. While watching TV, he gets a call from his friend, Darius. Darius is the opposite of Steven. While Steven is a laid-back person, Darius is a hothead who will do what he has to do to get his point across, as he has been arrested a few times. At the same time, though, Darius is a loyal friend of Steven's, and they always have each other's back.

"My boy Steve! what the move is?" Darius said. "You tell me, bro?" said Steven. "I'm on the block right now waiting for some people to come buy this product; you coming out today?" "You already know be out there by 12."

Steven takes a shower and gets ready to go on the block. Before he gets ready to go out, he gets a knock at the door. "Who's at the door?" He yells from inside, and a voice yells back, "It's the motherfucking police." Recognizing the voice, Steven opens the door and says, "Man, stop playing. I know that's you, Rich." Rich is one of Steven's childhood friends, and they went to school together. When kids used to pick on Rich about his height in middle school, Steven would always defend him. Rich is now the best High School Basketball player in their town and is being highly scouted by recruiters. As he comes through the door, Rich says, "My boy, what you about to get into?" Steven replies. "Man, I'm about to go on the block to get some money."

A frown is on Rich's face as he hears Steven say that, "Man, you need to get yourself a real job instead of selling on the block." Steven and Rich situations were different. The only support system Steven ever had in his life was his Mom, his grandma, who sadly passed away when he was twelve, and other people in the neighborhood who are trying to find a way to make it out just like him. In contrast, Rich was raised in the suburbs and had full support from his parents and family. "Now you are sounding like my momma; not all of us got a support system; we got to get what we need by any means." Rich feels like he made a mistake with his choice of words. "I didn't mean it like that, bro; I'm just saying it's more out of life than just selling on the corner," Steven says what he feels in his mind. "I feel you, bro; it's just that I see my momma struggling. I want better for her and me. And this is the only way I know how to get money quickly." "My guy, there are other ways; you got to let it come your way." "I hope it comes soon." "It will, my guy; trust and believe. Well, I got to get to work. I will talk to you later." "Alright, talk to you later; get that dough."

Steven finally leaves the house and makes it to the block to sell products with Darius. Steven pulls up on the block in his 1996 Black Chevy Impala, blasting Jeezy and Bankroll Fresh "All There". Dripped out from head to toe as he has on a black Tupac Shakur tee, black skinny jeans, and white vans." Darius daps Steven up and says. "Yo bro, where you been at?" Steven tells Darius about the conversation he had with Rich. Steven says, "Man, Rich came by the house, and I talked to him for a minute." Darius is curious about what Rich is talking about. "What fam was talking about?"

Steven tells Darius and asks how business has been on the block. "Just talking about life. Has it been busy out here?" Darius tells Steven what's been going on. "Naw, it's been just a few people out here." "People bound to come out soon." "True, it's a Friday, so we are bound to have a lot of people out here by 5 today. Going to be getting that guap and getting some girls phone numbers." "Yes, sir," Steven says with excitement. "Yes, sir, it's about to be lit!"

The guys are approached by Dee. Dee is one of the big homies that stay in the same neighborhood as Steven and Darius. He also ran the streets with Steven's Dad back in the day. Steven and Darius both see Dee as an Uncle. Dee daps both of the guys up as he says. "Little homies what your doing out here?" Steven tells Dee what he has planned on doing. "Man, trying to make some dough. What about you?" Dee, with a smile on his face, answers Steven's question, "Same thing; I'm going to throw a cookout on the block tomorrow; you're down?" Steven and Darius excitedly agree to attend Dee's cookout. Darius says. "I be hungry out here; we definitely need some grub." Steven agrees with Darius. "Yes, we do." "I'm going to throw it down tomorrow. Watch and see."

Darius finally sees customers coming to get products from him and Steve. Darius says. "Finally, some customers is coming our way; we are about to get paid." From 1 p.m. to 8 p.m., Steven, Darius, and Dee make $500 each from the products they are selling. Steven only sells Weed, pills, and lean. While Dee only sells weed on the side to make some extra money for his family. And Darius sells almost every drug on the market.

After hustling for the day, Dee talks about the money he made and the importance of it. "We got paid today, going to save up and make another 5 tomorrow. Darius says, "You aren't gone spend none of it." "Youngin, let me tell you something: when you save, you will have more. Remember this: it doesn't matter how much money you got that counts; what counts is what you do with the money," Dee responds. This helps Steven learn the value of money. Steven says, "That's deep. I never thought of it that way." Dee says, "It's facts; you got to appreciate the value of the things you have in life. Steven responds, "Yes indeed, I am most definitely going to do that." Darius also responds, "Me too, big homie."

Dee tells Steven and Darius how he wants to see them do good in life. "I want to see you win. You youngins have a better advantage in life than us old heads." Steven responds, "Best believe we going to make some things happen." Darius says, "Yes, we will." "Alright, homies, I got to get home; see you tomorrow," Dee adds.

After talking to Dee, Steven and Darius are trying to figure out what to do next. Steven asks Darius, "Aye, bro, what time is it?" Darius responds, "It's about 8:30; you trying to get into something." "I hear Diamond was throwing a party tonight; you want to go?" Asks Steven. "Hell Yeah, it's going to be some fine girls up in there. Even though I know you mainly hoping Dani be there," Darius adds. Dani is Steven's on-and-off again girlfriend. Steven starts laughing. "I'm not stressing over her, bro. The party starts at 9; let me call Rich so he can meet us at the party; you can ride with me," says Steven. "Alright, Bet," Darius responds.

While on their way to the party, Steven and Darius starts talking about life. Steven says, "I been thinking all day what Rich was telling me today." Darius asks, "What fam was talking about?" "He was talking about it was more out of life than what we are doing," Steven responds. "Bro isn't lying, but a nigga got to eat. I got my momma and a little brother to take care of," Darius adds. "I feel you, bro; we don't have no father or nobody to teach us how to be a man. We got to do that on our own," says Steven. "Sad truth only people that been through the struggle can understand the reason why we do what we do," Darius continues. "Big facts; I hope we can make it out of this place one day," says Steven. "We will, my G, best believe," says Darius. "I see Rich right behind us in his whip," Steven chips in.

Rich pulls up in his 2007 Ford GT Mustang, excited for the party. Rich says out of his window, "Y'all ready to get lit tonight?" Steven responds, "Let's Get it." Rich, Steven, and Darius walk into the party. Rich says, "Your it's lit in this place." Steven looks around the house and is ecstatic by the scene of the party, "Yes, it is, and the honeys are looking absolutely stunning tonight." Darius laughs and responds, "Bro, these girls got you talking like Carlton Banks, but they are looking fine as hell." Rich peeps out a girl, "I see a shawty I know from school. I'm about to put the key into the ignition." Steven and Darius wish Rich good luck. Steven says, "Alright, my dawg, good luck." Darius says, "Don't get shawty pregnant?" Rich says, "I know to put the mustard on the hot dog."

Steven and Darius get approached by Diamond. Diamond is also one of Steven, Rich, and Darius's friends whom they grew up with. Diamond stays two doors down from Steven. Steven and Darius always see Diamond as their little sister. Diamond says, "Well, well, well if it isn't the poor version of Lil Boosie and Webbie." Darius responds back, "Well, if it isn't wannabe Moesha, how you doing?" "I'm doing good, D; how you doing, Steve? Steven responds to Diamond, "Doing good; you about ready to graduate?" "Yeah, I wish y'all would have never dropped out of school; y'all should be on the stage with us," Diamond answers. Darius states his case on why he dropped out, "We had to do what we had to do." Steven says, "Facts, we had to get that dough; school wasn't teaching us how to do that." Diamond responds, "Y'all two smart boys, but so naïve that you can't see your potential." Darius doesn't want to hear what Diamond has to say. "Anyway, where the drinks at?" Darius asks. "Over there to the left," Diamond responds.

After Darius leaves to have drinks, Steven and Diamond have a deep conversation. Steven asks, "What you got plan on doing after graduation?" Diamond responds, "Plan on going to nursing school; why you still out here slinging Steve? I can understand with Darius; he always been a hothead, but you, why?" "This all I know what to do, to provide for me and mines," Steven adds. "I'm just saying, though, you're one of the smartest people I've met. You can be great and special. I see that in you; how come you don't see that in yourself?" Diamond continues.

Steven tells Diamond the main reason why he sells drugs, "I do see it. I just haven't found my way. I don't like slinging dope, but I do this shit because it helps me and my Mom out. You know, I started due to my Mom getting sick, but the amount of money I have made has helped us a lot. I used to have people laugh at me because of the clothes I wear; I got tired of that shit. Now I got people looking up to me." "Do you really think this is it for you?" Diamond asks. Steven responds with a sad look on his face, "I honestly don't know; I'm just trying to find my way." "I hope you find it soon," says Diamond. "I hope so too, but let's party," Steven responds.

Everybody starts partying and having a good time. While dancing, Darius enters into a pool game with Nikolas, a jock from his and Steven's former high school. Nikolas used to bully Darius and Steven when they all went to school together. He is a well-scouted football player for Norris High School. Darius yells out, "Yo bro, how much you want to bet?" Nikolas responds, "I will bet $50 we play three times." "Alright, bet," Darius adds. Darius and Nikolas play three games, and Darius beat him in all. "Tough luck, homie; better luck next time," Darius continues. Nikolas gets mad and starts roasting Darius, "You can have that money; at least I've an education. You don't have nothing without money and drugs." Darius gets angry, "What the hell you just said? Is there a problem we can take it outside?" Diamond sees the commotion and tells Steven to stop the argument. Diamond says, "Steve, you need to get your boy before something pops off." Steven looks over at the argument and says, "Not on my watch."

Steven runs toward the confrontation and says, "Aye, chill, what is going on?" Nikolas starts downing Steven and Darius. Nikolas says, "You need to get wannabe 21 Savage over here. Y'all nobodies without the drugs and the money." Darius starts getting angrier, "You're out of pocket!" Steven calms Darius down and defends them, "Hold on, bro, I got this; you are saying we nobodies, but you got seven dudes behind you like you're Donald Trump. You isn't nobody without them or without football. See, one thing about me and D is we loyal and real to ourselves. We don't need people to validate us. You got seven people around you to make you feel good and worthy about yourself; that's sad, bro." Nikolas responds back, "Whatever, I'm out of here; guys, let go, and Steve, good luck with just being another regular dude in the hood." Steven responds, "Whatever you say, Faker Mayfield." Everybody starts laughing after Steven says that.

After the argument, Darius expresses his gratitude toward Steven, "Man, thanks for looking out for me, bro." Steven says, "Always my G." Darius and Steven dap another up. Diamond gives Steven his props, "That's one thing I can say about you, Steve, you always helping and keeping it real with people." Steven says, "Got to stay real; can never be fake."

Rich comes downstairs while trying to put his clothes on after the argument and says, "Aye, I heard all the arguing upstairs; what's going on?" Darius responds with a laugh and asks, "Bro, you were knocking the whole time while everything was going on?" Rich has a big smile on his face and says, "Dang straight, shawty said she wanted a blessing, so I gave her blessings on blessings." Steven starts laughing and says, "Man, you something else. What time is it?" Rich tells Steven the time, "It's about 1 a.m. You want to call it a night?" "Yeah, we can call it a night," Steven responds. While Steven and Rich have plans on going home, Darius has his eyes on a fine girl. Darius says, "I see a fine shawty that been looking at me all night. I'm going to try to get the digits before I go." Steven smiles and tells Darius he will see him later, "Alright, my G, see you tomorrow."

Steven talks to Rich in his car before going home. Steven says, "So, how was it between you and homegirl?" Rich responds back with a smile on his face and also expresses his experience with women, "Man, that shit was amazing, but I get tired of messing with the same girls all the time." "What you mean?" Steven asks. "I'm a star basketball player, and I got girls wanting me because of my popularity. I want a girl that wants me for Rich, the person, not Rich, the basketball player," Rich responds. "I feel you, bro, but with you finna be going to college, you about to have a whole bunch more coming your way," Steven adds. "True. I might need you to come with me to help with that, lol," says Rich. "You are tripping, bro," Steven responds. What about your love life? You trying to talk to some other girls? Or are you still sprung on Dani?" Rich asks. "So, I guess our conversation done turned into an episode of Iyanla, Fix My Life." Rich starts laughing and says, "Bro, just answer the question."

Steven talks to Rich about his relationship status with Dani and what he dreams of in a relationship. Dani is Steven's girlfriend. Steven says, "Me and Dani been talking to one another for six months; I want us to have a great relationship. But she scared of how people might perceive her if it was known she was talking to me, with her being a cheerleader and a top student at her school. Granted, I'm a drug dealer, but I'm a good man. I know I'm a great man for her; the question is, 'Do she think that way of me?' I know I'm going to see her tomorrow at Dee's cookout, so I'm going to have a conversation with her about our relationship. Overall, I want a girl that brings pure happiness to my life, and one that accepts me for the person I am."

Rich gives Steven some encouraging words, "You are a good dude, bro; one of the realest people I ever met. The right girl is out there for you. It might be Dani, or it might not be." "I hope so, my G," Steven responds. "You going to be something special, bro; you just got to see it in yourself," says Rich. "I believe I will," Steven responds. "Do you really?" Rich asks. Steven takes a long pause after Rich asks him the question and he truly can't answer the question, then says, "To be honest, I don't really know." "You going to be straight, don't worry," Rich adds. Rich and Steven dap one another up. "Alright, paper chaser, talk to you later, and remember what I said," Rich continues.

Steven walks into his house, and suddenly, a light turns on in the kitchen. It's Steven's Mom standing in the kitchen with an angry look on her face. Steven's Mom asks, "Boy, where the hell you been at?"  Steven answers, "I was at Diamond's birthday party."  "Oh, ok, that girl is going far in life. I wish I would've known; I would've gotten her something. Did you look for a job today?" His Mom asks.

Steven tells a bald-faced lie to his momma, "Of course, momma, I did. I went looking for a job at the new furniture place downtown." Steven's Mom shakes her head and expresses her concern toward her son, "Boy, you are lying. I can always tell when you lying, just like your daddy. The streets isn't going to do shit for you, but either put you in jail or in an early grave, son." Steven tries to calm his momma down, "Momma, why are you acting like something bad is going to happen to me? I'm being careful out here."  "Look at your daddy, son; he used to say the same thing; now he in prison for life. Do you want that to be you?" Steven's Mom asks. Steven answers, "No, ma'am, but momma, I'm just doing what I know. What I'm doing right now is helping us pay bills." Steven's Mom sadly accepts her son's decision with tears falling from her eyes. She bangs her hand on the kitchen table and yells, "Forget the money; I want my son; that money don't mean shit if you dead or in jail. Son, you're old enough to make your own decisions. It's up to you with what you want to do in your life. Goodnight!"

After the conversation, Steven starts thinking about his life. He finds a journal and starts writing in it. "What do I really want to be in life? I don't know. Deep down, I know I'm a good man; I'm a man who's trying to find his way. It's like darkness crowds my environment, but all I want is love and peace before my soul rests. I want to be happy, and all the stress and pain just drift away; I want to buy my Mom a house; I want to be a great man, but how can I be a real man if I have never even been taught how to be a man." Steven puts his journal up and goes to sleep.

It's Saturday morning, and Steven's Mom is cooking breakfast. Steven finally wakes up. Steven walks to the kitchen and says, "Yes sir, momma you are throwing down in here like our house is Waffle House." Steven's Mom responds, "Well, I know I got to throw down sometimes; Paula Deen ain't got nothing on me. So, what you have plan on doing today, son?" Steven responds, "You know Dee supposed to cook out today on the block, so I'm going to go out there." Steven's Mom says, "Ok, you be safe. Hold up somebody knocking at the door." Steven's Mom opens the door and sees it's Darius.

"Oh, it's Darius," says Steven's Mom. Darius says, "Hey, Ms. Connie, is Steve here?" Steven's Mom responds, "Yes, he is how you been doing?" Darius answers, "I been doing good, just out here living." Steven's Mom asks, "How your momma doing?" Darius says, "She doing good; she actually just got a new job at the hospital." Steven's Mom says, "OK, Jeanette, getting to the money. Well, look, I made some breakfast; help yourself to something to eat in the kitchen with Steven." Darius responds, "Yes, ma'am, I will." Darius walks into the kitchen as Steven gets done eating. Steven asks Darius, "Yo, what's going on, bro?" "Nothing much." Steven's Mom says goodbye to Steven and Darius, "Well, guys, I'm about to go on a little getaway with one of my homegirls; y'all stay safe and stay out of trouble." Steven says goodbye to his Mom and asks Darius what he plans on doing. "Alright, momma, see you later, so what's the move? What you trying to get into, D?" Darius is trying to go to the mall and wants Steven to go with him. Darius says, "I got my momma vehicle. I was thinking we could go to the mall before the cookout today." Steven responds, "Let me see how much I got saved up real quick, bro." Steven looks in his shoebox to see how much money he has saved up. "Aye, D, I got about three bands saved up, so I will go," Steven continues. "Alright, bro, I will be waiting for you in the car," Darius adds. Steven finally gets dressed up and goes to the mall.

While on their way to the mall, Steven and Darius discuss everything that happened last night. Steven says. "So, did you get with that girl that you were talking to last night?"   Darius laughs. "Hell Yeah, shawty was something special, bro, been thinking about her ever since; I hope I didn't get her pregnant, though." Steven gives a weird look toward Darius and says, "Yo, wait, I know dang well you didn't forget to put the mustard on the hot dog. As much as you be getting on to me and Rich about that." Darius puts his hand on his head and smiles. "What can I say? We had a great, passionate moment that made me feel alive."  "Shawty got you hypnotized out here talking like you Wale," Steven adds. "Whatever, bro, but I do appreciate you for having my back, bro; that was some real stuff you did," says Darius. "And I will do it again. I will forever ride for my brothers till the wheels fall off," Steven responds. "Grateful to have you as a friend; you like the brother I never had; we going to make it, bro best believe," Darius adds. Steven and Darius dap one another up. Steven asks Darius what he plans on doing at the mall. "No doubt what you got plan on doing at the mall?" "I got plan on buying a fresh fit for the cookout today," Darius responds. Steven thinks about how the day will turn out. "We going to be making some dough too. I know it's going to be a lot of people out there." "Hell yeah, it's going be a good day today," says Darius. "So, your momma going to let you have the car all day?" Steven asks. "Yep, I'm glad she is letting me hold it, bro; she got a new vehicle, so it mines now. I feel like Mitch in Paid in Full (The Movie) driving this thing," Darius answers. "So, I guess this makes me Ace?" Darius starts laughing. "I was going to say Calvin, but I guess so." "Bro, you play too much," responds Steven. "I know, but we're finally at the mall," says Darius.

Steven and Darius go into the mall and buy a couple of clothes and food. While there, Steven spots this beautiful girl at the Hollister store in the mall and is stunned by her beauty, as she has beautiful ebony skin and hair glowing like a gazelle. It's like looking at a model in a magazine. She has on an Aaliyah shirt tee, white skinny jeans, and Tommy Hilfiger White tennis shoes. Even though he has a girlfriend, in his mind, he feels there's something special about the girl he's looking at. "Yo D check out homegirl in the Hollister store; thinking about stepping to her," says Steven. Darius takes a good look at the girl and says. "Shawty is beautiful; she seems like an intelligent girl. You need to try to holler at her." Even though Steven is dating Dani, he is mesmerized by the young lady's beauty; in his mind, it's like he is looking at an angel and is scared to approach her. "Bet, but I don't know what to say," Steven lets out. "Just be you; your realism will impress her," responds Darius. "We about to find out." "Don't use no corny jokes either." "I won't."

Steven walks into the Hollister store and approaches the beautiful girl. Steven says. "Excuse me, beautiful. I had to come over and get your name." The beautiful lady turns around and says with a smile, "My name is Lily; you do that with all girls?" "What you mean?" Steven asks. "You always ask a girl her name as a first approach to get to know her?" Steven starts laughing and says, "No, you seem like a beautiful and intelligent woman. I could not help but to approach you. It's like what my guy Tevin Campbell says." Steven starts singing. "Can we talk for a minute, girl? I want to know your name." Lily starts laughing. "I know you didn't just disrespect Tevin Campbell with that terrible voice." "I never said I had a beautiful voice, but hopefully my good looks is impressing you," Steven responds. Lily smiles as her eyes sparkle. "You something else; you are asking me my name. What's your sir?" "Steven is my name, beautiful." "Ok, Mr. Steven, where you from?" "I'm from Thomson, GA; what about you?" "I'm from down here in Augusta. Just graduated about to start college in a few months. I actually work at this store; maybe I can help you find a great outfit?" Steven hits Lily with a great pickup line. "Well, you do have beautiful eyes, so maybe you do have the right eyes for a great outfit." Lily is charmed by Steven as her eyes sparkle. "Well, let me show you around wannabe Prince Charming."

Lily shows Steven around the store and finds him a great outfit. "So, what you think about this?" "I love it. I'm going to be dripping like a faucet; you do have a great eye for things," Steven responds. "Well, thank you." "So, you always be this nice and always looking out for your customers." Lily plays with her hair as she answers the question. "Only the ones that I'm attracted to." Steven is stunned and is excited by Lily's reaction. "Ok, so I'm attractive?" "You're alright." "Hmmm, if you say so, but could I have your number? I would definitely like to get to know you better." Lily smiles at Steven for a second and asks for his phone. "Give me your phone." Lily gives Steven her phone number. "Ok, let me have yours." Steven gives Lily his number. "There you go, beautiful; well, I have to go. I would love to talk to you again." "Ok, let me guess, talk to other girls in other department stores. Steven laughs with a smile on his face. "If they special like you maybe so." This makes Lily's eyes sparkle again in Steven's direction. "Just kidding. I got a cookout I got to go to, though," Steven adds. "Alright, well, Mr. Steve, you have a nice day and have a fun time at the cookout and don't be a stranger." "I most definitely won't be you have a nice day." Steven was super happy after meeting Lily. Lily is the type of girl any man would dream of being with. Steven loves the way she talks, dresses, and smells. And loves the way her eyes look into his eyes. Lily is different from any girl he has ever met, including Dani. He hopes he sees Lily again.

Steven walks around the mall and goes looking for Darius. Steven calls Darius, "Bro, where you at?" Darius responds, "I'm in the food court; come meet me there." "Alright, Bet." Steven meets Darius in the food court. And Darius asks him how it went with Lily. "So, did you get her number?" "Yes, indeed I did." Steven is excited to tell Darius what happened. "Bro, this girl is something special definitely going to try and get to know her more."

Darius tells Steven what he was doing in the meantime. "Well, while you were getting homegirl's number, I ran into this dude that be selling in the Hawks neighborhood two miles from here. Bro has a lot of clientele out here; he said we can sell out there sometimes; we just got to ask him first." "It's like 12'o clock right now. If you got some stuff with you, we could go out there right now and sell some stuff," Steven responds. "The cookout is supposed to start at 5, so we can make it back in time. I'm going to give bro a call and see what he says." Darius calls the guy he met. After the phone call, he gives Steven an answer. "He said we can come out there right now." Steven is curious about the guy Darius contacted. "Alright, but what you know about this guy?" Darius tells Steven he has nothing to worry about. "He seems legit; I'm not no dummy. I know he's not 12, plus I done heard about him from around the way. I'm not going to put us in a situation that will mess us up, trust me." "Alright, bro, let's go ahead and go out there," Steven responds.

Steven and Darius arrive in the Hawks neighborhood to sell product. Steven looks around and asks, "Where he at?" Darius sees him and says, "There he goes right there, the dude with the Braves jersey and hat." The guy spots Darius and Steven. Darius yells out, "Tony!" Tony is one of the biggest plugs in Augusta and wanted Darius to sell on his turf. Tony goes over and meet with Darius and Steven. Tony says, "Yo, Darius, what's going on, bro? Glad you took me up on my offer." Darius says, "Well, hey, got to stay on the hustle." "Big facts, who's your friend?" Darius introduces Steven to Tony, "This my homeboy Steven, Steven, this is Tony." Steven says, "What's up, bro," Tony says, "What's going on, little homie? One thing about me you guys should know is that I make sure my people eat. I got you all a corner off Jefferson Street; it be a good amount of people looking for product out there. How long your got plan on being out here?" Steven says, "Probably about three hours, then we going to head back to town." "Alright, sounds good to me; well, you go ahead and walk on the corner. Let me know If you need anything." Darius thanks Tony, "Alright, thanks for the opportunity." Steven plans on making a lot of money in Augusta. Steven says, "Alright, let's get to this money."

Steven and Darius sell their product on the corner for about three hours. They have customers coming to them almost every minute and getting money like crazy. Steven asks Darius what time it is, "Aye, bro; what time it is?" "It's 3:15, alright, we got to bounce," Darius responds. Steven and Darius walk from the corner of Jefferson Street to where Tony is at. Darius says, "Yo Tony, we about to head out." Steven says, "Yeah, we got to head back; how much we owe you for selling on your block?" Tony asks, "How much did you guys make?" Steven tells Tony the total amount, "About a whole band each." Tony says, "Alright, I will take 20% of what you earned." Darius and Steven agree with Tony's deal.

Steven says, "Alright, sounds good to us; here you go." Tony says, "Alright, you guys have a nice trip back home, and if you ever want to come back out here again, you let me know." Steven says, "Alright, appreciated, bro." Darius is amazed at how much money he and Steven made. Darius says, "These boys be getting paid out here." Steven was amazed, also. Steven says, "Man, Yes, indeed; imagine if we would've been out here longer." "We going to come back out here, but for right now, we going to go and get our grub on," Darius responds.

Darius and Steven drive all the way back to Thomson and go to Darius's house to get ready for the cookout on the block. Darius says, "Your I'm back in the hizzhouse; anybody here?" As Darius returns home, he is greeted by his younger brother, Danny. Danny says, "Yeah, me, bro." Steven says to Danny, "Yo, what's going on, Dan, see you getting bigger." "Well, you know, got to stay in shape for the ladies," Danny responds. Darius starts laughing and says sarcastically, "Ain't nobody checking for you?" Danny responds, "Nobody checking for you with that messed up hairline." Steven starts laughing and says, "Your some fools." Darius asks, "Anyway, did momma say when she was going to be back?" "Yeah, she said she will be back by eight," says Danny. "Alright, me and Steve going to go to the cookout on the block; you want to go with us?" "No thanks. I plan on having a couple of homies over, and we plan on playing a couple of video games." "Alright, do you need something to eat?" "Momma left me some money for me to order some pizza just in case I get hungry." Darius gives his brother some money. "Alright, here's forty dollars; get your homies some wings and stuff, bro." "Alright, appreciated, bighead." "You welcome, Junebug. Come on, Steve, let's go upstairs and get ready for the cookout."

Steven and Darius put on the outfits they bought from the mall. Steven looks in the mirror at himself as he has on a white button-down polo shirt, white shorts, white vans, and sunglasses on his face as he says. "Man, me and you are out here dripping. We going to have people looking at us like how them dudes was looking at DMX and Nas in Belly." Darius responds, "You always going to have people hating; that's how you know you winning. Man, you should've probably invited shawty from the mall to the cookout." Steven starts blushing, "Man, she does not seem like the hood type, and I don't want her to come around and see what we do. She's special, bro. I don't know if somebody like her would understand the life we live. I don't want her to think less of me, for what I don't have, the guy she met at the mall, that's the guy I want her to remember. Plus, you know Dani is going to be at the party."

Darius keeps it real with Steven, "I'm going to keep it real with you, bro; you a good dude, like I said before, one of the realest people I know. With Dani, she knows what you all about, but she doesn't act like she is fully committed to you. Don't waste your time with a girl who isn't giving her all toward you. Now, for the homegirl you met at the mall, for her to really like you, she got to get to know the real you. That means everything about you; sure, you might hide who you are and where you from, but the truth always comes out at the end." Steven responds, "True, you are not lying, bro, but I got to get her to know me for who I truly am. I feel it in my soul; I will see her again." "If it's built to last, it will. Anyway, you're about to be tested because it's going to be some hot girls at the cookout." "I already know, but most of them probably don't got the looks or beauty like Dani." Darius starts laughing, "Shawty got you whipped, boy." Steven starts laughing, "Man, whatever, let's go to this cookout. Alright, bro, Alright Danny, don't have no girls over." Danny responds, "Don't you get none pregnant."

Darius and Steven finally make it to the cookout. The whole neighborhood is outside for the cookout. Darius says to Dee, "Man, you're still cooking?" Dee responds, "I'm finna be done with the ribs and chicken, but we got mac and cheese, potato salad, collard greens, dressing, some hot dogs, sweet potato pie, pecan pie, and some red velvet cake." Steven asks, "You did all this cooking by yourself?" "Yes sir, I did. I'm one of a kind." As Dee says that, his wife slaps him on the back of his head. Dee's Wife says, "Negro stop lying. Boys, if you want some food, by all means, help yourself." Steven says, "Say no more. Anybody looking for some product?" Dee says, "Yes sir, especially with this free food, people coming around here about every five minutes. And, of course, the girls going to be here; you got some across the street right now checking you out." Steven and Darius wave at the ladies as they see them waving at them.

Darius tells Dee about Steven's love interest, "Oh no, Mr. Steve got his eyes on a girl already." Dee asks Steven questions about the girl, "Where she from?" "Her name is Lily; she from Augusta." "Ok, how long you known her?" "I literally met her today at the mall. This girl is something special by the way she look and the way she talks." "That's what's popping right there."

Dee asks Steven about Dani, who is actually his wife's cousin, "So, what's going on between you and Dani? I know you and her been talking for a while." Steven says, "Man, I want to take our relationship to the next level, but she acts like she is ashamed of me. I dreamed of being with her since middle school. Finally made it happen a couple of months ago, but I want us to be exclusive. I can see her and me being together forever, but don't treat me like I'm a nobody. Treat me like I'm your man."

Dee gives Steven some real dating advice, "Listen, she might be my cousin-in-law, but don't stay with a girl that don't treat you like the king that you are. She is supposed to be showing up here in a few. I will say this: have a conversation with her and ask her how she views you guys' relationship. The main question is, does she see a future with you? Either way, time will reveal itself."

After eating, Steven and Darius start dancing. While dancing, Dani approaches Steven as she is wearing a lovely white jumpsuit. Dani has a girl-next-door personality. Every guy wants a piece of her. She is smart and beautiful, but she only got her eyes on one man, Steven. Dani touches Steven on his back and asks, "Excuse me, may I have this dance?" Steven accepts her offer for a dance. "Yes, I will be glad to dance with you. Steven and Dani start dancing.

After dancing, Steven and Dani start talking. Steven asks, "So, how's everything been? It's been a minute since we last talked." Dani says, "Everything has been good; I've just been super busy with school and cheerleading. Sorry if it seems like I been distant. I have just been doing my best to focus on my future. The main reason why I came out here was to speak to you." "I'm glad you said that because we do need to talk about our relationship." "Can we go to your house and talk so we can have some privacy?" "My mom is out of town, so most definitely, you can come to my house; let me get my things, and we will go."

Steven goes to tell Darius he is about to bounce. Steven says, "Darius, I'm about to bounce; me and Dani about to go back to my house and chill." Darius says, "Alright, bro, express how you feel about her. If she still wants to keep your relationship a secret, send her back to the streets." "I'm definitely going to express how I feel; pray for the best."

40

# Chapter 2: Loverboy

Dani and Steven finally go to Steven's house to talk about their relationship. Dani asks, "So, how has everything been going with you?" Steven says, "It's been going good, mainly hustling and getting to this money. I want to talk about the future of our relationship. What do you see us being in the future? Are you ashamed of me?" Dani holds Steven's hands and says, "Look at me, Steve, ever since we met at our Debate match in High School. I have been in love with you. I love everything about you, including your mind, body, and soul. If I wasn't, I wouldn't be coming over here every weekend to come to try to see you. I'm not thinking about no other guy, but you. Plus, I'm not ashamed of you, but you are like one of the biggest drug dealers in Thomson, probably the biggest one. If it was known I was dating you, people would look at me a certain way. But I do see something serious in you. It's about time I show the world who my man is. I love you, Steve." "That's what I wanted to hear." This makes Steven feel truly loved by Dani, as he wants her to stay by his side.

While watching "All Day and A Night" on Netflix on his living room couch, Dani lies on Steven's lap. Steven asks Dani an important question while looking at the movie. Steven says, "Hey babe, if I was to ever go down, would you be there for me?" Dani looks into Steven's eyes and responds, "I'm the Clyde to your Bonnie; I'm your ride or die and will forever be by your side. Wherever you go, I will be there by your side. Do you ever think you will stop selling drugs one day?" Steven actually thinks about the answer, "I honestly don't know; I've been doing this since I was 15; this is the only occupation I know, and I'm good at it. Plus, I make a lot of money doing it. If I wasn't doing it, I wouldn't be able to afford the gifts I buy you. Then again, you never know how life works out."

The next morning, Dani and Steven wake up together in his bed. Dani says, "Well, good morning, sir; I must say last night was magical. You definitely know how to take care of a woman." Steven laughs, "Well, hey, I'm just a great man who provides great service; glad I was able to satisfy you." "It was my honor to be serviced by you, Sir Steven. Well, I shall be going home; see you later, Steve." Dani and Steven kiss one another as Dani walks out the door. Steve says, "See you later, my love."

Steven calls Darius after Dani leaves. Steven says, "Yo Day, what's going on?" Darius talks very sluggish as he smoked a lot of weed the night before, "Faded as hell, got super high last night, and I hooked up with shawty, who I met at Diamond's party. How did everything go between you and Dani?" "It went well; she decided she is going to be more open when it comes to our relationship. I love her, bro; as long as she stays riding for me, I forever got her back." "I hope shawty stays honest with you; if she's truly a real one, it will show. Just remember to value yourself even if she don't value you. You still going to try to talk to the homegirl you met at the mall?" Steven is glad that Dani wants their relationship to prosper, but he is still mesmerized by Lily. Steven say, "I can tell Dani wants to take our relationship seriously; I'm not going to mess with any other woman. Are you going on the block today?" "Naw,, bro I'm going take me a day off and just chill. Plus, Brock and Trey supposed to be doing their thing on the Block. What about you? What you going to do?" "I got plan to go with Rich to Warrenton to play some basketball with some people. He just texted me; he said you could come if you want." "Naw, I will mess with bro another day; I'm going to chill with family today. Me and you got to back to Tony's block in Augusta to get some more dough; them dudes be getting straight cash up there." "Hell yeah, I'm probably going back on the block tomorrow." "Alright then, I will see you tomorrow, bro." "Alright bro, take it easy."

As Steven gets off his phone call with Darius, Steven's Mom arrives back home after spending time with her homegirls. Steven goes downstairs to greet his Mom. Steven says, "Mom, you finally made it back. Did you have a good time?" Steven's Mom says, "Baby, yes I did; that retreat was something special; got my nails done, got my hair done; out here looking like Mary J. Blige, got some great massages, and did some karaoke singing with my girls." "But Momma, you can't sing." Steven's Mom shakes her head at Steve, "Boy, hush, I was in choir when I was a kid; just to let you know; I did get you something while I was gone." "What did you get me?" Steven's Mom pulls out a black Bible from her purse and gives it to Steven. Steven says, "You got me a Bible?" "Yes, I did. I don't know if this means a big thing or a great value to you right now, but I know it will one day. My son, you are a great man, a man that has endured a lot, but one that stands tall through the hardest times. I can't wait for the day that you become the full man God designed you to be. I have accepted that you're a drug dealer, but I don't see that lasting long. I know God has a higher calling in your life than you just being on a block." Steven takes the Bible, stares at it, and says, "Well, Momma, I can't wait for that day to come." "I want you to take this Bible and try to read it as much as you can. God's Word is the greatest and best word of all. But enough with what I did on my getaway; what did you do while I was gone, son?"

Steven tells his Mom about his relationship with Dani, "Well, the main thing that happened while you gone was I had Dani over the house. We talked about our relationship, and she decided she would make it publicly known that I'm her boyfriend. I feel like me and her relationship is stronger, Mom. I'm going to do everything in my power to be the man she deserves." "Happy for you, son. Dani is a great young lady. At the same time, that girl has a lot going on. And a lot of people are counting on her. Don't do anything to jeopardize your relationship." "I won't, Momma." "Son, let me ask you something: do you love yourself?"

Steven looks confused as his Mom asks him that question. "What you mean, Momma?" "What I mean is, do you love the man that you are? Do you love the way you live life? That's what I'm asking, son?" Steven thinks long and hard about his life before he answers his mother's question. "Honestly, Momma, I really don't know; I don't love being a drug dealer; I do it because I need to survive. And I do not want to be broke. I'm not going to lie; I do love the things it has brought my way: the money, the clothes, and being recognized. It makes me feel important; I did not feel that way growing up. I'm sorry, Momma if I embarrass you with what I do; I'm sorry for not being the son you wanted." Steven starts breaking down, crying, and thinking about the choices he has made in his life. Steven continues, "I guess I do not love the person that I am, but God knows I try. I do my best to be great; it gets so hard, Momma. I hope I will be able to make you proud one day."

Steven's Mom starts crying while seeing her son vent his frustrations. "Son, I never knew you felt like that. I'm sorry you did not have a lot of love in your life; I really am. Trust and believe, though; you're the son I have always wanted. We all have our faults in life; I love you for who you are. You are humble. I noticed how you give other kids some of your money so they can have something. You always help people in need. The other day, Ms. Arlene, down the street, was talking about how mannerable and intelligent you are. Son, you are something special; you are bright, and I am proud of you. Am I proud of what you do? No, I'm not, but I know one day you are going to be big. You already got kids looking up to you. Just wait; you are about to shine bright like the star you truly are. I love you, son, always and forever; don't you ever forget that." With tears coming from both of their eyes, Steven and his Mom hug one another. Steven says, "I love you, Momma!" "I love you too, Son! Let's wipe our tears and talk some more, my son," she responds.

"I got a letter from your father a couple of days ago. He wrote one for me, and you let me get you the letter so you can read it," says Steven's mom. While his mother gets the letter his Dad wrote, he wonders whether what his Dad said in the letter was good or bad stuff. "Alright, here is the letter your father wrote you; it's a long letter, but I think you might enjoy what he wrote for you," she continues. "Alright, Mom, I will read the letter," Steven reads the letter his Dad wrote for him.

Steven reads, "Dear Son, how are you doing? Fine, I hope; as for me, I'm good. You might not believe me, but I think about you all the time. I think about all the years I missed you growing up; I blame myself for why you are in the streets. Yeah, I know; your Mom told me you be slinging, plus I keep my ears in the streets behind these walls. I remember when you was a baby when I was out here doing my thing. I would have you with me at the trap houses while I was doing my thing. Looking back, that's something I'm not proud of. When I was on the block, I allowed the money to take over me. Not only me, but a lot of my other homies also became the same way. That's the reason I'm in here today; my homeboy Rico and I robbed this plug we knew to get more weight; in that process, the plug tried to get his gun, and Rico shot him. Me and him ended up getting caught 10 days later and charged with second-degree murder and other charges. Fucked my whole life up trying to get this fast money. I didn't have plans on being a drug dealer; believe it or not, my goal was to be a doctor. I was nineteen when you was born. I did not want you to struggle like I came up, but sadly, I was not thinking clearly like I should have. My mindset at that time was to provide the best way I knew how for you and your Mom. My father wasn't in my life either. When your mother had you, I told myself I was going to be a better father than he was, but I was wrong. Son, promise me, but also promise yourself when you have kids; do not let them struggle like we did. I created a group in prison a few years back that helps young men vent their frustrations and start seeing who they really want to be in life. End the generational curse that we've in our family. I believe you will get out the streets one day; you smarter than I am. I can tell by the way your Momma brags about you. I come up for parole in two years; hopefully, I can make it out, and we can have a father-son relationship like I always hoped for. I put visitation papers in the envelope just in case you might want to see me. I understand you probably got anger toward me, but just in case you want to see your old man, just fill out the letter. I love you; please stay safe and trust in Jesus Christ always. Tell that boy Dee I said wassup."

Steven gets done reading the letter his father wrote for him and sits back and thinks about what his father said in the letter. Steven's Mom asks him how he feels about the letter. Steven's Mom asks, "So, Son, what you think about the letter your father wrote?" Steven responds, "I did not know all that stuff about him. It's weird; it's like I'm reliving his life." "That's the cycle that most Black kids like yourself deal with in this world, but son, you will break that cycle. You might not see that now, but you will one day." "Mom, let me ask you something: what made you get with my Dad?" Steven's mom laughs and smiles, "What made me get with your Dad was he was charming, but what made me get with him was people looked up to him. Kind of like how people look up to you; that's something you and him both share." "Did he really want to be a doctor?"

Steven's Mom smiles as she reminisces about Steven's Dad. "He was a smart guy in school. He was an a-honor roll student who used to have all the women crazy about him, but as much as he was dedicated to the books, he was dedicated to the streets. He helped me get through nursing school; he also had a side job. He put down his dreams to try to make my life and yours better. I used to tell him he did not have to be a dope boy, but he used to always say he would get out one day. Your Father always been a good person; he just got caught up; that's one of the saddest things that happens in the hood. I hope he makes it out one day. Do you still hold anger toward your father?" Even though Steven is glad to get a letter from his father, he still has anger toward his father, mainly because he had to learn how to be a man on his own. Steven says, "That was a great letter he wrote. I finally felt like I got to see a glimpse of who he truly is, but I'm not going to lie; I still hold anger toward him for not being in my life." "There's nothing wrong with that; hopefully, one day, you can tell him how you feel face to face." "Me too, Mom."

Steven and his mother start eating breakfast. After they are done eating breakfast, they hear a knock on the door. Steven's Mom asks, "Who at the door?" Steven says, "Well, it is a Sunday morning, so we know it's not somebody trying to get us to go to church." As Steven's Mom opens the door, they see it's Diamond at the door. Diamond says, "It's me, Ms. Anderson, Diamond. Can

I come in?" Steven's Mom smiles and hugs Diamond. "Diamond, girl, yes, you can come into this house. How you doing, baby?" "I'm doing good, wassup Steve. I wanted to give you and Steve an invitation to my high school graduation." Steven responds, "When it's going to be?" "It's going to be this Friday," Diamond answers. Steven starts smiling. "You know we going to be there; you like a sister I never had. I'm always going to be there and support you, best believe." Steven's Mom responds, "Me too, baby doll. I see you as an honorary daughter; you know we got you. I'm going to buy you something nice. I know your father smiling down from heaven at you, girl." Diamond says, "Yes, he is, and I thank you for always being there for me; you guys are my family and always will be." Steven says, "I think this call for a hug, guys." Steven, Steven's Mom, and Diamond hug one another. Diamond says, "That was a good Moment; I know I was telling Steven that I wish him and Darius would be on that stage with me and Rich." Even though Steven's Mom is happy for Diamond, she wishes her son was also graduating. Steven's Mom says, "Well, I know they both will be there to support you. Hold up, somebody calling my phone; I will be back."

Diamond and Steven sit down and have a one-on-one conversation. Diamond asks, "Well, what's you been up to, Steven?" Steven smiles and can't wait to tell Diamond what's been going on. Steven says, "Mainly getting to this money, hustling seven days a week." "Hmmm, anywho, I see Dani put a pic of you and her on Instagram. Seems like you guys are finally making your relationship public to everyone." "I'm glad she mines. She's the only one I'm trying to mess with." "Happy for you, Steve; both of you stay real and loyal to one another." "Most definitely, what would be the main advice you would give a guy about a woman?"

Diamond gives Steven advice on ladies, "My main advice would be to recognize which one truly cares for you. Some women see a guy getting money or winning out here and want to be with them because of what they have, not for who they are as a person. And they start showing them off like they won a grand prize at a fair. Then you have smart-minded women like myself. We like guys that are smart minded, but a man with a plan. I mean, granted, a man who gets a lot of money is great to have. You know he can spoil you, take you on vacation, all of that fun stuff, but a man with a plan is way more powerful." Steven asks, "How is they more powerful?" "Boy, you got me feeling like Oprah talking to you; they are more powerful because they are thinking about the man and impact they will make in 5-10 years from now. In other words, the man with a plan and a vision knows he has a purpose in this life, which makes him stand out from other men. Like with you, for example, what do you have plan out in your life? Where do you see yourself being in 5-10 years from now?"

Steven doesn't know what he wants to do in life. He never really thought about his future a whole bunch. "Honestly, Diamond, I do not know; I got to find my way, I believe I will find my path to greatness one day." "You know what I notice about you compared to all the other dudes that be on the block?" "Naw, what do you see?" "You the only one on the block that don't be with a crowd of people all the time; like granted, you do be with Darius. The thing about you is that you do not need people with you to stand out; you just need yourself." "That's deep right there I never thought about it like that before."

"Also, I wanted to say I hope what Nikolas said at the party did not get to you." The words that Nikolas spoke to Steven didn't leave a negative impact on him. Steven responds, "I have been used to people like that all my life telling me I won't be nothing. Plus, that privileged white boy don't have no freakin idea what we go through in the hood. If he lived or been through the things me and Darius been through, he would not survive." "You always going to have people doubting you and looking down on you for whatever reason; the key thing is always to believe in yourself." "Big Facts, I'm not finna have nobody get my spirit down."

"That's what I'm talking about; you can't. I'm curious: do you think Darius will come to the graduation?" Even though Steven and Darius aren't fond of their old High School, they will always support their friends. "For you and Rich, I know he will be there; that's a rule me and him both live by. Always be there for the people that always show you love through the good and the bad." "That's love. I will always appreciate what you and Darius have done for me." "I will forever have your back, Diamond, we family; best believe." Steven and Diamond hug one another. 'Thank you. I shall be going now; my Mom is cooking Sunday dinner, so I got to get back." "Alright, sis, you take it easy. I'm going to get you something for your graduation."

Steven plays his video games until Rich picks him up to play ball. Steven's Mom tells Steven that Rich is at the house to pick him up. "Rich, out here to pick you up." Steven says, "Ok, I'm on my way down." Steven goes to hang out with Rich. As Steven goes in Rich's car, Rich says, "Loverboy, what's been going on with you?" "Diamond came over the house and gave me an invitation to your graduation?" "You coming to it, ain't you?" "Most definitely, I'm not going to miss it. You and Diamond always been there for me, but I got to ask how your Dad will feel about it?"

Rich's Dad is the High School's principal, Steven's mentor while attending High School, and Steven's coach on his debate team. He was very disappointed in Steven when he dropped out of High School. Rich says, "I know you and my old man had issues, but I think he would love to see you there, mainly because you are going to be there to support me." Rich responds, "I appreciated that, bro; I know your Father probably sees me as a Hoodlum or a thug, but that ain't me. In my mind, I feel like I got to do what I do; I don't care who you're; when you see your mother or parents struggle, that shit get to you." "I feel you, bro; I apologize if I ever made you feel like I downgraded or made you feel less as a person for what you do." "It's all good, bro. I know you be speaking from the right place; that's what I appreciate about you." "Just like you got my back, I got yours. I remember when I used to get picked on in Middle School about my height, you was the main one that stood up for me; that's something I will never forget." "That's love, my guy; you know I got you."

"I know word has been going around town about you and Darius being the biggest plugs in town." In reality, Steven and Darius are some of the biggest drug dealers in Thomson, as they make a lot of money off the product they sell.  Steven is curious about who has been talking about him and Darius. "Let me ask you this, though, who you heard this from?" "I was in Washington the other day. Some white girl was talking about these two black guys in Thomson on Harmony got that good stuff, then about four more people said the same thing about you." "It wasn't nobody on no hating shit or nothing like that, was it?" "Naw, it wasn't none of that, but if I was you guys, I would still watch out; you never know who watching you guys. I don't want to see your in jail." Steven takes what Rich says as a compliment rather than a warning sign, saying, "We going to do our best not to get caught up, best believe. So, have you decided which college you want to go to?"

Rich decides to tell Steven which College he is going to. "You promise you won't tell nobody, will you?" Steven is the first person to know about Rich's decision. Steven responds, "Nah, fam, I won't." Rich reveals to Steven his decision. "Your boy going to UGA; going to be the starting point guard for the team." "Let's go, I'm proud of you, boy, you are about to be big time. I see that now. What time your press conference supposed to be?" "At 11:00 on Tuesday morning, Nikolas got his at 10:30, so I'm after him." "That dude something else. I would not be surprised if somebody knocks him out by the way he talks." "I feel you. He is something else; hopefully, he changes his ways. We're finally here at the court, don't get those ankles broke." "You better tell that to your homeboys; I'm about to go Ja Morant on these boys."

"We about to see there; they go right there." Rich yells out for his homeboys, "Yo guys, this is my homeboy, Steven, Steven this is Jack, Kurt, and Lance." The three guys embrace Steven and start playing basketball for an hour. Lance says first, "Guys, I got to take a break; it's hot as hell out here." Rich responds, "I feel you I got to take a break myself." All the guys take a break from playing basketball. Kurt says to Steven, "Aye, Steve, you got some moves on you, bro; you must play a lot." Steven responds, "Nah, bro, I haven't played in like a year." "Sure, don't look like it. Bro out here playing like Allen Iverson, shooting fadeaways and everything." Steven appreciates the compliments, "Man, I appreciate all the love guys."

Jack and Lance eventually leave, while Kurt stays to get to know Steven better. Kurt asks Steven a few questions, "So, how you and Rich know one another?" Steven answers Kurt's questions, "We went to school together; we basically grew up with one another." "What school you go to now?"

Steven is hesitant to tell Kurt he is a dropout, but he decides to tell him anyway. "I dropped out after 10th grade to help my Momma out." Steven was scared of Kurt's reaction, but it turned out to be pleasant. "I understand you got to do what you got to for your family. My father dropped out of school, and now he is a real estate developer. I don't judge people; we are all God's children. We are not better than anyone else. Only the man upstairs can judge us for our actions and decisions." Steven feels great hearing Kurt's response and says, "That's real. I thank you for understanding my situation and not judging me; that means a lot." "No problem; we got to uplift one another. I hope you can hang out with us more in the future." This conversation makes Steven feel good, appreciated, and admired, something he has hardly felt in his whole life. "I appreciate you guys; I would definitely like to hang out with you guys more."

The guys go back to playing basketball; during the game, while playing, a beautiful girl starts shouting out Steven's name. Kurt asks Steven about the girl. "Aye, bro; who's shawty calling your name?" Rich says, "Bro got his own personal cheerleader; dang, I need to step my game up." Steven smiles as he notices who the young lady is and says, "That's the beautiful Dani; excuse me, guys, I got to talk to the beautiful lady."

Steven walks up to Dani to talk to her. Dani says, "Well, hello, handsome. I'm surprised to see you up here." Steven says, "Playing some basketball with a couple of friends of mine." "Well, I'm not surprised you play basketball; I found out last night you was good with the D." Steven starts laughing. "You're funny; what are you doing here?" "I was playing some volleyball with a couple of homegirls. Do you have anything planned right now?" "No, I do not; you trying to have some more fun?" "Yes, my Mom will be going to church within an hour. You can come back to my place, and we can have a great time." "That sounds great to me." "Let me give you a good luck kiss for your game." Steven and Dani kiss each other.

Steven goes back to playing ball. Kurt says to Steven, "Every dude down here been trying to get with her; you are one lucky son of a gun." Rich also says, "That's my boy; forget calling you Steven; we calling you Playboy Steve for the rest of the day." The guys play basketball for another hour and call it a day. Kurt gives Steven his number. "It was nice meeting you, Steve; we got to do this again." Steven says, "Alright, guys, I appreciate it; let's do it again."

As Rich gets ready to take Steven home, he sees Dani staring at Steven. "Welp, I guess I won't be taking you home I see you got a beautiful girl waiting for you to come her way. Go and enjoy yourself, bro. And remember, put the mustard on the hot dog." Steven walks toward Dani as she stares at him. Dani says, "You ready to come back to my place?" Steven says, "Yes, I am; let's have a great time and enjoy each other's company."

Steven and Dani go back to Dani's house to hang out. Steven walks into Dani's house. Dani asks Steven, "You want to smoke some weed?" Even though Dani has a girl-next-door personality, she also has a wild side. Steven answers, "You know dang well I don't smoke." Even though Steven sells weed, he doesn't smoke it. When it comes to selling drugs, he doesn't believe in using the product that you sell. Dani says, "Alright, I guess more grass for me; why don't you go upstairs? I'm about to put on something cozy." "Alright, sounds good. Don't take too long; which room yours?" "The one with the excellent smell in it; go in there, and we will have an excellent time." "Ok then, well, I will wait for you to come upstairs." Steven goes upstairs to Dani's room and waits for her to come in. Dani finally comes upstairs, stands in the doorway wearing beautiful black lingerie, and says, "So, Steve, you ready to have some fun?" Steven smiles like a little kid in a candy store and says, "I most definitely am." Steven and Dani start having sex.

After getting done having sex, Steven hears a door open downstairs and says, "Aye, I believe somebody downstairs." A lady yells out for Dani. The person downstairs is Dani's Mom. Dani's Mom says, "Baby, I'm back home!" Dani gets scared when she hears her Mom's voice. "Oh shit, that's my Mom, you got to go!" Steven wonders how he will get out of the house. "How I'm going to get out of here? How I'm going to get home?" "I don't know; you got a phone; call somebody and jump out the window." Steven gives Dani a crazy look and says, "Jump out the window? This ain't Fast and the Furious!" "If my Mom catches you in here, it's no telling what she will do." "Fine, help me open the window so I can get out." Dani helps Steven open the window, gives him a kiss, and says, "I will call you when I want to do this again." Steven responds, "Alright, I will text you when I get home."

Steven walks to the nearest gas station five miles from Dani's house and calls Rich to pick him up. Rich answers the phone, "Yo, Playboy Steve, what's going on?" Steven says, "Aye, bro, I need you to pick me up at Shell Gas Station off Davis Rd." Rich is curious about why Steven is at a gas station. "What you doing there for?" "Man, I will explain once you pick me up." "Alright, bro, I will be there in about 20 minutes."

Rich finally picks up Steven from the gas station and asks Steven why he wanted him to pick him up at the gas station. "Yo bro, why in the hell you want me to pick you up from the gas station? What happened?" "Alright, so Dani and I are getting busy when suddenly I hear somebody downstairs; then I hear the person say, Baby, I'm home." Rich is intrigued by the story. "She had another dude up in there?" "No, It was her Mother." "What The Hell." "So shawty like, you go to get out of the house, so I'm like, how am I going to get out of the house? Shawty talking about jumping out the window, like, what the hell? I ain't no Jet Li, but I had to do what I had to do. She gave me a kiss; before I jumped. I told her I would text her once I got home."

Rich is shocked by this story. "Dang, shawty got you jumping out of windows and hiding from Ma Dukes, bro; that might be a sign." "What sign what you mean?" "A sign that she might bring drama into your life." "I'm not going to lie; before we had sex, she wanted me to smoke weed with her, but you know me, I don't smoke. Bro, I ain't going to lie to you; she starting to remind me of the regular girls that be buying grams from me." "You just got to keep a close eye on her and protect yourself." "Best believe I will." Rich drops off Steven at his house. "Alright, bro, take it easy and remember who's real and who's not."  "Best believe, I will."

Steven goes upstairs to his bedroom and texts Dani. Steven texts, "Aye beautiful, I made it back home safe, that's if you care?" Dani responds to his message, "Of course, I care. If I didn't care about you, I wouldn't have had you at my house. I will try my best to make sure something like that never happens again."  Steven texts back, "Alright, when the next time you want to link?" Dani responds, "I will let you know. It will probably be in a few days, but for now, you have yourself a good night." Steven starts smiling and responds by saying goodnight.

Steven falls asleep and rest for the next day. It's Monday morning, and the sun is shining brightly outside. Steven wakes up and tells himself today is going to be a good day. Steven's Mom has already gone to work for the day, so he starts getting ready for the day. He fixes himself some frosted flakes and watches TV.

After eating breakfast, he calls up Darius. Steven says, "Yo, Darius, you ready to make some money on the block today?" Darius responds with some good news. "Hell Yeah, I'm out here right now. I got some news I got to tell you, but it got to be in person; it's some big stuff, bro." "Alright, bet, say less. I be out there in twenty minutes."

Steven irons his clothes, puts on his shoes, and heads to the block. As Steven heads to the block, he wonders what news

Darius has for him. "Yo Darius, what's the move?" Darius and Steven dap up one another. "Man, I got some exciting news." "What's going on, bro?" "So yesterday I got a call from Tony. He was talking about how much money we made out there on his block. And people been asking about our products. He was wondering if we could come back out there this week and sell some more stuff. I told him I got to get with you before I let him know. I told him I would let him know by the end of the day." Steven thinks about how much money he made last time. He thinks it would be best for them to go to their plug for more product. Steven says, "We made a killing last time we was out there. I will say before we go we got to get with Big Mike. He can give us a little bit more merchandise, and we can make more." Big Mike is Steven and Darius's plug; he's the one they go to whenever they need more product. Darius agrees with Steven. "Alright, let's go to bro house and get some more merch."

Darius and Steven go to Big Mike's house to get more products. Steven and Darius pull up to Big Mike's house. Steven and Darius are amazed by Big Mike's house. The guys look up to Big Mike. He's a big-time hustler who now lives in the suburbs and is from the Harmony Projects, just like Steven and Darius. A random guy answers the door, "Yo, what you need?" Steven says, "We here to see Big Mike; tell him it's Steve and Darius from the 500 block off Harmony Street." The guy tells Big Mike that the guys are there to see him. The guy comes back to the door and lets the guys in.

Steven and Darius walk to the kitchen and meet up with Big Mike. Big Mike is excited to see Steven and Darius, as he respects their hustle and ambition. Big Mike is a tall dude, super slim, and built muscles. He's nicknamed Big Mike as he has always been a tall person since he was a teenager. Big Mike daps up Steven and Darius and says, "Well, look who it is: the two main trappers out of Thomson. How can I help you out?" Steven tells Big Mike, "We was wondering if we could get some product from you." Big Mike responds, "How much you need?" Steven says, "We need to buy about three more bags of product." "Alright, that will run you up to $500; you got the money to pay?" "Yes, I do, here you go." "Alright, aye, Angie, get me some bags of kush grams and ounces. And a few bags of pills from the garage, that's all you want today?" Darius says, "Yeah, or else you got something that might interest us." Big Mike has something in mind. "Your interested in some more guns; I know last time your came, your got two 9mm handguns. I just got four 12 gauge's a couple of days ago. Your want to go and test them out." Both of the guys say, "Hell Yeah."

Big Mike takes Steven and Darius to his backyard to shoot some rounds off. Steven decides to shoot first. Big Mike says. "Alright, Steve, be careful of that kickback." Steven responds, "I got this, my guy." Steven shoots the gun, and it makes his shoulder go back. Steven slowly drops the gun, grabs his arm, and says. "Damn, that thing ain't no joke. Almost blew my shoulder up." Big Mike and Darius start laughing. Big Mike says, "You got to start lifting some weights, youngin. Darius, it is your turn."   Darius shoots off the gun; the gun does kick back, but Darius stays shooting as he lets off four more rounds." Big Mike says, "It's my go; let me show you youngins how it's done." Big Mike shoots 10 rounds straight like he's the Terminator. Big Mike continues, "See, your don't got a lot of weight on your shoulders, which is okay—got to go to a gym. It's all good; I had fun watching you guys. I'm going to give you guys some advice. No matter what this life brings, never fold under any type of pressure. Meaning, never give up; your strong guys, and I got nothing but love for you. Steven says, "We most definitely appreciate your advice. Thank you for everything you do for us. We going to go ahead and head out." Big Mike responds, "No problem, your take care of yourselves and be careful. And thank you guys for hustling on my block; your helping me make a lot of money."

Steven and Darius head back to Harmony Projects, and Darius calls Tony to let him know that him and Steven will be in Augusta this week. After his conversation with Tony, Darius speaks with Steven. "Alright, he said we could come out there all this week if we want to; he said we could come out today if we want." Steve says, "What time it is?" "It's about 12 noon." "Let's go out there tomorrow; we be down there for the whole week." "Sounds good to me; let me text him and let him know." Steven is happy thinking about how much money he's going to make this week. "We about to get paid, bro; we still got to keep things on the low."

"I feel you, bro; while you down there, you can visit that girl you met at the mall. It won't be like messing with Dani, who got you jumping out of windows like Jeff Hardy." Steven starts laughing. Even though Steven will be hustling in Augusta this week and is in an official relationship with Dani, he can't wait to see Lily. "I might pull up on her. Don't get me wrong, I love Dani; even though I met Lily once, it just something special about her." Darius smiles, "Well, you never know who might be the right one for you."

Steven and Darius sell product from 12-7 pm. Steven counts the amount of money he makes. Steven says, "We got paid today, getting that money over here." Darius responds, "Yes sir, how much you made?" "Made about $600; what about you?" "I made about $570 dollars; just think about what we going to make tomorrow. It's going to be a great week in Augusta."

As the guys count their money, Dee goes to speak to them. Dee says, "Young homies, what's going on?" Steven says, "Packing up for the day, me and Darius made a lot of dough out here today." Darius says, "How the new job going at the factory?" Dee responds, "It's going well so far; who knows, I might be able to hook you guys up." Steven considers the idea. "If it pays good, I will take it." Darius says, "I got Destiny calling me. I will talk to you guys later."

After Darius leaves, Dee and Steven have a one-on-one conversation. Dee says, "So, what you been up to, Steve?" Steven tells Dee everything that's been going on. "Mainly getting to this money, but also me and Dani talked, and she decided to publicly acknowledge me as her boyfriend. I hope me and her relationship prosper in the right direction." Steven smiles while thinking about

Dani. Steve continues, "Do you think it could work out between me and her?" Dee keeps it real with Steve. "I mean, I ain't God or a psychic, now, if her Mom find out about you and what you do, it's going to be a problem, but God and the universe always find ways to show you who real and who's not. Here's the main question: she know you a drug dealer; if you ever went down for something, do you think she will be there?" Steven wonders to himself if Dani is a ride or die. "I don't know. I hope it don't come down to something like that." "Either way, I hope it works out between you guys."

"I appreciate you, Fam. I got a letter from my father over the weekend; he wanted me to tell you hello." "I haven't heard from your father in years; what he been up to?" "He started a group in prison to help young people, and he comes up for parole in two years. Let me ask you something: did you look up to my father?" Dee tells Steven about how he looked up to his father. "Most definitely did; your father was a street genius. He was like a visionary, one of the smartest people I have ever met." "In your opinion, when did everything go wrong for him?" "He got in too deep. It happens a lot; a lot of guys get addicted to the money, the women, and want more. When I first found out what he did, I was surprised and sad. Your father looked after me many times on these streets, and made sure I had some money in my pocket. That is something you and him got in common: your make sure that your people eat. Try your best not to end up like him."

Steven reveals to Dee the reason why he joined the streets and stayed.  "When my Mom was diagnosed with breast cancer three years ago, I only had plan to do this for a quick minute. I got addicted to seeing more money than I have ever seen in my life. People respecting me, showing me love, making me feel important. Dee asks Steven a very important question. "Why you keep on doing this? I know you probably got a good amount of money saved up. Plus, you ain't like everybody else around here. You are one of the smartest people I ever met. You are more than a drug dealer."

Steven looks around and starts thinking about his life. He thinks about his future, asking himself what his purpose in life is. He realizes he can't be on the streets forever. Because if he stays slinging, he will end up just like his father. He makes an important decision. "Between me and you, I got about $5,000 saved up. I'm going to go for my GED once I have everything situated."  "Are you close to having everything situated?"  "Well, me and Darius got plan to go to Augusta this whole week to sell product. I know me and him are going to make a killing enough money that will make sure me and mines be straight for at least a year."  "So, you about to shut everything down, huh?"  "I got to. I can't end up like my father; this my last week doing this."

"How you think Darius going to take the news?" Steven has made the decision to be done with the street life after this week. He thinks about how Darius is going to take the news. Darius is a brother to Steven, so his opinion matters. Steven says, "I don't even know; I hope he accepts it, but not only that, I hope we can still be friends." "Your mud brothers, nothing ain't going to tear you guys apart." "I hope so; it's time for me to move on. I can't be out here no longer; this my last week. "I'm proud of you, bro." Dee and Steven hug one another. Dee asks, "You going to tell your Mom?" Steven plans to tell his Mom he is done slinging after his last day in the streets. Steven says, "I'm going to wait till I'm officially done, but Dee, I appreciate you, my guy. I got to get back home." Steven finally decides he had enough of selling drugs. He thinks to himself, "How will his life be once he is officially done?"

# Chapter 3: One Last Dance

Steven arrives back at his house and is greeted by an unexpected guest. As Steven goes to open his door, somebody yells out his name. Steven is stunned to see the person is Dani as she is standing behind him next to her car. Steven says, "Dani, what you doing here?" Dani responds, "I wanted to see how you were doing after everything that happened last night." "I'm doing fine even though I had to jump out of a window. Felt like I was Wesley Snipes doing that shit., but it's cool though. How was your day?" "It was great, mainly preparing for graduation next week and trying to see what colleges to attend." Steven walks up to Dani, puts his hand on her face, and says, "What I have always told you, you are smart you are intelligent. You can do anything that you put your mind to. You are a freaking rockstar, baby. You going to do some amazing things." "That's why I love you, baby; you always empower me." Dani and Steven kiss one another.

Steven invites Dani inside his house. "You want to come inside the house? My mother probably cooking dinner right now." Dani agrees to come into the house. "Most definitely, I haven't talked to Ms. Connie in a minute, so let's eat."

Steven and Dani walk into his house and look for his Mom. Steven says, "Mom, Where you at?" Steven's Mom responds, "I'm in the kitchen. I just got done cooking dinner; come get some of this food. Well, I see we have some company; hello, Ms. Dani, you are looking beautiful as always." Steven's Mom and Dani give each other a hug. Dani responds, "Thank you, Ms. Connie. You are looking beautiful, as always. Would you mind if I have dinner with you and Steven?" "I don't mind, sweetie pie; your come in here and eat before the food gets cold."

Dani, Steven, and his mother sit down for dinner. Steven's Mother asks Dani some questions, "So Dani, how's your mother doing?" Dani responds, "She's doing well; she's still doing her thing as a lawyer. I'm just doing my best to try to be like her." "Well, always remember to just be yourself and stay true to yourself. I know you are getting ready for your High School Graduation; you have any plans what you going to do after you graduate?" "I got a scholarship offer from Georgia Southern University to be a Nurse Practitioner. But I'm still undecided what I'm going to do." "Well, like I always tell Steven, follow your heart, but also follow the footsteps GOD has laid upon you. My precious son, how was your day today?"

Steven wants to tell his mother he is getting out of the drug game. Instead, he decided to keep it to himself. "My day has been great. I believe this week is going to be a beautiful one." "What makes you so sure of that?" "GOD been speaking to me, Momma; I just feel great things are going to come my way. Just know I'm going to do my best to be the man you raised me to be." "I know you will, son; you are a great man. Dani, my son has his ways, but stay believing in him. He's going to be a force to be reckoned with." Steven smiles at his Mom as he says that. Dani smiles in Steven's direction.

After eating dinner, Steven walks Dani outside to her car. Steven asks. "What are you doing this Wednesday evening?" Dani responds, "I don't have nothing planned; why?" Steven wants to take Dani out on a date. Steven says, "I want to take you out on a date and treat you like the queen you are." Dani only has one answer to that. "Well, my Prince, I shall have a wonderful night with you on Wednesday. I love you, Stevie." "I love you too, Dani." Steven and Dani hug and kiss one another.

After talking to Dani, Steven goes to his room and starts writing in his journal. Steven writes, "Made a tough decision today, finally decided to drop out of the drug game; it's time. I can't end up like my father; I feel it in my heart. I'm destined to be somebody special; granted, do I know what I'm destined for? No, I don't, but I ask that God show me the right path, that he shows me the way to be great and be a powerful man. I feel like I might actually be getting love and happiness now in my life with Dani. I hope and pray that our relationship prospers in the right direction. I feel like everything is finally coming together."

Another day has come, and Steven wakes up and gets ready to go to Augusta with Darius. Steven thinks about the potential money he will make this week and is thinking how his life will turn out once he is done with the street life. Steven and Darius go to Augusta to sell product. On their way there, Steven is slightly nervous to tell Darius he is leaving the drug game. Darius says, "This week is going to be a huge week for us; we going to make a whole bunch of money out here." Steven says, "Yes indeed, have you ever thought about how life would be like if we wasn't selling drugs?" "I do think about it sometimes, you know, growing up, I had dreams of being my own businessman, but I love the money that I'm getting out here." "You ever think about getting out?" Darius grows suspicious of Steven's Questions. "One day, but this is really all I know: getting this money all at once. Not only does it help me out, but it helps my mother and brother out, too. Let me ask you something: why all of a sudden you asking me these questions?"

Steven tells the reason why he asked Darius those questions. "Man, the real reason why I asked you these questions is I decided this is going to be my last week selling drugs; man, I got to get out." Darius pulls over the vehicle with tears in his eyes. "I knew one day this day would come. What made you decide to finally quit?" Steven tells Darius the reason why he is quitting the drug game. "I can't be like my father; that's why I got to be better. With the amount of money you and I are going to make this week, it will keep me and my Mom straight for a good while." "What you got plan on doing then?" "I'm going to try and get my GED. I don't know where this life is going to lead me. I'm going to do everything in my power to be successful."

Darius gives Steven encouragement, "You're one of the smartest people I've ever met; I remember when your Mom got sick, you came to me, and you said I got to get some money. I didn't want to put you in the game, but I know how it is seeing your mother struggle and you feel like you can't do nothing about it. Me and you been out here since we was 15; we ain't blood, but I will always consider you a brother and family. You're more than a drug dealer; when we was in school, you was the smartest person there. You got potential; I know you are going to do something great." "I appreciate it. What about you? You ever think about getting out?" Darius keeps it real with Steven. "This is all I know. I'm able to get my Mom and little brother stuff. Not only that I never want my brother to struggle and do like me and you. It's hard out here when you don't have a father, but also not a lot of support. You got to fend for yourself; it's hard. I will get my life strengthened out one day; when that day be, I don't know. I support your decision, and I'm always here for you no matter what." Darius and Steven hug one another. "Same here, my dawg; let's get back on the road so we can get to this money." "This is our last week together in these streets. Let's go off with a bang."

Steven and Darius also talk about their love interests. "I also got a date with Dani on Wednesday." Darius is amazed. "Bro, you something else; what you got plan on taking her to?" "I got plan on taking her to Red Lobster. I feel like wining and dining with my lady." "I see you, my boy, getting fancy out here." "So, what about you and Destiny? Are your just hooking up, or your dating?" Destiny is Darius's girlfriend. "I'm kind of in the same predicament you in; I'm just trying to get to know her." "I hope it works out for you." "I hope so too; we almost by Tony's spot; be prepared to make some bread."

Steven and Darius arrive at Tony's spot to start selling products. Tony claps his hands and smiles when he sees Steven and Darius. Tony says, "Well, if isn't the two country boys, how you're doing?" Steven says, "We doing good; we ready to make some cash."  "I heard that. How long your got plan on being out here this week on the block?" Darius says, "We was wondering at least six hours every day this week if that's ok with you." Tony responds. "I see how much money you guys made in three hours, so most definitely. I'm going to get your to go on the same block you guys was on before." Steven asks Tony if they pay the same percentage as before. "We still give you 20% of our profit, right?"  "Yes, sir, I'm going to get my boy Lenny to walk your down to the block. Lenny about the same age your is, so I think your will get along fine. Yo, Lenny, come over here; this is Steve and Darius. Steve and Darius, this is Lenny."

Lenny is one of Tony's best distributors on the block and the youngest on the block. Lenny says to the guys, "What's going on, guys? You're ready to make some money?" Darius responds, "Yes indeed." Lenny says, "Alright, let's go to the block." From 12-6 p.m., Steven and Darius make $1,500 each. Steven smiles brightly as he counts how much money he made. Steven says, "Man, we got paid today; this is probably the most money we done made in a day." Darius says, "Yes indeed, imagine what we are going to make this whole week." Lenny is impressed by the way Steven and Darius hustle. "Your some dangerous motherfuckers. I've never seen nobody like your sell product like that. Where you're from?" Darius responds, "We from Thomson." Lenny says, "Ok, I done heard about Thomson before, so you're going to be out here all week?" Steven responds, "That's the plan; let me ask you something what is the most money you done made out here?" "The most I done made in a day is $2,000; believe it or not, that was on a Saturday. Saturdays are the best days to come out here and get more clientele, which equals more money in your pockets."

Steven and Darius get to know Lenny. Steven says, "I feel you on that; how old are you?" Lenny says, "I'm 17; been doing this for about a year." Darius asks, "What made you start slinging, bro?" Lenny reveals his life story to Steven and Darius. "I had a tough life; my father been in and out of jail my whole life, so it just been me, my Momma, and my little sister. Last year, my mother lost her job; she started struggling with her bills. I tried applying for jobs, but due to my record, nobody would hire me, so I decided to come out here and get some dough." Darius says, "So, do your Momma know you be out here?" "She do; she always tell me I will find my true potential." This reminds Steven of what his Mom tells him. Steven says, "My Mom says the same thing to me, so what did you do to go to jail?" Lenny says, "When I was 15, I was a part of a home invasion. I was charged with armed robbery. I did 2 months in juvenile jail. I'm still on probation till this day for the crime I committed." Steven responds, "Dang bro, your story is kind of similar to ours, but we got your back; we going head back home; you stay safe." Lenny responds back, "Appreciated, and your do the same." While talking to Lenny, Steven notices the similarities between the both of them. It was like looking in the mirror and seeing himself.

The next day, Steven and Darius return to Augusta and make the same amount of money they made the day before. After hustling for the day, Darius drops Steven off at Dani's house. Darius says, "Alright, bro, handle your business; you want me to wait for you?" Steven responds, "Naw, meet me at the gas station nearby. I will call you once I get done."

Before Steven even knocks at the door, Dani opens the door, pulls him in, and starts kissing him. Dani and Steven have sex. After having a fun time, Steven and Dani relax and watch TV. Dani smiles and looks at Steven. "I needed that great exercise today." Steven responds, "I'm glad I was able to help you with your cardio and squats."

Dani asks Steven for a favor, "I was wondering, could you give me a 3.5? You still selling it for me at $25 right?" Usually, Steven sells a 3.5 for $35, but for Dani, he gives her half price. "Yeah, same price, you got to stop smoking that stuff when it comes to your stress. Either way, any issue or situation you have, you going to have to face heads on." "I know I'm going to stop smoking one day. I can't wait for our date tomorrow." "I feel like one of the old guys in the movie. I'm going to wine and dine with you." "I appreciate your generosity and can't wait to see more of it tomorrow on our date. And I promise I will reward you for your generosity." "I'm going to hold you to that; well, I'm going to go before it starts getting dark. You have a great night, my love."

Steven calls Darius to pick him up. Steven says, "Aye, bro, I'm headed to the gas station to meet you." Darius says, "Alright, I'm going to meet you halfway." Darius picks up Steven. "This is one big neighborhood; the time I dropped you off, I hurried up and went to the gas station. I didn't want this bougie folks to think I was staking out the house." Steven starts laughing. "Bro, you hell them people don't know you." "When you black and brown, you always got to be careful. I see that our boy Rich going to the University of Georgia to play basketball. Steven and Darius are happy for their friend's accomplishments. Not too many people make it out of Thomson, so for Rich to get a scholarship offer, it's a huge deal. "This is a proud Moment for the city; I'm proud of him; bro about to do big things."

"Facts, I know this: when bro make it to the NBA, he better give me some tickets; I'm trying to sit courtside with Lil Baby and them at the Hawks game." "Out of all of the people you would want to sit next to, you pick Lil Baby. Why?" "He's a real dude; not only that, when you trying to be a boss, you always got to try to hang around boss people. If you had to choose, who would you sit courtside with?" "It would be between Floyd Mayweather and Zendaya." "Why?" "See, with Floyd got millions of dollars, I can get a lot of game from him just by sitting next to him, and with Zendaya, she fine as hell. She's the type of girl I would marry." "I feel you on that; those some good choices. Darius drops Steven at his house. "Alright, boss, we will get back at it tomorrow." "Alright, bro, take it easy."

The next day, Steven and Darius go back to Augusta and make double the amount they made the two days prior. After coming back from Augusta, Steven drives back home. Steven walks into his house, and his mother has his outfit laid out for him for his date. Steven's Mom says, "My son, I got everything prepared for you. Are you ready for your date?" Steven responds, "I'm a little bit nervous. I got to meet her Mom, but I think I will do fine." "Son, I know you will. You're charming and intelligent, and you got this. Now go get ready." Steven puts his clothes on, gets his car keys, and goes to Dani's house.

Steven pulls up to Dani's house and knocks on her door. Dani's Mother answers the door. Dani's Mother says, "Hello, how may I help you?" Even though Steven and Dani have been dating for six months and have known each other for a while, this is his first time meeting Dani's mother. Steven says, "Excuse me, my name is Steven, and I came here to pick up your sister." Dani's Mother starts laughing, "I'm her mother; you are a very charming young man; please come inside. Dani, your date is here to pick you up." Dani yells out, "Ok, I will be down in a few minutes." "Ok, sweetheart, so Steven, where are you from?" Steven doesn't want to tell Dani's Mother all about his life, so he gives false information about himself. "I'm from Thomson, Ga. I go to school at Norris High School." "That's great to hear. It is always great to hear a young black man doing great things." Dani finally comes downstairs. Dani says, "Well, I'm ready to go; my stomach is calling for some food." Steven is amazed at how well-dressed Dani is as she is wearing a beautiful red dress. Steven says, "Well, I must say you're looking very stunning tonight." Dani responds, "Same here; you look very handsome." Steven says to Dani's mom, "Well, Ms. Martinez, we are going to head out. Do you want us to bring you anything back?" "No thanks. You guys have a great time. Be safe."

Steven and Dani arrive at Red Lobster for their date. Dani says, "So since we are here, let's eat up and enjoy ourselves." Steven responds, "Most definitely enjoy yourself, beautiful." Steven decides to tell Dani about the big decision he made in his life. "Babe, I made a huge decision in my life. This is going to be your boy last week selling drugs. I'm officially retiring from the game. I can't end up like my father. I've always told myself I can't be like him. Plus, with the amount of money Darius and I are going to make, it will have my Mom and me set for a good couple of months. And Dee told me he will hook me up with a job at the Mcduffie County Factory. And I'm going to school to get my GED. I'm going to start making the correct moves and be the person I know I'm destined to be. Tell me what you think about everything?"

Dani gives her reaction to Steven's decision. "Babe, I'm so happy for you. I'm glad you decided to go back to school. I mean, you are the smartest person I know. Your intelligence is what impressed me the most about you. You was a great captain for the debate team at your high school. Somebody with your mindset and expertise is destined for great things. You are going to be a great businessman, and I can't wait to be the leading lady by your side."

Dani decides to talk about her passions in life, too. "Even though I do have a couple of scholarship offers, I'm not going to lie; I feel like dancing is for me. You know better than anybody I'm a good dancer. I would love to open a Dance Academy for kids. Be like the Debbie Allen of my city. My Mom, though, feels like dancing isn't a real career. I honestly don't know, Steve, what to do when it comes to my future." Steven gives Dani his honest advice. "Forget what anybody got to say; do what you love. You don't want to live your life with regrets. Go for everything you want, and don't let a damn thing stop you." Dani is motivated by Steven's statement. "Thank you Steve; seriously, I needed that. Tell me, what is special about me?"

Steven spits a freestyle for Dani. "Indeed, it was your good looks had me hooked on you like a crack addict; looking into your hazel eyes is like looking at a butterfly in springtime. You are as fine as a dime that I want to make mines forever.." Dani is amazed by the beautiful description Steven gave of her. "Ok, Mr. Kendrick Lamar Jr., you know how to make a lady feel special." "Every time you look in the mirror, you should feel special." Dani starts smiling. "You are one amazing man, Steve."

After their date, Steven and Dani go back to her house. Steven says, "Well, that was a great time. I hope you had fun?" Dani says. "I did. Aren't you forgetting something?" "Oh yeah." Steven gives Dani a kiss. "Not just that, the weed." Steven goes to the back of his car and gets the weed. "Here you go, don't let your

Momma see that weed." "I won't. I guess I will see you on Friday." "Yes, I will.

Steven goes back home after taking Dani home, and his Mom is waiting to hear how the date went. Steven's Mom asks, "How was the date?" Steven responds, "It was good; I met her mother, and she seems like a nice lady. We had a great time, and I believe Dani might be the one for me." "I'm happy for you, son; she's a lucky lady."

The next morning, Steven tells Darius and Lenny about his date. Darius asks, "So, bro, how was the date with shawty?" Steven says, "It was amazing. I know this might sound crazy for an eighteen year old to say, but I feel like Dani is the one for me." "I'm glad everything is working out for you." Lenny says, "I can't wait to experience that one day." Steven says, "It will happen, bro." Darius says. "Aye, guys, your see that black vehicle."

The black vehicle had been passing by the neighborhood for the last couple of days, and it never stops by to buy any product. Lenny says, "Hell yeah, fam been passing by here for about two weeks, never buy any product." Steven is skeptical and says, "We need to watch for him. It could be 12 or an opp." Darius responds, "I will tell Tony about that."

Steven thinks about the graduation party in Thomson tomorrow. The party is being thrown at Rich's house. Steven says, "We got to get ready for the graduation party tomorrow." Lenny asks, "What party?" Darius and Steven respond. Darius says, "It's a graduation party tomorrow in our hometown." Steven says, "If me and Darius would've never dropped out, we would be graduating, too." "Dang bro, so why your dropped out?" Darius explains, "I was a hothead when I was in school; they kept on sending me to alternative school. Not only that, my mother was struggling to raise me and my little brother, so at 14, I dropped out and been out here hustling ever since." Lenny asks Steve also," What about you Steve?" Steven answers, "When I was in school, I was one of the smartest students you would ever meet, but when I was 15, my mother was diagnosed with breast cancer. She couldn't work, so I had to step up. I got with Darius; me and him been out here ever since." "That's a story. Is your mother ok now? Is she in remission?" "Yes, she has been in remission for two years. I honestly don't know what I would do without her."

Hearing Steven's story, Lenny resonates with him. "I feel you; I feel the same way about my Momma." Steven invites Lenny to the graduation party. "You know something? You should come with us to the graduation party tomorrow." Darius says, "Yeah, bro, it would be a great way for you to get out of town, but not only that, make some more money." Lenny accepts the invitation, "I appreciate guys. I most definitely will go with your to the party." Steven responds, "Alright, bro, we are going to be going to the graduation first, then the party, just to let you know." Lenny says, "Alright, no problem." "Alright, fam, we going to head out; we will talk to you tomorrow."

Before Steven and Darius leave, they tell Tony about the black car. Tony says, "Hey, you guys about to head out?" Steven responds, "Yes, sir; here's your twenty percent." Darius says, "I know me and the guys been noticing this black car passing by the neighborhood, but never buying product; you know who that person is?" Tony already knows about the black car. "No, I don't know. You are not the first person to tell me about this black car. Some of the other guys on the other blocks are saying the same thing; all I would say is just watch your back, even when you're in Thomson. This is just part of the game; you always got people looking at you for whatever reason. Now you have a safe trip back to Thomson, and I will see your tomorrow." Steven responds, "Alright, Tony, we will catch up with you." In Steven's mind, he had a bad feeling about that black vehicle; he had a feeling that the person in that vehicle would finally reveal themselves.

As the guys walk away, Darius asks, "What's your opinion on that black vehicle?" Steven responds, "I agree with Tony; we just got to watch our backs." Darius asks Steven about how he feels about going to the graduation, as he feels Steven might feel a certain way about not graduating. "So going to the graduation tomorrow won't be hard for you?" Deep down, Steven wishes he was graduating tomorrow, but he hides his feelings. Steven says, "Why would it be hard for me?" Darius responds, "Because you was supposed to be up there graduating tomorrow." "No, it won't. I'm just mainly going to the graduation to support our friends." "Alright, bro, just wondering; I know the graduation party tomorrow is going to be lit." "It's going to be something special;

we going to make a lot of bread." "Big facts, alright bro, I will see you tomorrow."

While Steven walks into his house, he gets a text from Lily. The girl he met at the mall a couple of days ago. Lily texts, "Just to let you know, every time I listen to Tevin Campbell, I think of you now." Steven laughs as he reads the text.

The next day, Steven and Darius come back on the block in Augusta. Darius puts his arm around Steven and says, "Well, one more day, and it won't be no more Day and Steve out here." Steven wants to go out in a big way for his last day. Steven says, "Yeah, man, I was thinking since tomorrow is our last day together, we should go back to the Harmony block and sell one last time." "I think we should sell everything 20% percent off." "That's a great plan; go off on top." "Are you going to miss it?" Steven thinks about the work he done put in the streets. "Honestly, bro, I really don't know; only time will tell."

Lenny comes on the block and talks to the guys. "Yo, my guys, what's going on?" Darius says, "What's going on with you fam? I see them fresh J's you wearing." Steven also says, "For real, bro, you dripping out here." Lenny smiles. "I got to be fresh for the party later tonight, don't I." Steven responds, "True, it's going to be a great night, aye bro; what time it is right now?" "It's 12 o'clock." "Aye, I'm about to head to the mall then." Darius responds, "What for, oh, you trying to see homegirl in the Hollister store, that's why." "She texted me last night; I want to go up there and surprise her. A man and woman can be friends. I'm with Dani, and I'm not trying to play around." "Alright negro, I will give you the keys to the car and let you drive up there. I'm not going to leave Lenny out here by himself." "You can come with me if you want." "Nah, I'm trying to make some more bread; you can take my car, Steve. Just don't mess it up." "I won't. I know how your Momma is appreciated fam."

Steven takes Darius' Car and goes to the mall to see Lily. Steven goes into the department store where Lily works. Steven walks up to Lily and says, "Excuse me, I'm looking for a beautiful girl to help me look for a great outfit." Lily acts sarcastic and says, "Of course, sir, I'm a lady that has a great eye for beautiful things." Steven starts laughing. "Let me stop playing. How are you doing?" "I'm doing great, especially now that you are here; I actually got you a gift just for you." Steven is impressed by the gift. "You got jokes; you got me a Tevin Campbell CD." "I was looking at steps that can make an awful singer turn into a great singer, but I had a feeling you will like the CD better." "You funny. I should take you to a karaoke bar just to see if you can sing or not." "I got some vocals on me, but I got to get back to work. I will hit you up; we need to hang out sometime." "Most definitely, Lily; you be blessed." The only girl Steven is seeking is Dani, but he feels a genuine connection between him and Lily.

Steven returns to the block after going to the mall. Darius wonders how it went between Lily and Steven. Darius asks. "So, Steve, how did it go?" Steven says, "It went great; she gave me a

Tevin Campbell CD. I'm not trying to get with her, but it's something about homegirl I just can't explain." Darius says, "You never know; it could be a divine connection." "True; anywho, how much money your done made?"

Lenny says. "I done made about $500." Darius says also, "I done made about $600." Steven counts his money, "I done made about $400." Lenny sees the black car from yesterday. "There go that black car again!" Darius says, "It's finally pulling up, Steve; since you got the less amount, go ahead and see what homeboy wants." "Alright, let me find out about this mystery man." Steven walks up to the black car and tries to see who is inside. "Hey, bro, anything I can help you with today?" Random guy says, "Yeah, I heard you guys got the best product out here. I was wondering I could buy three zips of weed and some ecstasy pills from you." "Man, you must be throwing a party or something like that." "Something like that, how much will that cost me?" "It will cost you about $200." "Sounds good to me." "Alright, let me get the weed and pills for you." Steven goes and gets the weed and pills for the random guy. "Alright, bro, there you go." "Appreciated; me and my guys are definitely going to love this." The random guy drives away.

Lenny asks, "What bro wanted?" Steven responds. "He wanted three ounces of weed and some pills; that's what he wanted." Darius asks, "Did he seem suspicious?" "No, he seemed like a dude that smokes weed." Darius responds, "Probably just a regular dude, we probably stressing about nothing." Lenny asks,

"So, what time are we leaving for the graduation party?" Darius responds, "Well, first, we got to go to the Graduation, which is at 6, so we need to leave at 4." Steven says, "It's about 1:30 now, so we got to hustle some more." Steven, Darius, and Lenny stay selling on the block until 4. Darius says, "Alright, guys, we did a good job; let's call it a day."

The guys give their 20% percent to Tony and head to Thomson. Steven, Darius, and Lenny arrive at Steven's house. Lenny says, "I must say you have a nice house, Steve." Steven responds, "Appreciated; we going to introduce you to some of our people at the party. I'm going to go upstairs to call Dani to see if she needs us to pick her up or find out if she's going to meet us there."

Steven calls Dani. "Hey beautiful, do you need me to pick you up for the graduation party?" Dani responds. "I'm going to meet you guys at the party; I expect us to have a magical night." "Yes, indeed, it's going to be a special night." "You better save me a dance." "I got you; see you tonight, love."

Steven and Darius get dressed for the graduation. Darius looks at Steven and says, "Brother, you looking sharp." Steven has on a red denim jacket, white Derek Jeter jersey, blue denim pants, and Air Jordan 12 Retro Cherry. Steven responds, "You are too, bro; we going to be dripping like hell." "It's going be a lot of girls around us tonight." "I'm just trying to be around Dani tonight." "Well, like Rich always says, make sure your mustard is on the hot dog." "You already know." "Your mother going to meet us there?" "Yeah, she pulling up right now in the driveway."

Steven's Mom comes back home and sees Lenny on her couch. Steven's Mom says, "Steve, I'm here; who is this young man sitting down on my couch?" Steven introduces his Mom to Lenny. Steven says, "Mom, this is Lenny, a good friend of mine from Augusta; Lenny, this is my mother." "Hey, nice to meet you, ma'am. Steven and Darius invited me to go with them to the graduation party tonight." Steven's Mom responds, "Well, that was nice of my son and Darius to do that; any friend of my son is like family, so I know you won't be no trouble, so please make yourself at home." Steven asks, "So, Mom, do you have Diamond's gift?" Steven's Mom says, "Yes, I do. Do you have your gift for her and Rich?" "Yes, I do." Darius says, "Hey Ms. Anderson, you looking beautiful today; Steven and Lenny, ready when you guys are." Steven's Mom responds, "Well, Darius, you looking sharp tonight. Don't get involved in nothing crazy tonight." Darius smiles. "I will try my best not to, ma'am." "The same goes for the both of you, Steven." Steven responds, "We will be safe, Mom; we will see you at the graduation."

All of the guys go to the auditorium downtown for the graduation. As the guys walk into the auditorium, they see a lot of people in there. Darius says. "Well, Lenny, welcome to the famous Norris High School Auditorium." Lenny says, "This is a big auditorium." Steven says, "We had some great times up here. We used to have all of the debates here, competing against other people." Darius reminisces also, "I had my first kiss in the first row." Lenny laughs, "You is one wild boy."

As the guys are hanging out in the auditorium, Steven and Darius are greeted by a former teacher of theirs. Their former teacher says to Lenny. "Yes, he is a wild boy; this is one of the most obnoxious students I ever had. Steven, what's going on? I haven't seen you in years. Steven is one of the brightest students I've ever had." Mr. Dixson is not just Darius and Steven's former teacher, but also Rich's father. Mr. Dixson shakes Lenny's hand and asks, "What's your name, young man?" Lenny says, "My name is Lenny; I'm good friends with Darius and Steven." "They both got their ways, but they're good people. They looked out for my son when he used to get bullied, and for that, I'm forever grateful to them. Steven, do you mind if I talk to you by yourself for a minute?" Mr. Dixon was Steven's debate coach and mentor during his time in High School. Steven responds, "Sure, Mr. Dixson."

Steven and Mr. Dixson step away from the guys to talk and reconnect; this is their first time talking in three years. Mr. Dixson asks, "How's your mother doing?" Steven responds, "She's doing good; she will be here tonight, so you will have a chance to see her." "Well, that's good to hear. Can't wait to see her. The main reason why I wanted to talk to you is to see what you are doing in your life."

Steven didn't know how to reply to Mr. Dixson's statement; he didn't want to tell him that he had been selling drugs ever since he dropped out of school. "I been mainly making sure that me and my Mom are straight; I also been thinking about signing up for GED classes." Mr. Dixson says, "You know something, Steve, out of all the students I taught, you was the smartest and most knowledgeable one out of everybody. The way you can utilize your skills and the way you could analyze a problem and solve it in great detail is something special. I'm not a fool; students talk about what you and Darius do. Rich told me what you said about me thinking that you are a hoodlum. I don't think that way about you. You are a smart, intelligent young man who has been given great skills by God, but with what you are doing, you are wasting your life away. It pains me that you are not one of the students walking on the stage tonight because a person with a great mind like yours should be up there tonight. Steve, I see you being a successful man in the future who can make a great impact on this world. Overall, a man who can be an inspiration to others. I hope and pray that one day, you see that in yourself and be that person. It was great seeing you, I got to get ready for the graduation." Steven thinks about what Mr. Dixson told him, which motivates him to turn his life around.

Darius asks, "What Mr. Dixson was talking about?" Steven responds, "He just wanted to know what I was doing in my life." "Man, always wants to know what his students up to." "Yeah, well, let's go sit in the stands and wait for the graduation to get started."

Steven, Darius, and Lenny sit in the stands as they watch the graduates walk across the stage. As Steven watches the graduates walk across the stage, he looks at his mother and feels disappointed in himself for not being on the graduation stage. Small tears come out of Steven's eyes, which he quickly wipes away.

After the graduation, the guys go and congratulate Diamond and Rich. Diamond says, "Hey guys, thanks for coming." Darius responds, "You know we wasn't going to miss your big day." Steven says as he hugs Diamond, "Not a chance in hell; happy for you, girl; you looking very beautiful tonight. Here's the present I got for you." "Who is this handsome guy standing next to your?" Steven introduces Lenny to Diamond, "This is Lenny, Lenny, this is Diamond." Lenny says, "Hey, I agree; you look very beautiful tonight." Diamond responds, "Thank you. Are you coming to the graduation party tonight?" Lenny responds, "Yes, that's the main reason why I came." "Well, save me a dance at the party." "I most definitely will." "I see your Mom waving at me, Steve; I'm going to go talk to her and get my gifts. See your later tonight."

Rich walks up to the guys and says, "My guys, what's going on; your boy is officially done with high school. I'm out of this place!" Steven hugs Rich. "Happy for you, bro; here's my present, man. I hope you enjoy it." "I know you're coming to the party; it's going to be huge, bro. Who's the new guy?" Darius introduces Lenny to Rich. "This is Lenny, Lenny, this is Rich." Lenny says, "What's going on, man? I seen you play in Augusta; you got some hops on you, bro." "Appreciated, man. The only thing I got plan on hopping on tonight is a fine woman. I got to talk to some more people. I will see your at the party." Steven, Darius, and Lenny talk to some more people and head to the party.

Lenny says to the guys, "We finally at the party, it's so many baddies up in here." Darius says to Lenny, "You better cuff one tonight." Steven looks at the crowd and focuses on the amount of profit he and the guys will make. "Alright, guys, let's have some fun, but also let's make some money." Steven, Darius, and Lenny make $500 to $1,000 selling product for the next hour. Darius says, "It usually takes us a whole day to make this, but we made it in an hour." Steven responds, "We just that damn good money makers and hustlers over here." Lenny smiles as he sees how much he made. "I'm glad I met you two; your done helped made me more money than I have ever made." Darius says, "You remind us of how we was when we first started." Steven says, "Sure do you like a little brother to us. We know you a real one." Lenny says, "I appreciate it; I haven't had a lot of people look out for me." Steven and Darius hug Lenny, and Steven says. "We got your back, bro."

As the party continues, Dani shows up and finds Steven. Dani says to Steven, "Hey, handsome." Steven responds, "What's going on, babe? You are looking sexy tonight. Let me take you to the squad. You already know Darius, and this is my other homeboy, Lenny." Darius says, "What's good, Dani; it's been a minute; you looking good as always." Lenny says, "It's nice to meet you. Steve's a real dude definitely stick by his side." Dani responds, "I most definitely will, speaking of which. Steven, do you want to dance?" Steven says, "With you anytime of the day." Dani and Steven dance for the next 30 minutes. Steven says, "Girl, you can get down. Do you want something to drink?" Dani responds, "Yeah, sure, I will have a soda."

While Steven goes and makes Dani something to drink, Nikolas tries stepping to Dani. Nikolas says to Dani, "Excuse me, would you like to dance?" Dani responds. "No thanks, the only man I'm dancing with is my man over there." Nikolas laughs when he sees the person Dani is pointing to is Steven. "Oh, you talking about fake ass Nino Brown over there? Steve don't have as much money I got; dude don't even have an education; he's a nobody." Darius warns Steven about Nikolas. "Aye, Steve, Nikolas trying to get with your girl; you want me to intervene?"

Steven looks and sees Nikolas with Dani and runs straight to them. Steven says, "No, I got this." Nikolas says to Dani as he grabs her hands, "You need to be with a man who can really give you nice things in life." Steven pushes Nikolas and says, "And you need to leave her alone, begging for a woman's attention, clown ass boy." Nikolas laughs, "What you going to do about it, huh? Without your popularity of being a drug dealer, you will still be that kid who didn't have a damn thing to his name." Steven responds, "And without football, you will just be an average country boy living off his parents." Rich tries to calm the situation. "Nick, man, you need to chill." Nikolas says, "Steve's not going to do nothing; he's lame; what you going to do, huh, cry to your Momma like you did in High School, Mr. Dropout."

Steven punches Nikolas. Darius cheers for Steven and says, "Beat him up, Steve." Steven beats up Nikolas for two minutes before people intervene." Rich says, "Get Nikolas drunk ass out of the party." Nikolas is thrown out of the party. Steven yells out loud,

"Don't play with me, boy; you going to learn to stop messing with me." Rich says, "Steve, calm down." Dani says, "Yeah baby, calm down; at least now he knows not to mess with you." Lenny says, "Man, you messed bro up; you was hitting bro like you was Michael Jai White." Darius says, "Nikolas been had that coming to him; dude always been arrogant since we was little kids." Steven says, "Well, he learned his lesson, your get back to the party; let's have a good time." Dani grabs Steven's hand and says, "I want you to come with me to my car; I want to show you something."

Dani and Steven head to Dani's car. Dani says, "Get in the backseat." Steven gets in the backseat, and Dani does too. "Just know, Steve, I love you; forget what homeboy was talking about. You are worthy enough to be with me, so let me show you how much I appreciate you." Dani and Steven have sex inside the vehicle. Steven is less stressed out after talking with Dani. "I needed that; you made a brother feel all better." Dani smiles, "Well, that is what I'm here for. I will always have your back through thick and thin." "It's the same with me, too; I always will have your back, but let's go ahead and go back to the party."

As Steven returns to the party, he talks to Rich. Rich asks, "Hey Steve, you alright?" Steven responds, "Yeah, I'm straight. Dani made sure I was taken care of. Where Lenny and Darius at?" "Well, last I saw Lenny, he was getting a little bit cozy with Diamond on the dance floor. And Darius was with Destiny last time I checked." "Alright, so when you leaving for UGA?" "In Two Months, I'm going to miss it down here; I hope you and

Darius stay out of trouble." "We will try our best." "I got this fine snow bunny waiting for me, so I'm going to bounce your take it easy."

After Rich leaves, Steven talks to Dani. Steven asks, "So, what you want to do now?" Dani says, "I would love to hang some more, but I have dance practice in the morning." Steven responds, "Alright, I will call you tomorrow." "Okay, I will talk to you tomorrow, boo." Steven gives Dani a kiss goodbye.

After the party is over, the guys reminisce on how good the party was. Lenny says. "Man, tonight has been a fun night." Steven says, "Yeah, I heard you and Diamond was getting cozy on the dance floor." Lenny smiles, "She got some great moves on her." Steven says, "Be careful now; she like a sister to me and Darius." Lenny responds, "I understand." Darius asks, "Aye, Steve, you good?" Steven says. "Yeah, I'm going to call it a night, but Lenny, just to let you know, tomorrow is going to be my last day in these streets." Lenny is shocked, "Wait, what, why?" Steven explains, "It's time for me to move on, I got a bigger destiny in life than this." Lenny responds, "I'm surprised, but I understand you got to do what makes you happy in life." Darius says, "Facts, Steve, you know I'm going to miss you. I love you, bro; I want you to be great. I'm sorry if I was one of the people that set you back." Steven says, "No, you didn't; you was there for me when most wasn't. I will never forget that." Darius responds, "Brothers for life." Steven and Darius hug one another. Steven says, "That goes for you too, Lenny. Alright, I will see your tomorrow."

It's Saturday Morning, and Steven wakes up feeling good, knowing today is his last day on the block. Steven tells himself today is going to be a great day in his life. A new beginning in his life. Steven drives his 1996 Black Chevy Impala on Harmony Street, bumping Yo Gotti's "That's Wassup Intro" loud with the windows down. Before meeting up with Darius and Lenny, he meets up with Brock, who also sells on the block. Along with Darius, he taught Steven how to make money in the streets. Brock is an OG on the block, as he has been selling drugs in the Harmony Projects for ten years.

Steven daps up Brock, "Yo Brock, you looking fly as hell in those Jordans, man." Brock responds, "I can say the same thing about you. You got the white tee and white forces on. And got the impala outside today; looks like you going to a celebration." "In a way, you can say I am. I don't know if Darius told you, but this is my last day on the block. Your boy is about to stop being in these streets." Brock is proud of Steven. "I'm proud of you, homie; when you first joined us out here, we looked at you as the little homie. Always wanted to make sure you was straight so you could help your Moms out. You was a quick learner; you started off as a rookie at the beginning but became a Pro toward the end. You might have looked it up to me, but I looked it up to you, too. You are the biggest trapper I know; you stayed stacking your bread. I salute you, bro, and I wish you nothing but success. Make everybody in the Harmony Projects proud, my nigga." Steven and Brock hug one another.

After talking to Brock, Steven goes to meet with Darius and Lenny. "Guys, what's going on? How your feeling today?" Lenny says, "I'm straight." Darius says., "I'm doing great; time to make them stacks back to back one last time." Steven looks around the block and smiles. "Our last day out here together, let's get that skrilla." Darius says, "Let's do what we always do." Lenny asks, "And that is?" Steven says, "Make some money!" From 9 am to 5 pm, Steven, Darius, and Lenny make $500-1000 dollars each. Steven is so happy that he buys ice cream for all the kids in the neighborhood, who are outside playing curveball. Darius says, "We made a whole bunch today." Steven responds, "This was great for our last time." Lenny says, "Steve, thank you, bro; you helped me out in many ways." Steven says, "No problem."

As the guys are about to stop selling for the day, they see a white car approaching. The person in the car says, "Aye, I'm looking to buy some Larry Bird?" Steven says, "How much you want?" "I will take all you got." "I got 5 grams left; I will have to sell it for $100." "No problem." Steven walks up to the car and gives the guy in the car the merchandise."

The time Steven walks away from the vehicle, cops start swarming in. As he sees the cops, Steven yells. "12; run!" The cops start chasing all of the guys on the block; the cops catch Darius while Steven and Lenny run away and try climbing over a gate. Steven says to Lenny, "Come on, bro; we can't get caught; you climb over before I do." Lenny climbs over the gate; by the time Steven gets ready to climb the gate, the cops grab him. Lenny yells,

"Steve!" Steven yells, "Go! Don't worry about me!" This day was supposed to be a new beginning for Steve, but instead, it looks like a new hurdle that Steve has to overcome. Will Steven overcome this, or will he just be another black man who is a product of his environment?

98

# Chapter 4: Jailbird

Steven, Darius, and the other guys who were arrested arrive at the police station. After getting booked, Steven and Darius go into the interrogation room, and they wait for the detective to walk in. Darius, with a sad look on his face, looks at Steven as he blames himself for why Steven is in jail. Darius says, "Aye, bro, I'm so sorry about this; this was supposed to be your last day doing this; now you're in jail. I'm sorry I got you involved in all of this." Steven is thinking of a way to get out of jail. The reality of him being in jail hasn't set in yet. Steven says to Darius, "Don't blame yourself. I made my bed; now I got to sleep in it, but for right now, let's not speak until we get a lawyer." "I got 7 bands saved up, so I know we can get somebody to defend us other than a public defender." "I got 6 bands saved up; we can get somebody. Somebody coming; let's be quiet."

A detective walks into the room, and Steven quickly recognizes him. The detective says, "Well, hello guys, if it isn't the Shaq and Kobe when it comes to selling drugs in Thomson. We been watching you guys for a couple of months; I must say you guys are good at what you do." The detective shows evidence of Steven and Darius selling drugs. Steven says, "I remember you; you was the white guy in the black car I met a couple of days ago." Detective responds, "Yes, that was me; I done my research on the both of you. Steven, you seem like a clean-cut guy. I don't see how you got into slinging drugs. On the other hand, you, Mr. Darius, I see that you have a couple of priors Marijuana possession and aggressive assault on your record. Now selling with intent to distribute drugs, Marijuana possession, and Gun possession, you looking at some years in less you give us some information." Darius doesn't hesitate to reply, "Mr. Detective, I have no information to provide you." "Ok, sit yourself."

Steven wonders how much time he is facing. "If you don't mind me asking, how much time I'm looking at?" The detective says, "Well, we're charging you with intent to distribute drugs, marijuana possession, and gun possession; you looking at least a year in jail, might not have to serve no time if you give us some information." Steven thinks about the potential of him being in jail for a year but doesn't fold. He was taught that if you do something, you are the one who has to deal with the consequences, not tell on somebody to save yourself. Steven says, "Just like my friend Darius said, I have no information to give to you, detective, and we aren't saying anything until our lawyer comes." "Ok then, well before we take you guys to your cells, your mothers wants to see you guys. I will give you guys five minutes."

Steven's Mom and Darius's Mom walk into the interrogation room. Darius's Mom talks to Darius while Steven's Mom talks to Steven. Steven's Mom has a sad look on her face as she sits down to talk to her son. She is sad to see her son in jail as she knows he is meant for more in life. Steven's Mom asks, "Steve, are you okay?" Steven responds, "I am Mom; how did you guys find out about this?" "The whole neighborhood knows about you and the guys getting arrested. Dee is the one who told me that you got arrested."

With tears in his eyes, Steven apologizes to his mother as he thinks about how he disappointed her. "Mom, I'm so sorry; I wish I would have been a better son for you. I actually had planned on today being my last day on the block, but I should've just stopped. I understand if you don't want nothing to do with me after this, Mom." Steven's Mom starts tearing up, touches her son's hands, and says, "Steven, look at me. I will never turn my back on you. I'm your mother, and I love you. I will never turn my back on you. I remember when you was a baby, I used to sing Whitney Houston's "My Love is Your Love" to you; you would just go to sleep so peacefully after I would sing it. My favorite part about that song is when she says it would take an eternity to break us. That's how I feel about you, my son. I'm always going to be there for you during the good and the bad. That is what a real mother is supposed to do." "I love you, Mom; I'm forever thankful for you.

Have you and Darius's Mom got a lawyer for us yet?" "Not yet. When I get home, I'm going to get somebody." "Is My Car back at the house?" "Dee returned it back to the house for you." "Could you ask the guard if I could write a note?" Steven's Mom asks the guard, and he says yes. Steven writes down where he keeps all his money. "That's where all of the franklins at, Mom. Use that for the lawyer fees; Darius going to do the same thing for his mother." The Detective comes back into the room and says, "Alright, guys, it's time to take you guys to your cells. You guys will be arraigned on Monday at 10 A.M." Darius's Mom says, "We will have a lawyer for the both of you by then." Steven's Mom says, "We sure will; we love the both of you; your stay strong."

The detective takes Steven and Darius to their cells. Both Steven and Darius are in separate cells. As Steven walks inside his cell with an orange jumpsuit on, it sets in his mind that he is in jail: no windows, two bunk beds, and one toilet. He stares at the wall and starts thinking about his life. Once destined for great success in High School, he is now in a jail cell. Steven remembers people telling him he would be nothing. In his mind and heart, he knows he is meant for more in life and starts thinking about how he can overcome this situation.

In his cell alone by himself, Steven starts praying and crying, "Dear God, I'm so sorry for all the times I disappointed my mother and for not being the best son I should've been. I'm sorry for disappointing my Mom. She did her best to raise me; I don't know what your plan for me is. Growing up, I didn't want to be nothing like my father. Now I'm sitting in a cell just like him. I pray that you give me another chance to make things right. Deep down, I know I'm destined to be somebody great. Please stay watching over me and my guys. And give me strength to make it through this storm in my life. In Jesus name, I pray. Amen."

The next morning, Steven wakes up in his cell and gets breakfast. It's nothing like the warm-cooked meal his mother would make for him as he is served with grits, two pieces of ham, a fried egg, and butter on a piece of bread. After he gets done eating, one of the correctional officers tells him he has a visitor. "Anderson, you have a visitor." Steven responds, "OK." Steven thinks it must be his Mom, but as he walks into the visiting room, he is greeted by a tall white guy wearing a suit and tie. The tall guy says, "Steven, hey, my name is Dave, and I will be representing you on your case." Steven responds, "That's great to hear; my mother called you?" "Yes, she did; she is a great lady. She told me you and your friend Darius needed my assistance, and trust me, I'm the best man for the job." "Has she paid you?" "You and Darius's legal expenses are taken care of, so don't worry about that. I'm looking at the charges against you. They're not major charges, but they aren't minor at the same time. With you pleading guilty, you are looking at least six months in jail since it's your first offense. And you are looking at, at least two years of probation. So, do you got plan on pleading guilty?" Steven decides to plead guilty. "I might as well. I'm not dumb; I know they got solid evidence on me that I was distributing drugs and had a gun on me." "Your mother told me you was a smart, intelligent kid; what I want to know is who is Steven Anderson." "What do you mean by who am I?" "Like what type of a person you are, what led you down this path?"

Steven tells Mr. Dave his life story. "I was a good kid growing up; I always got As and Bs on my report card, and I was a part of after-school programs. During my high school tenure, I was captain of the debate team and had the highest grading average in all my classes." Mr. Dave is impressed by Steven's accolades. "I didn't even do all of that when I was in high school; what made you quit school and start selling drugs?" "When I was in tenth grade, my mother was diagnosed with breast cancer; due to her having cancer, she couldn't work, so in my mind, I felt like I had to step up. So, I seen a lot of guys I grew up with making quick money in the streets, so I told myself, why not do that? And that's how everything began." "Your story is something fascinating. I had a whole bunch of clients that were your age, but not with your intelligence. Is there anybody I can talk to who can speak on your behalf on how good of a student you were?" Steven has one person in mind. "There is somebody, but after hearing that I got arrested, I highly doubt he would want to speak on my behalf." "You never know; just give me the person's name." "His name is Richard Dixon Sr. He's the principal at Norris High School. He used to be my former teacher and debate coach. He will be able to tell you how great of a student I was. I'm friends with his son, Rich. I can give you Rich's phone number, and that can put you in communication with Mr. Dixson." "Thank you. I will definitely be giving him a call."

"How does the future look for me, in your opinion?" "Well, you are going to be doing some time. I will say use your time in jail wisely, but when you get on the outside, if I was you, I would definitely try to get my GED." "That's exactly what I want to do; I want to change my life for the better." "Believe in yourself and GOD, and everything will fall in place. Now, just a heads up, I will be representing you and Darius separately. By doing that, the both of you guys can get a good sentence, in my opinion." "Do you know how much time he will be serving?" "I'm going to let him talk to you about that. Now, I'm going to leave and prepare for your defense tomorrow. I will see you in court tomorrow at 9 to talk to you about your case and what to expect." "Ok, thank you." "Try to have a nice day and get some rest for tomorrow."

The correctional officer takes Steven to the recreation room where all the other inmates are. Steven sees a whole bunch of people in the room. As Steven walks around, somebody yells out his name. Darius yells, "Steven, come over here!" Steven sees Darius and other people from their neighborhood in a pack. He walks over to where they are and daps all the guys up. He is excited to see his homeboys. Steven says, "The whole crew over here, what's going on, Brock, Jai, and Trey." Brock, who also taught Steven how to sell drugs, got locked up along with Steven and Darius. Trey, who also stays in the Harmony Projects, got locked up along with the guys. Jai is the oldest out of the guys and has been hustling since he was ten. He is looked up to as one of the biggest drug dealers from Harmony. All three of them are facing major years in prison.

Brock says, "What's going on, Steve? When they got you going to court?" Steven responds, "They got me going tomorrow." Darius says, "Me too." Steven asks, "How much time they say you looking at Brock?" Brock says, "With me being on parole, they said I'm looking at some years in prison. I don't have no money for no lawyer; I'm making sure my kids have all the money I got." Steven says, "Dang, bro, sorry to hear that." Brock responds, "It is what it is; we know what we be getting ourselves into when we do this.

What about you, Day, how much time they say you going to get?" Darius says, "I talked to my lawyer, and he told me due to me being on parole, I'm looking at 1 to 5 years in prison. What about you, Steve? How much time you looking at?" Steven responds, "My lawyer told me I'm looking at six months in here due to this being my first offense." Trey says, "Bro, you lucky." Jai says, "Just know we got your back, and watch out for the crazy people up in here." Steven asks, "What is there to do up in here?" Trey says, "Mainly, what we doing now is just talking to fellow inmates, but if you do end up in here for six months, I highly suggest that you do a work release program." Darius says, "A guy like you will be perfect for that, especially since this is your first time being up in here." Steven says, "I'm definitely going to look into that."

Darius asks Steven, "So, what happened to Lenny?" Steven tells Darius what happened. "Me and him was trying to climb over the gate. I knew he was on parole, so I let him climb first; the time I attempted to climb, the police got me." Darius responds, "You a real one for that; he owes you for that one." "We brought him down here. I would have felt super guilty if he would have got caught." Brock says, "You always look out for your boys; that's why you well respected in these streets, Steve." Trey asks, "Have your made any phone calls yet?" Darius responds, "I made one to my mother, and that's it." Jai asks, "What about you, Steve?" Steven says, "I haven't made one yet. I had plan on making phone calls tomorrow, but I will call my mother before the end of the day." Trey explains how the phone system works in jail. "You get like three free phone calls when you first get in here. After that, you got to pay for your own calls. Now, if you want, I got a connect; they can get you a cellphone in here for about $200." Steven and Darius decline Trey's request. Darius says, "We got to get our mom's to put money on our books." Steven says, "We will be straight by tomorrow."

Darius asks Steven about Dani. "You ain't going to call Dani, bro?" Steven hasn't really thought about Dani since he got locked up. "I will call her tomorrow. I don't know if she still going to want to deal with me or not." "Well, you said yourself, you will find out if she was real or not. Now, with you being behind these walls, you will definitely find out if she's for you." Brock says, "You are not lying about that; when you behind these walls, you will find out who real or not." Trey says, "Facts, when I first entered this place for my first bid, my girl left me no phone calls; I found out through my brother she was messing with somebody else." Brock says, "We got you, bro. Hopefully, you will stay in this section." Jai says, "With you possibly getting sentenced, they probably going to put you with a roommate tomorrow, so be prepared." Steven responds, "As long as bro don't be on no weird stuff, we good."

The guys stay talking and give Steven more insight about jail. And introduce him to some of their fellow inmates. Steven says, "Thank you guys for showing me around. I'm going to make a phone call to my Mom."

Steven calls his mother. Steven's Mom asks, "Son, how are you doing?" Steven answers, "I'm doing good, Mom." "Are you prepared for tomorrow?" Steven is ready to accept the consequences of his actions. "Yeah, I'm willing to accept the judge's decision when it comes to my case. Has anybody been asking about me?" "The whole neighborhood been asking about you; Dee came by earlier and brought some food. He said he going to be in court to support you and Darius." "Glad to hear that. Have you heard from Dani?" "No, I haven't, son. Rich called and asked about you. He said he going to pray for you." "Glad to hear I got some support; well, I got to go. I will see you tomorrow." "Alright, son. I'm going to put money on your books tomorrow, and I was told I could bring you a few things. So, I will give that to one of the officers to give to you. I love you, and I will see you tomorrow, Son." "Love you, Mom."

Steven goes to his cell and thinks about what will happen to him tomorrow and what will be his outcome. Steven prays to GOD before going to sleep. "God, my life is in your hands, please God, give me another chance to make things right. I know I don't pray to you often, but I'm begging you to give me a second chance."

The next morning, Steven is woken up by one of the correctional officers. The officer says, "Anderson, time to get dressed." The officer gives Steven a black Suit and Tie. Steven asks, "Where the suit and tie come from?" "Your mother bought it; now hurry and get dressed. You got 20 minutes to get ready before we go to the courthouse." Steven gets dressed and gets escorted with the other fellow inmates who are getting arraigned in Court onto the county jail bus. Steven and Darius see each other and wave at one another on their way to court. The inmates arrive at court and wait for their case number to be called. Steven and Darius's case numbers are the last ones to be called.

Before his number is called, Steven's lawyer talks to him in one of the rooms at the courthouse. Mr. Dave asks, "Hey Steven, how are you doing?" Steven responds, "I'm mainly nervous." "I understand. Well, I made a great deal with the DA by you pleading guilty. You are looking at serving six months in jail and serving the other six months on probation. I also got in contact with Mr. Dixon. He spoke very highly about you; I plan on using the words and information he gave me to show the court the type of person you are. Mr. Dixon wanted me to tell you that he is praying for you and wants you to know that this mistake doesn't define you, but you still have a great chance at a bright future." "I'm glad he still believes in me; now, you say the DA has worked out a deal for me to serve six months, but isn't it ultimately up to the judge?" "Yes, he has to agree to the deal, but you never know; he might decide you will have to serve less time partly due to this being your first offense." "So, how will everything start off once we in the courtroom?" "Well, he will ask you what you plead, and you will say guilty. Then, he will go over the deal that me and the DA came up with and give his judgment. And probably ask you if you got anything to say before he gives his sentence. I believe everything is going to work well for you; just keep your head up when you enter that courtroom. Your mother wants to speak to you before you go into the courtroom."

Steven's Mom walks into the room to talk to her son and hugs him. Steven's Mom says, "Son, how are you doing?" Steven responds, "I'm doing good, Mom, now that I'm seeing you." "I wanted to ask you something before you enter that courtroom." "What is it, Mom?" "Do you know why I got you that Suit and tie for your court appearance?" "For me to look nice and professional in front of the court." Steven's Mom smiles, stares at her son, and says, "No, to show you who you can be. I remember when you was in middle school, you would always tell me, Momma, I'm going to be a businessman. Today starts a new beginning in your life, and that suit and tie symbolizes the man I believe you will become. That future businessman you always wanted to be. I believe GOD put you in jail for a reason: to wake you up and guide you in the right direction. Now I want you to walk in that courtroom with your head up and know that God and his son are going to guide you to your destiny." Steven and his Mom hug one another. "Thank you, Mom, I love you." "I love you too, son; I will see you in there."

The correctional officer walks Steven back to where the other inmates are. After waiting for about an hour and half, Steven's name and case number is called. An Officer says, "Alright, inmate Anderson, time to head into the courtroom."

Steven walks into the courtroom with his head up high and sees a couple of his friends in the courtroom supporting him. Dee, Rich, Diamond, and even Lenny are in the courtroom to support him. He was looking to see if Dani was there, but he didn't see her.

And, of course, his mother was sitting right behind him, supporting her son.

Judge Brown says, "Mr. Anderson, I see that you agree to accept a guilty plea. Is that correct?" Steven responds, "Yes, your honor." "Before I give you your sentence, is there anything you would like to say to the court?" "Yes, your honor."

Steven steps in front of the courtroom with full confidence and honesty. Steven says, "I would first like to say I am disappointed in myself; my mother did not raise me to be this way. I got caught up in a fast-living lifestyle that I thought could give me and my mother happiness, but right now, I see that all it has given us, mainly her, is pain. Mom, I am so sorry for this. I promise I will make up for it. I will be successful in a legit way; I'm going to make you proud, Mom. Your honor. I don't know how you view me as a person as you read my case file, but I am a man who is trying his best to provide a better life for his family. I'm guilty of the crime I committed; I'm not afraid to admit that I made a huge mistake that I am learning from right now. When you are behind these walls, you have a lot of time to think about your life. I don't know how long I will be in jail, but I'm going to make sure while I'm in jail that I use my time wisely and better myself every day. Whatever judgment you bring my way, I will accept and respect your honor."

Judge Brown responds, "Thank you for your statement, Mr. Anderson. Mr. Dave, do you have anything to say on behalf of your client." Mr. Dave says. "Yes, I do, your honor. My client,

Steven Anderson, is a great kid who sadly went down the wrong road, but he is a very smart individual person who I honestly believe can be a great influence on kids in the future if he believes and takes his time in jail as a learning lesson and use it wisely. He started selling drugs to help his mother out with bills when she was sick with breast cancer. He wasn't thinking that what he was doing was wrong; he was thinking of the best way he could help and provide for his mother. He was a young boy put in a grown-man position at an early age. Most of us in this courtroom would probably do anything for our mothers. I'm not justifying that what my client did was right; he told you himself he was wrong for doing the crime he committed. I do not believe my client deserves a hard sentence. I believe he's a great kid with a lot of potential; as you can see from the files I have given you, all this young man needs is the right guidance. Don't set back his future. Give him the footsteps to be a successful man in life; that's all I have to say, your honor." Judge Brown asks, "Ms. Nicole, do you have anything to say."  "No, I don't, your honor."

Judge Brown is prepared to give his judgment. "Ok then, well, it's time for me to give my judgment." All of Steven's family and friends are patiently waiting for the judge's verdict. "I have been a judge for 30 years, and in all of my years, I have never had anybody be as honest as you about the crime that they committed. I'm looking at your file. You had great academic scores while you were in school. You had the highest SAT score out of anybody in your whole school. And captain of your High School Debate team. When I read this file, I see a kid with a lot of potential who can make a great impact on this earth. As I look at you today in court, I don't see a boy; I see a man who is admitting his wrongs, a man who has realized how his mistakes have impacted himself and the people around him. Young man, that is the first step you have to take in order to move forward in life, and I applaud you for admitting your wrongdoings. I'm deciding to show you some leniency; I hereby submit that you serve two months in county jail, and that you also participate in a work release program during your time in jail. After your release from jail, you will be on probation for 10 months. Also, I request that after your release from jail, you start attending GED classes at Brooks Technical College in Augusta, Ga. If you don't apply for any GED classes within 30 days of your release, you will be sent back to jail and serve out the whole six months that was originally requested. Mr. Anderson, I hope you take full advantage of this opportunity. Don't let me regret my decision. This is your second chance; make the best of it and make your Mom proud." Steven and his Mom start crying with tears of joy.

Tears of joy pour down Steven's face. "Your honor, thank you; you will not regret this; the next time you see me, you are going to see that you made the right decision." Mr. Dave shakes Steven's hand. Mr. Dave says, "Well, Steven, I wish you the best. This is your second chance, be that great guy God designed you to be." Steven responds, "Thank you so much for helping Darius and me. I don't know how I will ever repay you." "You don't owe me nothing. You won this case today, not me; the only way you can repay me is by being great. When you get out of jail, give me a call."

Steven's Mom and Darius's Mom hug him. Darius's Mom says, "We love you, Steve. I always consider you a child of mine; make the best out of this opportunity." Steven's Mom says, "Son, this is GOD giving you a second chance. He is giving you the footsteps to follow so you can reach your destiny; I know you will succeed." The Correctional Officer yells, "We got to go, Anderson." Steven says, "I will call you tomorrow, Mom." As Steven is escorted out of the courtroom, his friends give him words of encouragement. Diamond says, "We love you, Steve." Rich says, "Stay Strong." Dee says, "You got this little homie." Lenny whispers, "Thank you." Now that Steven has been sentenced, how will jail life be for him?

j

# Chapter 5: Life Behind the Gates

The correctional officer puts Steven back on the bus with the other inmates and takes him back to jail. Steven returns to jail and finds out he is moving to a new section of the jail. Correctional Officer says, "Anderson, you moving to Pod D." Steven asks, "Why?" "That's where everybody go to who is sentenced."

As Steven moves to Pod D, he sees Darius looking at him in the recreation room. Steven wants to say goodbye to Darius as he knows it will be the last time they will see one another for a while. Steven asks the Officer, "Could I say goodbye to a couple of my friends before I move?" The officer says, "You got five minutes." Steven walks over to where Darius is at. Darius asks Steven, "So, they moving you out, bro." Steven responds, "Yeah, I'm moving to Pod D." "My Mom told me you got two months up in here." "Yeah, I got to do a work release program while in here and attend GED classes when I get out of here." "I'm happy for you; in a strange way, this might been one of the best things to happen to you." Steven asks, "Appreciated; how much time they gave you?" Darius responds, "I got a year in prison due to me being on parole. They supposed to ship me out tomorrow; it supposed to be in Columbus, GA." Steven is saddened by Darius's sentence, but keeps his composure. "I'm going to be praying for you, bro; we going to make it through this." "I appreciate you, bro; we are not blood, but we forever brothers. Love you, thug." "Love you too, bro." Steven and Darius dap one another up as they know it would be the last time they see one another for a good while. The

Correctional Officer says, "We got to go, Anderson." Darius says, "Stay being that soldier that you are, Steve." "You, too, forever stepping everywhere we go."

The Correctional Officer walks Steven to Pod D and shows him to his new cell, where he meets his cellmate. Correctional Officer says, "Alright, Anderson, this is your cell, and this is your cellmate, Robert. Don't start no trouble, you too." Robert is just a few years older than Steven. Robert is a tall black guy with a slim figure. He and Steven look at one another as the Officer introduces them to one another. Robert responds, "We won't." The officer walks away, and Rob starts talking to Steven. "Alright, youngin, listen, here are the rules in this cell: make sure your bed is clean, don't leave nothing smelly in here, don't sit on my bed, and please don't leave the toilet nasty." Steven is going to do his time but is not going to be pushed around. Steven says, "I won't, but just to let you know, I'm not finna be pushed around." "I respect that; I'm just here to do my time; trust me, you don't have to worry about me. I'm not going to push you around.

Steven and Robert get to know one another. Robert asks, "So, tell me your story?" Steven responds, "What you mean?" "Why are you in here?" "I was caught selling drugs and had a gun on me." "A young dude like you should be in school; how much time did they give you?" "I got two months up in here, then when I get out, I got to be on probation for 10 months and attend GED classes." "You got yourself a great deal, so take full advantage of that. How old are you?" "I'm 18." "What made you start selling drugs?" "When I was 15, my mother was diagnosed with breast cancer; she had to stop working for a while. We were struggling for money. I had to do something, so I decided to start selling in the streets. I made a lot of dough out there. I had planned on last Saturday being my last day doing it, but I got caught, and now I'm in here."

Robert explains why he is in jail. "I feel you. I was the same way when I was your age, except I was in a gang. We did everything, all types of stuff. When I was your age, I got arrested for armed robbery and did three years in prison. When I got out, it was hard for me to get a job. So, I started selling drugs. I rounded up getting caught two years after getting released, and now I got to do a whole year up in here. I got a three-year-old son growing up without a father. I hope and pray he be better than his old man."

As Steven hears Robert's story he relates to it a whole bunch. "I understand; my father been in prison all my life growing up. I didn't want to be anything like him, but now I'm in a cell just like him." "Are you mad at your father for the decisions he made?" "Yeah, I believe if he would've never made those decisions, I would've had a better life and probably be in a different predicament in my life right now." "That's the same way I felt about my father; my Dad was never in jail. He never wanted to be a part of my life. I watched my mother struggle to raise me and my four siblings. I got with a homeboy of mine who was in a gang; they were getting money, so I wanted to be down with them. I look back on that now, and I wish I would have chosen a better route. When my son was born, I told myself I can't let him struggle like I did, so that's why I sold drugs while being on parole. I don't know your father, but I understand why he did what he did. When you have a kid, you don't want them to struggle for nothing, but when we out here in the streets, we are caught in the Moment, and we don't think about how our actions will impact our loved ones."

"I wish I would've got that installed in my brain before being behind these walls." "You have a chance to turn everything around. It's not too late. Don't be like me, little homie. When you get out of here, get your GED and do positive things." "What made you have the mindset that you have now?" "I got closer to God during my time in here. I learned that you can always change your life, but it doesn't matter what you go through; God is always there for you." "I hardly ever went to church growing up, but I have been praying a whole bunch to him since I been in here. How did you find God?"

Robert explains his relationship with GOD. "I read the Bible and pray every day, but I found God by going to the Sunday services that they have here every Sunday. When I first went, I was like this ain't for me, but I started going and developed a deep connection with GOD. You should come join me and the fellow inmates on Sunday." "I will check it out; they got me doing this work release program. I'm supposed to be doing lawn care with the other inmates starting tomorrow." "I'm in the same program; you will like it. Granted, you will sweat real quick in the heat, but me and the guys have a good time doing lawn care for the community."

Steven sees people in the recreation room. "That's what's popping. I see they letting us hang out in the recreation room. Do you mind introducing me to some of the fellow inmates?" Robert agrees. "Yes, sir, I will show you around."

Robert introduces Steven to the other inmates in the Pod; while introducing him to the inmates, he notices two of them playing chess. Steven asks, "Hey Rob, I'm going to play a chess game." Robert responds, "Good luck. Michael is undefeated, never been beaten." Michael is the smartest guy in the jail and has never been beaten in chess. Steven smiles, "Well, that's going to change today." Steven walks over to where the inmates are playing chess and asks them if he can play. Steven asks, "Excuse me, could I join you guys and play a game of chess." Michael laughs as he looks at Steven and says, "You think you can play this game, little man?" Michael is this medium-slim fit white guy who looks like a school teacher. Steven responds, "There is only one way to find out." "Well, have a seat and play me." Steven and Michael play chess for about 35 minutes. The inmates look on as the game is starting to get intense. Michael says, "I must say you make some great moves, but against me, you got to go all the way against me." Steven yells, "Checkmate, I just did!" Michael and the rest of the inmates are shocked. "How did you do that?" "You let your guard down against me; you probably thought I didn't know anything about Chess, so you left an opening for me to get to your knight. With Chess, it's all about paying attention to detail."

Michael is impressed by Steven as he smiles as he looks at Steven. "I have never met anybody like you up in here; how you know how to play chess so well?" "I learned to play when I was in middle school and was the leader of my chess and debate club when I was in High School." "I would love to play with you some more. We usually be playing all the time, so try and face me again. My name is Michael; what is yours?" "My name is Steven." "Steven, if you ever need anything in here, by all means, hit me up." Steven responds, "Alright, bet."

A Correctional Officer gives Steven some items. The Officer says, "Anderson, here's your tablet and the Bible your mother brought for you, and your mother has put minutes on your phone time; use both of the privileges wisely." Steven responds, "I will, sir." Robert gives Steven his props for beating Michael in Chess. "I have never seen anybody beat Mike in chess I can tell you got one of those Albert Einstein minds." "It's a gift that I'm just blessed with." "I see they gave you a tablet." "Yeah what do you guys usually do on it?" "Mainly play games, listen to music; I read the Bible with mine, and you can Facetime people with it. You got to schedule an appointment to do it." Steven asks, "Who all you Facetime?" Robert responds, "Mainly my son. To make sure he straight. Who do you got plan on Facetiming?" "My Mom, a couple of homies, and my girlfriend." Robert asks, "What Shawty's name?" Steven talks about Dani. "Her name is Dani; we been together for six months. I thought I would see her in court, but she didn't show up." "When you get locked up, you will find out super quick who got your back and who don't. I had a girl before I came in here, but after she found out how much time I had, she left me." "What do you suggest I do?" "Give shawty a call; that way, you will find out if she's a ride or die or if she for the streets." Correctional Officer yells, "Alright, guys, time to shut it down for today." Robert says, "Well, it looks like you got to wait till tomorrow to make that phone call." Steven responds, "Yeah, let's get some rest to prepare for tomorrow."

As everybody go to their cell, a fight breaks out between two inmates. Correctional Officer yells, "Everybody in their cells now!" Steven sees the fight. Steven says, "They swinging like hell up in here." Robert explains how jail operates. "That's Hector; he's the big boss up in here; that man stay making money up in here. The guy he fighting owed him some money; that's one of the major things you never want to do in here. You never don't want to owe nobody in jail. Because if you do, you will have to pay back in some type of way." "I'm going to make sure that ain't me."

Before going to sleep, Steven opens his Bible and reads a message his Mom left in the Bible. The same Bible his Mom bought for him before he went to jail. Steven reads the message, "Darkness doesn't last forever; sunshine is just around the corner; stay strong, son."

Steven and the rest of the inmates go to sleep. It's 8 am in the morning. Steven and Robert are awakened by a correctional officer to prepare for their work release program. Correctional Officer says, "Anderson and Davis, it's time to wake up; we need you guys to come and help us get all the equipment we need for today's task." Robert asks, "What we got to do today?" Correctional Officer explains. "We are going to be cutting grass and mainly lawn care. Anderson, since you are new, we will have you plant flowers." Steven never planted anything in his life. Steven says, "But I've never planted flowers before." Correctional Officer responds, "No worries, we will get Hector to teach you; he's the best Gardner in this jail. I know he will be glad to teach you. Hector is the same guy that got in a fight with another inmate last night. Now, come along and help us with this equipment."

Steven and Robert go to help the officers load up the equipment. Steven asks, "So, how many days out of the week we usually do the work release program?" Robert responds, "Four days out of the week, every Tuesday, Wednesday, Thursday, and Friday." "How much we get paid?" "We be out here for at least 6 hours a day, so we make 6 dollars each day a week." "Well, at least we get something up in here." Correctional Officer asks, "You guys have everything equipped yet?" Steven responds, "Yes, sir, we do." Robert asks, "So where are we going to today?" Correctional Officer says, "We are going to the mayor's mansion today and do lawncare on his yard. You must be Steven; my name is Officer Brown. You will be seeing a lot of me. If there's any trouble, let me know." Steven responds, "Ok, thank you, sir." Steven asks Robert, "So, do we usually do lawncare at the mayor's mansion?" Robert answers. "Yes, about every month; he a cool guy, he got big property we joke around quite a bit, so be prepared for that."

Steven responds, "I'm a jokester, so I'm going to fit right in." Correctional Officer says, "Alright, guys, time to get on the bus."

All the inmates get on the bus and head to the mayor's house. As the inmates arrive at the mayor's house, Officer Brown introduces Steven to Hector. "Steven, this is Hector; he will show you how to plant flowers today." Steven remembers Hector from the fight from last night.

Hector says to Steven, "What's going on, Homie? Have you ever planted anything before?" Steven answers, "No, I haven't." "Say less; I'm going to show you how to grow some plants. So today, we are growing lily flowers. To me, these are the most beautiful flowers in the world." "How long have you been planting stuff?" "Really, all my life, my grandmother taught me how to plant at an early age." "Growing up, I used to think that planting was boring." "I used to think the same thing until I found the true beauty in planting flowers." "What is the true beauty in planting?" "The true beauty in planting flowers is you can create something that is looked as ugly by most people but turn into a beautiful masterpiece and is loved by many. It's the same thing with us as people. Some of us are born into difficult situations and have to live a hard life, but the beauty of this thing called life is we can be something powerful and be the great masterpiece GOD designed us to be. That's the same thing I see in flowers." "You are a deep individual. What is your favorite flower?" "The flowers we are planting now; the water lilies, mainly because it is the queen of all aquatic flowers. To me, it's the one that shines the brightest.

I love to see them blossom; it's wonderful to see something so small grow into something great. Can't wait till I get out and I can make my own garden."

Steven asks, "If you don't mind me asking, what did you do to be in jail?" Hector is honest with Steven. "Drug possession, gun possession, and intent to sell. I got sentenced to six months in jail. I got two months left before I get out. I tried to get this money the fastest way I could, trying to provide for my Senorita and my daughter. I'm a good guy just trying to correct his wrongs." Steven asks, "Why were you fighting last night?" Hector answers, "One of the guys stole one of my snacks and owed me money. You can't let nobody walk over you in here. If you do, everybody will try to get over you. So, what did you do to get in here?"

Steven answers, "Kind of the same thing you did: drug possession, gun possession, and intent to sell." "How much time they gave you, and what type of product you was selling?" "I got two months up in here; I'm going to be on parole for a good while when I get out, and I was selling weed and pills." "Ok, you were selling that gelato. I know you was getting that paper." "I was making them stacks for real, bro." "You look young as hell; how old are you?" "I'm 18; how old are you?" "I'm 25; even though you in here, look at the bright side; you got another chance to turn everything around in your life. Granted, will it be easy? No, but to get to the destination we want to reach in life, we have to overcome obstacles to achieve our goals." "Big facts, bro. You know the funniest thing about us growing lily flowers is I met this girl named

Lily before I got locked up." "That's funny. Well, when you get out, you should give her some lily flowers; trust me, that will impress her." "I might just do that." Officer Brown comes to get the guys. "Alright, guys, time to hang it up; we going back to the jail."

Steven and the inmates get on the bus and return to jail. As Steven arrives at the jail, a fellow inmate gives Steven a note. Steven asks, "Aye, bro; who is this from?" Inmate says, "It's from Darius; he wanted me to give that to you. He was shipped to Columbus just an hour ago." Steven goes into his cell and reads the note Darius wrote for him. Steven reads, "Steven, what's going on, bro? If you reading this, you know I've been sent to Columbus already. First of all, I wanted to say I apologize for getting you involved in the game. A person like you is meant to be something big in life. I know you are going to do great things. I hope when you get out, you be the guy you are supposed to be. While I'm here, I'm going to try my best to turn my life around. Also, I got to try and set a good example for my little brother, which is why I need a huge favor. When you get out, I know you are going to be busy, but could you look out for my little brother? I don't want him to end up in here like me and you. He's a good kid; I know you will be a good influence on him. We grew up together and been through many situations together. We will overcome this; next time we see each other, it will be in person, and we will be in better positions in life. Stay keeping your head up. Don't give up. Love, Darius."

As Steven gets done reading the letter, Robert walks into the cell. Robert asks, "What you reading?" Steven answers, "It's a letter from a friend of mine, me and him got locked up together; they just shipped him out to Columbus." "I know how that is; how much time he got?" "They gave him a year because he was on parole." "Your will make it through. I wish the best for your friend. So, have you talked to your girl yet?" "No, I haven't. I'm going to go ahead and do that; wish me good luck."

Steven nervously walks over to the phone and calls Dani. Doesn't know what is in store for him; Steven hopes Dani is still riding for him. Dani answers the phone, "Hello, who am I speaking to?" Steven is excited to hear Dani's voice. Steven says, "It's your man, beautiful. Do you miss me?" Dani doesn't sound so happy to talk to Steven. "Oh, hey Steven, how are you doing?" Steven is surprised by Dani's tone of voice. "Well, that's not the response I was waiting to hear. Are you mad at me for getting locked up?" Dani nervously says, "I'm going to be honest, Steve, this isn't going to work out." Steven is in shock at Dani's remark. "Because I'm in jail! But I thought you said you love me. Remember, you said you are my ride or die. You the Bonnie to my Clyde. They sentenced me to Two months in here; I'm not going to be in here forever. GOD gave me a second chance to make things right. Everything I said I'm going to do when I took you out to dinner is still going to happen. Don't give up on me; stay believing in me, baby. I'm begging you; I'm going to do great things when I get out of here; just watch." Dani starts crying on the phone as she still loves Steven. "Steve, I love you with all my heart, and I will always care about you. We can no longer be together. My Mom found out you got arrested, and she don't want me nowhere near you. And I'm trying to be a positive figure in my community, but it's not a good look for me to be with you. You give me so much inspiration and hope. I'm going to miss you, but it has to end."

The comments Dani has made have downed Steven's spirit, but he keeps his composure. Steven can tell by the tone of Dani's voice she is serious. Small tears are flowing out of Steven's eyes. In his heart and mind, he knows he has to let Dani go. "I remember when I first met you, I was like, I have to get to know her. I'm grateful that I made that decision; you brought joy into my life when my world was dark. One thing my grandmother taught me before she passed away was you got to accept any consequences that come with your actions. I'm accepting my consequences right now; sadly, one of those consequences is me losing you. I hope you find a guy that can treat you better than I did. Stay prospering and stay believing great things will happen for you. I'm going to do big things once I get out; I wish you would stick by my side. But I guess you just wasn't meant to be my ride or die. Even though we no longer together, I still wish the best for you. Have a nice day, my love."

A disheartened Steven goes back to his cell with tears in his eyes. Robert asks with concern in his voice, "Aye, Steve, are you okay?" Steven responds, "My girl just broke up with me; she saying it's not a good look for her to be with me due to me being in jail. It hurts, man; she was the first girl I ever gave my heart to." "Bro, listen, shawty is for the streets; she was never real. If she was, she would've been in court when you were arranged. You have a lot of people who are there for you when you are winning, but when you take a loss, they just disappear. She is one of those people; the best thing you can do is prove her and everybody else out of a lie. When you are behind these walls, you have some people who give up on you; they don't see us people in jail being successful in life. The main thing is to believe in yourself and never give up. Great things will come your way. And when you become successful, them same people that gave up on you going to want to be in your life." "Facts, it hurts, though, when you open your heart for love, but instead you get rejection and pain. I will be alright, though. I been through way worse. Either way, I'm going to bounce back in a big way."

After calming himself down, Steven plays chess and beats everybody that faces him. Michael says, "Little man, you are one vicious dude on this board; you got to give us your secret." Steven responds, "The main secret is paying close attention to detail. You got to see the weakness that your opponent gives you. Once you find that out, that's when you attack their vulnerability." Hector says, "You are a special talent, little man."

Over the next couple of days, Steven gets close with the rest of the inmates in his pod. It's Sunday morning, and Robert gets ready for the Sunday service at the jail and invites Steven to come with him. Robert says, "Aye, Steve, I'm about to go to Sunday service. Do you want to come with me?" Steven responds, "Nah, bro, I'm good." "You been talking about how you want to get close to GOD; if you truly are trying to get close to GOD, you need to come." Steven, in his heart and mind, knows he needs to get close to God, especially after he gave him a second chance. "My apologies, bro. I'm going. He gave me a second chance to get my life straightened out; I need to go." Steven gets dressed and goes to the Sunday service with Robert.

As Steven walks into the jail room where Sunday service happens, he notices almost everybody is in the room. Steven says, "Almost everybody is up in here." Robert responds, "Yeah, most people come in here just to get out of their cells, but you actually have some people here trying to get the spiritual word." "Who preaches Sunday Service?" "Officer Brown, here he comes right now." "Never knew Officer Brown was a preacher." "He always has the days off on Sundays, but he comes in here and preaches the good word to us every Sunday morning." Officer Brown says to all of the inmates, "My fellow men, how you're doing today?" The Inmates respond, "Good!"

Officer Brown starts preaching and tells the story of Joseph, how Joseph's brothers betrayed him, and how God turned that evil betrayal into something good. Officer Brown says, "The main meaning behind what I'm preaching is that God can turn something meant for bad into something good. For example, with you guys being here, you can use your time in here to develop into being an impactful person in the outside world and in your community. You all have a chance to turn your life around. I see potential in all of you guys. I'm going to leave you guys with this final message: for every minor setback, is a setup for a major comeback. I believe and have faith that when most of you guys get out of here, you are going to do something special in your lives. Well, that is my message today. Robert will you lead us in prayer." Robert prays, "Yes sir, GOD, thank you for this day, thank you for giving us a second chance; I hope and pray that you touch everybody's soul in here and stay helping us to get closer to you. In Jesus' name, we pray. Amen." "Amen, you guys have a nice day."

After the service, Robert and Steven talk to Officer Brown. Robert says, "Officer Brown, great service today." Officer Brown says, "Thank you. Steven, great to see you in here today; so what did you think about the service?" Steven answers, "I actually liked the service and your preaching." "What was your favorite part?" "My favorite part was when you said for every minor setback, it is a setup for a major comeback. I got plan on using my time in here wisely; when I get out, I want to be a positive influence for the people in my community." Officer Brown says, "Robert, you mind leaving us for a minute? I want to talk to Steven one on one." Robert responds, "Yeah, sure."

Officer Brown and Steven have a one-on-one conversation. Officer Brown says, "Robert told me you are trying to change your life and get close to GOD." Steven says, "I am; when you get behind these walls, it makes you appreciate the outside life more. When the judge gave me two months in here, I saw that as God giving me a second chance. When I get out, I got plan on getting my GED. Officer Brown asks Steven an important question. "That's good to hear, but let me ask you something: what is your main goal in life?"

Steven thought long and hard before he gave Officer Brown an answer. "I mainly want to be successful and make my mother proud of me; I can't end up like my father." "Where is your father?" "He is in prison; he been in prison since I was a little kid. I don't want to waste my potential like he did." "I mostly definitely understand that. I have been keeping a close eye on you since you been in here. Something I noticed about you is that you're very intelligent. The guards were bragging about how well you can play chess the other day." "I appreciate; I was just born with great gifts." "No, God gave you those talents; you was meant to be an intelligent, gifted kid. I want to give you something; here is a journal. While you in here, write down your goals and dreams in that journal and read that Bible your Momma gave you. By doing that, you will find what your main goal in life is, and it will help you get closer to GOD." "Appreciated, Officer Brown. I will definitely be writing a whole bunch in this journal. "You welcome; always remember this: when hard times come, just know they don't last forever. I will see you tomorrow; you have a nice day."

Steven goes back to his cell and starts reading his Bible. While reading, he learns that his mother is at the jail to visit him. Correctional Officer says, "Anderson, your mother is here to see you." Steven goes to the visitation room to see his mother. Steven and his Mom hug one another. Steven says, "What's going on, Ma dukes?" Steven's Mom is happy to see her son. "Son, you looking good; how you been doing?" "I have been doing good in here. I'm learning a lot in here; just came from Sunday Service and schooling these people in chess." "That's my son. I'm glad you doing well. I need to tell you about Lenny."

Steven asks, "What about Lenny; is he ok?" Steven's Mom says, "He got shot last Thursday. He's ok and is back home." Steven is shocked to hear about Lenny. "What happened?" Steven's Mom explains, "According to his mother, he was on the block doing you know what, and some guys were shooting at somebody else, but instead, the bullet hit him. He got shot in the leg; he on crutches now." Steven is stunned to hear about Lenny as Lenny reminds him of a younger version of himself. Steven says, "When you get a chance, tell him I say wassup and that I hope he has a speedy recovery. I talked to Dani on Tuesday."

Steven's Mom rolls her eyes and says, "What was her excuse for not being in court to support you?" "She didn't give one; she basically dumped me, and she basically stated me being with her would tarnish her image." "Son, I'm sorry; it's her loss because you are going to be something in life. There's a better girl out there right now waiting for a guy like you to come their way. I know her Mom probably had something to do with that. When hard times come, you find out who truly got your back." "It hurt me. I saw her being the person right by my side, but she ain't for me. I'm going to make something out of myself; don't matter who don't believe in me." "I know that's right; I wanted to let you know that your father knows that you are in here. He called me a couple of days ago."

Steven laughs and says, "What fatherly advice he trying to give me this time." "He wanted me to tell you to be strong, and you will overcome this. He also said don't be like him and take advantage of the opportunity the Judge gave you. And that he loves you." "Well, tell him I said thanks; one of the officers in here gave me a journal. I'm going to start writing down my goals and dreams in the journal. And read the Bible you gave me so I can get closer to GOD. And thank you for the message you put in the Bible." "I'm so glad to hear that; like I said before, I believe GOD did this for a reason. My son, you are going to be something special. I been known this since you was a little kid. Now, I think you finally starting to see that in yourself. This has made my day."

"Well, I'm glad I made you happy, Mom. Have you talked to Darius Mom?" "Yes, she doing good; me and her been spending a lot of time with one another; she will be alright. She actually wanted me to tell you to stay keeping your head up, and you will make it through." "Tell her I say thank you. How's Danny doing?" "He's doing good; of course, he misses his brother, but he seems like he doing good despite everything that's going on." "That's good. When I get out of here, I got plan on hanging out with him and being a positive role model for him. I know that Darius wants me to lookout for him; that what I got plan on doing." "Danny will be lucky to have you as a role model."

"How everybody else doing?" "Well, I know Rich is about to get ready to go to UGA in a few months; Diamond is also getting prepared for college and just got a car. I know Mr. Dixon wanted me to tell you that he is praying for you and wishing you the best. And Dee and Steph about to have another baby." "I'm glad everybody doing great. Tell everybody I thank them for the love and support they been giving me; it means a lot to me." "I will; the whole neighborhood is behind you, but the main thing is GOD is behind you. With him by your side, you can overcome anything." "I appreciate Mom; your boy going to be better than ever when he gets out from behind these walls." "I know, son, well I got to go. I love you, son. Always remember your mother loves you." "I love you too, Mom, and I know you always got my back.." Steven and his Mom hug one another. As they both walk away from one another, small tears fall down from their face.

After his mother leaves the jail, Steven calls Rich. Rich answers, "Hello, who is this?" Steven says, "This Steve, bro, what been going on with you?" Rich is happy to hear from Steven. "Man, I'm glad to hear from you. I'm about to go to UGA in about a month. I'm excited, and I believe I will have a fun experience at the University. How are you doing?" "I'm doing good. Being here is giving me a better insight into life. When I get out, I'm going to get my life straightened out. I'm using my time in here to better myself." "I'm glad to hear that; you got this. You never know; a couple of years from now, you might be an inspiration for a lot of kids in our town." "That would be amazing." "So, have Darius been shipped off yet?" "Yeah, they shipped him to Columbus last

Tuesday. I already know he going to be alright. He a soldier; he done survived many things; I know he will survive this." "Both of your going to be alright. I talked to some of my friends, and they said they wouldn't mind helping you out once you get out." "Which friends?" "The ones we was playing basketball with: Kurt, Lance, and Jack." "As long they are not going to judge me for what I have done, I'm cool with that." "They are not going to do that to you; these guys are positive people who I believe can help you out. Have you talked to your girl? She should've been in court with us."

"She dumped me. I talked to her a couple of days ago. Her Mom told her to stay away from me, and she scared I might ruin her image." "Don't worry about shawty; there is a special girl out there for you." "I believe I will find that right lady, too, but right now, my main focus is to get my life straightened out. You do your thing on the basketball court; show the boys who the boss is." "You already know I'm going to show out; you never know; in a few years from now, your boy might be in the NBA." "Something that I learned from your father is you can always turn a dream into a reality." "Facts; one thing about my father is he got great choice of words." "How is he doing?" "He's doing good; I know he put in a good word for you with your lawyer. He praying and hoping for the best for you, just like I am." "I appreciate the love and the support; it means a lot to me. Hopefully when I get out of here, I can school you in a game of Basketball." "If you say so, be well, my friend." "Likewise, and remember to put the mustard on the hot dog." Rich laughs, "I will try my best to remember that; stay keeping your head up." "Will do, fam."

After he gets done talking to Rich, he plays chess and plays some basketball before going back to his cell. As Steven goes back to his cell, he walks in on Robert, talking to his son on his tablet. Robert says, "Your Daddy loves you. Steve, come here. I want you to meet somebody. Son, this is a good friend of mine; this is Steven, Steven, this is RJ." Robert's Son says, "Hey, Steven." Steven responds, "Hey RJ, how old are you?" Robert's Son says, "I'm 4." "That's wassup; you have a good father; he done helped me out a lot. You are lucky to have a father like him." Robert's Son asks his father, "Thank you, Daddy. When are you coming home?"

With tears in his eyes, Robert tells his son that he is coming home soon. "Daddy coming home soon; when I get out, we are going to have so much fun together. I got to go; Daddy loves you." "I love you too, Daddy, bye Steven."   "Bye."

Robert says to Steven, "Thank you for saying that about me to my son."  "No problem. If I didn't mean it, I would not have said it. I can tell he misses you." "I miss him too; five months from now, I will be reunited with my son. So how did you like Sunday Service?"

"I actually liked it. I'm not used to going to church every Sunday, but you know I definitely got plan on going every Sunday while I am in here."  "I'm glad to hear that. GOD has a special calling for all of us in our lives. It's up to us to follow the pathway he has set up for us. By going to the Sunday service, I have gotten closer to God, but I have also found out what my goals in life are."

"Officer Brown gave me a journal, and my Mom sent me my Bible, but I don't know where to start." "With the journal, write about your goals and dreams; just write what you want. If I was you, I would start by writing what you want to do when you get out of here. And with the Bible, start from the beginning: Genesis to Revelation." "Have you read the whole Bible?" "No, I'm close to being done with reading it; in my opinion, it's the greatest book to ever be written." "What is your favorite story in the Bible?"

Robert reveals his favorite and explains why. "My favorite story is the Book of David. Nobody believed in David, not even his own father, but God saw his potential and greatness. He chose David to be the chosen king of Israel. David beat the biggest person on the earth; his name was Goliath. Nobody didn't believe David would beat Goliath. David was a short guy, while Goliath was this big giant. David defeated him with no problem. I look at that story as how we deal with obstacles in life. You know, we deal with big obstacles in life; sometimes, it seems like we will never overcome them, but we can overcome them. Hard times and situations happen, but it doesn't last forever. That is what keeps me going; we are not going to be in here forever. I guarantee you that within a year, we will be in a better position in our lives."

"That was real stuff you just said there; what are your main goals when you get out of jail?" "First, being a father to my son, I want to be a great role model for him. Second, Is get my CDL license, so I can start driving Trucks. What I want to do is have my own trucking business and provide employment for people who have also gotten out of prison or jail." "That's a great plan. I know my main goal is to make my Mom proud." "Well, start writing down your goals so one day, you can make that happen." "I got plan on reading the Bible tonight, then in the morning write in the journal." "Do you want me to read the Bible with you? Time goes by fast here when you have something to do." "I wouldn't mind. I appreciate you helping me out." "No problem, bro; I wish I had somebody who would give me advice when I was younger. Now, let's start reading The Holy Word." Steven and Robert read the Bible until it is time to go to sleep.

. The next morning, Steven wakes up and starts writing in his journal. Steven starts writing down what he is going to do when he gets out of jail. "Dear Diary, I have been in here for a week now. I can't wait to get out of here and make my life better. The first thing I plan on doing is attending GED classes and getting my GED. The second thing is getting a job, a legit job. I can't be in streets no more. I look at where I'm at and where my friends at. I want better than this. The third thing is being there for Danny. Darius wants me to look out for him; not only that, I want the best for the little homie. I want to be a positive influence on him and the rest of the kids in my neighborhood. I'm going to make my Momma proud of me. I'm going to be that special person that I was destined to be."

After Steven gets done writing in his journal, he works out a little bit in his cell and then heads to the recreation room with the other inmates. Hector calls Steven to where he and his homeboys are at. "Aye, Steve, come join us." Steven responds, "What are you guys doing over here?" "We doing some rapping and poetry over here; my boy Luis over here plays the beats off his tablet, and we just bust a freestyle." Luis says, "You got bars, little homie?" Steven responds. "I got a little something." Hector says, "Why won't you do a freestyle and talk about how you feel? I know the perfect beat for it, too. Luis plays that Goapele "Closer" beat." Luis starts playing the beat. Hector says, "Show us what you got." Luis says, "Wait, hold up, we got all the time in the world up in here. Let little homie listen to the beat for a few minutes, and let him write something down, and then he spit something. Here's some paper and a pencil; write down how you feel."

Steven listens to the beat for a couple of minutes and writes a beautiful poem. Steven says, "Alright, ready when you guys are. Hector says, "Luis, drop the beat." Steven starts his poem. "I name this poem Beauty. Her beautiful eyes brighten up my day; when she is nears me, I want her to stay by my side forever. In this world of darkness, she helps bring light to my day. She's the type of beauty that can turn a demon into an angel. She's got a great mindset. The way she talks about her future makes you glister in the sunset as you think about her great potential in this life. I know she is going to be something special in this world because she is an angel sent from the heavens above. I hope and pray that she takes this young man under her wings and teach him the true meaning of love and beauty. Beauty, Beauty, thank you for giving a young man great insight into what true beauty truly is."

All the inmates and even some of the officers start clapping after Steven gets done reading his poem. Hector says, "That was a great poem. It was like I was listening to Common or Chance the Rapper spit a bar in a song." Luis asks, "That was great, little homie; what was your inspiration behind that poem?" Steven explains, "I hope for love one day in my life; when I find that special lady, I hope she has a pure heart, but a beautiful soul that can give me a great insight on what true beauty and true love really is." Luis responds, "You got talent; you mind teaching us how to write poems in a very detailed way?" "I don't mind; let's get started."

Steven teaches the inmates how to write poetry for about three hours. Hector asks, "So how can someone as young as you know how to write poetry so well?" Steven says, "Growing up as a kid, my mother used to listen and play a lot of neo-soul music in the house. I grew up listening to Jill Scott, Erykah Badu, D'Angelo, Maxwell, and Musiq Soulchild. I'm a huge fan of soulful music; the rhythm and the melody in the beats speak to me. When it comes to writing down the words, for me, I visualize the topic I'm talking about and describe it in the most detailed way." "Man, you something special; it's like you are a gifted genius. I wish I had a brain like yours." "And I hope I'm able to plant flowers like you. Something that my former teacher used to tell me is we all are given talents; we just got to know how to utilize them in the best way." "Big facts, I can tell you a real dude. I'm not just saying that." "I appreciate it. I got to make a phone call to a friend of mine; I will talk to you later."

Steven calls Diamond to check and see how she's doing. Diamond answers, "Steven, what's going on, bro?" Steven says. "I'm doing good; you know I'm holding it down up in here. What about you? How are you doing?" "I'm doing good. I'm preparing for college. I got plan on going to Brooks Technical College this fall." "OK, so me and you will be on the same campus as old times. I can't wait for that. So, what are you taking up?" "I got plan on taking up Nursing. You know me, I love to help people out, so why not do that for a living." "That's great. I'm happy for you; that's a perfect role for you. You are a generous person. I know you will do well and succeed in college." "I appreciate you, Steve; you always support your people and show love to people. That is what makes you special. I heard you and Dani broke up."

"Yeah, she dumped me. It is what it is; she gave up on me, but I'm not finna give up on myself. She wasn't meant for me. I'm going to be alright. It's somebody out there for me; wherever she is, I will find her one day." "You are a good man, Steve. There is a special lady out there for you. You have a great heart, and I hope one day you find true happiness."

"I appreciate the words of comfort. Have you talked to Lenny? How is he doing?" "Yes, he is doing better. I think him getting shot might have made him appreciate life more. He's been talking different; he talks more about his future, and he also is thinking about getting his GED. I think he also feels guilty about what happened to you. I'm the one that took him home after you got arrested. He told me what you did for him; you sacrificed your freedom for him; that was a courageous act. A lot of people would not have done that; that proves that you are loyal to your friends." "He's a good kid, and I hope he gets his life straightened out just like me. I couldn't let him get arrested; he would've done more time than me. I'm going to pray for him and hope he heads in the right direction in his life. So, do you have feelings for Lenny?" "I mean, he is good-looking. If he gets his life straightened out, I will definitely try to get with him." "All you can do is wish and pray for him. Well, I got to go; I wish the best for you. I know you are going to do well, my friend." "I appreciate, Steve; you stay strong; you going to be out sooner than later."

After Steven gets done talking to Diamond, he plays chess with Michael. Michael says, "Steve, the way you make your moves is outstanding. Steven responds, "Appreciated, Mike; I must say I done faced a lot of people, but you probably my best opponent. I have to think sometimes for a couple of minutes before I make a move against you." "You got to have a strong defense, which is something I taught myself how to do at an early age." "You seem super intelligent; how did you end up in here?" Michael laughs as he is about to tell his story. "Believe it or not, I was very successful before I got locked up. I got a bachelor's degree. I was a Doctor for six years, and then I got addicted to drugs and alcohol after my divorce. My wife fell in love with another man and left me for him. I saw her as my muse, the one that would be mine forever. I started drinking and using Cocaine after we broke up. I thought to myself, there was no one out there for me. I been arrested five times in two years for DUI and drug possession. I lost my doctor's license in the process. Last Year, I was thinking about killing myself; I had planned on jumping into the Savannah River. On my way there, the police stopped me, and I got arrested for DUI and drug possession. I was sentenced to do one year in here; so far, I've done six months."

Steven is shocked to hear Michael's story. "That's one hell of a story. I'm sorry you had to go through that. Are you still on drugs now?" "I have been clean since I got in here; I'm not going to lie, it was hard dealing with the withdrawals, but I have overcome. I done gotten close to GOD while in here; that has helped me out a lot." "What do you have plan on doing once you get out?" "I got plan on attending AAA meetings when I get out. I hope one day to regain my doctor's license; I want to treat and heal people. The main thing I got plan on doing is following the footsteps God has laid out for me. Officer Brown gave me some of the best advice; he told me GOD always has a better plan than the one we have. So why not follow the path God wants us to follow." "That's real; you look at me. What is the best advice you can give me?"

"Learn to love yourself and do not try to seek validation from other people. If I would have done that, I probably wouldn't be here. You remind me of myself when I was young; you have a powerful mind. Never let anybody take advantage of you or belittle you. Know that you can do anything and be who you want to be in this life. When you instill that into your brain, the sky is the limit, my friend. You should watch Hybrid Theory on YouTube. It has helped me out a lot." "I will check it out; thank you for opening up to me, but also for the great advice. I deeply appreciated it." For the rest of the day, Steven watches Impact Theory videos on YouTube on his tablet.

The next day, while picking up trash alongside the road, Steven is approached by Hector. Hector says, "Aye, Steven, word going around in jail about how good you are at poetry. I'm not just talking about the people in our pod, but almost the whole jail. You should start your own poetry business here, and you could make a good amount of money here." Steven asks, "Isn't that illegal to do in here?" "No, I sell cigarettes in here. It's a side hustle; the guards know about it. I think your poetry can help a lot of people here; everybody needs some positivity in their lives." "Ok then, who will be my first customer?" "Me, I talk to my girlfriend every night. I want to pay you 5 dollars to write me a poem for her." "Alright, that's no issue. What you want the poem to be about." "I want it to be a poem that shows her that I love her and I miss her. And when I get out, she and I will create beautiful memories together with ourselves and our lovely daughter." "Alright, when we get back to the jail, I will write one for you; I will give it to you by tomorrow morning. If you think the poem is great, you put the word out for me that I'm writing wonderful poetry that can help people out." "Say less, bro; I got you." "Do I owe you anything for giving me this advice?" "No, little homie, I just don't want to see somebody's gift go to waste."

When the inmates return to the jail, Steven returns to the cell and writes the poem Hector wanted him to write. Steven gets done writing the poem within 30 minutes before giving it to Hector; he lets Robert read the poem. Steven says, "Hey, Rob, tell me what you think about this poem I wrote?" Robert reads the poem for about five minutes before he gives a response. "This is one amazing poem; you are one great poet. You are on some Tupac Shakur type stuff. You writing this for a shawty?" "Hector wanted me to write a poem for his girlfriend. I'm about to start a poetry business in here." "OK, look at you; how much are you going to charge people for a poem?" "One dollar, I believe some of these poems can help a lot of people out in here." "I'm proud of you, bro; you using your gifts for good. When you get out of here, I know you are going to do great things." "Appreciated, bro; well, let me give this to Hector."

Steven walks over to Hector. Hector says, "You got done with the poem that fast; you are a true artist. Let's do the exchange in my cell." The guys walk to Hector's cell. Steven says, "Here's your poem. I wrote it in a beautiful way; hopefully, you like it." Hector reads the poem for a few minutes and then gives a response. "Bro, I almost cried reading this poem; she is going to love this, thank you. If we wasn't in jail right now, I'm not going to lie; I would give you a hug, amigo. I'm supposed to talk to her in an hour; I will let you know how she likes it. I'm going to put the word out on the great poet we have in this jail." "My dawg, I appreciate it. I will see you later." Later that night, Hector walks to Steven's cell and tells him that his girlfriend loved the poem. "Steve, she loved the poem. She started crying when I read it to her; again, thank you, and I just put the word out, so be prepared. You are about to have a whole bunch of people asking you for poems." How will Steven's poems affect the jail?

# Chapter 6: The Poetic Plug

Over the next two weeks, inmates in every pod and even correctional officers request Steven to write poems for them. Steven starts making a lot of money off these poems, but the main thing that made him happy was that the poems was giving inspiration and joy to the inmates.

One day after Sunday Service, Officer Brown talks to Steven about his poems. Officer Brown says, "Steven, you been in here almost a whole month; the work you doing in here is phenomenal. The inmates love the poems you wrote; it has even caught the Sheriff's attention. He was wondering if you would teach a poetry class here every Saturday while you in here. He thinks it can help some of the inmates express their feelings in a great way." Steven quickly responds, "I would love to do that; writing these poems has helped myself, but I'm glad it has helped out the other inmates in here."  "You know when you get out, this will help you get a job. It says in the Bible that in order to receive, you must give. And Steven, that is what you doing; I'm proud of you; keep it up."

As Steven goes back to his cell, one of the inmates stops him to thank him for his poem. Inmate says, "Excuse me, are you Steven?" Steven responds, "Yes." "Bro, I just wanted to say thank you for the encouraging words in the poem you wrote for me."  "I appreciate. What was your favorite part about the poem?"  "My favorite part is 'days come and go, I shall not look back at my past mistakes; I shall do my best in the present so I can be great in the future.'"   Steven explains the meaning behind the poem. "Sinner, the poem was inspired by my life. I made mistakes, but as I wake up every day, I'm making sure I'm a better man than the man I was the day before. So, one day, I will be the great, powerful man I was destined to be."   "That's powerful, man. I would definitely like some more poems."   "Well, I'm actually about to start a poetry class this Saturday. I would love to see you in the class."   "Most definitely would love to learn. I will tell everybody about it; you keep on doing your thing."

Steven returns to his cell and tells Robert that he will be teaching a poetry class. "Just got some great news. I have been told that the sheriff wants me to teach a poetry class in here." Robert responds with joy, "That wassup; my boy on his professor shit in here. When are you supposed to start?"   "This Saturday, I want you to be my co-teacher." Robert isn't sure about that decision. "I don't know nothing about poetry."   "It's all about describing things or situations in a detailed way. Like the way you gave me advice when I first got here. With this class, we can possibly help the inmates and ourselves be better people. Are you down?"   "Yeah, I got you."

During the whole week, Steven and Robert prepare for the poetry class. It's Saturday Morning; Steven and Robert walk into the classroom that was set up for them for the poetry class. Robert looks around and says, "This is one big classroom; never been up in here." Steven says, "It sure is, Officer Brown; how many people signed up for the class?" "We have thirty inmates in this jail coming in here today to learn poetry." "That's a lot, and I'm glad about that." "So, what is going to be the main topic you guys are going to talk about today?" Robert says, "We are going to be talking about goals." Steven says, "Yes, we have plan on teaching the inmates to go for their dreams and goals. I believe it will be a great class."

The inmates walk into the classroom, and Steven starts teaching the class. Steven says, "What's going on, everybody? Most of you know who I am; my name is Steven. This is my co-teacher, Robert, and today we are going to be talking about achieving goals in life. What I want you guys to do today is write down your goals. Then, in your best way, express the way you want your life to be in words. I will give you an example of my goals. I want to be somebody special and make my mother proud of me, so this is what I came up with for my poem. I call it The Underdog. Trying my best to be a better man. Obstacles and barriers steady coming my way, but I shall overcome each and every one. I shall strive for greatness as I live in this world of madness. Young brother praying and hoping for happiness because all he knows is sadness. I shall not give up on myself because I know in my heart I am destined for greatness. I'm in a storm now, but I know the darkness won't last forever; sunshine is on the other side. Jesus Christ is my ride or die, so I know I'm going to make it to the other side."

All of the inmates start clapping after Steven gets done reading his poem. Hector says, "Masterpiece, bro." Steven says, "I'm glad you guys loved my poem; now let's get started." Steven and Robert teach the inmates how to write poems, format words, and express their feelings.

After the class, all the inmates thank Steven and Robert for teaching them poetry. Inmate says, "Thank you, guys. This been an amazing class. Do you got plan on teaching more?" Steven says, "Yes, we do every Saturday."

Over the next three weeks, Steven and Robert teach the inmates more about poetry and teach them to appreciate themselves and value life.

It's Friday morning; the guys are in Columbia County doing landscape work. Hector goes over to Steve and says, "Look at you, Steve, planting flowers by yourself; I taught you well." Steven responds, "Yeah, you did; I appreciated it. I owe you a lot, Michael and Robert; your done taught me a lot up in here. If it wasn't for you, I wouldn't be teaching a poetry class. Thank you." "You welcome, bro, but it really wasn't me. That's something you been had inside of you. You just had to discover the talents and gifts you already had. Like with me, it's planting flowers; I have been doing it since a little kid, and while being here, I discovered that's my passion. When I get out of here, I'm going to get a job and try to start my own flower business." "Wouldn't be a bad idea; I mean, I would definitely buy some flowers from you; you are great at what you do." "Not only do I want my daughter and wifey to be proud of me, but I'm also going to do everything in my power to ensure they have everything they want and need." "I feel you. I feel the same way about my mother. When I get out, I want to do something with poetry, not necessarily be a poet, but create something that inspires people." "You ever thought about doing a clothing line with poetry or motivational words on the clothes?"

Hearing Hector's idea about starting a clothing line sparks a great idea in Steven's mind. "I never thought of that, but by doing that, I can make a huge impact on a whole lot of people." "It just an idea, but with your creativity skills, you going to make a great impact on this world; just watch and see." "I appreciate, and best believe big things are going to pop off for the both of us."

After the inmates finish landscaping in Columbia County, they head back to the jail. On the way back to jail, Steven sees a Corvette driving on the highway. He visualizes himself driving the vehicle. Steven looks at Robert and says, "Robert, you see that Corvette; your boy going to be driving it one day." Robert responds, "In order to have what you want, you got to see yourself having it first; you will have it one day." "That's what we need to talk about tomorrow in class: dreaming and having a vision." "That's a great idea, so let's do that."

The next day, Steven and Robert teach the poetry class, and the main topic they talk about is Dreams and Vision. Steven says, "What's going on, guys? Today, we will be talking about dreams and visualizing. I been watching a lot of motivating videos on YouTube; one video I watched is this Lil Baby video, where he tells the interviewer he envisioned himself having millions before having millions. That is something we all have to do as people; some of us here want to open our own businesses, some of us want to get our lives straightened out, and most of us want to be successful. In order to do that, we have to see ourselves achieving that before we actually do. Here's the poem I wrote for this topic. "Going for better in life." Writing letters to myself telling myself I'm going to be big, I'm a true believer in my dreams, I'm like the eagle in the sky, I'm flying to greatness, Times get tough, but I have to stay patient, See myself as a future success story. Once I make it big, my Mom won't have to worry about no bills because her son is going to put her in the hills; as long as I believe in myself and God, I can achieve any dream I envision for myself. I shall fly high for my dreams because before I die, I don't want to regret a thing."

Everybody in the room starts clapping. While looking around the classroom as everybody claps, he notices this man with a cowboy hat he never seen before. After the class is over, the inmates greet Steven. After they get done greeting him, Officer Brown introduces him to the mysterious man with the cowboy hat on. Officer Brown says, "Steven, I want to introduce you to somebody; Steven, this is Sheriff Scott, Sheriff Scott, this is Steven." Sheriff Scott says, "Mr. Steven, I done heard a lot about you. I been told you been doing a lot of good for your fellow inmates in here." Steven says, "Well, I'm the type of person that's trying to help out people the best way I know how. I'm glad I have greatly impacted some of the people in here." "Have being in here made you a changed man?" "Most definitely, my first day here was the realization that I needed to change my life, but also disappointing my mother. I promise myself when I get out of here, I will never disappoint her again. I'm going to be that guy GOD designed me to be. Going to the Sunday Services has given me great insight on what I can be and do." "I love to hear that. I read your file; the Judge gave you a great deal. What is your plan once you get out of here?" "I'm going to start going to GED classes, get my GED, and look for a job. I believe I will do great things once I get out of here." "Well, Mr. Steven, I got great news; your beginning of a new start in your life starts today. The judge has granted your release; he and me believe you have learned your lesson." Steven is shocked, and with a big smile on his face, he asks, "Are you serious?" "Yes, I am; you are a free man."

With tears of joy, Steven hugs Sheriff Scott. Steven has been given a second chance to go in the right direction in his life. "Thank you, sir; I promise you and the judge will not be disappointed or regret this decision." "I got a feeling we won't be disappointed. Like you said in that poem you wrote, believe in yourself and believe in GOD. I wish you the best of luck, Steven. Do great things."

When Sheriff Scott leaves, Steven hugs Officer Brown, tears falling from his eyes. "Can't believe I'm a free man." "This is GOD giving you a second chance. Out of all my years as a correctional officer, I have never met an inmate special like you. That journal and the Bible your mother gave you, stay using them both. Stay writing down your goals and reading the Bible; it's going to help you out. You are going to do great things, young man. While in here, did you find your purpose in life?"

One great thing about being in jail is that Steven did find his purpose in life. "Yes, I did, being an inspiration to people. I want to inspire people, but also I want people to learn and know they can do anything they put their mind to." "I'm happy to hear you are going to inspire a lot of people. What's your favorite verse in the Bible?" "I haven't read the whole Bible, but my favorite verse is Philippians 4: 13: "I can do all things through Christ who strengthens me." It mainly says that with GOD on our side, we can overcome any situation." "Yes indeed. Are you going to call your Mom?" "You mind if I use your phone?" "By all means."

Officer Brown lets Steven use his phone to call his Mom. Steven's Mom answers the phone. "Hello, who is this?" Steven says, "Mom, it's me; I got some great news. They are letting me free, Momma. I'm a free man." Steven's Mom is happy to hear her son is free. "For real Steven?" "Yes, Mom, can you come get me?" "Yes, baby, on my way to you right now." Steven's Mom hangs up the phone and rushes to her son. Steven says, "Well, I guess I will get the rest of my belongings and say my goodbyes to everybody; again, Officer Brown, thank you for everything."

As Steven heads back to his cell to get the rest of his belongings, all the inmates start clapping and saluting Steven. Michael says, "I heard that you was getting out today. Is that true?" "Yes, it is. I'm going to miss playing chess with you, and I won't forget the advice you gave me." "It's time for you to spread your wings and be great, so don't waste this opportunity. I guess I'm back now being the King of Chess. Make the right moves and let GOD guide you in the right direction." Steven and Michael hug each other. "Thank you. Here's my phone number; call me sometimes."

Other inmates, including Hector, talk to Steven. Hector says, "Bro, I just heard the news. Congratulations; now you can chase your goals and dreams. I get out within a month; I would love to link up with you once I get out." "No problem, thank you for everything. I know how to plant flowers because of you, and I was able to help a lot of inmates here. Thanks to you making me freestyle and writing poems." "You helped me out, too; the poetry class has helped me out a lot. I been writing poems to my wife and daughter, thanks to you. With you gone, I don't know who's going to teach the class." "I have a great replacement that's going to do a great job. I'm going to talk to him right now. Here's my phone number; hit me up whenever, bro. Hector and Steven hug one another.

Steven goes to his cell and is greeted by Robert. Robert stands up with a smile and says, "I heard you getting out; congrats, bro." "Yeah, man, I'm about to go home. Thank you, big homie, for everything. Out of everybody in here, you was the main one who helped me and made me believe in myself. You like a big brother I never had; I will never forget what you did for me. I forever got love for you." "It was my honor, bro; you are going to do great things. I'm grateful that God has made me one of the people to inspire you on your path to greatness. Stay bettering yourself, stay away from the streets, and read your Bible. I love you, bro; stay focused and stay looking up." Steven and Robert hug one another.

Steven has one request for Robert. "I need one more favor from you." Robert responds, "What is it?" "I need you to teach the poetry class." "I'm not good at it like you, plus I don't have a crafty mind like you." "You was able to show this crafty-minded guy how to believe in himself and how to find his purpose. To me, you are very qualified for this job." "Since you asked me, I will do it." "You are going to do well; just speak what's in your heart." "I will, my brother; all of us rooting for you makes us proud. One last question for you, Steve: what is your purpose in life?" Steven responds, "To be an inspiration to people." "Your light shall shine bright, young king. Steven and Robert hug one another one more time.

As Steven walks out of the jail, he gets a standing ovation from the inmates. Steven walks out of the jail with tears of joy and is greeted by his mother. Steven runs straight into his mother's arms like a little kid. Steven yells, "Mom!" Steven's Mom yells, "Son!" They both embrace one another with tears in their eyes. "I missed you so much; I'm so glad you are out." "Mom, I promise you I will never put you in this position again. I'm about to do great things; today starts a new beginning." "I already know, son; I can't wait to see what you do. Now let's go home."

As Steven arrives back home, he notices a couple of his friends on his front porch. As Steven gets out of his Mom's car, they greet him with hugs. Rich says, "Welcome home, bro." Diamond says, "Welcome home, Steve." Dee says, "Welcome home, little homie; I can tell you were lifting weights up in there; you done got big." Steven responds, "A brother always got to stay in great shape." As Steven walks into his house, he is greeted by Darius's Mom with a cake. Darius's Mom says, "My son, glad to see you, Steve. I made you a cake. I hope you like it. Danny is at basketball practice; he wanted me to tell you he glad you home. You mind if I talk to you in private?" "No, I don't mind. Let's go to the backyard."

Steven and Darius's Mom go into the backyard to talk. Darius's Mom says, "I know it's been a minute since you talked to Darius; just to let you know he's doing fine. I found out last week I'm going to be a grandma."

Steven is surprised and excited to hear that Darius is going to be a father. "Darius is about to be a father?" "Yes, he found out a couple of days ago. The mother of the baby is some girl named Destiny. I haven't met her yet, but I got plan on meeting her in a couple of days." "I done met her before; she's cool; I can't believe my boy is about to be a Dad. Just know I'm going to do everything in my power to make sure his baby and Danny are straight. I know if the shoe was on the other foot, he would do the same thing for me." "I appreciate, Steve; I'm glad that Darius has a friend like you. He calls every Sunday at 1 o clock; come by the house tomorrow so you can speak to him." "I most definitely will; now, let's get back to this party."

As Steven returns to the party, more people in the neighborhood come by to celebrate Steven's release from jail. The party lasts all day long. As the guest leaves, Dee, Diamond, and Rich stay to talk to Steven about helping him out. Steven's Mom says, "Well, guys, thank you for showing up for the party. Steven, all of us have created a plan to help you out. Even though you have your own car, it's best not to drive the car out of town until you get your license." Steven responds, "Then how am I going to get to school and take care of business." Diamond says, "I will be taking you to school, I got to go Brooks Tech early in the morning for my classes. If you got to stay over, just call me and I will come back and pick you up." Rich says, "When it comes to hanging out, I got you, even though I'm going to be gone within two weeks. I got friends that will help you out." Dee says, "And with me, I done started a side hustle. I'm cutting grass now, and I need a second man. Would you work with me from time to time?" Steven says, "Yeah, I'm down." Steven's Mom says, "Steven, we got your back, and we are going to do everything in our power to make sure that you succeed. Steven says, "I appreciate that, and I'm going to do better than I did before, I promise." Steven's Mom says, "Let's hug guys." Steven, his Mom, Dee, Rich, and Diamond hug one another. Dee says, "Love you, youngin, talk to you later." Rich says, "See your bro; we going to link soon." Diamond says, "I will see you first thing on Monday morning."

The next morning, Steven talks to his lawyer on the phone about what he needs to do since he is out of jail. Steven says, "Hey, Mr. Dave, how you been doing?" Mr. Dave responds. "I been doing good. Congratulations on getting out; I can't wait to see what you do. Now, let me break down everything you have to do now that you are out. First thing is to apply for GED classes. Do that first thing tomorrow morning. Second is reporting to your probation officer every Friday. Third is getting a job; you must show you can get a job and make legit money. And fourth, but finally, stay out of trouble and be around the right people. Do you have any questions?" "No sir, there are no questions." "Alright then, come by my office on Tuesday; I have a great opportunity for you that I believe you will like." "Alright, sounds good; I will see you on Tuesday."

Steven goes downstairs to eat breakfast. His mother cooked him an all-star breakfast: Cheese Grits, Bacon, Toast, Pancakes, and Orange Juice on the side. Steven says, "Mom, you went all out. This food is way better than the food in jail." Steven's Mom responds, "Well, them cooks don't know how to throw down like your Momma; now eat up."

After eating breakfast, Steven and his mother have a conversation. Steven's Mom says. "I'm so glad you are home; I was praying day and night for you. I heard you was teaching a poetry class while in there." Steven says, "Yeah, I did; I was able to help out a lot of inmates by doing that. Hopefully, I made a great impact on them." "You are intelligent. I know for a fact you made a great impact on the people in there." "So, I got to ask how much money we got left? I made a couple of dollars while in jail." "Steve, I don't want you worrying about no money. We have a good amount; you have about 2 bands left over in your shoebox. Please use that money wisely, and don't even think about going to the streets." "Mom, I promise I won't; I'm going to try and get a job. Hopefully, I find one that pays well and comes with great benefits." "I believe you will find a good job; do you have planned out what you want to be in life?"

"Being a successful man, but I believe in my heart I am destined to make a great impact in this world. I just got to follow in the footsteps God has made for me in my life. Granted, it might get hard sometimes, but I'm not going to give up on myself." "Well, son, just know Momma is not going to give up on you; I'm forever going to support you. While you was in jail, your father wrote you a letter I read it. It's nothing bad; he's not judging you, mainly just giving you some advice."

Steven's Mom gives Steven the letter to read. Steven wonders what his father wrote. "Dear Son, I heard that you was in jail. A part of me wishes I was out there, and maybe this could have been prevented. I'm not trying to make it about me; I want you to have the best son. Your mother told me about the deal the judge gave you; that's a great deal. Take advantage of that. You have so much potential to be great and do great things in this life. We all have a purpose in life, so go out and find yours. Trust me, it's not in these streets; the streets don't love nobody. I wish I had known or found my purpose before I got locked up. Steve, you don't want to end up like me every day. I'm around people who are what-if stories, including myself. I'm praying that you get on the right path and find your way in this life. Sadness and hard times come our way in life, but we cannot let that get us down. We have to stay fighting for better and going for greatness. I love you, Steve; you will bounce back from this. People might count you out and give up on you. Just always remember: never give up on yourself. I'm going to leave you with this verse; it's Joshua 1:9: Be strong and courageous. Do not be afraid; do not be discouraged, for the Lord your God will be with you wherever you go. I love you, son; keep your head up; better days are coming."

Steven says after reading the letter, "I appreciate the support; I'm actually glad he wrote me. With me being in jail with other people, I understand why my Dad did what he did. He was wrong for what he did, but he felt like he had to do it to survive and take care of his family." Steven's Mom responds, "It seems like you have forgiven your father for not being there for you?" "Honestly, I don't know if I forgive him, but I understand him more." "Well, that's the first step, and you will forgive him one day."

After talking to his Mom, Steven goes to Darius's house to wait for his phone call. Steven hugs Darius's Mom and says, "Hey, Ms. Jeanette, has Darius called yet?" Darius's Mom responds, "Not yet." As soon as Darius's Mom responds to Steve, she gets a phone call. Darius's Mom says, "Hello." Darius says, "Ma dukes, what's going on? How you doing?” “I got somebody that wants to speak to you.” “Who is it?”

Darius's Mom hands the phone to Steven. Steven says, “Well, well, if it isn't the money-making Mitch to my ace boogie.” Darius is surprised and happy to hear from Steven. “I know this isn't who I think it is. Steven, this you?” “Yep, it's me.” “Bro, I'm so happy to hear from you; when did you get out?” “I literally got out yesterday.” “Glad to hear that you free; you got my note?” “Yeah, I got it. You already know I'm going to look out for Danny. And congratulations to you; I heard you got a baby on the way.” “Yep, it's true; Destiny got in contact with me in here; the baby is mine.” “How do you feel about the whole situation?” “A part of me is happy, but a part of me is sad too at the same time. I'm glad I'm going to be a father, but I wish I could be out and help Destiny out with the baby. Hopefully, I make it out of here before the baby comes; I want my kids to have love in their lives. I want my kid to know that their Daddy loves them. With me saying all of this, I'm going to need another favor. I know you trying to straighten your life and everything, but I need somebody to watch over my kid. Could you make sure that Destiny is straight?” “I will do my best; you know I got you. So, what all you doing in prison?” “Believe it or not, I'm cutting hair in here and started GED classes. When I found out I had a kid on the way, I told myself I got to make sure my kids have more than I do. I got to do right; my father never cared about me, but it isn't going to be the same with my kids. I have to be better, and I will be. So, what do you plan on doing now that you're out?” “Mainly getting my GED and getting a good job.”

"Did Dani ever reach out to you?" "I talked to her on the phone when I was in jail; she dumped me. She believes it would look bad for her to be with me due to me going to jail." "Man, forget shawty; she is going to wish she stayed with you. It's better fish out there in the sea. You a good dude; you going to find a good woman. Your phone number still the same?" "Yes." "Alright, I'm going to call you later this week; stay keeping your head up." "Likewise."

As Steven goes outside, he notices Danny and other kids in the neighborhood playing football. As Steven walks up to the kids, they start running his way. All of them start yelling out Steven. They celebrate the guy they remember buying them ice cream and giving them money. Danny runs and hugs Steven. Danny says, "Steven, I'm so glad to see you; you want to play football with us?" Steven responds, "Let me school you guys really quick." Steven plays football with Danny and the rest of the kids in the neighborhood.

After playing football, Steven talks to Danny. "I bet you didn't know I was that good." Danny nods his head to the side. "You alright; you aren't better than me." "So, I hear you playing football for the middle school now." "Yep, I'm the quarterback; I'm going to be the next Patrick Mahomes. I have a game on Wednesday at 4. You should come." "I won't miss it; you better go lights out." "Watch me work; I'm going to put on a show. I was born to be a star." "Talk your stuff, bro." "I wish my brother was out to see me play. He prepared me for this Moment; he taught me everything I know." "I know, bro, just know I'm here for you. If you need anything, just let me know." "Thank you, Steve." "I'm going to talk to you later; stay working on that arm."

Steven goes back to his house and reads his Bible. Right before he goes to sleep, he says a prayer to God. "Dear God, thank you for giving me a second chance; I pray that my brothers in jail be alright; tomorrow is going to be special. I thank you for the blessings you have coming my way. In Jesus' name, I pray, amen."

It's Monday morning; Steven wakes up excited as he is about to start this new journey in his life. Steven goes downstairs to eat breakfast and talks to his mother. Steven's Mom says, "Well, son, how are you feeling?" Steven responds, "I'm feeling great, can't wait to get back in a classroom. I'm going to take great advantage of this opportunity; I believe I will have a great experience in the GED class."

Diamond picks up Steven, and they head to school together. Steven smiles as he returns to school for the first time in three years. Steven says, "If you would have told me two months ago that me and you would be going to be in school together again, I would call you a liar." Diamond responds, "God works in mysterious ways. On Mondays, I have classes from 8:00- 2:00. Can you wait that long for me?" "Yes, no problem; you never know, I might find a lady to hang out with." "There you go, but you are going to do great things here. Just remember to stay believing and never give up." Steven and Diamond arrive at Brooks Technical College. Steven looks at the front of the campus and thinks about his future. "Well, today starts a new beginning in both of our lives; we shall do great things." "Yes, we should."

Steven walks anxiously to the GED class. As Steven walks into the classroom, the whole class turns toward Steven's direction. Steven asks, "Excuse me, is this the GED class?" Mr. Marcus, the GED teacher, responds. "Yes, it is. Are you here to sign up for the class?" "Yes, sir, I am." "Well, by all means, have a seat, and I will give you a paper to fill out. After Steven is done filling out the paper, he is given four tests to see where his education level is. After Steven finishes taking the tests, he is let go for the day. Mr. Marcus says, "Alright, Mr. Anderson, it seemed like you did well on your tests. Come back on Wednesday, and we will have you working here. Before you go, go ahead and get your ID from the school. And one final thing, Mr. Anderson, to get this GED, you have to be fully committed." Steven looks straight into Mr. Marcus's eyes and says, "Sir, I am fully committed. I can't wait to show you what I'm made of."

As Steven walks out of the classroom, one of the people in the classroom walks out with him. The person says, "Do you need help getting to the library to get your ID?" Steven says, "Actually, I do. Do you mind helping me out?" "Sure, you look awfully familiar. I feel like I know you from somewhere." "Well, you know what they say: all black people look alike." The person starts laughing. "You're funny. Now I know who you are; you are a plug. I remember seeing you a month ago in one of the streets in Augusta." Steven wants to refrain from the past lifestyle he used to live. "I no longer live that lifestyle; I'm no longer a plug. I'm just a man who is trying to change his life for the better." "I understand; I'm trying to do the same. I have a one-year-old kid, and I'm doing my best to provide for her." "Things will get better; you just have to have faith in GOD and believe in yourself." "Thank you. I needed that." Steven and Ashley walk into the library to get his ID. Thank you for showing me where the library is; I will see you on Wednesday. By the way, my name is Steven." "My name is Ashley, and it was nice meeting you."

As Steven gets done getting his ID, a young, beautiful lady gets attracted by his appearance. The beautiful lady taps Steven on his shoulder and sings. "Can we talk for a minute? Boy, I just want to know your name." Steven turns around and sees that it is Lily. The beautiful girl he met at the mall before he got locked up. He wonders in his mind: this is just a coincidence or maybe fate.

# Chapter 7: Finding My Way Back

Steven is ecstatic to see Lily as he thought he would never see her again. She looks more stunning than ever before. There are a few other people around, but Lily is the only person who got his full attention. Steven says, "Lily, it's so great to see you." Steven and Lily hug one another. Lily responds, "It's so great to see you too, Steve; you go to College here also?" Thinking about telling her a lie, he decides to tell her the truth. "I'm signing up for GED classes, and I'm going to try to get my GED. And then hopefully go to college." "I'm proud of you, and don't say try; say when you get your GED. When you say that, you are saying you are going to get it in the future." "Well, thank you, Mom." Lily laughs. "You welcome, and I'm not your mother, even though she's probably a wonderful lady." "You right, you are not; you are a beautiful queen. I know my mother would agree with me on that. Lily starts smiling and touches her hair. "I will give you credit; you know how to make a girl smile. Are you doing anything right now?" "No, I'm not; I'm done with my class for the rest of the day." "Great, you can keep me company until my next class."

Steven and Lily talk for almost two hours. Steven asks, "So, what are you taking up here?" Lily says, "I'm taking up nursing. I love helping people out, so I think it would be a perfect occupation for me. I hope you are not mad at me. I tried texting and calling you, but I didn't get a response." Steven doesn't tell Lily about him being in jail. "My apologies. I been having a lot going on in my life. I'm not going to lie; I thought you might have met another guy and decided to ditch me." "No, well, it was this one guy I met who caught my eye."

Steven wonders who this guy is. "Who was this guy that caught your eye?" Lily says, "I met him a couple of months ago; he wanted me to help him find a great outfit. The way he spoke to me charmed me like nobody has ever done. He's a great guy despite being a bad singer." Steven starts laughing. "So, I'm guessing this wonderful guy is an intelligent man named Steven, right?" "Yes, indeed, you are right; I'm not going to lie. Ever since I met you, you have always stayed on my mind. You have this light about you. I don't know everything about you, but you are a special person. You are going to do great things." This makes Steven smile and feel like there may be true love out there. "I must be super special if I surprised a girl like you in that way. I'm not going to lie; you been on my mind since I first met you, too. Your beauty is like the essence of an angel. I hope I'm not doing too much with my words of choice." "No, you ok. I actually love to hear you speak. I wish I could hear you speak some more, but I must go to class and hear my boring professor speak. What days are you usually here?" "I will be here every Monday and Wednesday from 8-2." "Well, I can't wait to see you again this Wednesday; you have a nice day." "Likewise."

After talking to Lily, Steven waits for Diamond. While waiting for Diamond, he sees a guy struggling with his paper. He decides to help the guy out. Steven asks, "Excuse me. If you don't mind me asking, what are you working on?" The guy says, "I'm working on this essay about Martin Luther King." "What part are you struggling with?" "The opening sentence, I don't know where to start." Steven wants to know how does the guy views Martin Luther King Jr. "Who is Martin Luther King Jr to you?" "A man that changed how we as people look at one another." "Ok, then put something down like Martin Luther King Jr, a man who made a great impact on this world and changed how we in the human society look at one another." "Man, that's genius; that helped me a lot. I appreciate it, man. What's your name?" "My name is Steven." "My name is Garrett; what are you taking up here?" "I'm actually in GED class; I do got plan on going to college here once I get done." "That's wassup, man; you are a smart dude; you should take up what I'm taking up." "And what's that?" "Computer Programming is all about paying close attention to detail; I believe somebody like you would love this program." "I might take that up; you never know. My main goal is to be my own businessman. I want to be somebody that people can look up to." "I like it. That's amazing. Listen, I got to go, but I would definitely like to talk some more. Since you helped me, if you ever need anything, hit me up." Garrett gives Steven his phone number.

After Garrett leaves, Diamond shows up and Steven and her return to Thomson. Diamond asks Steven, "So, how was your first day?" Steven responds, "It went well; I took some tests, and I will find out my results on Wednesday. That will determine where my academic knowledge is at. I also ran into this girl named Lily, whom I had met before I got locked up. It was great seeing her; she is the embodiment of an angel. I know that sounds weird, but if you see her, you will know what I'm talking about." "Shawty got you Sprung, so how did the conversation go?" "It went great; she's something special. She told me she haven't stopped thinking about me since she met me." "Well, I'm glad she knows the type of person you are and appreciates you. Did you tell her everything that has happened since you last saw one another?" "I told her I was in GED classes, but I didn't tell her anything about me going to jail. I don't want to scare her off; I want her to get to know me before I reveal my past to her." "Well, if she truly likes you, she probably will not care about that. My Mom taught me that if a person truly likes you, they going to hold you down through thick and thin. Just like God showed you Dani's true colors, he will also show you Lily's true intentions."

"You're right; I appreciate the advice. I talked to Darius yesterday; you know he about to be a father." Diamond is shocked to hear the news. "Darius, about to be a father, man, we are growing up. All I know I want to know is who the mother of the baby is." "Destiny is the mother of the baby?" "The girl he was dancing with at my party a few months back?" "Yeah, I told him while he is in prison, I will look out for Danny and the baby. You know where shawty stays at?" "She stays in the apartment complex behind Walmart; she's about two years older than we are. So, Darius might have found a great lady, but what do you mean by being there for the baby?" "Being there for appointments if she needs somebody or if she and the baby need some financial assistance, I will help out with that also. I'm doing this because he would do the same for me." "Well, that's great to hear, but don't do nothing illegal to get money." "I'm not. I'm done with that stuff. I'm a changed man."

Diamond drops Steven at his house and is greeted by Rich on his front porch. Rich says, "Bossman, what's going on with you?" Steven says, "I'm doing good. I just came from GED class." "That wassup. I'm about to go and shoot some hoops with some of my guys. Do you want to go?" "Yeah, bro, let me school you and your boys really quick."

Steven and Rich head to the basketball court. Steven asks, "So, what you been up to, bro?" Rich says, "Been working out to prepare for basketball season. Also, I been tutoring kids and teaching them the fundamentals of basketball." "Proud of you, bro; I know I better get tickets to the game." "I got you, bro, going to have you sitting courtside." "How your pops doing?" "He's doing good; he also happy that you out and trying to get your GED. When he found out you got arrested, he had tears in his eyes. He thought you had messed up your whole life, but God gave you another chance."

"Yes, he did. I know some people probably laughed and celebrated my downfall." "You talking about Nikolas?" "Yeah, bro, was the main one talking about I wouldn't be nothing, but I'm going to prove him and everybody else out of a lie." "He probably did, but while you was in jail, Nikolas had his own downfall." "What happened?" Rich explains, "Well, when he went to Georgia Tech for his physical to play football there, they found out he had an enlarged heart. So, he can't play football no more." Even though Nikolas bullied Steven, Steven is still saddened by the news. "Man, that's tough; my prayers are with him and his family. Even though me and him don't like one another, I don't wish that on nobody."

"Yeah, that was a tough blow, but how was the first day?" "It went great. I took a couple of tests, and then I ran into the most beautiful girl I have ever seen." "Who's the girl you are talking about?" "Her name is Lily, and she's a girl I met at the mall before I got locked up. When I first met her, I felt a connection. It was great seeing her." "You never know; it might be fate. I know. I see that your other girl has moved on with another dude." "You talking about Dani. Who's the guy?" "The dude's name is Chris. He a star baseball player; he goes to Beckerman's Academy." Steven is not surprised he still has love for Dani; he hopes that she finds true happiness. "She got herself a prep school guy. I'm not surprised; hopefully, he treats her well." "Well, if you ask me, she missed out on a good person. It's like what J. Cole said in 03' Adolescence show old girl what she missing the most illest nigga alive. She going to regret ever dumping you; just watch and see."

Steven and Rich arrive at the basketball court and are greeted by Rich's friends, with whom they previously played basketball with. Kurt smiles as he sees Steven and says, "There he goes." All the guys run and dap Steven up. Jack says, "Glad to see you out of jail, bro; I know you going to do positive things now you out." Lance says, "Steve, it's so good to see you, bro; now I can school you." Steven laughs and responds, "We are about to find out." The guys play basketball for about one hour.

After playing basketball, the guys talk to Steven. Kurt says. "So, Steve, if you don't mind me asking, what was jail like?" Steven says, "It was a learning experience; when they first put me in my cell by myself, I knew the street life wasn't for me. My Mom seeing me behind those walls made me feel disappointed in myself; she didn't raise me to be a drug dealer. Plus, I want better in my life; I know if I stay in the streets, I'm either going back to jail or worse. I did meet great people and learned new things. I learned to plant flowers; I got great advice from the inmates while I was inside. I started my own poetry class while I was in jail. Overall, I thank God for sending me there because I believe that being in there has made me go harder for my dreams and goals."

Jack says, "Glad to hear that; even though we haven't known you as long as Rich has, we've got your back." Lance says, "Yes, we do; we would love to hang out with you sometime." Kurt says, "We know Rich is going to be leaving us next weekend, and you going to need somebody to hang out with. We would be glad to support and be there for you. One thing about our crew is we look out for one another. And we are there for each other through the good and bad times." Rich says, "Yeah, Steve, these guys are going to support you while I'm gone." Steven says, "Guys, I appreciate; thank you. I'm down to hang out with you guys any time of the day. So, what you're going to do since your graduated?"

Kurt says, "I'm taking a year off from school and working for my Dad." Lance says, "I'm going to college this fall; I'm going to be taking up Business Management." Jack says, "I'm in college right now taking up classes in technology." Steven says, "Well, guys, just know that by believing in ourselves and GOD, we can accomplish our goals and dreams. It might get tough sometimes, but remember, never fold under the pressure no matter the circumstances." Jack says, "Big facts."

As the guys leave the basketball court, Steven notices a young lady staring at him. He looks closely and sees that the young lady is Dani. This is Steven's first time seeing Dani since being released from jail. As they both stare at one another, Steven taps Rich on the shoulder and says, "Hey Rich, I will be back; I got to talk to somebody." Rich sees that the person he got to talk to is Dani. Rich says, "Alright, bro, good luck."

Steven walks over to Dani to talk to her and wonders what she will say to him. Steven says, "Well, I didn't expect to see you here. I'm guessing you probably surprised to see me." Even though they broke up, Dani is happy to see Steven. Dani says, "I heard that you got out; even though we are not together anymore, I am glad that you are free." "Appreciated. I actually just started my first day in GED class. Being in jail made me wiser and made me go harder for my dreams. I'm officially done with the streets; I'm retired from the game. I'm about to do great things." "I'm happy for you; you deserve happiness. I hope everything you dream of comes true. Listen, I was in a tough situation two months ago; you was the man

I wanted to be with. I am thankful for everything you did for me. When you got arrested, I had multiple people calling me about it and some of those people advised me not to no longer date you. Of course, I thought about how this would affect me and you. I broke up with you because I was scared it would tarnish my image. Plus, my Mom told me to stay away from you. She said all you are is a hoodlum and a thug. Just know, Steve, I will forever have love for you."

Steven vents himself toward Dani. "First of, your Mom had good reasoning for saying that about me. Even though I am more than a hoodlum and a thug, I made my mistakes in life. I'm not going to let those mistakes define me as a person. We had a great relationship; you broke my heart when you broke up with me. I was already at my lowest when I was in jail; you made me bend a little bit more. I saw you as my ride-or-die, but like I said on the phone that day, you just wasn't meant to be on my side. We had love between one another, but with everything that you just stated, it was never real love between us. I still wish you nothing but the best, sweetheart." This has Dani looking disheartened.

As Steven finishes talking to Dani, her new boyfriend shows up. Dani's Boyfriend says, "Hey baby, you are looking sexy today; who's your friend?" Dani and her boyfriend kiss; Steven still keeps a straight face. Dani says, "This is Steve, Steve this is Chris." "Steve, I know you from somewhere. Oh yeah, he's the plug guy you was telling me about. Dani told me you sell the best weed. You got some on you now?" Steven laughs and smiles. "No, I no longer sling any product; I'm just a man trying to be legit." "I heard you and your boys had got arrested; that could scare a lot of people from selling drugs again." "I'm not scared of nothing or nobody, homie; the only person that I fear is GOD. I forgot to ask how long you guys been dating?" "We been dating for a month, been trying to get with her for a long time. This girl right here is a delightful angel to be around." Steven doesn't show any weakness. He just starts smiling. "That is amazing; it's great to see two wonderful people together." "Yes, it is. Well baby, we got to go; it was nice meeting you, Steve." "Goodbye, Steve. Good luck with everything I wish you nothing but the best."

Steven smiles and walks off. As he returns back to Rich's vehicle, Rich asks, "So, how was the conversation?" Steven says, "I spoke my peace, and I met her boyfriend. Either way, I found peace with Dani; I wish her nothing but the best." "I'm glad you found peace with that situation. Appreciated; my parents are throwing me a going away party for me next Friday. I would love for you to come." "I'm down; as long as your parents cool with it, I will be there." "They will be cool with it; I know my father will be excited to see you." Rich drops Steven off at his house. Rich says, "Alright, bro, I will talk to you later." "Yes indeed, appreciate, bro. I needed to get out of the house."

Steven walks into his house and is greeted by his mother. Steven's Mom asks, "Hey baby, how was your first day?" Steven says, "It went great. I took a couple of tests. I find out Wednesday about my results. I made a couple of friends there also." "I'm happy for you, son; you are going to do great. Show these people who you are." "I will, Momma; I'm tired. I'm going to bed, goodnight Mom." Steven hugs his mother and goes to bed.

The next morning, Steven goes to see his lawyer, Mr. Dave, at his office. Mr. Dave hugs Steven. Mr. Dave says, "Steven, what's going on, man? What was your first day in GED class like?" Steven answers, "It went great. I'm going to do well in my GED class. I do got to ask how long I got to wait to get my driver's license?" "It's up to your parole officer; you probably got to wait at least thirty days due to the drug charges. If you driving without a license, I will say do your best not to get caught." "I'm going to do my best to stay out of trouble. So, what is this opportunity you want to talk to me about?" "Well, since you are on parole, your probation officer is going to want you to get a job. So, I want you to work for my brother, who owns a landscaping business. I told him about you, and he wants you to work for him." "How much will I be getting paid?" "With you working part-time, it would be about $500 every two weeks. I know it's not the same amount of money you was making when you was selling drugs, but it can help you out. So, will you accept the offer?" Steven is happy about the offer. "Yes, I sure will; when do I start?" "My brother is here now waiting to meet you. Let me introduce you to him.

Mr. Dave introduces Steven to his brother. Mr. Dave says, "Joe, this is Steven, the kid I was telling you about. Steven, this is Joe, my big brother." Mr. Joe says, "Nice to meet you, Steven; my brother told me so much about you. He told me you are in GED class. What are the best days for you to work?" Steven says, "I go to class on Monday and Wednesday. If you can work around my schedule, that would be great." "Yeah, we can work around that; come meet me at my spot on Thursday morning at 8 a.m. sharp. Then we will get you started." "Ok, that sounds great. Thank you, Mr. Dave and Mr. Joe, for this opportunity. I promise you guys won't regret it." Mr. Dave says, "I know we won't; you going to do great things."

As Steven leaves his lawyer's office, one of Mr. Dave's assistants criticizes his decision to help out Steven. Mr. Dave's assistant says, "Why you wasting your time on that thug? All he is going to do is go back to the streets. It's no use in trying to help that kid." Mr. Dave responds, "First of all, you should be ashamed of yourself for judging him without even getting to know him. We have had a lot of clients who were found guilty of their crimes. That kid, though, he's something special. I never met somebody like him before; all he needs is support and people being there for him. Joe and I are going to make sure he succeeds. Steven Anderson will be a success story; just watch and see."

After Steven leaves his lawyer's office, he heads back to the Harmony Block to speak to his former crew. While driving on the block, memories start popping in his head, thinking about the many times he had hustled out here. As Steven pulls up on the block in his vehicle, some of the people who look up to him on the block run up to his vehicle like he is Michael Jordan. Steven daps all of the guys up. Steven says, "What's going on, guys?" Randy says, "Oh, snap, Steven, what's going on? Glad to see you out?" All the other guys come and speak to Steven, as all of them look up to him. These kids are sixteen years old; Steven put them under his wing, taught them the game, and looked out for them. Deshawn says, "Man, when we found out you and everybody else got arrested, it had everybody messed up. We miss your, especially you and Darius; your two ran this whole block." Steven says, "Yeah, we had some good times out here. What your been doing while I was in jail?" Deshawn says, "Things were tough when you and Darius went away, but Big Mike stepped in and made sure we were straight. Speaking of which, here he comes now."

When Steven and Darius got arrested, Big Mike returned to Harmony Block to make sure everything ran smoothly, as he made most of his profit from the Harmony Projects. Big Mike approaches Steven. Big Mike smiles and hugs Steven. Big Mike says, "My boy Steve, so happy to see you, glad to see you out; let me speak to you for a minute. So, you good when it comes to money?" Steven says, "Yeah, I'm straight; I'm not trying to get back out here." Big Mike is shocked to hear Steven's answer, as Steven is one of the best drug dealers he has ever seen. "Why not? You can run this whole block all by yourself. You could be the biggest drug dealer down here." "That's not my goal in life; I'm aiming for something bigger than this. This isn't for me, Mike, no offense to you. My time in jail showed me I have a bigger purpose in life than this." Big Mike recognizes Steven is a changed man as he looks directly into Steven's eyes. "I can respect that you can walk free. Darius made sure to pay me back for my product being taken. I have seen a lot of youngins out on these blocks, but you were the main one I always mainly respected. The main reason being that you have this confident integrity about yourself, and you are not a showoff, just like your father."

Steven is surprised that Big Mike knows his father. "You know my father?" "Everybody looked up to your pops; that man ran this whole block back in the day. When I was young in the game, he took me under his wings and looked out for me. He looked out for everybody out here, just like you did. You remind me a lot of him; both of you are leaders. I didn't tell you I knew your father because I wanted to know who you were. A lot of these guys Daddies were in the streets, and they feel entitled because of it. While with you, you made a name for yourself in these streets. A lot of people look up to you out here; you never know; with you changing your life, you might help save people. I wish I could've been like you when I was younger; you don't want to be like me. I been doing this since I was 14, been to jail and back." "Well, you never know; things might change."

Big Mike laughs. "I'm too deep in the game, young blood. I wish I could go back in time. I'm ok with the man that I am because I chose this life. Steve, you go out there and make a name for yourself. Show these people how powerful a Black man from the projects can be. Even though you are not going to be out here no more, if you need anything, hit me up. I will make sure you are taken care of. Just know the whole hood got your back; we love you. You going to be something special; stay rising, young king.

Love you, young nigga." Big Mike and Steven hug one another and go their separate ways.

After talking to Big Mike, Steven heads to Destiny's house to talk to her. Destiny asks, "Who's at the door?" Steven responds, "It's me, Steven, Darius's friend." Destiny opens the door and lets Steven in. "I heard you had gotten out of jail. Congratulations. What you been up to since you been out?" "I'm trying to get my life straightened out, mainly trying to get my GED. I just got a landscaping job; I start that this Thursday, so everything going good so far. What about you? How long you got left before the baby comes?" "I got two months left before the baby is here. Darius told me you was somebody I can count on. I don't want you to feel obligated to be there for me and my baby." "I don't feel obligated; if I was in the same situation as Darius, he would do the same thing for me. That's my brother; we are going to forever make sure we and our people are straight. Just know, I got your back; if you need anything, just give me a call. When's your next doctor's appointment?" "Next Wednesday at 3; do you want to come?" "If you want me to, I will be there to support you and the baby." "I would love for you to be there. Out of all Darius's friends, you the one that seems like he got his head on straight. I'm grateful that our baby is going to have you as their godfather." "Appreciated, if you don't mind me asking, once Darius gets out, what are your plans?"

"Well, me and Darius wasn't really boyfriend and girlfriend before he got locked up. We were friends with benefits, but I have always had feelings for him. We don't want our kids to grow up like we did. So, we decided once he gets out, we are going to try to date. Hopefully, it works out for everybody's benefit. If it doesn't, at least we can say we gave it a chance. I know Darius is a hothead, but I believe deep down he can be a great man. We just need to support him and be there for him." "We got him; our boy is going to succeed, and so will that child in your womb. Here's a little something that might help you out." Steven gives Destiny $500. "OMG, Steven, you didn't have to do this." "No problem. Like I said, I look out for my people." Destiny and Steven hug one another. "Well, I got to get going; I will check on you later." "Alright, stay safe."

The next morning, Steven wakes up for school. While getting ready for school, Steven gets a text message from Lily. Steven reads, "Stay rising through the dark and the light. You're a star, and you shall shine bright. Keep your head up, and you shall fly high." Reading the motivational message from Lily brings a smile to Steven's face.

When Steven arrives at GED class, his teacher approaches him to discuss his test results. Mr. Marcus says, "Steve, let me talk to you about your test results." Steven asks, "How did I do on the tests?" Mr. Marcus responds, "You did great; I was impressed. You did great on all the subjects except for math. We going to get you working on that in class. I looked at your background; I see that you were a great student when you were in high school. And that you have a high IQ. With the knowledge you have from school and your test results, I think you should try to take the GED test in three weeks. I believe you can pass. I also read about you getting arrested and trying to change your life. You can do this. All you got to do is believe in yourself and work hard. I support my students, so I will do my best to help you. Remember, though, it's all up to you, but I have reason to believe you going to put in the work." "I most definitely am going to be putting in the work. The main reason why I'm in this class is because I want a better life. Yes, I dropped out of school and went to jail, but a wise man once told me that for every minor setback, there is always a major comeback. I'm going to be successful. I don't care who believes in me." "I believe in you, Steve; you are going to do great things."

As class starts, Mr. Marcus gets Steven to introduce himself to the whole class. Mr. Marcus says, "Steven, will you please introduce yourself to the class." Steven says, "My name is Steven; I'm 18 years old. I'm mainly in here to better my life and get my GED." After Steven introduces himself to the class, the rest of the class introduce themselves to him. After introducing themselves, Steven and the rest of his class start working on their work.

While working, another student with crutches walks into the classroom. Steven turns around and is shocked to see who the student is. Mr. Marcus says, "Well, Mr. Lenny, glad to see you in here; how's the leg doing?" Lenny says, "It's doing well; the doctor said my wound has healed up. So, I will be in here every day." As Lenny sits down, he notices Steven. They both wave at one another with a smile on their faces. Mr. Marcus says, "I usually let you guys out at 12, but since you guys have worked so hard today, I'm going to let you guys go 30 minutes before 12. You guys have a nice weekend, and be safe."

As Steven and Lenny leave class, they hug one another. Lenny says excitedly, "My boy Steve, what's going on? I'm so happy to see you." Steven says. "Man, I'm doing good, glad to be out of jail. What about you? How you been doing?" "I been doing good; I already know you know about me getting shot." "Yeah, if you don't mind me asking, how did it all happen?" "I was on the corner with my guys. We were joking and whatever. All of a sudden, this car came by, driving recklessly and started shooting at my boy, Myles. They ended up hitting me and him. I'm grateful that I survived; that was a sign from GOD that I needed to change my life. My boy Myles wasn't so lucky; he ended up getting shot three times. He can't even walk right now; just like you, I got to better my life also."

"Sorry to hear about your friend; hopefully, he will be able to walk again. Stay off the streets, man; it's nothing out there for us but bad consequences." "You're right, and thank you for looking out for me when the police was after us. A lot of people would've left me there, but you helped me get over that gate. You saved me; for that, I'm forever grateful." "I'm the one that invited you to Thomson; I didn't want you to get caught. That would have made me feel guilty. I would have rather for me being caught than you. Where did you go after you climbed over the gate?"

"After I climbed over the gate, I saw that you got caught, and you told me to go. I ran like I was Adrian Peterson. I rounded up going to Walmart and called Diamond to pick me up. And she took me back to Augusta. I told Tony what happened, and he shut down the whole block for the whole weekend because of that. I started slinging by myself after you guys got caught, but after I got shot, that was my wake-up call." "You and I have been through some hardships and battles. We can and will overcome the difficult situations in our lives. Let's be a great example for other kids in the hood. Me and you are going to be something in life." "Yes, we are; I appreciate you, bro. I forgot to ask: what you doing for money now that you're out?" "I got this landscaping job, and I will start tomorrow. I'm going to try to start my own clothing line also." "I hope it goes well. I'm looking for a job right now, but with my record, it's hard to find work. I still got a little bit of money saved up from what I earned in the streets. Hopefully, I will find something soon." "You will, bro. I'm going to pray for you. GOD is going to work everything out for us." "Most definitely."

One of the guys' GED classmates approaches them. Jose says, "Lenny, what's going on with you?" Jose is Lenny and Steven's GED classmate, but has known Lenny since their years in High School. Lenny says, "Nothing much, bro, just talking to my boy Steve. Steve, this is Jose. Jose, this is Steve. Jose says, "What's going on, Steve? Where you from?" Steven says, "I'm from Thomson. What about you?" "I'm from Augusta; Lenny and I used to go to school with one another back in the day. I got to say I mess with them J's you wearing; they look fresh as hell."

"Appreciated, bro; you got to stay looking fresh out here in these streets." "Sure, do; if not, you better be walking on the sidewalks. So, what's your story, man? Why you in here with us?" "Mainly trying to better my life. I want to do better for myself and my family. I'm trying to do everything in my power to be a success story." "I feel you, bro; I'm the same way. I dropped out mainly because I didn't mess with school a whole bunch. My parents really want me to have a diploma, so I told them I will get my GED." "Why didn't you like school?" "The High School me and Lenny went to, the teachers didn't care about us. Not only that, but I also didn't really learn anything important while I was there. I honestly like GED class more than High School because Mr. Marcus cares for us and makes sure that we understand our work. I wish more teachers like him were in the public school system." "I feel you, man, so what is your main goal?" "My main goal is to be my own businessman. I'm trying to have my own design business, clothing store, and everything. I got some designs made right now."

This reminds Steven of what Hector was telling him about creating a clothing business with poetry and motivational quotes on the clothes. Steven starts thinking about having his own clothing business. Lenny says, "Steve, this dude is the living truth. This guy is the best drawer I know. He can do any design you want." Jose says, "For real, if you need any design or anything like that, hit me up." Steven says, "Alright, bet I got you. I want to start my own clothing line, so if you can help me with the designs, that would be great." "Say less; I got you, bro. We will make something pop off. Well, guys, I got to go. Nice meeting you, Steve; see you later,

Lenny." Jose made a great impression on Steven. "He seems like a cool dude." Lenny responds, "He is; he will look out for you and help you out if you need something.

So, who bringing you up here?" "Diamond, she brings me up here every day. She goes to college here, too." "Ok, I didn't know; she didn't tell me nothing. I am most definitely going to be looking forward to seeing her." "So, you have feelings for Diamond?" Lenny has feelings for Diamond, but is scared he is not good enough for her. "She is a beautiful girl; she has a nice soul. The way she smiles can brighten up a room. I would love to be with her." "I got a feeling that a part of you feels like you are not good enough for Diamond. That's not the case. Diamond is a nice, caring person. She already knows your life and accepts you for who you are, so why not go for it? You are trying to change your life; that shows her right there you are a man on his purpose. If you truly a changed man, she will get with you." "You're right, bro; I should at least try. When you are not used to being loved and admired by somebody, it feels amazing when somebody shows you appreciation for the person you are. I hope and pray for love in my life." "It will happen, man; just stay believing." "I will do my best. Well, my Mom is here to pick me up; I will talk to you later."

After Lenny leaves, Steven heads to the student lounge. While in the student lounge, he is greeted by Lily. Lily says, "Hello, Mr. Steve, how are you doing today?" Steven responds, "I'm doing well. Thank you for the inspirational message you sent me. It helped brighten up my day, just like seeing you smile." "You are so sweet; the main reason why I sent you that text is because I want to see you win. You different from most people I meet; you have a humble spirit. Every time I see you, it also brightens up my day. I don't know your life; I don't know why you dropped out of school. And that is none of my business. While on the other hand, I would definitely like to know who you truly are."

Steven is wondering what Lily is leading to. "What are you getting at?" "I want to go on a date with you." This has Steven excited. Usually, the guy asks the girl out, but Lily decides to ask him first. In his mind, he hopes that Lily will be somebody who can help him have more love in his heart. At the same time, he's not having his hopes up high after what happened with Dani. "Well, I'm surprised by this. Usually, the guy asks the girl out." "Well, with me, I really want to get to know the wonderful gentleman I see sitting in front of me. Plus, when you didn't respond to my messages, I thought you might've found somebody else, thought I might have lost my chance with you." "No, you didn't. I had a lot going on around that time. Ever since I met you, I can't help but think about you. I even think about the Coca Chanel perfume you wear. I would be honored to go on a date with you. Where do you want our date to be at?" "Let's do Stars and Strikes; I mainly want to get to know you and have a fun time. Are you busy on Saturday?" "I got to work, but I should be off by 4 p.m." "OK, great. Do you mind picking me up at 7?" "I don't mind, so I'm guessing I will also be meeting the parents." "Slow your roll, brother; I don't stay with my parents. I have my own place. I stay in an apartment two miles from the mall. If you play your cards the right way, maybe you will get to meet my parents one day." "Trust me, I will play my cards right. When your parents meet me, they are going to love me." "Well, we shall see how you play your hand, Steve. Well, I got to go. I have a lunch date with a homegirl of mine. I will call you on Friday and see you on Saturday. You stay shining." "You too beautiful."

After talking to Lily, Steven walks to the library. While there, he runs into his GED teacher, Mr. Marcus. Mr. Marcus says, "Steve, I'm surprised that you are still here." "I'm waiting for my friend to get done with her classes. I came in here to read some books." "What type of books are you trying to read?" "Mainly inspirational books; while I was in jail, I watched a lot of inspirational videos. You got any suggestions?" "Yes, I do. I got two books you should read that I believe might help you out. I got them in my classroom; follow me." Mr. Marcus and Steven go to his classroom. "These are two books that I believe can help you strive to be a great man in life. Letters to a Young Brother by Hill Harper and Jordan Peterson's 12 Rules of Life. Read those books and tell me what you think. When you get done with those books, let me know, and I will give you some more." "Alright, appreciated."

Before Steven leaves, Mr. Marcus asks Steven an important question. "Wait, hold on, don't leave yet. Let's get to know one another. What inspires you, Steve?" "What do you mean?" "What inspires you to get a GED?" Steven explains his ambitions in life. "Because I want a better life. I want to be a success story and an inspiration to people in my hood. I want to show them it doesn't matter where you are from or how you grew up. You still can make it out. It's not how you start; it's how you finish. I see myself as a great businessman one day. Not only that, I want to make my Mom proud and be the great man she raised me to be." Mr. Marcus is amazed by Steven. "I love the story and the great wisdom you have. A lot of people your age don't have an intelligent mind like you. The main reason I asked you that question is to never forget what inspires you. Before you ever think about quitting, think about why you started. I have seen many people come in here and then quit once things get hard. You never don't want to live life in that way. When you quit, you stay in the same position you are already in. When you stay pushing and working hard, you are one step closer to your goals and destiny." "I appreciate the advice, and I'm most definitely going to use it to my advantage." "I haven't known you for a long time, but I believe you are going to do something special in your life. Well, I got to go. I will see you on Monday, young man; you have a nice weekend."

After Diamond finishes her classes, she and Steven head back to Thomson. While on their way back, they have a lengthy conversation. Diamond asks, "Well, how has your day been like?" Steven smiles as he thinks about his day. "Diamond, this been one of my best days in a long time." "What happened to you today that got you so happy?" "I talked to Lily today; she asked me out on a date." Diamond lightly punches Steven's arm. "Look at you, Mr. player; where are your going on your date?" "We are going to Stars and Strikes. When I was in jail, I thought I would never see her again. I'm so grateful to have the chance to show her the type of person I am. Hopefully, everything will work out." "It will be like I said before; you are a good guy, and she already sees that. You never know; she might be the one for you. My question is, are you going to drive your car to pick her up? Knowing dang well you don't have no license."

Even though Steven doesn't have a driver's license, he plans on driving to Augusta. He doesn't want to look like a guy who has nothing toward Lily. "Of course, I'm going to drive my car; sure, I don't have my license, but I can drive in Augusta. I will try my best not to get caught. I just really want to impress Lily; I want her to love me for the man that I am. Saturday Night is going to be a beautiful night for your boy.

How do you feel about Lenny, though?" Diamond expresses her feelings. "Between me and you, I like Lenny. My only issue with him is that he needs to be more mature." "What do you mean by that?" "For example, you have learned from your mistakes, and you are being a person that is on their purpose. While with Lenny, I don't know if he learned from his mistakes or not. Or is he a person on their purpose? I don't know about most women, but with me, you got to show me some action. Words don't mean nothing to me." "I agree; that's why I hate it when people tell me they love me without meaning it. That's fake, in my opinion. Just like my mother always taught me as a kid, never tell somebody you love them if you never show them love." "Facts.

Love is out there for everybody. Love will find both of us, Steve. Hopefully, Lenny gets his act together not for me, but for himself."

After Diamond drops Steven off, he gets a call from his parole officer. Steven answers, "Hello?" Parole Officer says, "Yes, is this Steven Anderson?" "Yes, ma'am, who am I speaking to?" "This is your parole officer; as you know, we will be meeting one another every Friday in my office. I was wondering when would be the best time for you to come to the office on Friday?" "I just got a landscaping job, so I will be working on Fridays. So, I should be off by 5 p.m. I will say we can meet up every Friday at 5:30." "OK, that sounds great; the main thing we will be talking about is what you are doing in life. What are you able to do or not to do? Also, you will have to take a drug test every time you come here. Does that sound good to you?" "Yes, ma'am, I will see you on Friday."

After talking to his parole officer, Steven gets a phone call from Darius. Darius asks, "My boy Steve, what's going on with you?" Steven says, "Your boy doing good; I'm about to watch your brother play football at the brickyard." "Today is his first game; I wish I was able to be there in person. Lil bro going to show out on everybody in there. I'm proud of him; he's got great potential." "Indeed, he does just know I got him. I'm going to look out for him and your mother." "I appreciate. I talked to Destiny earlier today; she told me you came by her apartment yesterday. I appreciate you for showing my girl encouragement and giving her a gift." "No problem, bro. I know if I was in the same situation, you would do the same for me. How's everything going in the inside for you?" "It's going well; of course, I have my hard days, but I'm going to survive. I been attending GED classes here. I'm even learning how to cut hair in here." Steven starts laughing. "Please tell me you haven't messed up nobody's hairline." "Naw bro, my roommate in here teaching me; dude is like 40-something years old. He stays dropping gems on me.

You heard about Brock?" "No, I haven't. What happened?" "They sentenced bro to five years; I pray for him and his kids. When I heard that, it made me want to change my ways. I don't want my kids to grow up and see me in and out of jail. It's sad how a lot of people we grew up with in the hood are locked up. We got to change that narrative. The kids in our neighborhood look up to us, and we need to inspire them to go in the right direction. I'm going to try my best to be a changed man once I get out of here." "You will be bro; GOD got you. I'm proud of you for going in the right direction. Stay believing in yourself and him. You do that, and you will accomplish a lot of things in life." "I'm proud of you bro; you seem like you're back on the right track. What's been going on with you since you got out?"

"A lot of great things. I got a job; I started GED class earlier this week. And I got a date this Saturday." Darius wonders who Steven is messing around with. "Who are you messing around with?" "Lily shawty I met at the mall before we went to Tony's for the first time. Found out she also attends Brooks Tech as a College Student. We reconnected last Monday, and she asked me out today. I hope everything works out between us. She told me I been on her mind ever since she met me. I'm not going to tell her nothing about my past until she gets to know me." "I'm happy for you, bro. If she's a real one, she's going to stick by your side through the good and bad. You deserve love and happiness, Steve. I hope and pray that you finally get it." "I hope so too; that's something in my life that I need. I have felt more hate in my life than love. My heart needs more love. I just want to experience having a girl who loves me for me and is there for me. Lily is something special; I believe and hope she is the beautiful angel I believe she is." Steven hopes that Lily is the person he believes she is. "If it means to be, my brother, everything will fall into place."

"Yep, I also ran into Lenny today. I found out he is also in GED class." "How's he doing? I heard he had got shot." "He's doing good; he mainly trying to do the same thing I'm doing. Trying to turn his life around." "I'm happy for him. I hope you and him be great men. Well, I got to go, bro. I will talk to you later." "Be easy, bro."

After his phone call with Darius, he goes to Danny's football game. When Steven arrives at the brickyard, he is greeted by Danny and Darius's mother, who gives him a hug. Darius's Mom asks, "My other son, how are you doing?" Steven says., "I'm doing good. I just got off the phone with Darius." "What my boy was talking about?" "He was mainly talking about how he is going to try and change his life. So, he can be a good role model for his kid." "You know something, Steve, I'm glad Darius went to jail. He still would've been out in these streets if he had never been locked up. I tried my best as a mother to raise him the best way I knew how. I had Darius when I was 16. When he was growing up, I tried my best to provide for him. I wasn't there for him sometimes when he needed me. His father didn't want nothing to do with me or him after I had him. Darius just needed love as a kid. He still does to this day. I have apologized for my sins. I'm going to do everything to show both of my kids true love. I'm going to make sure Danny doesn't follow in the same footsteps as Darius did. I thank GOD for you, Steve; in my opinion, you probably the best thing that ever happened to Darius. He looks up to you. I think just by you trying to turn your life around, it's inspiring him to turn his life around, also. I believe you and him are going to be great men. Don't give up, Steve; you are a special young man. Remember to always believe in yourself, even when people might not believe in you. I see you as a second child; if you need anything, just ask me. I got you. I love you, Steve." "I love you too."

Steven and Darius's Mom hug one another. "Let me stop being so emotional; how are you doing in GED class?" "I'm doing good; my teacher suggested to me that I take the test in three weeks. So, I'm working hard to make sure I pass and succeed. I also got a date this Saturday." "Look at you, boy. What's the lovely lady's name?" "Her name is Lily; this girl is one in a million. I never met nobody like her before. I feel like she sees the good in me. She told me I have been on her mind ever since we first met. Everything is good between me and her; the only problem is she doesn't know nothing about my past. She knows that I'm in GED class and dropped out of school. She doesn't know nothing about me selling drugs and going to jail. I plan on telling her once she fully gets to know me for the person I am. I hope she still wants to get in touch with me once she finds out." "I'm going to give you some real advice, Steve. When a woman truly likes or loves a man for who he is, she is not going to turn their back on them. If this Lily girl truly likes you, she will accept you for who you are. You are an intelligent young man; if she doesn't see that, something is wrong with her." "I appreciate the advice." "You welcome, my son; let's get to our seats so we can watch the game." Steven and Darius's Mom go to their seats to watch Danny play football.

While watching the game, Steven is approached by Mr. Dixson, Rich's father. Mr. Dixson asks Steven, "Are you enjoying the game, Mr. Anderson?" Steven responds, "Yes, I am; I'm surprised to see you here." Mr. Dixson and Steven hug one another. "Well, I love supporting the kids in our community, plus my nephew is on the football team. So, how has everything been going for you since you been out?" "It's been going well; I been doing good so far in GED class. I plan on taking the GED test in three weeks. I believe I will do well." "I believe you will do well also; I will be praying for you. If you don't mind me asking, how was your time in jail?"

"To be honest, it wasn't that bad. That's not me saying that I love jail, but I learned a lot of great things there. I learned how to plant flowers. I started back playing chess. I even taught a poetry class during my last couple of weeks in jail. The main thing that I am glad I learned in jail was learning about God. I got closer to him and found my purpose while I was there. Jail made me into a better man. And I want to thank you for putting in a good word for me." "I'm so glad to hear that, Steven. When I first found out you had been arrested, I was heartbroken. I prayed that you find your way on the right path. When your lawyer came to see me to ask me questions about you, I spoke the truth. For somebody your age to have the mind and intelligence that you have is something special. I was grateful to have taught you. I never thought of you as a thug or as a hoodlum. All of us on this planet has the potential to be great. It's like what Denzel Washington says in American Gangster: you either a somebody or a nobody in this world. We pick who we want to be in life. I'm glad that you found yourself while you were in jail. I can tell the difference; you are more mature than the last time I saw you. Steven, you have been given a second chance to do great things in this life. Don't waste this opportunity; there are many young men in the world today who wish they were in your shoes right now. Be a leader, but overall, be that great man GOD designed you to be. Your life story can inspire so many people. Be an inspiration to others so they can follow in your footsteps and be something special, also. If you ever need anything, I'm a phone call away." "Thank you, Mr. Dixson, you are definitely the best teacher I ever had. My goal and purpose is to be an inspiration to others. Hopefully, my story will inspire people in the world."

"I got a great feeling it will, Steve. You should come by the school sometimes and visit the debate team. I think hearing from you can give them great insight on how to be a great team." "I would love to visit; I probably can give them some pointers."

"Great to hear also; Rich's mother and I are throwing him a going away party next Friday. We would love for you to be one of the guests at the party." "I will be honored to be a guest at the party. If Mrs. Dixon is ok with me being there, I will be there." "She will be delighted to see you. She actually wanted me to make sure you get an invite to the party. Me and her are so grateful that Rich is friends with you. When he was going through his issues early in his life, you helped him out with that. I don't think Rich would be where he is today without your friendship. His mother and I are forever thankful that Rich became friends with a kind person like you." "I'm grateful to have Rich as a friend also. He is going to do great things." "Yes, he is. Well, it looks like the game is over. Nice talking to you, and see you at the party."

After the game, Steven congratulates Danny on his game. Steven says, "Congratulations on the win. You were making plays out there like you were Lamar Jackson. I didn't know you had moves like that." Danny says, "I tried to tell you I'm going to take my team to the championship." "Now that's the right mentality to have; you keep it up, and you might make it to the league." "I want to, but one of the old guys in the neighborhood said I need to stop dreaming. He told me that would never happen for a kid from the hood." Steven gives Danny advice that changes his mindset. "Don't ever let nobody tell you, you can't be something in life. When you dream or envision things in life, you can turn them into reality. Believe in your vision and dream, Danny. If you see yourself being a quarterback in the NFL, you go for it. Never let negativity get you down." "Thank you, Steve; I'm going extra hard so one day I can be in the NFL." "That's what I like to hear. I will talk to you later; stay doing your thing."

After leaving the football game, Steven goes to visit Dee. Steven and Dee dap one another up. Steven says, "Big homie, what's going on?" Dee says, "What's going on, youngin? How you been doing?" "Bro, I been doing good. I got this new landscaping job I'm doing tomorrow. And I got a date this Saturday." "Man, look at you, haven't been out of jail for a week, and you doing big things. How did you get the job?" "My lawyer hooked me up with it; his brother owns the company. I believe everything will go well there." "I'm happy for you; now, who's the girl you got a date with? I know it's not Dani."

Steven laughs, "You must have heard about me and Dani breaking up?" Dee has a smirk on his face. "No, after Dani's Mom found out you got arrested, she came storming inside my house and asking me and Stephanie why we let Dani get with that thug. We went back and forth. She mainly said she doesn't want her daughter to be associated with somebody who has a low life." "That's probably the reason why she didn't show up in the courtroom and dumped me." "No, that is not the reason. Dani is her own woman; she old enough to make her own decisions. She knew you was hot in these streets. She saw you as an opportunity for her to be hot in these streets also. Always notice who on your side during the good and bad times. You will find out who really on your side and who is not. She didn't stay down once you got arrested; she showed you that she wasn't loyal. In my opinion, that's a blessing in disguise."

"I agree. I actually ran into her a couple of days ago with her new boyfriend. I'm glad I was able to make peace with her I'm not mad at her. GOD might have blessed me with somebody better."

Dee smiles and laughs. "So, who's the lady you macking with?" "Her name is Lily, and she is wonderful." "Have you told her about your past?" "No, I have not. I got plan on telling her once she gets to know me. She do know about me being in GED class; that's all she knows. She told me I been on her mind ever since she first met me. Just hearing her voice lightens up my soul. I never felt this way before about anybody." "You in love, my guy, but remember to take things slow. I was the same way when I met my wife. I wasn't getting a lot of love from home, but Steph showed me the true meaning of love." "When did you know she was the one for you?"

"I had got locked up for having a gun on me and selling drugs. Luckily, I beat my case, but I lost all my money in the process. I remember breaking down one night and crying while I was at her house. I told her what was happening, and she told me we would make it through. She gave me $300 to help me out. It wasn't her giving me the money that meant so much to me. It was her saying we will make it through, meaning we were a team and stuck by each other through thick and thin. Now, 10 years later, we have a house together and two beautiful kids. And I got my landscaping business going on right now." Steven is inspired by Dee's story. "I'm happy for you; that's inspiration right there." "It is, but I could have had more if I didn't waste my time out here in these streets. You going to do something special. You going on the right track. You never know; you might be an inspiration to other kids in this neighborhood. Stay doing what you doing; the hard work you putting in now is going to pay off in a big way."

"Best believe, big homie, I'm about to do big things. I talked to Big Mike yesterday." "What he was talking about?" "He talking about how he wanted me to be to go back slinging on these streets. He was saying I could be the biggest drug dealer out there. I told him I'm no longer in these streets, and I'm trying to change my life for the better." "What did he say?" "He said he respected my decision. He said something that stuck with me." "What did he say?" "I told him he might change his life around also. He started telling me that it was too late for him to turn his life around. He said he was too deep in these streets. My question is, why do a lot of people in the streets think that way?"

Dee explains. "Mike and I came to the game together. Mike been out here since he was 14; he's 33 now. This all he knows. He didn't have a lot of people on his side growing up. A lot of us don't have any love from home, so we go to the streets to find that. There is one problem: the streets don't have love for nobody. When you out here, you get addicted to the fame and recognition that come with it. The money coming your way and the many girls that are steady trying to get with you. It's so easy for us to fall into that trap." "I know you sold some stuff with me and Darius for side money, but what changed for you?"

"Well, first of the main reasons I started working with you guys on the side was to get money for my landscaping business. What made me stop full-time from slinging drugs was my kids. I didn't want them to think of their father as a drug dealer. I wanted to be somebody that they are proud of. Granted, has it been easy? No, it hasn't. I done lost jobs and gained jobs. The beauty in that journey is that I learn from each experience and that helps me grow into a better person. With Mike, he made that path in his life. He knew what he was getting himself into when he first got on the streets. He knows the benefits and the consequences that come with the game. We all decide which way we want to go in life. It's up to us to choose which way we go. Now my beautiful wife is cooking dinner. You want to come in and have a bite?" "Most definitely."

Before the end of the night, as he lies down in bed, Steven starts thinking about his first day at an official job. He says a prayer, "Dear GOD, I thank you for giving me a job. I pray that this job brings great benefits my way and helps me grow better in life. In Jesus name, I pray. Amen." How will Steven like his first legit job?

206

# Chapter 8: Going Legit

It's Thursday Morning, and Steven wakes up excited as he starts his new job today. Steven walks downstairs as his mother cooks him a wonderful breakfast for his first day at work. Steven's Mom smiles as she sees her son in his uniform, and says, "Working man, are you ready for your first day?" Steven responds, "Yes, I am ready to make this money." "Son, let me just say I am so proud of you. I have been waiting for this day for you to have a job. You are something special, and your light is starting to shine." "This is just the beginning of something special, Mom. Just watch and see."

Steven eats his breakfast and heads to his workplace. As Steven arrives at the workplace, he is greeted by his boss. Mr. Joe says, "Steven, welcome to Joe Davis Landscaping. We here at this company make sure our customers and clients are satisfied. We are like family around here; we are there for one another through the good and bad. I'm going to have you working every Tuesday, Thursday- Saturday from 8:00 a.m. to 4 p.m. Sometimes we do overtime. I believe this will be a great experience for you. I know this is your first job, so it might get hard sometimes, but just know we are here for you. Let me introduce you to the crew. This is Corey, Zach, Jamal, Cody, Nate, Derek, and Shane. We work in fours, so I'm going to have you work with Corey, Zach, and Jamal. You guys show him the ropes and show him how things are done. Now, let's head to the location where we will be working today."

While heading to his working location, Steven gets to know his new co-workers. Corey asks, "Steven, do you have any experience when it comes to doing landscaping?" Steven responds, "While I was in Jail, I cut grass, planted flowers, and pulled weeds. So, I do have some landscaping background." Steven looks nervous about how his co-workers will react as he awaits his co-workers' reactions. Jamal says, "You got more experience than most people your age." Zach says, "Sure, a lot of people as young as you have never even cut anybody's grass." Corey says, "Yes indeed; also, we don't judge nobody; it doesn't matter if you been to jail or not. What matters to us is that you are a good co-worker and a person who will be there for his co-workers." Steven responds, "Sounds good to me. I'm a cool person once you get to know me. I believe we will get along just fine." The guys finally arrive at the location. Corey says, "Alright, Jamal and Steven, your two work with one another in the back. Zach and I will take care of the front."

Jamal and Steven do lawn care in the backyard. While in the backyard, Jamal and Steven get to know one another. Jamal says, "Cut a little bit more to the side; you always got to make sure the grass is cut great, so it looks beautiful." Steven says, "Got you, bro." "So, if you don't mind me asking what did you go to jail for?" "I got caught selling drugs and had a gun on me. I wounded up doing two months in county jail. I just got out last Saturday. Mainly trying to change my life for the better. I'm doing this, but also trying to get my GED. Trying my best every day to be a better man." "I respect that and commend you for trying to change your life around. I also spent some time in jail myself. I used to sell guns without a license. I ended up getting caught and did two years in prison. I got out two years ago. Ever since I been out, I have better myself. I got this job, but also I have been a better husband and father. I'm not going to lie to you; it gets tough sometimes. The main thing is to stay striving for better. And always remember your why."

Steven is curious about what Jamal means. "What do you mean by remember my why?" "What I mean by that is that we have something or somebody that makes us want to do better. For me, it's my wife and kids. They help me strive for better in my life. Always remember your why; it's like that old saying: before you quit, think about why you started. I believe you are going to be alright though; let's get back to working on this yard."

After finishing the yard, the guys go to their next location. Zach asks, "So, Steven, how was that first yard?" Steven says, "It was pretty easy. Is that how it usually is? Corey says. "Sometimes, this next place we going to is a doctor's office; it's pretty big. You think you can handle it?" "I'm ready for the task; bring it on."

The guys arrive at the doctor's office; they stay out there for four hours. Jamal asks, "Steven, are you tired?" Steven says, "Yes, it's hard work, but that's life." Corey says, "Welcome to the crew, rookie." The guys work on two more yards and then decide to call it a day.

After Steven gets off, Mr. Joe asks, "Steven, how was your first day?" Steven enjoyed his first day working. "It was pretty easy. I believe this is going to be a great job for me. Thank you again for the opportunity." "No problem. My brother and I believe in giving people second chances. I already know you are going to do great things here. Just know all of us here got your back. Don't we crew?" Everybody yells out, 'Yes, Sir.' I will see you tomorrow, Steve. Have a nice day."

Steven arrives back home and enters the house. As he enters the house, he hears his Mom talking on the phone with somebody. Steven's Mom asks, "Hey, son, how was your first day at the new job?" Steven says, "It went well; the people I work with are cool people." "I'm so happy to hear that. It's somebody on the phone that wants to talk to you."

Curious about who wants to talk to him, Steven takes the phone and starts talking. Steven says, "Hello, who am I speaking with?" The person on the phone says, "This is your Daddy, son. Man, I haven't heard your voice in so long. In tears right now; you was just a little boy since the last time I spoke with you on the phone. Now I'm talking to a young man. How are you doing, son?"

Steven is surprised to hear from his father. He doesn't know whether he should be happy to hear from his father or tell his father how he is still mad at him for not being there for him. "I been doing great. I just got out of jail last week. Mainly trying to get my life straighten out." "I'm so happy to hear that; just remember you are somebody special. I pray for you night and day. I believe that GOD will guide you in the right direction. He has given you a second chance, so please take advantage of that. I see so many people your age in here. Some serving life sentences in here. There are a lot of young people in the world today that wish they were in your position. Be an inspiration for them; show them the right path for them to follow." "That's the plan. I want to be a great example for kids and show them a better way."

"We have to; I'm sorry for not being there for you. I know it was times in your life you needed me there. You were actually my motivation for starting my motivation group here. I started it about five years ago, and there are about 100 inmates in the group. I try my best to help them out. To the ones that have a second chance of getting out here, I tell them there are many ways to be successful and have money in this life other than being in these streets. To the ones that are in here for life, I tell them they can still get close to GOD, and he will forgive them for their sins. Even though we make mistakes, GOD is still on our side through the good and bad. Don't you ever forget that. I understand you also taught your own class while you were in jail." "Yes, I started a poetry class while I was in jail. It helped out a lot of people in the facility. The Sheriff heard how well the inmates loved my poems and offered me to teach a poetry class. Since I'm out, I got my boy Robert taking over the class now. I already know he's going to do well teaching the class." "I love it; that's proof right there. God has a special hand on you. Well, I got to go. If you want to see me, fill the visitation papers I sent you. I really would like to see you face to face. Take care, son; love you." "Alright, take it easy."

Steven feels good talking to his Dad, but he is sad because his Dad can't see what he is doing in life. Steven's Mom says, "Well, that sounded like a great conversation you had with your father." Steven replies, "It was great talking to him; I will say he has a lot of wisdom. I'm not going to lie. I wish he was a mentor to me like he is to his fellow inmates. I will see him one day, though. We need to see each other face to face." "Your definitely need to see each other face to face. I'm glad to hear that your first day went ok. Have you talked to your parole officer yet?" "Yes, we talked. I got to go meet her tomorrow." "Alright, I also got some great news." "What's the good news?" "I got a promotion from my job today. You are looking at the head nurse at McDuffie County Hospital!" This is huge for Steven's Mom. She was diagnosed with breast cancer three years ago, has been in remission for a year and a half, has been working at the hospital for a year, and has already gotten a promotion. "You go, Ma dukes. I'm so happy for you. I know how hard you worked to get to this Moment. I'm proud of you, Mom." Steven gives his Mom a hug, as they both cry tears of joy as they reminisce how far they come. "I'm proud of the both of us; I guess this is the new beginning for the both of us." "Yes, we are about to do great things." "GOD done brought me and you a long way; people think they have seen something but haven't seen nothing yet. Now I done cooked dinner, so let's eat."

The next day, Steven arrives at his workplace and gets straight to work. While on his lunch break, Steven talks to Mr. Joe. Mr. Joe says, "Steven, I got to say, for a young fellow, you sure can work. A lot of people don't like to work mainly because they don't have any determination. I can tell you are a different breed, though." "I appreciate. I learned how to do most of this stuff while I was in jail. So, how long have you owned this business?" "I created this business in 1993. I was fresh out of high school; I needed some money, so I created my own landscaping business. My father gave me a loan to start this business. Granted, when I first started, it was hard, but with great support and with Jesus Christ on my side, I made it." "It's wonderful to see how you and your brother are successful. How did you and your brother become successful?" "That's all thanks to our parents. At an early age, our parents taught us we can do anything or be who we want to be in life. And to also put GOD first in our lives." "That's amazing, so how did you find out about me?" "My brother doesn't usually ask me for favors when it comes to his clients, but he saw something special in you. He told me you were a kid who needed a second chance, but not only that, with great support, he said he believed you can go far in life. Plus, I had already seen you in action when you was locked up." Steven is puzzled by Mr. Joe's answer. "Wait, so how did you see me working while I was in jail?" "The first time I saw you in action was when you guys were at the mayor's house. I saw how hard you were working; I also saw how you were learning to get better at working in landscaping. I asked my good old friend Officer Brown who you were, and he told me you were a new inmate at the time. I kept tabs on you; Officer Brown was actually the one who suggested to me that I should hire you. I didn't know my brother represented you until you got out. So, I guess it was GOD's plan for you to work for me. You seem like a great kid. I'm going to do everything in my power to make sure you succeed; I promise you." "I appreciate Mr. Joe; that means a lot to me. I promise you I won't let you or your brother down." "I know you won't, Steve; you are going to do some amazing things. Let's get back to making this money."

After getting off work, Steven heads straight to the parole office to meet his parole officer. Due to him not having his license, Steven parks his car one block away from the parole office. As Steven walks into the parole office, one of the workers yells out: another thug has walked into the building. Steven says, "I'm not a thug; my name is Steven Anderson. You better get your facts straight." The worker sits down and goes back to work.

Steven's parole officer comes from the back to greet him. "Are you Steven Anderson?" Steven responds, "Yes, ma'am, that's me." "I'm your Parole Officer, Ms. Harris. Please have a seat. So, the first thing I want you to do is go to the bathroom and pee in this cup. To see if you have any drugs in your system." Steven goes to the bathroom and pees in the cup. Steven comes back and gives the cup back to Ms. Harris. "We will have your results back within 24 hours, and we will let you know if you tested positive or negative. So, tell me, what have you been doing since you got out of jail?" "What I have mainly been doing since I got out of jail is improving my life. I am in GED class, trying to get my GED. I also got a job; just started yesterday. I'm doing everything in my power to be a better man." "I can respect that; now let me tell you all the rules you have to follow. You can't be on any drugs or be around them. You can't be in possession of any firearms. Everything else is basic knowledge you already know. And for your driver's license, you will be able to get them once you have completed 30 days in GED class. If you are caught driving a vehicle without your license, you can be sent back to jail to finish the rest of your term. And that's go for all the rules. That's everything, Mr. Anderson. You have a nice day, and stay safe." "You do the same."

After Steven leaves the parole office, he returns home. As he walks inside his house, Steven gets a phone call from Robert. Steven answers, "Hello, who is this?" Robert says, "What's going on, little homie? How's the outside world treating you?" "It's been treating me well; I started GED class last Monday. And I started a new job yesterday as a landscaper. So, everything goes well." "I'm so proud of you; everybody in here is rooting for you. What you are doing inspires so many people. Don't ever stop. Are you still reading your Bible and writing in your journal?" "Every night before I go to sleep. It helped me out when I was in jail, and now it's helping me out at home. How have you and everybody else been doing?" "Everybody in here doing good; we all do miss you. With me, I been doing the same old thing, steady motivating people in here and motivating myself. I'm not going to lie; I am nervous teaching the poetry class tomorrow." "You got this; don't try to speak what's in your head; speak what's in your heart. Not only that, everybody in there has respect for you, so everybody is going to listen to what you say." "I appreciate you. I got this. That's what's special about you as a young person; you have knowledge and power." "Thanks, I got to thank you for some of the knowledge I have. You kept dropping gems on me. And I need some more advice from you?" "Lay it on me, homie?" "Well, I have a date this Saturday with this beautiful girl tomorrow." "You are living a lot of people's dreams right now. Congrats on the date, but I can tell there is an issue by the way you are talking." "She knows that I dropped out of school and is in GED class. However, she doesn't know anything about my past. So, I was wondering when I should tell her the truth." "Do you know anything about her past?" "No, I don't; she seems like a sweet, delightful person, in my opinion." "Let her reveal herself to you; by doing that, you will see if she will accept you for your past or not. If she truly cares about you, she is not going to care about all of that. Remember this also, Steve, what is kept in the dark shall come into the light one day." "You are right. I appreciate man; you always keep it real with me." "I want to see you win, bro; you are something special. I want to see you go in the right direction. Always remember to believe in yourself and GOD. I got to go, little homie; I will let you know how the class goes tomorrow. Stay safe, my guy." "You too, bro."

After getting off the phone with Robert, Steven thinks about the advice that was given to him. A few minutes after getting off the phone with Robert, he gets a phone call from Lily. Steven answers, "Ms. Beauty, it's so great to hear from you. How are you doing today?" Lily says, "I'm doing well; I been thinking about our date all day. I got this great outfit picked out and everything." "I'm glad to hear that; knowing you, I know you are going to wear something extraordinary. I'm happy about our date. We are going to have a great time. When we get to bowling, it might be a hard time for you. I'm the goat when it comes to bowling. Lily starts laughing.  "You clearly haven't met a woman like me before. Honey, I'm the queen bee; nobody can mess with me when it comes to bowling. I'm going to have you crying your way back to Thomson." "Well, we will see tomorrow night who has the best control of the ball." "It's going to be a wonderful date. I'm glad we are not doing any karaoke because you would break some people's glasses." "What you talking about? I will have to let you know that people call me a young Michael Jackson." "More like Tito Jackson." "On the real, though, I think we should do that one day. I believe me and you can create some heavenly magic together." "I would love to do that one day; we already got great chemistry, so we definitely can create something special. Well, I have to go. I will see you tomorrow. Get some good rest and sleep tight." "You do the same, beautiful."

After talking to Lily on the phone, Steven writes in his journal. "Dear Journal, I lost a precious Jewel, but I believe one that's brighter has come my way, with more value and with more beauty. I pray that the Jewel lightens up my soul and brings happiness in my life."

The next day, Steven works on four properties; while working on the last one, he bonds with Jamal. Jamal says, "Young buck, you are a beast out here; you did good teaching the high schoolers how to do the yard." Steven says, "Appreciated, man. Can I ask you something?" "Sure, bro, what you need to ask me?" "When you first got out of jail, how were you perceived?"

Jamal keeps it real with Steven. "To be honest, I was perceived both ways. I had people down me to my face telling me I won't be nothing. Then, I had people who supported and encouraged me. The main thing to remember is how you see yourself. If you see yourself being powerful in life, you can be it. To me, the most powerful image in this world is the one we see in the mirror every day. Never let somebody's perception of you downgrade the great perception you see in yourself. Remember that, Steve, it's all about how you see yourself." With the advice Jamal has given him, Steven starts caring more about how he sees himself than what others see.

After getting done working on the last property, the guys go home for the day. Jamal asks, "Steven, what you got on plan on doing tonight?" Steven says, "I actually got a date tonight with a beautiful girl." "Ok, Mr. Mack, you got any cologne?" "No, I honestly forgot to get some." "That's no issue." Jamal heads to his truck and gives Steven his cologne. "This is Ralph Lauren Polo Cologne here, my guy; you put this on, and you will have that girl of yours all over you." "Man, I can't take this from you; I know that cost you a lot of money." "No, it's ok. I got plenty at home; take this. Youngblood, whenever you go on a date, you always have to wear some type of fragrance. See, you a powerful man. The polo cologne is the most powerful cologne in the world. That symbolizes to the girl that you are a powerful man. I believe the date will go well for you; I will see you on Tuesday. Have a nice weekend."

Steven leaves his job and returns home to get ready for his date. After getting ready, Steven lets his mother see his outfit, as he is wearing blue skinny jeans, a white polo shirt, and Air Jordan Mid 1. Steven asks, "Mom, how do I look?" Steven's Mom answers, "You look handsome, son, and you smell good. Out here looking like a model. Ms. Lily better watch out cause you are truly going to take her breath away. Just remember, son, you are special and unique." "I appreciate it, Mom; tonight is going to be great." "You be careful; please don't get stopped by no police. Can't have them catch you driving without no license; I'm not trying to see you go back to jail." "Mom don't worry I will be just fine. Now, you have yourself a good night."

Steven drives to Augusta and goes to Lily's apartment. How will Steven's first date with Lily go?

220

# Chapter 9: Finding Love and Happiness

Steven arrives at Lily's apartment as he can't wait for his date with Lily. Steven knocks at Lily's door as he can't wait to spend time with her. Lily answers the door; Stevin is just in awe of Lily as she stands in the doorway looking magnificent. Steven says, "Well, hello, queen, you are looking stunning as always. Here is some Lillie flowers I got you." Lily starts laughing while wearing grey sweatpants and a white tank top. Lily says, "These are some beautiful flowers; I appreciate. I haven't even finished getting dressed yet. You look sharp yourself, looking like a movie star." "Thank you." "I'm going to go to the back and get dressed. Going to put the flowers in my room. And don't look at my behind as I walk to my room." Steven starts laughing. "I will try my best not to. Who's that you listening to?" "That's Brandy; it's the Full Moon album. I thought you would know since you are a huge fan of throwback slow jams." "I do. I'm going to put you on game. I like your spot; how long you been in here?" "For about three months, my parents paid for it. I try my best to keep it clean and peaceful." "So, you keep the house just like yourself?" This brings a smile to Lily's face. "You can say that." "Hold up, this is my jam." Steven starts singing. "Now, this is the time to relax your mind." Steven sings out loud to Brandy's "When You Touch Me" as it plays on Lily's phone.

As the song plays, Lily presents herself in a lovely outfit, wearing a beautiful black jumpsuit. "Well, what do you think?" Steven stares at Lily for one Moment and is amazed by her beauty.

As he says to himself, GOD took his time with you, pretty boo. "You look marvelous; it's like I'm looking at a precious diamond." "Thank you for the kind words; you look amazing yourself. What I want to do is replay this song, and you dance with me." "Play it, and I will let you lead the way." "That's probably best because you look like you got a bad two-step." "Well, let's find out." Lily replays the song, and she dances with Steven. While dancing, they both gaze at each other's eyes. The connection between the two gets stronger. Lily says, "I got to say you are one great dancer; I guess you know how to sweep a woman off her feet." "Yes, I do know how to sweep a woman off her feet as long she don't come with a lot of baggage." "You are funny; let's head out and have a fun time."

Steven and Lily go to Stars and Strikes. While there, they participate in a lot of activities, including bowling. Steven is bowling and says, "Knocked all of them down; told you I was the best at bowling." Lily responds, "Since you are the best, show me how to knock down all of the cones." "No problem. See, the main key is to focus on the cones and how you hold the ball. See, you want the ball to roll in a good motion so it hits the right spot. It's just like going in the right direction in your life to live in your destiny. Now, on my count, we are going to release the ball ready in 3,2,1." "I knocked down all the cones!" Lily jumps in Steven's arms. "You are one intelligent guy, Steve; the way you describe stuff, I can hear you talk all day." "Well, with the way you look and act, I don't mind talking to someone as unique as you." "Well, I need a bite to eat, so let's do some talking."

Lily and Steven go sit down and talk to one another. Lily asks. "So, I got a question to ask you, Steve. You are intelligent and smart; how come you dropped out of school?" Steven decides to tell Lily the truth about why he dropped out of school. "After my tenth-grade year, my mother was diagnosed with breast cancer. Other than myself, there was really nobody to help her out. So, I dropped out of school to make sure she was straight. My apologies. I got tears in my eyes just talking about it." "No, it's ok. I want to hear your story. Is your Mom okay now?" "Yes, she been in remission for about two years; she recently just got a promotion at her job. I'm so proud of her." "I'm so happy to hear; would love to meet her. If you don't mind me asking, what about your father?"

"My father has been in jail since I was about three years old. He was deep in the streets, and just like most people, he just wanted more. Sadly, the greed took over, and that's what put him in prison." Steven still decides not to tell Lily all about his past. "I'm sorry you had to go through all of that."

"No, it's ok, but enough talking about me. Tell me about your upbringing?" "Well, I was raised by my Mom and Dad down here in Augusta, GA. My mother is a teacher, and my father is a Doctor. I have one older brother who's in college in Statesboro. I grew up in a great neighborhood, and I have always been an A honor roll student." "So, no B's?" "No, I was the queen bee boo. I was even captain of my soccer team in High School." "That's something you and I share in common. I was captain of my debate team in High School, I was a pro in chess, and I did write some poetry on the side." "Ok, spit something for me." "You putting me on the spot like that?" "Well, if you are that good, it shouldn't be that hard."

Steven decides to speak from the heart and spits something. "I'm on a date with a beauty. I don't know if she's destined to be my mate. When I'm with her, I feel electric and powerful; she brings light to my day. Even though our souls are just getting attached to one another, I hope and pray that she stays around me for a long time so our souls can enlighten one another." Lily smiles and claps. "Wow, I have never had any guy do that for me. Most guys just try to approach me with corny pick-up lines." Steven says smoothly, "Well, I'm not most guys. I just love showing a woman true appreciation." "So, you show every woman appreciation?" "Only a lady that is deserving of it like yourself." "So, you aren't talking to any other ladies right now? You are a pretty smooth guy; that's the only reason why I ask." "Right now, no, but I was in a relationship with somebody a couple of months ago." "Why did you and that other person break up?" Steven reveals his breakup with Dani to Lily. "She found somebody better; she didn't think I was going to amount to anything. I'm not going to lie; it broke my heart. I thought she really cared. I learned that sometimes what seems good might be bad." "In my opinion, she's the one that lost out. You are a great person. I can tell by the way you talk that you are going to be somebody special. Never let anybody downgrade you. If I didn't think you would be something in life, I wouldn't be on this date with you right now." This brings a smile to Steven's face, and he can tell Lily is nothing like Dani. Steven and Lily stay talking some more.

Lily asks. "So, what is your favorite movie of all time?" Steven answers, "By far, 'Good Will Hunting,' mainly because I can relate to Matt Damon's character in the movie." "How do you relate to the character?" "The main character in the movie is smart and intelligent but is overlooked due to his hard upbringing and life. Not only that, he is scared to open up to people because he doesn't want to deal with disappointment with people like he has in the past. Overall, he's a great person; with the right guidance, he can be successful." "That's deep. I got to check that movie out." "It's a great movie, you will love it. So, what is your favorite movie of all time?" "Love Jones' is actually my favorite because it shows true love between two people, but it makes you want to find great chemistry with somebody. That's the type of love I hope for." "I hope for that type of love myself, somebody that generates good energy in my soul." Lily and Steven stare at one another and smile.

After talking and playing more games, Steven takes Lily home. Steven says, "I had a great time with you tonight; hopefully, we can do this again." Lily says, "I would definitely love to; if you are not busy next Saturday, I would definitely like to take you to this spot I hang out at." "Anytime I can be around you, I'm always down for it." Steven walks Lily to her door. "So, am I supposed to give you a hug or a kiss like they do in the movies?" "Just express what you feel in your heart." "I'm just trying to be respectful." "Come here." Lily grabs Steven and kisses him. "I always wanted to do that; it was my first time doing that. I wanted to do that to a guy I truly desired." Steven is shocked and happy as he knows that Lily truly desires him. "I got to say you are a great kisser. I loved having a taste of your beautiful, warm lips. So, what does this make us?" "I want to take this slow; just know you are the only person I'm talking to. I believe this can go somewhere; let's stay getting to know one another." "Yes indeed, you have a nice night, and hopefully, I'm the blues in your left thigh." Lily smiles as Steven walks to his car.

As Steven is on his way back to Thomson, he notices a traffic stop up the road. As Steven looks to go in another direction, the police stop him. Steven is super nervous; he doesn't want to go back to jail. He starts praying to GOD. "Dear GOD, please let me go free. My life is just getting back right. This has been one of the best days of my life; please don't let nothing happen to me. The police approach Steven's vehicle, and he lets his windows down. "Hey, Officer, what's going on?" "This is just a routine traffic stop. Can you show me your license and registration?" As he doesn't know what to say, he nervously tells the officer he does not have any license. "I don't have no license, officer; just do what you got to do." "Why are you driving if you don't have no license?" "I had a date tonight; I wanted to impress this girl. I see her as someone special; I just wanted to make a good impression on her." "We all been there before. Listen, what your name is, son, and how old are you?" "My name is Steven and I'm 18." "Steven, I don't know you, but you seem like a good kid. I'm going to let you go; it will be bad to arrest a young man after he's been on a date. You stay safe and have a nice night." "Thanks, Officer."

Steven drives off with tears in his eyes as he thinks he might get arrested. Steven says, "Thank you, GOD!" As Steven returns to his house, he writes in his journal. "Dear Journal, This has been one day I will never forget. Despite being pulled over by the police, I had a wonderful night. Lily is something special. I know me and her are taking things slow, but I hope she's the one for me. From the way she talked, walked, and from the way she looked she took my breath away. When she's in my presence, she enlightens my soul. Kissing her was something special, and I will never forget that amazing Moment. Hopefully, we are meant for one another. Maybe she is the person who can teach me the true meaning of love."

The next day, Steven gets a surprise visitor. Steven's Mom hears a knock at the door and answers the door. The person at the door is Officer Brown. Steven's Mom asks. "How may I help you, sir?" Officer Brown says, "Hey, my name is Reginald Brown; I'm a correctional officer at the county jail here in Thomson. Your son Steven was one of the inmates on my block; I just wanted to see how he was doing." "Yes, please come in, Steven you have a visitor! So, you, Officer Brown, Steven has told me so much about you. Thank you for looking out for him." "It was my pleasure; your son was an inspiration to many people while he was in jail." Steven is happy to see Officer Brown. "Officer Brown, it's so great to see you." Steven and Officer Brown hug one another. Officer Brown says, "How you been doing since you been released?" "I been doing good. I started GED classes earlier this week. I'm doing well in there; I also got a job." "Look at you, I'm happy for you. We at the jail miss you; the great work you did there has inspired so many inmates. This one inmate wanted me to give you this letter to show his gratitude towards you."

Steven reads the letter. "Dear Steven, I know you don't know me, but the poems you wrote have deeply inspired me. I'm going through so much in my life right now. I even thought about taking my life until I read your poem "The Great Light that's in the Dark." My favorite part of that poem is I'm living in darkness right now, I'm looking all around to find a way out. A small voice tells me I'm the light; even though people can't see me shine, I shall rise so people can see the great light in the dark shine bright and spread his wings. Even though in my mind I'm down, I got the Most High on my side, so I shall shine bright as the star. That inspired me in many ways. You don't know how much that means to me. I'm 17. I got a year in here for gun possession. I want better out of life; I'm trying my best to be a better man. I been going to the poetry class you created. I wish I could have introduced myself. What you created has changed my life forever. Thank you."

Steven finishes the letter with tears in his eyes. "I didn't know I made that type of impact on everybody. I just mainly created something that was fun for me to do." "That shows how special you are. You are gifted; GOD has a special hand in your life. I have seen a lot of inmates, but not one like you. You have a great gift; you are destined to do great things in this life." "Thank you, Officer Brown. I'm doing everything in my power to be the person GOD wants me to be. I forgot to ask how well Robert did teaching the class?"

"He did a wonderful job. He wasn't nervous. He was calm and collected. The inmates loved the words he spoke. You taught him well; he's going to do a great job." "I know he will; Robert is a great guy. I learned a lot of great things from him and from you, too, Officer Brown. I loved going to the Sunday Service every Sunday to hear you preach. I'm still writing in my journal and reading my Bible. I know this might sound crazy, but being in jail changed my life. It has given me a new outlook on life and made me a better man." "That doesn't sound crazy at all; that is what jail is for: to rehabilitate people. I'm glad that you have changed your life, especially somebody your age. I have seen people spend their whole lives in jail, and most of them change their ways when it's too late. Not you, though. I got a feeling you are going to inspire a lot of people. GOD is about to make you shine, young man. Be prepared." "Most definitely, and thank you for hooking me up with my landscaping job." Officer Brown starts smiling. "It was no problem; you did a marvelous job doing community work for us. You deserved that position, but not only that, you earned that position. Take care of the opportunities GOD has given you. I got to go; if you ever need anything, I'm just a call away. And Steven, you can also call me Mr. Brown." "Alright, thank you for coming by. I definitely will give you a call if I need something. Thank you again for everything." "No problem, come visit us; some of the guys will love to see you." "Will do."

After Officer Brown leaves, Steven's Mom walks back into the living room and says, "I overheard the conversation you had with Officer Brown. Just by hearing that conversation, I'm more proud of you. GOD has designed you to be somebody who will inspire the whole world, my son."

After the conversation with his mother, Steven gets a phone call from Darius. Steven asks, "Darius, what's going on with you, man?" Darius responds, "Nothing much, just out trying to survive, bro. You know the reason why I called, right?" "To see how the date went with Lily. Bro, it was amazing, one of the best nights I have ever had in my life." "Give me details, bro. Did you get some on the first date?" Steven starts laughing. "No, I didn't hit on the first date, which was actually a good sign, in my opinion. So, I knocked on her door, and she answered the door, looking stunning. It was like looking at a star at nighttime. She ended up getting dressed; we danced to one of the songs she was playing on her phone before we left."

Darius starts laughing. "Bro, you can't even do a good two-step; I would've paid money to see that. With your Dancing With the Stars ass." "It went well; it was like one of those ballroom dances you see in the movies. So, we went on a date, and we had a lot of fun; she did ask me about my parents and why I dropped out of school." "Did you tell her the truth?" "I was honest about those two things; I didn't reveal to her about all my past and being arrested. However, she was supportive when I told her about the other stuff in my life. She's very different from Dani. I can tell she truly cares about me. And at the end of the night, she gave me a kiss." "Man, she sounds special, bro; I will say stay getting to know her before you reveal everything about your past to her. You never know, though; she might be a real one." "I hope so; enough talking about me. How are you doing?" "I'm doing good out here cutting people's hair and everything. Making some money up in here, but it's nothing like being outside these walls. Being here makes you appreciate life more. It might be hard for you to believe I been reading books lately." "You definitely changed; you reading a book? I never would have thought. Which books are you reading?" "Letter to an Incarcerated Brother by Hill Harper; that book done helped me out a lot. Also, I been reading the Bible; my cellmate and one of the people in my dorm got this Bible group they created. So, I started going to that. I been told you; I'm doing everything in my power to be a great father figure for my kid. My kid is not going to see their father as a dude in the streets. They going to see somebody powerful and somebody they can look up to. We got to be a great example for the kids that come after us. We might not have nobody from the hood and the projects be successful, but we can change that. We can show the kids the right path to follow." "Most definitely so; that's the type of stuff I'm on. We can help prevent kids from going down the same path we went on."

"Yes indeed, Destiny sent me a pic of the baby's ultrasound. According to her, the baby is healthy. A part of me do hope it is a boy, but I will be just satisfied if the baby is just 100 percent healthy." "I can't wait to meet my godchild; that kid is going to be spoiled." "Also, Danny told me how you was there for him at his football game. I appreciate that; thank you for the great advice you gave him. I wish I could be there alongside him and help him out, but I'm glad you are there to help him. When I get out, everybody going to see a better version of me. I'm going to do big things just like you." "When you do get out, just know I got you. We going to be popping out here in these streets legit and be a powerful force that many people can look up to." "That's on everything, Steve. We are going to show out in a big way. I got to go, man. I will talk to you later." "Alright, be easy, bro."

The next morning, while on their way to school, Steven talks to Diamond about his date. Diamond asks, "So, how did the date go with Lily?" Steven responds, "It went amazing; it was one of the best nights I have ever had in my life. She even gave me a kiss at the end of the night. We are going back out this Saturday; she going to take me to this spot she likes going to." "Ok, Mr. Certified Lover Boy over here, I'm happy for you; you deserve happiness. I forgot to tell you Wednesday, but Lily is actually in one of my classes. I plan on introducing myself to her. I promise I won't tell her nothing about your past street life. She's smart and she could help me out a lot in class. Plus, I think me and her can be great friends." "I would love for my sister to be friends with somebody that could be my potential lady. You could put in a good word for me." "You know I got you; I will say good things about you."

As Steven goes to GED class, he gets better acquainted with his classmates. Ashley says, "Steven, tell us your back story on why you dropped out." Jose says, "This is a judgment-free zone; we won't judge." Steven speaks his truth. "When my Mom got sick, I started slinging in these streets to help support her. I got addicted to all the money that I was getting. I ended up getting caught a couple of months ago. I rounded up serving two months in county jail. I just got out about two weeks ago. I'm mainly here just to turn my life around. Hopefully, we can help and support one another while getting our GED." Jose says, "Most definitely, bro, we support you and thank you for telling your story. It took a lot of courage for you to tell your story." Will, the oldest person in Steven's GED class, says, "Yes indeed, little homie, I'm 39; when I was your age, I was in and out of jail. I wish I had your mindset when I was your age. Keep on doing your thing; you are on the right track." Steven says, "Appreciated, bro, and it's not too late for you either."

As class starts, everybody do their work during the middle of class. Mr. Marcus starts talking about finding purpose in life. "Today, I want to talk about finding your purpose in life. In life, we all deal with trials and tribulations, but those trials and tribulations help define who we are. Some of you are in this class today trying to find your purpose in life. The best way to do that is to do things you are passionate about, but also believe in yourself and believing in your dreams. Believe in the person you envision yourself being. Look at Tyler Perry; he knew his purpose was to be a writer and a director. He went through many situations that probably made him want to give up, but he believed in his purpose. It's the same way with getting your GED; in order to get your GED, you have to envision yourself having it. Granted, it might be some hard times you endured on your journey to get your GED, but always remember why you started before you ever think about quitting. I'm going to give you guys an assignment. I want you to write down where you see yourself in five years and share it with the class on Wednesday. I don't care how silly your purpose and dreams might sound to others; it's all about whether you believe in them, which counts."

After class ends, Steven talks to Will, one of his classmates. Will asks, "Excuse me, little homie, what is your name again?" Steven responds, "Steven Anderson is my name, but most people call me Steve." "Is your father named Steven too?" "Yeah, you know my father?" "I used to go to school with your pops, and we was in the streets together. Your father was something special; he is one of the smartest people I have ever met. Dude was super educated; everybody looked up to him for help. And he was that dude in the streets; he was book-smart and street-smart. He made sure I was straight many times when we were on the block together. I remember he used to have you with him sometimes at the trap houses. He loved you, man; he wanted to give you a better life. He just got caught up, and it saddened me when I found out he had got arrested. Everybody thought he was going to do something big in life. You ever talk to him?" "I actually spoke to him a couple of days ago; he doing good." "Glad to hear that. I hope he makes it home one day." "Me too, so tell me your story. Why are you in here to get your GED?"

Will tells his story. "I was a hoodlum in my younger days. I dropped out of school at the age of 17. After that, I was deep in these streets. I was selling drugs left and right; I was the man. I rounded up finally getting caught when I was 30. They got me on Drug trafficking and a whole bunch of stuff; I ended up doing five years in prison. I'm not going to say Prison changed my life. It was me being away from my kids that changed me. I missed so much of their lives; I wish I could've been there for them. When I got out, I started working at a factory; I still work there to this day. I admire you, little homie; I heard about you before you joined this class. People from our hood always brag about you. They used to always say Steven's son is a hustler just like him." "I didn't even know all of that, but I put that part of my life behind me." "I can tell; I heard you tell your story to everybody in class. It's very inspirational someone like you can make a big impact on the young kids in the ghetto.

It's something an old man told me while I was in prison that I want to share with you. He told me people in the streets are lowkey the smartest and most blinded people in the world. So, I was like, how that is? And he told me most guys in the streets know how to sell a product or drugs the right way. They know how to market their product and get customers coming back for more, which means they know how to make a profit, which makes them smart. So, then I asked him what made us the most blinded people in the world. He told me the same thing we do in the streets is the same thing people in a Fortune 500 company do. People in a Fortune 500 company know how to market their products and how to get customers coming back, which helps them make a great profit for their company. Overall, he was stating that we really don't see our potential. We have the mindset and skills to be legit businessmen, but we don't see it in ourselves. In life, we all have the potential to be great. It's up to us to see the vision GOD is putting in our brains and take full advantage of our potential so we can live in the foundation that is laid upon us." "Those are wise words, Will, it's funny when we be out here in these streets; we don't think nothing about that. We just think about the present; we don't think nothing about the future." "Facts, little homie, I got to go, but I'm going to give you my phone number. If you need anything, hit me up; your pops looked out for me. I just want to return the favor."

The next day, Steven goes to work and talks about his date. Jamal asks, "Young, buck how the date went?" Steven says, "It was amazing. I been telling people it was one of the best nights I have had in my life. She even gave me a kiss at the end of the night. I guess you were right about that cologne." Jamal starts laughing. "I told you, boy, you put that fresh scent of cologne, and you are going to have some girls that want a taste of you. Reminds me of my first date with my wife; I took her to this fine restaurant; she was the finest thing in the room. They always say the men sweep the woman off her feet, but that night, the woman swept the man off his feet." "When did you know that your wife was the one for you?" "Me and my wife been together for fifteen years and been married for ten years. What made me find out she was the one for me was when I went to prison. She could have left me and gave up on me, but she chose to stick by my side. A couple of months after I got out, I asked her why she didn't leave me. She told me she made a vow the day we got married, for better or for worse. Not only that, but she also told me she loves me, and she got me through the good and bad. That's how I found out she was the one for me. See, you a young guy; you probably going have women all over you. Here's the key thing to remember: if a girl loves the person you are, she will stick by you through the good and bad. You will find out sooner or later on whose the one for you; you just got to pay close attention." Steven takes Jamal's advice.

After he is done working and returns home, Steven receives a call from Robert. Robert asks, "Steve, what's going on with you, bro?" Steven says, "Nothing much, bro, mainly focus on positivity. What about you? Officer Brown told me you did a great job teaching the poetry class." "I did, man. I'm not going to lie; I was nervous, but Officer Brown told me to speak from within. And that's what I did. I spoke from the heart. I spoke my truths and passion. A lot of people open up to me due to that. I'm glad that I'm inspiring people in jail like you did, bro. You don't have to worry; the poetry class is in good hands. I forgot to ask how the date with homegirl was?" "It went well; me and her are actually going back out this Saturday." "That's what's popping, bro; happy for you. I hope everything works out. Hold on, Steve. There is somebody who wants to speak to you."

Michael gets on the phone to talk to Steven and says, "Mr. Chess King, what's been going on with you?" Steven says, "My boy Mike, glad to hear your voice. I been doing good, man, mainly focus on my future." "I'm happy to hear that; your future is bright, man. Always remember your potential and wake up every day to become a better man than the man you was the day before." "That's deep; I'm definitely going to do my best. How have you been doing?" "Well, since you been out, I have returned to being the chess king in jail. You the best competition I had in here. However, I decided to start teaching people how to play chess, mainly Robert; he's my new cellmate. They moved me into his cell after you got out. I have got some other news. I been preparing myself to get my license back. A good friend of mine came to visit me a couple of days ago. She used to be my assistant. Now she is a doctor, and she told me she's going to put in a good word for me to get my license back when I get out. I feel back to my old self except more mature. I feel like I owe you for that, in a way. Being around you really inspired me. Hopefully, when I get out, I can get my life straightened out. Not only that, I want to inspire other people who have been addicted to drugs and alcohol to get clean. It doesn't matter what pain or sorrow they feel; they still can make it and be somebody in life." "My guy, you already inspired me, so you already have inspired other people. You taught me how to find validation within myself. I learned to love myself because of that, and for that, thank you. Stay focused on the positivity and your future. You are going to do great things when you get out, so stay believing in yourself and GOD." "I appreciate that, Steve; I'm definitely going to do my best. Can't wait to see five years from now where we'll be at in life. I know it's going to be way better than where we are now in life. I'm not going to hold you for a long time. I'm going to give the phone back to Rob. Take it easy, my friend." "Will do."

Robert says, "Alright, man, I got to bounce; my minutes finna run out. Hector wanted me to tell you he said hey; he couldn't come to the phone. Just know all of us in here are rooting for you. Even though we behind these walls, we with you in spirit, bro." "Appreciated, bro; got nothing but love for you guys."

The next day, during GED class, Mr. Marcus asked Steven and one of his classmates to work out some math problems. Mr. Marcus asks, "Who wants to work out some math problems on the board? C'mon, it's got to be somebody who wants to work out some problems." Jose says, "Not me; I'm good." Mr. Marcus says, "Steven, I pick you to come up here and work out some problems." Steven isn't fazed by the decision. "No problem, I will show you guys how it's done." Steven works out the math problems and amazes his classmates in the process. As Steven sits down, he looks outside of the classroom and sees Lily pass by as she gives him a wink.

Before class ends, Mr. Marcus gets everybody in the class to share where they see themselves being five years from now. Everybody in the classroom share what they see themselves being in five years. Finally, it's Steven's turn to share where he wants to be in life in five years. Mr. Marcus asks, "Where do you see yourself being five years from now?" Steven says, "I didn't write nothing down. I decided to speak from the heart. Five years from now, I see myself being a better man and in a better position in life than where I'm at today. I hope to be a great businessman one day and be an inspiration to the people in the community."

After Steven says his statement, the whole class cheers him on. After class is over, Mr. Marcus has a one-on-one conversation with Steven. Mr. Marcus says, "Steven, let me talk to you for a minute. I loved what you said when you were talking about your future. I can tell you want to be your own businessman, but my question is, what type of business you got plan on running? And after you get your GED, what you have plan on taking up?" Steven doesn't have a plan mapped out yet but has an idea. "To be honest, I was thinking about Business Management, but I want to get a job out the gate." "I know you want to go to College, so here's my advice: take up something you are passionate about. The more you love what you do for a living, the more it is super easy to make money.

I also saw the way you were working out those problems. You got some great math skills. I know you take your GED test in two weeks, but I believe you can help out some of the students in the class. Everybody in this class is really not that good in Math except for you, so I was thinking every Monday and Wednesday, me and you work out problems on the board. It will help a lot of people out in here." "I'm down, but let me ask you something: what subject do I struggle the most in?" "I look at your classwork and the tests you have taken so far; I will say Science. I will say study harder in it, but still take the test. You never know; you might pass." "I most definitely will. I appreciate it; you have a nice weekend. I will see you on Monday."

After class, Steven talks to Lenny and Jose. Lenny asks, "So, Jose, you should help my boy Steven make a clothing line?" Jose says, "Yeah, bro, I'm making these designs, but I want to create something that makes a great impact on the fashion business. I want to do something that uplift people. We need to link up, and we can create something special for the culture." Steven says, "Most definitely, you have my number; let's make it happen soon." "Sounds like a good plan to me. We will be in touch; I will talk to you guys later."

Steven and Lenny have a one-on-one conversation. Lenny says, "I'm a happy man today, bro. I'm getting off these crutches and getting this big boot off my foot. I can finally walk on my own and be able to do more things, man." Steven is happy to hear the good news. "I'm happy for you. I can finally get you on the basketball court and school you." Lenny starts laughing. "Dude, I played basketball for my high school team. I got real skills, my guy. I will break them ankles super-fast." "We shall see my friend."

As Steven and Lenny talk to one another, Lily approaches them. Lily says, "Hey Steve, how are you doing today?" Steven says, "I'm doing well, doing better now that you are in my presence. Lenny, this is Lily. Lily, this is Lenny. Lenny says, "Nice to meet you." Lily responds, "I appreciate. You know something? You look awfully familiar.

Steven gets nervous after Lily makes that statement. Lenny says, "I live in Augusta. I be all over the place, so it could be from anywhere. Wait, hold on now, I remember you; I met you at the hospital after my surgery. Her father is the one who performed my surgery. He introduced her to me, and she prayed for me. I appreciate that you didn't even know me, and you said a prayer for me. Lily says, "No problem. I'm glad that you are doing better." Steven asks, "So, you pray for all your father's patients?" "When I go and visit my Dad, that is something we do. Plus, I got plan on being a nurse, and that is one of the things I want to do for my patients." Lenny interrupts, "I got to go, guys. Steve, talk to you later, bro; it was nice seeing you again, Lily."

After Lenny leaves, Steven and Lily have a lengthy conversation. Lily says, "I saw you working out problems on the board, and I must say I was very impressed." Steven says, "So, you were watching me?" Lily starts smiling. "I was not stalking you; you have great skills." "Or maybe I had a good luck charm helping me out." "Well, maybe I do have that magic touch. I can't wait for our date on Saturday. You will love the place I got plan on taking you." "And you still are not going to tell me where we are going on our date." "It's a surprise one you will enjoy. I also met a friend of yours named Diamond; she's cool. She told me a little bit about you, which made me admire you more." "She's a good friend of mine, more like a sister; she always had my back. I forgot to say I love that perfume you wearing; it's making me tingle." Lily starts laughing. "My good looks ain't making you tingle?" "I mean, it's alright, and it's decent." Lily joyfully punches Steven on the shoulder. "OK, I see how it is; well, I got to go to class. I will see you on Saturday." "See you on Saturday, beautiful."

While waiting for Diamond, Steven is approached by Garrett, the kid he helped out last week. Garrett says, "Steven, isn't it? I don't know if you remember me, but you helped me with my essay last week." Steven says, "I remember you, man; how did you do the essay?" "Dude, I owe you; I ended up getting a 100 on the essay. I owe all of that to you, man." "No problem, man. I used to have to write some in High School, so I know how it is. Are you from down here?"

"Me and my family is well-known down here; my father owns a lot of properties across town. His name is Christopher Banks; you might have heard of him." "I have heard of that name before; your father got a lot of money." Garrett starts laughing. "Yes, he does; look, you help me out; I would love to help you out. If you need anything, let me know. Where you from?" "I'm from Thomson. I got into some trouble a couple of months back, and I was required to take GED classes down here. I am mainly trying to get my life straightened out." "I feel you, bro; I got arrested for marijuana possession last month. Things happen in life. We just got to move forward from our past mistakes in life. I had a few people turn their back on me due to that. I bounce back, though. When you go through hard times, you find out who's really got your back." "How did your parents feel about that?" "Surprisingly, they were super supportive and had my back. I don't smoke weed a whole bunch, just when I got a lot of stress going on." "You can't use the drugs to numb the pain; granted, the pain will be gone for a minute, but it will be right back once that high is gone. I learned in life, you have to deal with your pain head-on; if you stay running away from it, you will never find peace."

"I never thought of it like that before. I broke up with my girlfriend a couple of weeks ago; it just had me in a depressed state." "I was in a relationship myself a couple of months ago with a girl. Shawty didn't like me for me; she desired me for how powerful I was and what I had. Forget the homegirl who broke up with you, though. If she don't support or love you for who you are, she isn't for you." "I needed that, bro; I got to have more people like you on my squad. My parents are throwing this party in a couple of weeks, and it's a great way to network with people." "If I'm not the only black person there, I will be there. Garrett starts laughing. "There will be plenty of black people there; you will love it. Plus, I told some friends of mine what you did for me and some of them want to meet you. This could be a great opportunity for you, and you seem like somebody I can be good friends with." "Alright, I'm down; keep me posted on the party, and I will be there." "Sounds good. I got to get to class. I will talk to you later."

After leaving school, Steven and Diamond talk on their way back to Thomson. Steven says, "Lily told me she met you." Diamond says, "Yes, she did; she's cool and very genuine. You definitely made a great impression on her; she stayed bragging about you." "Well, I'm not surprised by that; what all did you say about me?" "It wasn't nothing bad. I spoke very highly of you. I spoke about who you are as a person, the person she deeply admires. Me and her exchanged phone numbers; I believe she can be somebody that uplifts me also."

"Glad to hear that; so, are you going to Rich's going away party this Friday?"  "I am; he invited me to be there, so I'm definitely going to be there. What about you? Are you going?" "Most definitely, Rich has always been a real friend of mine, so I'm definitely going to be there for him. Plus, his father actually invited me to the party also."

"Ok, so you and Mr. Dixson are back talking; that's good to hear." "You making it sound like he's an ex or something like that." Diamond starts laughing. "The reason why I said that is you looked up to him. Plus, everybody at our school knew that you were his favorite student; he probably saw you as one of his kids. He stayed asking about you after you dropped out; some of these teachers probably didn't care about you. Mr. Dixson, though, he deeply cared about you." "I know he did and still does; me and him had a great conversation at Danny's game. He even said he would like me to visit the school sometimes to help the kids with the Debate team." "Do you got plan on doing that?" "I might; you never know. I could give them some great pointers." "Well, you were a beast when you were on the Debate team. So they could learn great things from you. There are going to be some people at the party who will be surprised to see you. Are you prepared for that?" Some of Steven's former classmates and teachers will be at the party. "I don't really care what them people got to say about me. I guess they're just going to be surprised when I walk up in there. I believe it's going to be an amazing night."

It's Friday evening, and Steven is getting ready to go to Rich's going away party. He wears the same suit and tie he wore at his court appearance. Steven asks, "Momma, how do I look?" Steven's Mom comes downstairs and sees Steven with his suit and tie on and starts crying. "Mom, why are you crying?" Steven's Mom says, "When I first bought you this Suit and tie, I envisioned you wearing it once you got out. To me, this navy blue set signifies who you are as a person, somebody who is powerful. When you walk into this event tonight, you are going to turn so many heads. Steven Terry Anderson, you are an extraordinary young man; don't you ever forget that." Steven's Mom kisses him on the forehead. "I love you, son, and you tell Rich I wish the best for him." "I will."

Steven goes to Rich's party looking super sharp with his navy blue suit and tie on. As Steven arrives at the party, he is greeted by Rich's Mother. Mrs. Dixson says, "Steven, OMG, it is so awesome to see you; you are looking well-groomed." Rich's Mother hugs Steven. Steven says, "Mrs. Dixson, it is so great to see you; you are also looking wonderful this evening." "Well, thank you, Steve. I saw you at Rich's graduation, but I didn't get a chance to talk to you. I know a lot has happened since then in your life; I just wanted to say you are somebody special. Mistakes don't define our lives; what defines our lives is the impact we make in this lifetime. Always remember that; now, come inside. Rich and his father are waiting for you."

Rich greets Steven. "Steve, man, I'm so glad to see you here. You are dripping out here, bro; the fit is super nice, my guy." "Appreciated, bro, you dripping hard out here to man, bro got the tailor-made red suit on and everything." "It's my party; I had to dress up super nice. Come with me upstairs for a minute. I want to talk to you without everybody around."

Steven and Rich go upstairs and talk. "So, I'm leaving this Sunday to go to College. I got plan on balling out at Georgia and hopefully being the best college player in the nation. You played a huge part in this; just know that. The many words of encouragement you gave me I will never forget. I wish Darius was here to celebrate with us, but I'm glad you are here to celebrate with me." "The honor is all mine, bro; all I ask is when you make it to the NBA, you don't forget about your boy." Rich starts laughing. "I'm not going to forget about you, bro. I want you to visit me sometimes on campus. I'm going to send you some tickets to some of my games. I'm proud of us. We done come a long way; five years from now, we are going to have a lot of people looking up to us. Now, while I'm gone, don't you get in no trouble." "I won't, bro. I learned my lesson; I'm going to stay on the right path. I appreciate you for holding me down through the good and bad. You probably had many people that told you not to be friends with me. You never judged me for what I did; you always judged me for the person that

I am. I am forever grateful for that, and I appreciate you being a good friend to me." "We are not friends, Steve, we are brothers. We might not share the same blood, but we ride or die." Steven and Rich hug one another. Rich and Steven say love you to one another. Rich says. "Alright, man, let's get back to this party."

Even though Rich and his family are happy to see Steve at his party, there are a few people who are surprised to see Steve and are looking down at him. Mr. Michaels says, "Steven, I'm surprised to see you here; the last thing I heard about you is you and your obnoxious friend, Darius, were in jail." Mr. Michaels is Steven's former history teacher with whom he used to have issues with. Steven responds, "Well, I'm out now trying to turn my life around. I'm in GED classes right now." "You know, most people who get their GEDs don't become successful; some don't end up doing nothing in life. Now, what makes you so sure you are going to be successful with you being a drug dealer, high school dropout, and just another person with a GED?"

Everybody in the room become hostile when Mr. Michaels asks Steven that question. Steven is upset by the question, and instead of lashing out, he gives a great response to Mr. Michaels. "First of Mr. Michaels, I don't sell drugs no more; granted, I am a high school dropout, and I am a person in GED classes. My past doesn't define my future; I understand you judge me for where I am from and the stuff I have done. I will be successful in life; you mark my words. You said most people who get their GEDs don't amount to nothing. Well, I'm not most people. I'm Steven Terry

Anderson, a young man who is going to make a great impact on this world no matter the circumstances that come in my direction. Now excuse me; I lost a little bit of my appetite."

As Steven steps outside to get some air, Rich's father comes chasing after him. Mr. Dixon chases Steven and says, "Steven, wait, hold up! I'm sorry for what Mr. Michaels said back there. Just know me and Mrs. Dixon don't feel the same way. We fully support you in everything you do. I look back; I should have been there for you more when your mother got sick. I deeply apologize if you felt like I wasn't there for you and that you felt like I thought less of you. When I found out you dropped out, it upset me because I was seeing a young, intelligent man throwing his education away. Not only that, but like I said before, you are probably the best student I have ever had. I'm proud of who you are. You never let the hard times get you down. Now, you are in GED class trying to improve your life. Like I said at Rich's graduation, I see you being successful, and I see now that you are finally seeing that in yourself. And that's what truly counts if you see yourself being successful. Always believe in your vision and dreams before anybody else does." It means a lot to Steven to hear encouraging words from Mr. Dixson, but mainly that he supports him. "Thank you, Mr. Dixson. I apologize for letting you down in the past, but like I told you at the football game, I'm a changed man. What people say about my life doesn't define who I will be; the actions I make in my life will define who I will be." "Those were wise words you just spoke, Steve, and I can't wait to see the great impact I believe you will make on this earth. Now come on, and let's enjoy the rest of this party."

After talking to Mr. Dixson, Steven enjoys the rest of the party and talks to some of his former classmates. At the end of the night, Steven, Rich, and Diamond talk to each other before the party ends. Diamond says, "Well, cheers to new beginnings for you, Rich; we are so proud of you." Rich says, "I love you guys; it means a lot that you are here. I wish Darius was here to celebrate with us, but I'm going to go hard on the court for him and you guys. A lot of people from this small town don't make it out, but we will. Diamond, you are going to be a great nurse someday. And Steven, you are a visionary who will do big things in this world. We are going to have so many people looking up to us in a few years." Steven says, "Yes, we are; cheers to the great future that is ahead of us. Guys, I got to go and prepare for work in the morning. Diamond, I will see you on Monday. Rich, again, I'm so happy for you, brother; call me when you get settled on campus. And remember, always put the mustard on the hot dog." Rich starts laughing. "Will do, brother."

The next day, after getting off work, Steven prepares for his second date with Lily. Steven has his Mom look at him in his outfit. Steven asks, "Ma dukes, how I'm looking now?" Steven's Mom says, "You looking sharp; the look yells out to me: Young, fresh, and intelligent; it fits you perfectly. So where are you guys going to tonight?" "It's supposed to be a surprise; she is supposed to take me to this place she thinks I will like." "I hope you guys have a fun time and you be careful driving down there." "Will do Mom love you."

Steven heads to Lily's apartment for their date. Steven arrives at Lily's apartment and waits for her to open the door. While waiting for Lily to open the door, he hears somebody blowing their horn. Lily yells from her car. "Steven down here!" Steven starts laughing and smiling. "You could've called or texted me before I walked up these steps to see if you were at home or not." "I would apologize, but I did like seeing you walking up the stairs with your wonderful outfit on. Now hop in the whip."

Steven hops in Lily's ride. "You are looking extraordinary tonight, so where are you taking me tonight? You are not trying to kidnap me, are you?" Lily starts laughing. "No, I'm not trying to kidnap you; the place I got plan on taking you is going to be a place I believe you will love." "We shall find out if that's true or not."

After riding around town, Steven and Lily arrive at a Poetry Club. Steven looks on the outside of the place. "I have never been here before; what is this place?" "This is Tom's Poetry Club; me and a couple of my homegirls come to this place quite a bit. When you spoke your poem to me, I thought this would be a perfect place for you to come to. Let's go inside; you are going to love this place."

Steven and Lily sit down at a table and listen to poets tell their poems. Steven takes a look at Lily as she is enjoying the Spoken Word. "I look at the joy in your eyes when these people are doing poetry; what is your favorite part about the whole thing?" Lily says, "I love a lot of great things about it, but my favorite part of it is the storytelling. It gives you great insight into the situation or the person the poet is talking about. I love visualizing what people say when they are talking, especially when it comes to poetry. What about you? What is your favorite part of poetry?" "My favorite part is understanding the true meaning of the poem. Once you find out the true meaning of the poem, you can see the beauty and the sorrow in it. The same way we can see the good and bad in a person." "I have never thought of it like that before. You are very deep-minded." "You forgot charming and smart also." Lily smiles and laughs.

As all the poets say all their poems, the host asks if there is anybody in the crowd who would like to do a piece. The Host says, "Is there any individual in the crowd that wants to do a poem before the night is over?" Lily yells, "Yes, he does!" Lily points at Steven. Steven has a crazy look on his face. Steven looks at Lily and says, "What are you doing?" "I want to hear you do a piece." "You putting me on the spot like that?" "I just want to see if you really got it." The Host says, "Young homie, you want to come up here and speak?" "Yes, I would love to do a poem I had written a couple weeks ago." "Come on up and lay it on us."

As Steven walks up to the stage, he starts thinking about a poem he wrote for the future lady in his life while he was in jail. And he asks the DJ to play Goapele's" Closer" instrumental for him. "I dedicate this poem to my beautiful date. The name of my poem is Stars From Above.

"Me and my boo are lying down on a blanket as we look at the Stars From Above. Appreciating this lovely Moment, we have between one another as we manifested and dreamed of being tied together like roots to a tree. The love we have between one another is hotter than any degree; the forecast for us is we are two lovers who will make our love last forever, as when struggles come our way, we will hurdle over the pain as we know GOD will give us sunshine for the rain we went through. I love my lady with all my heart as she is my light and fire, as I will always cater to her desires, never have to worry about no depression, as all I have to do is see her happy expressions, as I will be fully healed. Enjoying the stars from above with my boo, telling her she's the brightest star I know, the way she smiles at me can bring true joy to the whole globe. Her pretty white teeth are like the pearly gates in Heaven. She asks me what makes her special. I tell her to look into the mirror, and she will see the most beautiful woman in this world as she shines like a black diamond in the sand. I stand by a woman who has drive and ambition, but mainly a loving soul that symbolizes what love truly is. As she is breathtaking and fascinating, she keeps me alive as every time I see her, my heart skips a beat. I look into her beautiful brown eyes, and I say, Baby, I love you; I thank you for being you and staying true, my pretty boo. We look into each other eyes and kiss one another as the stars from above centers around our love."

The crowd starts clapping once Steven is done with his poem. The whole room is in love with the poem, especially Lilly, as she smiles brightly like the sun and gazes at Steven with her beautiful eyes. As Steven goes back to his seat, Lily asks, "So, was that poem for me?" Steven says, "Well, you are the only star I see shining in this room." Lily gives Steven a kiss.

As Steven and Lily leave the poetry club, the manager stops Steven. The Manager says, "Hey, I'm Tom, the manager of this establishment. I heard your poem, and it was very beautiful. You have a great talent in poetry. I want to give you my card. It has all of my contact information; if you want to speak again in front of everybody, please give me a call." Steven says, "Appreciated, Mr. Tom; I might take you up on that offer."

After leaving the Poetry Club, Steven and Lily return to her apartment. Steven says, "Well, I had a great time with you tonight." Lily says, "Come inside. I want to look at the stars from above with you." Steven and Lily go to her balcony and look at the stars from above. Steven asks, "So, how did the poem I read affect you?" Lily responds, "I was taken away. I never had anybody describe me in that way. You really did make me feel like a precious jewel." "Because you are; I'm not saying that to get in your panties. I'm saying that because I see your true beauty." Lily sees something special in Steven and makes an important decision. "I want to make this official between me and you. I want to be your girl; I feel like it was meant for us to be connected."

This brings a smile to Steven's face as he wants Lily to be his girlfriend. Because in his mind, he feels like there is no one else like her. "I would love for you to be my girlfriend. Now I know I'm always protected because I have a beautiful angel by my side." Steven and Lily stare into each other eyes and start kissing. "I'm not the type of girl to agree to date a guy this quick, but I haven't met a guy that makes me feel special like you." "And I have never met a girl like you before as every time I'm in your presence, it feels like I'm in Heaven Gates. I want to show you how much I appreciate your beauty on the inside and the outside." Steven and Lily start making love as the stars from above truly centers around their love.

Over the next two weeks, Steven and Lily start officially dating and getting closer, as the love between them has grown unconditional. It's Wednesday morning, and Steven is getting ready to take the GED Test at Augusta Tech in Augusta. He and his mother pray together before he takes the test. Steven's Mom says, "Dear Heavenly Father, I pray that you be by my son's side as he takes this test; GOD, give him strength but also stay guiding him into the right path. What's in your will shall be done. In Jesus' name, we pray. Amen. Son, how you feel about taking the test?" "I believe I can pass it; who knows, when I leave this place today, I could become a GED graduate. "Remember to believe in yourself and GOD; you can do this."

Steven walks into the Brooks Tech building and takes his GED test. After three hours, Steven gets done taking his test.

Steven's Mom asks, "How did you do?" Steven has an unpleasant look on his face. Steven says, "I passed two out of the four subjects. I passed Language Arts and Math but failed Social Studies and Science." "Well, look at the bright side; you passed two out of four, so that means you only got two more to pass." "Yeah, you're right. I will get it next time. Lily is supposed to meet me here; she wanted to support me. And she wanted to meet you also. "I see a young lady walking upon us. Is that her?" "Yes, it is; that's the shining star I've been telling you about."

Lily meets Steven's mother for the first time. Lily smiles and asks, "Hello, so you are Steven's Mom?" Steven's Mom responds, "The only one so happy to meet you." Steven's Mom and Lily hug one another. Lily says, "I had plan on taking Steven to lunch after he took his GED test. Speaking of which, how did you do?" Steven says, "I passed two out of the four subjects. I wish I had passed the whole thing." Lily says, "Steve, you got this; your time is coming." Steven's Mom says, "Yes, it will, my son; well, I got to go to work. Lily, it was nice meeting you. Son, keep your head up." "It was nice meeting you too, Ms. Anderson."

After his mother leaves, Steven asks Lily, "So, how it was meeting my Mom?" Lily says, "I loved meeting her. I see where you get your great mind from. She seems like a sweet lady." "She is a sweet lady, so where do you got plan on taking me?" "I got plan on taking you to this restaurant downtown; you will love it. Come on." "Well, a brother could eat, so let's go."

Steven and Lily go to this fancy restaurant downtown. Steven says, "This is a beautiful restaurant; you sure do have good taste." Lily says, "Yes, I do, especially in men." "I definitely agree with you on that." "Just know, Steve, you are going to get your GED; I will do my part to help you get that." Steven and Lily kiss each other. "I'm so glad that I have you in my life." "I'm glad that you are in mine also."

As Steven and Lily continue conversing and eating, Steven hears somebody yell out his name. The person says, "Steve, amigo!" Steven looks and sees it's Hector. Steven says, "Hector, what's going on? When did you get out?" Steven and Hector hug one another. Hector says, "Just a couple of days ago, I'm here taking my senorita on a date." "I'm glad to see you out. My apologies, Lily, this is Hector, Hector, this is Lily." "Hey, how are you are doing?" "I'm doing good; look at you. Steven, you got yourself a beautiful girl after being in jail. Look at you, Mr. Big Pimpin." Lily has a shocked look on her face. "Wait, hold up, Steven, you were in jail?" Steven nervously answers Lily's question as he is scared of the consequences of his answer. As everything in his life is starting to look good, he is scared it might be about to crumble. Steven softly speaks, "Yes, I did two months in jail; that's the reason why you didn't hear from me." Steven's biggest fear has come true. Lily finds out Steven was in jail. Steven's secret has come to light. Will Steven reveal everything about his past? How will this news affect their relationship?

258

259

# Chapter 10: The Dark Light

Lily has found out that Steven was in jail just a couple of months ago. She is shocked and upset that Steven didn't tell her he just got out of jail. Steven nervously waits for Lily's response. With an unpleasant look on her face, Lily says, "Excuse me, I done lost my appetite; nice meeting you, Hector." Lily walks away. Hector says, "Steve, bro, I'm so sorry I did not know. I did not intend for that to happen." Steven is left scared of how this will affect his relationship with Lily, as he has just gained the girl of his dreams, and he is scared he will lose her. "It's not your fault; the truth was bound to come out sooner or later. I got to go and chase her down. Here's my number; hit me up later."

Steven gets an Uber and heads to Lily's apartment. Steven runs up the stairs and knocks on Lily's door. As he is hoping and praying he doesn't lose her. Lily asks. "Who is it?" Steven responds, "It's me. Please let me in so I can explain myself." Lily lets Steven in her apartment. Lily is angry at Steven and yells at him. "I trusted you; all I wanted from you was your honesty! Why didn't you tell me?"

Steven, with tears in his eyes, confesses everything about his past. "Be honest; if I told you about my past, you would not have accepted me. You are used to being around preppy guys; that's not me. I went to jail for selling drugs; that is not something I'm proud of. I sold drugs for three years. I did what I had to do to survive. Seeing my mother struggle hurt me to my core. Hardly nobody helped us out; I was 15, and I was tired of struggling. I was tired of seeing my mother begging people for money. I was able to put food on the table for my mother and help her pay bills. It made me feel powerful. I felt like somebody once in my life. Looking back, I don't know if I would do the same thing or not. It's hard being a man when you are just a young boy trying to find his way in life and have no father figure. Being in jail helped change my mindset; it made me view life in a different way. Overall, it helped me become a better man. I'm just a man who is trying to turn his life around and be an inspiration to people. I met you before I went to jail; when I first saw you, your beauty hypnotized me. I have never seen or met a girl as wonderful as you. I loved the conversations we had in the mall.

At the time, I was dating another girl; I thought she was my ride-or-die. The time I got locked up, she dumped me; she left me in my lowest moment. When I was in jail, I thought about having true love one day. After Dani dumped me, I thought I would never find anybody else, especially so soon. So when I saw you at the Library, I felt like it was fate. You don't know how good I felt when I saw you on campus in the library. Anytime I am in your presence, it brings joy to my life. I love you Lily; a guy like me getting with you is something you see in movies. At least, I can say I dated a true angel. Just know I enjoyed our time together; if you don't ever want to see me again, I totally understand."

Steven starts walking toward the door when Lily stops him as she grab his hands. "Steven, wait, I appreciate your honesty. I'm not going to lie; if I knew you were a drug dealer, I would not have nothing to do with you. I fell in love with the person who you truly are. I love to hear you speak; you are one of the smartest people I have ever met. As much as I uplift you, you uplift me also. Being around you has made me a better person. I will not leave your side. I am in love with you, Steve. All I ask from you is that you accept the man you are. Because that is the man I am in love with. And be honest with me." Steven is relieved that Lily accepts him. He has tears of joy coming out of his eyes as he is glad that Lily isn't going to leave him. "Thank you! I thought you was going to leave me once I told you about my past." "You paid for your mistakes already. I know it took a lot for you to open up to me. I just want to be there by your side through the good and bad. Just be honest with me, please. GOD put us together for a reason; it's like we were meant to be." "Yes, we were. I love you, Lily." "I love you too, Steven." Lily and Steven hug one another.

The next day, Steven goes back to work and talks to Mr. Joe. Mr. Joe says. "Steve, how did you do on your GED test?" Steven says. "I had plan on passing the whole thing but only passed two out of the four subjects." "Well, it's a start. It doesn't matter how many times you fall down. What counts is how many times you get back and try again. My brother is a successful lawyer, but he failed the bar exam four times. I never forget the first time he failed the exam for the first time; our dad got on to him. He said, boy, keep your head up; nothing great is going to happen in your life if you stay looking down all the time. My brother told him he tried his best, but he didn't think he was going to pass the exam.

This angered my father. He told him never to say that again. He told my brother that if you truly believe you can be a lawyer, you should believe in the vision you have of being a lawyer. Never let a minor setback get you down because, most of the time, a minor setback is set up for a comeback. My mother came in the room and read him Jeremiah 29:11: For I know the plans I have for you," declares the LORD, "plans to prosper you and not to harm you, plans to give you hope and a future. This motivated my brother, and he took it three more times and passed on his fourth try. He could have given up and not fulfill his dream, but he stayed working hard and became a successful lawyer. With you, Steve, never give up; it does not matter how hard it gets. You don't want to live your life regretting something that could have easily been accomplished if you just stayed going at it." "Thank you, Mr. Joe; I'm not giving up; I'm going to stay going at it." Steven instills Mr. Joe's advice in his brain.

It starts raining heavily toward the end of the day, and Mr. Joe lets the workers go home early. As Steven leaves his job and heads back home for today, he notices a car is flipped over. Steven gets out of his vehicle and runs toward the flipped vehicle. Steven is shocked to find out who's in the vehicle. Steven yells, "Nicholas!" The person in the vehicle is Nicholas, the same guy who always downed Steven as a person since their high school years together, and the guy that Steven got in a fight with at Rich's graduation party. Nicholas, with a beat-up face and a few bodily injuries, looks at Steven and says, "Let me die, man, just let me die. I have nothing to live for. I'm nothing, man, I'm nothing!" "No, you are somebody; GOD put you on this earth to do great things. I'm not going to let you die; give me a minute. Steven uses all his strength to pull Nikolas out of the vehicle. "Paramedics are on their way; stay with me; I'm not going to let you die." Paramedics arrive to assist Nikolas with his injuries.

Steven goes to the hospital with Nikolas. Steven waits in the waiting room for two hours to hear Nikolas's status. Steven sees the doctor talking to Nikolas's parents and approaches them. Steven says, "Excuse me, I was wondering how Nikolas was doing. I'm the one that found him in his vehicle flipped over." Nikolas's Dad says, "You the one that found my son?" "Yes, Sir." With tears in his eyes, Nikolas's Dad gives Steven a hug. "Thank you so much; if it wasn't for you, my son would be dead now. He had a couple of injuries, and they had to do surgery on his foot, but he will be alright. What is your name, Son?" "My name is Steven." "Steven, I am forever grateful for this. My son has been having a hard time in his life lately. He had planned on playing football, but during his physical, we found out he had an enlarged heart. He's been depressed ever since. His so-called friends hardly don't talk to him anymore. He never ever had something this bad happen in his life. I'm just glad my son is still here. I got to do better and stay being by his side." "I'm glad he is ok, and I'm glad that GOD put me there at the right time to help your son. If it's ok with you, can I come back and visit him tomorrow?" "Of course, I believe he will be happy to see you. You have a great night, Steven, and thank you again."

The very next day, after getting off work, Steven goes to see his probation officer. While visiting his parole officer, Steven gets some surprising news. Ms. Harris says, "Glad to see you again, Mr. Steven. Let me just say I am so proud of you. You are moving in the right direction. You got your driver's license, you are doing well in your GED classes, and you have a great job. I talked to Judge Brown about how well you are doing." Steven asks, "What did he say?" "He said he believes you learned your lesson and is proud of you. He told me it's up to me if I allow you to be off probation or not." Steven's eyes open very wide, "So, what is your decision?" "Mr. Steven Anderson, you are officially off probation." Steven jumps with tears of joy and hugs his parole officer. "Thank you so much; you will not regret this decision." "I believe I won't regret this decision; you stay on the right path, Mr. Anderson."

As Steven leaves the parole office, he calls his Mom to tell her the great news. Steven says, "Mom, I'm off parole!" Steven's Mom responds, "Stop lying, boy." "I'm not joking. My PO talked to the judge about everything. I'm officially off." "GOD is so good; he is making things happen in your life, son. Your light is starting to shine, and you are about to brighten the whole world." "Yes indeed, Mom, I got to make a stop somewhere, and I will be home."

Before Steven goes home, he visits Nikolas in the hospital. Steven knocks on Nikolas's door. Nikolas says, "You can come in." Steven says, "Hey Nick, just wanted to see how you were doing." "I'm still living, so I guess I'm ok. I messed up my ankle pretty badly in the accident, so I'm going to be wearing this boot for a long time. Thank you for saving me, but I do have a question?" "What do you want to ask me?" "I have downed you and said all types of nasty stuff about you. Somebody like you should hate me, but instead, you saved my life. Why?"

Steven explains his reason for helping Nikolas. "I'm not going to lie. I hated you for the way you used to down me and Darius. You judge and look down on me for where I was from and for me being a drug dealer. And you never took the time to get to know me as a person. The reason why I saved you is you are a child of GOD, just like I am. I wasn't going to let you die. I heard that you couldn't play football no more due to your heart issues. I know that it is tough for you to deal with, and you feel like you are a nobody. Everybody looked up to you; now, people acting like they don't even know you. I know; I have been there. I was in that situation when I dropped out of school and when I went to jail. When I first got locked up, I was mad at myself. I felt like I wasted my potential and also let my mother down. Being in jail, though, got me closer to GOD. Sometimes, we go through hard situations so GOD can humble us into being better human beings. I was sentenced to two months in jail; I was supposed to get six months, but the judge showed leniency. That was GOD giving me a second chance. During my time in jail, I became a better person. I been out for almost two months. So far, I'm close to getting my GED, got a fine girlfriend, got my license, and got a car. But overall, I'm becoming better each and every day. The moral of the story is that for every minor setback is a setup for a major comeback."

After Steven shares his testimony, Nikolas starts crying. Nikolas, with tears running down his face, says. "It's been so hard, man; I dreamed of being a football player since the age of seven. I feel like a failure, like I let everybody down." Steven says, "You are not a failure; you was put on this earth for a reason. If it was God's will for you to be a failure or a nobody, he would have you let you die in that car accident. GOD has you here for a reason; you will bounce back, but it takes time. It's tough now, but years from now, you going to look and testify about this moment in your life. Remember, tough times create tough people." "Thank you, bro. I needed that more than you know. And I apologize for downing you as a person all of these years. I should have never done that. So, are we cool?" "We good; before I go, if it's ok with you, I would like to pray with you." "I'm not the type of person to pray, but I will give it a shot." Steven and Nikolas pray together.

"Dear Heavenly Father, Thank you for this day you have given us. I pray that you watch over my good friend Nikolas and strengthen him where he is weak. Give him guidance on his path to greatness. I pray that he gets closer to you, GOD, and that he accepts you in his heart. I believe you got a plan for Nikolas to do big things in his life. Help him be the best man he can be, so he reaches his full potential. In Jesus' name, we pray, amen. Well, I'm headed out; you have a good night, and remember what I said." Nikolas says, "Thank you, Steve, for everything. I would love to talk some more once I get out of the hospital if it's ok with you. You have uplifted my spirits." "I don't mind, Nick. You have a good night."

The next day, while at work, Steven gets a surprise visitor. The surprised visitor walks up to Steven and says, "I remember being your age and doing landscaping, which put a good amount of money in my pocket." Steven turns around and says, "Judge Brown, it's so great to see you." Judge Brown shakes Steven's hand and says. "It's great to see you too, Steven; I wanted to talk to you for a minute if that's ok?" "Sure, I do not mind."

Steven takes a break from his job and talks to Judge Brown. "I usually don't keep tabs on individuals that come in my court, but you stand out from anybody that ever appeared to me." "I hope that's a good thing." Judge Brown starts laughing. "It's a good thing, trust me; I heard all of the things you were doing in jail, like motivating fellow inmates and creating a Poetry club. You helped a lot of inmates while you were in there. And now you are close to getting your GED. You are doing big things, Mr. Anderson; I am super proud of you. You are on the right track. That's the reason why I thought you didn't need to be on parole anymore; you learned from your mistakes. I believe you can inspire a lot of people with your story. I actually have a proposition for you once you get your GED. I'm not going to say nothing about it until you receive your GED. Here's my card; my personal number is on it. Give me a call once you get your GED. Stay striving for greatness, Steven; the future is bright. And never give up on your dreams; remember, give me a call once you get that GED." "Will do."

The next day, Steven has the day off and goes to visit Dee. Dee says to Steven, "Lil homie, what's going on with you? You been getting this money, and you act like you don't know anybody no more." Steven starts laughing. "You know it's nothing like that; what been going on?" "You heard about Big Mike?" "No, what happened?" "He got arrested last night; huge drug bust at his house last night." "Dang, bro, they got everybody?" "Everybody, they swept his place up. They said Big Mike is facing a lot of years for drug trafficking."

Steven is shocked to hear the news and saddened by the news as Big Mike was somebody he looked up to and due to Big Mike making sure he was straight when he was slinging. "This got me messed up. Mike's a good dude; he looked out for me and Darius." "That's how it be, man; you have good dudes out here, but you know the mentality is getting the money. Do what you have to do to survive. Mike is an OG in the game; he knew the consequences behind his decisions. You are taking the right path; hopefully, kids in the neighborhood look up to you and want to change their lives also." "I hope so, too; it's hard when you come from nothing. You try your best to do everything in your power to fight for better in life. Some of us try to find a quicker or easier way to provide better in life, but in the end, it puts us in a deeper hole." "Either way, it's going to be hard; life is hard, nothing is easy. That's something I wish I had learned when I was younger. When you get in the drug game, you going the wrong path; granted, you can make a lot of money selling kilos and 3for 5's out here, but there are harsh consequences that can mess up your life forever. We just got to try our best to do better." "We will do better; look at you; you already doing big things with your landscaping company."

Dee shares exciting news about his company. "I just signed a contract with the Board of Education; your boy going to be cutting all the grass for all the schools down here in Thomson." Steven says, "Congrats, bro; that's big news, man." "Appreciated man. I'm glad I'm able to provide for my wife and kids. I got tired of working for other people; I wanted to be my own boss. Not only that, when I'm dead and gone, this business can be passed down to my kids and theirs. Not only that, but I also hired some of the guys who used to be out here in these streets. I talked to Darius the other day, and told him he could come work for me when he gets out. He said he would love to work for me. We have to uplift and support one another. When one of us gets locked up, we always say free our boy, but did we do anything to help prevent our boy from going to jail? We got to change as people and as a whole society." "Me and you can do that for our community." "Youngin, me and you both are destined for great things."

"Yes indeed, big homie, we are destined for big things. I also finally told Lily the truth about my past." Dee asks, "How did she react?" "At first, I thought I was going to lose her. Then she told me she was glad that I told her. She just asked that I accept the man that I am because that's the man she fell in love with. We still going strong and doing our thing." "She sounds like a real one; you better keep her, man. When GOD gives you a beautiful companion, that's somebody who can help guide you in the right direction." "You speaking facts. Well, I'm going to head out; you be easy." "You to stay paper chasing, young homie."

After leaving Dee's house, Steven gets a phone call from Kurt, one of Rich's friends. Kurt says, "What's going on, Steve? I'm having a kickback out my house. I wanted to see if you wanted to come over." Steven says, "I'm down; send me the address, and I will be on my way." Steven heads to Kurt's house, and as he arrives at the house, he is greeted by Kurt. "My boy Steve, glad to see you; come inside. Some of the guys are already in here." Steven goes inside and reunites with Jack and Lance and meets a few more of Kurt's friends. Jack asks, "So, what you been up to, Steve?" "Mainly focused on my purpose, bro, trying my best to better my life." Jack says, "You got it, bro; just stay believing in yourself and GOD." Lance says, "Yes indeed, man. When you work hard and put your faith in GOD, great things will happen in your life."

As Steven gets to know more of Kurt's friends, Kurt introduces Steven to his father. Kurt says, "Steve, this is my father. Dad, this is Steven." Kurt's Father says, "It is so nice to meet you, Steven. My son has told me so much about you. Do you mind if I talk to you outside for a minute?" "Sure, I do not mind." Kirk's Father takes Steven to his garage. "You ever rode in a foreign before Steven?" Steven is shocked when he sees Kirk's Dad vehicle. "Woah, you have a BMW i8!" "I just got it last year; hop in; let's take a ride."

Steven and Kirk's Dad ride around town and talk to one another. Kirk's Dad says, "My son told me about you, all the stuff you dealt with and everything." Steven says, "You aren't finna start judging me, are you?" Kirk's Dad starts laughing. "I'm not going to judge you, my guy. You remind me a lot of myself when I was your age. When I was a teenager, I was deep in these streets. I was reckless out here; I was selling drugs and hitting licks. I didn't care at the time. I was getting the money, and that's all I cared about."

Steven asks, "What changed for you?" Kirk's Dad says, "When I was 19, my main partner got shot and killed while standing on the block. It messed me up badly. I was depressed for a good while over that. I even had a plan to get revenge on the person who did it. When I went to my homie's funeral, I looked at his Mom; she was crying nonstop. I told myself I didn't want my momma crying over me like that. I saw his son also crying. Seeing both of them cry the way they did made me want to change my life. So, I went out and got a job at a factory, worked my way up, rounded up, becoming the team lead of my shift. I had homies who told me I should have stayed in the streets; I would be making more money, but I knew if I had stayed in the streets, I probably would have been dead or in jail. So, I didn't really focus on what they were telling me. I stayed pushing forward and looking up." "So, how did you become a real estate developer and have your own real estate company?" "That's all thanks to my loving wife. I have to introduce you to her one day. I met my wife at the mall when I was 21. She's come from a very different background than I did. Her parents were in her life, and they lived in the suburbs and went to great schools. So, at the time, my wife just graduated from Augusta University with her Bachelor's degree in Business Management. With her expertise and knowledge, she helped me become a real estate developer and business owner. I told her my dreams and vision, and she believed in them and me. She encouraged me to go for my real estate license; at the age of 23, I got my real estate license. I worked for a real estate company for six years, and then I opened my own business. Now, twelve years later, I own almost 100 properties and have my own company, which I'm able to provide for people who are hustlers like me." "Man, that's inspirational. What made you go into real estate, though?" "I always wanted to be my own boss; that's one of the reasons why people love the streets. You can get up anytime and get that dough. I was always in love with properties as a young kid. I remember looking at big houses and telling myself that will be my house one day. I would also look at the properties in which people saw no value, but I saw something special in them. I see properties just like I see people. There is always a true value in both of them. It's value in all of us; the main thing is you got to make sure you see it in yourself." "Being in this vehicle with you has inspired me; you came from the bottom and made something out of your life." "You can do the same thing, granted. Will it be hard? Of course, but stay on the hustle so you reap the benefits of the hard work you have put in."

Steven and Kirk's Dad return to Kirk's house. Kurt's Dad says, "Here's my business card. If you ever need anything, you hit me up, Steven, ok?" Steven says, "Yes, Sir, thank you." Kirk says, "I see that you guys are back; how was the ride?" Kirk's Dad says, "It was great. Steven is a wonderful young man, and I would love for him to come by the house more often." "He is more than welcome. I know Rich isn't down here, but I got your back; if you ever need anybody to talk to, hit me up." "No doubt, I got to get up early for class tomorrow. I will see you guys later."

The next day, before class starts, Mr. Marcus talks to Steven. Mr. Marcus says, "Steven, let's talk about your GED test results. I know it wasn't the outcome you were looking for, but at least you passed two out of the four subjects. You are super close to being done. Don't give up; stay going at it." Steven says, "I'm not. I actually scheduled a retake for next week. I'm going to stay going at it." "That's great to hear. I also got some good news. The Technical System gives out a yearly award for GED students. The award is called The Rising Star Award. Us GED teachers nominate one of our students. And I want to nominate you for that award, with your blessing, of course."

Steven gets very excited. "Yes, I'm totally down; how does the process work? "Well, it's 21 other students you would be facing; all you guys have to do is write a paragraph on the impact you want to make in your life. Then, the committee will narrow it down to five students; then, you will meet in Atlanta and speak in front of the committee about being a GED student and the impact you want to make in your life. Whoever gives the best speech wins the award; I believe you can do it. You have an amazing story that can inspire people." "Since you believe I can win this award, I am most definitely going to go hard to win it."

After class ends for the day, Steven, Jose, and Lenny hang out with one another. Jose says, "Steven, do you want to work on your clothing line right now?" Steven says, "Yeah, let's do it." Lenny says, "Let's get some designing going on."

Right before Steven, Lenny, and Jose leave, Steven is stopped by Garrett. Garrett says, "Steve, been meaning to run into you; my dad is having the party I was telling you about this Saturday; here's your invite." Garrett gives Steven a flyer for the party. Steven says, "Thank you, my guy. Do you mind if I bring my girlfriend to the party also?" "I do not mind. I can't wait to see both of you guys there."

After the conversation, along with Lenny, Steven heads to Jose's house." Jose says, "Welcome to my crib, guys." Steven says, "Man, you got a big place." Lenny says, "For real, I didn't know you were living like this, Jose." "What can I say? My parents be getting to that guwop. This is where I make my shirts and where the love magic happens." Steven and Lenny start laughing. Steven says, "Chill, bro, let's come up with some slogans for the clothing line." For almost an hour, the guys create slogans to put on the shirts. Steven has the same idea that Hector gave him in jail about putting motivational words on a shirt, as his mindset is for people to be inspired and look fresh when they wear his clothes.

After getting done coming up with slogans, the guys discuss the price and the name of the clothing line. Jose says, "We got some great slogans, so how should we do the prices?" Steven says, "Do it how we do it in the streets?" Jose says, "What do you mean?" "On the streets, like we sell for 3 for 5 with the shirts, we can do a

2 for $10. Set up a website, create pages on social media, and market the shirts in an efficient way." Lenny says, "I agree; that's a smart strategy. We do it that way so that we can make a good profit off these shirts." Jose asks, "What should be the name of our clothing line?

Steven starts thinking about the struggles young men go through in life, thinks about everything he went through to get to this point, and comes up with a name for the clothing line. "I got it; the clothing line should be called The Boy That Comes From Nothing. This clothing line will represent the people that got everything they earned from the Dirt." Jose and Lenny love the name Steven came up with. Jose says, "I fuck with it." Lenny says, "I like the name too." Steven says, "So, it's official: our clothing line will be called The Boy That Comes From Nothing. This is a team effort. I want your to be co-owners of the clothing line with me. Plus, all three of us are Boys That Come From Nothing. Would you want to be co-owners of the clothing line?" The guys don't hesitate to answer. Jose says, "We gotcha, bro; let's inspire people together, bro," Lenny says, "I got your back, Steve. I'm down, Fam." Jose says, "I love the ideas; we going to make this happen. Give me a couple of days, and the shirts should be ready." "Thank you, guys, for helping me out. This means we are business partners now; let's motivate people with some drip." Lenny says, "Yes indeed, Steven, do you mind taking me home?" "No, I don't mind. Jose, I will see you later, bro."

As Steven and Lenny pull up to Lenny's house, they are approached by Tony. Tony daps up Steven and says, "Steven, my boy, haven't seen you in a while; how are you living?" Steven says, "I been doing great; just trying to straighten my life out." "It's nothing wrong with that. Lenny, how are you doing? Looks like your feet is doing well. Lenny says. "It's going well. I'm still recovering and everything. I will talk to you later, Tony. I will meet you inside, Steve."

After Lenny goes into the house, Steven has a one-on-one conversation with Tony. "So, I heard about you and Darius getting locked up." "Yeah, we got caught selling product on our block. I wounded up doing two months in county jail. Darius, he's still in prison since him getting caught selling drugs was a parole violation." "I was saddened to hear about you young brothers getting locked up. Your made a great amount of money out of here, but jail is also a part of the game. You have your good and bad, but if you a true hustler, you will find a way to bounce back some way. So, are you still interested in flipping some bricks?" "No, man, I'm done with that stuff. I do appreciate you for giving me and Darius an opportunity to make money on your block." "It's no problem; like I said when we first met, I like to see my people eat. You got my number; if you ever need anything, just let me know."

After talking to Tony, Steven walks inside Lenny's house and is greeted by Lenny's mother. Lenny's Mother asks, "So, you are Steven?" Steven says, "Yes, ma'am." Lenny's Mother gives Steven a hug. "Thank you for what you did for my son; if it wasn't for you, he probably would be in jail. You sacrificed your freedom for his; that right there makes you family. He looks up to you; you have inspired him more than you ever know."

Lenny comes from downstairs and says, "Had to go upstairs and get something." Steven says, "It's ok. I was talking to your Mom, great lady." Lenny's Mother says, "Steven is such a great young man; glad you are friends with him. Well, I'm still cooking. Bree should be home soon, but for right now, you guys should relax until the food is ready." Bree is Lenny's younger sister.

As Lenny's Mom cooks dinner, Lenny shows Steven around his house and talks to one another. Steven says, "Bro, you have a beautiful family and a beautiful house." Lenny says, "Appreciated, man, I appreciate what I have; me getting shot made me appreciate what I have in life." "I know I talked to Tony. Does he want you to go back in the streets?" "Of course, he does because he knows I can help him make a lot of money. After getting shot, I told him I was done with the streets. He respected my decision; I got to make it out of here to provide for my Mom and sister. I could have died out there, but I survived. When I was in the hospital, your girl Lily was visiting some of the patients. Her dad was my doctor. They both prayed with me and asked GOD to guide me in the right path of my life. They helped me realize that GOD had me here for a reason. Got partners that are in jail, and some of them are dead. Like you said before, we going to make it out and do big things." "Yes, indeed, bro, we are going to do big things; we just have to stay believing in the vision we have set for ourselves and put in the work to succeed." "Big facts, bro; we are going to do big things and inspire people at the same time.

Speaking of which, how is Darius doing?" "He's doing good; he got a baby on the way. He also is trying to get his GED in prison. Can't wait to see my boy out them gates. We going to do good things for our hood."

Lenny's sister arrives home. Lenny says, "Little B, how was your day at school?" Bree asks, "Who is he?" "Bree, this a good friend of mine; his name is Steven. Steven, this is my little sister, Bree." Bree says, "Hi Steven, do you know how to play Connect 4?" "It's her favorite game to play." Steven responds, "Yes, I do know how to play Connect 4; you want to play a game?" "Yes, I'm the best at Connect 4; let's play." Steven, Lenny, and Bree play Connect 4 until Lenny and Bree's Mom get done with cooking dinner. Lenny's Mom says, "Dinner is ready, you guys." Bree says, "You suck, Steven. I beat you four times." Steven laughs, "Today wasn't my day, but best believe next time, I'm going to show you why I'm the King of Connect 4."

Everybody comes to the table and eats dinner. While eating dinner, Lenny's Mom gets to know Steven. Lenny's Mom asks, "So, my son told me how you guys met. Even though I don't condone the things you and him did, I understand why he did it. But why did you join the streets, Steven?"

Steven explains. "Well, I wasn't raised to be a person in the streets. My mother raised me to be better than that. When I was 15, my mother was diagnosed with breast cancer. She ended up losing her job during that time; she wasn't able to get another job due to her condition. So, I had to do something. Seeing my mother struggle to pay bills made me feel sad. So, I got with my homeboy, Darius; he was slinging out here and getting dough. I told him I wanted to be part of the action; I started making a lot of money and was able to help my mother pay bills. I got addicted to the money and the fame it brought toward my way. A couple of months ago, I had plan on hanging things up because I felt GOD was giving me signs to leave the streets. On my last day in the streets, I rounded up getting arrested. I thought it was over for me. GOD gave me a second chance. I was facing a year in jail, but I only did two months in jail. My time in jail changed me as a person. It made me want to do better just learning from other people in jail. I also started a poetry class during my time in jail; I told myself once I get out, I'm going to do everything in my power to fight for a better life for me and my family."

Lenny's Mom applauds Steven on his efforts to be a better man. "I respect that and salute you for trying to change your life. You have been a great influence on my son; he definitely looks up to you." "I appreciate ma'am. Lenny is a cool dude who reminds me a lot of myself." "Mom, I am grateful to have a friend like Steve; he's like a big brother I never had." "That's what I like to hear; just stay loyal to one another, never turn your back on one another." "Never turning my back on him, I got his back, no doubt." "Yes indeed, ride for bro 4L." Lenny's Mom continues, "And Steven, even though we just met, I consider you family. You sacrificed your own freedom to help save my son. Like I said before, I'm forever grateful. If you ever need anything, do not mind calling us."  "I appreciate, Ms. Austin; that means a lot to me."

After everybody gets done eating, Steven gets ready to leave to go back home. Lenny's Mom gives Steven another hug and says, "Well, Steven, it was such a pleasure having you here in our house. Like I said before, you're family; you're welcome here anytime; we love you and support you." Lenny says, "Yes, indeed, bro, we got your back." Bree says, "You have to come back again so we can play Connect 4 again." Steven says, "I most definitely will, Bree; prepare to get beat next time. Thank you, guys, for having me. Good night." Steven feels delighted to feel the love and support of Lenny's Mother. For the first time in Steven's life, he is feeling real love and support from people.

As Steven returns to Thomson, he pulls his vehicle aside from the road and talks to GOD. Steven says, "GOD, thank you for what you are doing in my life. You have blessed me with so much in these past months. I hope I can use the blessings you bring my way to help bless other people. Just know, GOD, I'm going to do everything in my power to not let you down. I shall overcome my hardships and be the man you want me to be. In Jesus' Name, I pray. Amen."

When Steven returns home, he writes a paragraph for The Rising Star Award. He calls the paragraph "The Boy That Came from Nothing." After two hours of writing the paragraph, Steven is finished.

On Wednesday Morning, Steven turns in the paragraph he wrote to Mr. Marcus. Steven says, "Mr. Marcus, here's the paper I wrote. Hopefully, it's good enough." Mr. Marcus says, "You didn't waste no time writing this; knowing you, it is definitely good enough. I will turn this in later on today. I should hear something next week."

Before class starts, Steven and Jose have a quick meeting. Jose says, "Yo, Steven, can I talk to you for a minute?" Steven says, "Yeah, man, what do you want to talk about?" "Tell me what do you think about this." Jose shows Steven pictures of the shirts he created with the slogans he, Steven, and Lenny created. "Bro, this is nice; when are you going to start selling them?" "Just created a website for our clothing company." "You ain't wasting no time; this clothing line is going to be powerful in these streets." "Me, you, and Lenny, this is our business. All three of us came up with great ideas. Together, we will be great business partners. It will be perfect; I'm the guy that does the designs, Steven, you come up with the words that should be on the shirts, and Lenny does the marketing." Lenny walks into the classroom as the guys talk and smiles as he sees the shirts. Lenny asks, "Those the shirts for The Boy That Comes From Nothing?" Steven says, "Yes, sir." Lenny says, "We are going to take over the Streetwear game with this."

Jose says, "Yes, indeed, this is going to be huge." Steven says, "Together, we shall inspire the whole globe with our gifts and talents. I got this event I'm going to this Saturday that's supposed to have a lot of business people in it. I will try to make a lot of connections for us. There might be somebody there who can help us with the business." Jose says, "If you can make that happen, that will be great." "Sounds good; send me some pictures of the clothes, and I will work my magic."

After class is over, Steven gets a phone call from Hector. Steven answers, "My boy Hector, what's going on with you?" Hector says, "Nothing much, amigo, hope all is well with you and your senorita; sorry if I caused any issues." "No, you didn't. I actually should be thanking you. Thanks to you revealing to her that I was in jail, I was able to finally tell her everything about me and my life. It made our relationship stronger." "I'm glad everything worked out. I'm throwing a little get-together right now; you and your lovely lady should come by." "Alright, I'm about to call her right now to see if she's available to come with me. Either way, I'm going to be there; just send me the addy." "Alright then, I will see you soon."

Steven calls Lily to see if she wants to go to Hector's get-together. Lily answers, "Hey babe, how was class today?" "It was great. What are you doing right now?" "About to head to class, even though I don't want to." "Why don't you just skip and hangout with your boy? My homeboy Hector, who we met at the restaurant last week, is cooking out and wants us to join him." "I'm down. I hope he can cook; I will meet you in the parking lot."

Steven and Lily go to Hector's house. Hector says, "There he goes; what's going on, bro? I see you brought your lovely lady. Come inside and meet everybody. This is my lovely fiancé, Isabella; Isabella, this is Steven, the kid I was telling you about I met in jail, and this is his girlfriend, Lily." Isabella says, "It's so nice to meet you guys; Hector used to talk about you all the time while he was in jail. Thank you for looking out for him." Steven says. "No problem; Hector is like a big brother to me. He helped me out while I was in jail." Hector asks, "Lily, do you mind if I talk to Steven really quick?" Lily says, "No, I don't mind. I can talk to Isabella during the meantime."

Hector and Steven step outside to talk. Hector asks, "You want a beer, amigo, or a soda pop?" Steven says, "I will take the soda pop, so what you been up to since getting out?" "Man, really just enjoying my family and making sure I stay on the right track this time. I got to be a better man for my bae and my daughter; I want to be able to be the man my daughter can be proud of. I got this job at a factory. I start tomorrow. I'm about to get out here and make some money the legit way. I owe you, though, little homie."

Steven wonders how Hector owes him. "How do you owe me?" "The Poems you created for us in jail inspired me. It inspired me when it comes to life and inspired me when it comes to love. Not only that, going to Sunday Service every Sunday helps me get close to GOD. After you got released from jail, I actually started teaching the poetry club with Robert; that club is changing so many lives, bro." "Well, that's thanks to you; if you had never told me to start selling and making poems, it would never have happened. Let me ask you this: what encouraged you to tell me that?"

"It's something very special about you, man; you have this great gift of inspiring people. You are destined to do great things, my boy." "Appreciated man; my goal is to inspire and be a great influence for my people and the young kids in my neighborhood. So many of us don't make it to the side of success and happiness. I'm going to do everything in my power to make it to that side and bring my people with me." "I look at you now with your girl; it seems like everything is coming to fruition. Just like Officer Brown always tells us to stay believing and great things will happen. You stay doing that, and great things will come your way." "Big facts, bro. You know what's funny? On me and Lily's first date, I bought her lilies. I was inspired by you to do that." Hector starts laughing. "I wish I would have been out at the time. I would have planted those for you, bro."

"You still got plan on having your own flower business?" "Yes, sir, I got to save up for it, but that's my dream. It's the growing process I love about it. Getting to see something grow into a beautiful masterpiece is a wonderful thing to see. This business I got plan on doing can help my family out forever. Generational wealth is what I want for my family, especially for my daughter. That's why when I was on these streets, I went super hard to provide for my family. Now I'm going to do everything legit and provide for a better life for my senorita and daughter."

Steven also tells Hector about the clothing business he's starting. "I'm happy for you. I can't wait to see the great things you do. I know; I'm starting a clothing business, bro, with a few friends of mine. Something I didn't plan on doing, but I believe it can be a great thing for me. And that's thanks to you for giving me the bright idea to put my motivational quotes on clothes." Hector's face is filled with joy and excitement. "You a genius; in my opinion, you can do anything. Look at you, Puff Daddy; when you start selling clothes, let me know, and I will definitely buy from you. We might not be blood, but I see you as like a little brother. Any friend of mine is family, and I'm always going to support my family." "That's love, my guy; forever have love and respect for you." "Likewise. Now, let's get back into this house before our girls start looking for us."

The guys enjoy the rest of the cookout with everybody. Hector says, "I'm glad that you guys stopped by; we have to do this again." Lily says, "Yes, we do; you guys are so fun to be around." Isabella says, "You guys are welcome here anytime." Hector says, "Steven, remember, if you need anything or just need to talk, hit me up." Steven says, "I most definitely will; you have a good night."

After leaving Hector's house, Steven and Lily go to Lily's apartment. Lily asks, "So, what incredible things have you been up to?" Steven lets Lily know everything that's been going on. Steven says, "Well, your man is officially a businessman." "Stop lying for real." "For real." Lily smiles and hugs Steven. "What type of business?" "A clothing business, it's me, Jose, and Lenny. The Clothing Line is called The Boy That Comes From Nothing. Let me show you some of the designs; tell me what you think?" Lily is amazed by what she sees. "Bae these designs are awesome; do you guys have a website?" "The website is launching this Saturday; I believe the guys and I can make a great impact in the fashion world with this clothing line. And also, I have been offered to be the recipient of the Rising Star award. I submitted my paragraph to enter, I find out next Wednesday if I go to Atlanta to speak to the committee about being a GED student and the impact I want to make in my life. Whoever gives the best speech to the committee wins the award."

Lily is proud of Steven and has a great idea for him. "Did I ever say how proud I am of you; you are a star, bae. Now, people are about to see you shine like the star you truly are. I know you are doing this clothing business with your friends, but I also think you should start your own motivational website." Steven starts laughing. "You serious?" "Yes, I am, all the people you inspired in jail, and you started a poetry club while in there. Babe, somebody like you can inspire this whole world with your voice." "Since you see that in me, I'm going to do that, and I'm not just saying that. I thank you for being there for me." "I'm grateful to be by your side; we're going to shine brightly together." "This Saturday, we both are going to shine at Garett's party, boss man and boss lady taking over the building. Like we Jay-Z and Beyonce." "I actually got you something for the party; give me one second."

Lilly goes to her closet and pulls out a custom tailor-made suit. Steven is in awe when he sees the suit. Steven asks, "That's for me?" Lily answers. "Yes, it is; try it on and tell me what you think." Steven tries on the suit and loves it. "Bae, you are the best. I didn't expect this. This is one of the main reasons why I love you." "Like I said before, I got your back, plus you will wear this same suit when you meet my parents in a few weeks."

Steven wonders if Lily's parents will accept him. "Do you think your parents will accept me?" Lily holds Steven's hands, looks into his eyes, and says. "I already accept you; that's what truly counts. Plus, my parents know all about you. You will be fine; just remember, as long as you accept and love the person you are, it doesn't matter what anybody else thinks." "I thank GOD that he brought you into my life." "I thank him for letting me find you because you are definitely something special." Steven and Lily hug one another.

The next day, while at work, Steven gets a phone call from Destiny, the mother of Darius's Baby." Steven answers, "Destiny, what's going on? Is everything ok?" Destiny says in distress, "I'm in labor, Steven; the baby is on the way!" "I'm on my way!" Steven leaves his job and rushes to the hospital.

When he arrives at the hospital, he is met by Darius's Mom. "Got here as fast as I could. Has the baby arrived?" "Yes, I'm officially a grandmother; go ahead and go into the room so you can see the baby."

Steven walks into the room and sees Destiny holding her and Darius's baby as he is in awe of the baby. Steven says, "Man, he looks wonderful; he definitely got his looks from you, not Darius." Destiny starts laughing. As Steven says that, he hears another voice in the room. Darius says, "I know you ain't not talking with that big head of yours." Steven asks, "Darius, where you at?" "I'm on the phone. I got permission to be on an extended call to hear my son be born." "Glad you are here. So what have you guys decided to name the baby?" "Darius Steven Hampton Jr, of course, he was going to be named after his father, but we wanted his middle name to be named after his Godfather." "Like I said before, we are brothers; right now, I'm behind these walls, but I know you are going to lookout for my little man. I'm bettering myself so he can be proud of the man I am, but I want my son to idolize you, too. We both are going to be great father figures for my son. I thank you for what you have done, but guys, I have to go. Steve, I will call you later. Destiny, baby, I love you, and DJ, your daddy loves you. I'm going to make you proud, son."

Before he leaves, Steven wants to hold the baby. "Before I go, you mind if I hold the baby?" "Of course." Steven holds the baby and looks straight into its eyes. "Nephew, you are going to be a powerful person, and I'm going to be here for you." Steven gives the baby back to Destiny. "Call me if you need anything, alright?" "I will; thank you for everything, Steven; you are a real brother."

After leaving the hospital, Steven returns home and is greeted by his mother. Steven's Mom says, "Well, hello, son. I heard Darius's baby has arrived." Steven says, "It has; he's wonderful. Darius and Destiny decided his middle name would be Steven." "Well, that was very delightful for them to do that; I know you see Darius as your brother. So, I know you are going to look out for his son." "Most definitely, that is something you taught me: always look out for your people." "Yes, I did. I taught you well; you got mail, and it's a letter from your father." "Alright, I will see what he's talking about."

Steven reads the letter his dad sent him. Steven reads, "Dear Son, I hope all is well with you in your life. I was glad to speak to you on the phone; I missed a lot of your growth and can't wait for the day I see you in person. I want to send you visitation papers again; no pressure, it's up to you if you want to sign them and come see me. I want us to see each other face to face so we can speak our peace. I know you have questions and want answers, and I want to give you that. I never got a chance to speak to my father for not being there for me. I want to give you that opportunity to speak your peace. I can handle what you bring my way. Either way, son, I love you, and I will forever support you."

After reading his father's letter, Steven starts thinking about signing the visitation documents his father sent him. While thinking about the letter his father wrote, he gets a phone call from Darius. Darius says, "Big boy Steve, what's going on?" Steven says, "Still excited about the baby? How does it feel to be a father?" "It feels great. I can't wait until I get out so I can be with my little guy. I'm going to give my kid everything that I didn't have. Going to be a great father and a great role model for my son. Working on getting my GED in here, learning trades, and even reading books." "I can't believe you are reading books of all people." "My cellmate be putting me on; got me reading the Autobiography of Malcolm X; very inspirational stuff, even reading the Bible, too." "I'm proud of you, bro; you going in the right direction. When you get out, you are going to do big things." "We are going to do big things. We are going to put on for our hood and be a great example for the people."

"Best believe you heard what happened to Big Mike?" "Yeah, I did sad stuff, bro, but it's part of the game. I hope him and his family be straight." "Yeah, I also just co-founded a clothing line called The Boy That Comes From Nothing with Lenny and Jose, with whom I'm in GED class with. Working on some boss moves, they ain't ready for what I got in store." "That's what I like to hear: stay pushing, stay moving, bro. Don't matter what comes your way, stay going through it like the animal you are."

Steven asks for Darius's advice on how to deal with his father. "Best believe you know I will. I need your advice on something, man." Darius asks with concern in his voice, "What's up, bro? Everything good?" "So, I got this letter from my father;

he sent me these visitation letters so I can see him. He told me he wants me to visit him so I can speak my peace. Trying to decide whether to visit or not." Darius answers, "You know your life is going in the right direction right now; it's like everything is aligning in the right way for you. Not only that, you can't really judge your father. You were also in the streets just like him for the same reasons. Just like his actions affected you, your actions probably affected people close to you the same way. In a way, you should definitely understand why he did what he did. I'm not going to tell you if you should visit your father or not, but I know if my father reached out to me and wanted to see me, I would definitely take that chance. I got to go, bro; stay doing your thing, and thank you again for looking out for my brother and my son." After talking to Darius, Steven signs the visitation papers and mails them off the next day.

It's Saturday evening; Steven gets ready to go to Garrett's party. While getting ready for the party, he calls Jose." Jose answers, "Steven, what's going on, bro;. you about to go to that party?" Steven responds, "Yes, sir, about to make us some connections. Have we been making some sales so far?" "A few, not a whole bunch, but I got a great feeling we are going to be getting a lot of cash in the coming weeks." "We are, bro; let me work my magic tonight, and we will see how it goes. I'm not going to be at school on Monday because I am taking the GED test that day, so I will see you on Wednesday." "Alright, boss, you be easy and make those connections, bro."

Steven wears the same tailor-made suit that Lily bought for him. Steven asks his Mom how he looks in the Suit. "Ma dukes, how do I look?" Steven's Mom looks at her son and says., "That's my son, boss man. Steven, not going to lie; you remind me of your father wearing this. He used to dream of going to events wearing suits, and now you are doing it. Every time I look at you, son, I'm proud. Like I said before, GOD has a special hand in your life." "Well, Mom, I'm glad I'm making you proud. One of these days, I'm going to get you a mansion in the hills. All of our hard work is going to pay off. Momma, they are not prepared for us; we are about to pop out on them." "That's my boy; you have a good time at the party and tell Lily I said hello."

Steven leaves and picks up Lily from her apartment. As Steven sees Lily, he is in awe of her beauty. "Lord Jesus, heaven definitely lost an angel girl; you look stunning. People are going to drop dead when they look at you." Lily says, "You mean when they look at us because we are one killer ass couple that is always going to shine together." "Yes indeed, senorita, let's go before we are late."

Steven and Lily head to Garrett's party. As they arrive at the party, they notice a lot of people at the party. For living in the hood and never going out of his environment a whole bunch in his life, attending a party in the suburbs is a huge deal for Steven. Steven says, "Man, this is like something you will see in the movies. I have never seen this number of people in suits and ties in my life. I envisioned myself being at parties like this since I was a kid." Lily says, "Well, you have turned your dream into a reality, babe." "Yes, indeed, I'm glad I have a wonderful leading lady by my side; now, let's blow this people away."

As Steven and Lily walk into the party, they are greeted by Garrett. Garrett says, "Steven, what's going on, bro? Love the suit, man." Steven says, "Appreciated, bro; this is my girlfriend, Lily; Lily, this is Garrett." Lily says, "Hey, nice to meet you; thank you for having us at your event." Garrett responds, "It's no problem; my man Steve helped me make an A+ on my English paper. For that, I had to invite him to this party. Now come along; I will introduce you guys to some people."

Garrett introduces Steven and Lily to well-established people in Augusta and also to other college students. Steven makes a lot of connections and promotes his clothing business. Steven says, "Hey guys, I got to go to the bathroom; I will be right back." While in the bathroom, Steven meets somebody who will help change his life forever.

295

# Chapter 11: Making Things Happen

As Steven is washing his hands in the bathroom, a gentleman next to him starts talking to him. The person asks, "So, how are you enjoying the party, young man?" Steven responds, "I'm enjoying it; well, how about you? Are you enjoying this party?" "I have always been to parties like these for 30 years." Steven looks at the gentleman and recognizes who he is. "Hold on, I know you; you are Mr. Danny Scofield. You are the Mayor of Augusta." The Mayor smiles, "Yes, indeed I am, young man. You know I been watching you all night. You are something special. I watched the way you talked to people and made connections. You have great charisma for a young person. How old are you?" "I'm 18." "When I was your age, I used to be scared to talk to people, but I eventually grew out of it. What brings you to this event? Are your parents businesspeople in Augusta?"

Instead of lying to the Mayor, Steven decides to tell the Mayor the real reason why he was at the event. "No, my parents aren't businesspeople down here; I was invited by my friend, Garrett Banks, to come to this event. Me and a couple of friends of mine started this clothing business together; I got plan on marketing our business here at this event, and a motivational website I got plan on developing." "I do know Garrett, his father, and I went to school with one another back in the day. You and Garrett go to school with one another also?" "Sort of. I'm in GED class while Garrett is in college." "There's nothing wrong with that. It's always great to see a young person on a path to greatness. Do you have pictures of some of the clothes you and your friends are selling?" "Yes, sure, tell me what you think."

Steven shows the Mayor pictures of the clothes and designs he helped create with Jose and Lenny. Mayor Scofield is impressed by what he sees. "You and your friends have a lot of talent. Honestly, I think a clothing business like this can inspire a lot of young people. Plus, I love the designs of these clothes. When are you going to develop and put out the motivation website?" "In a few days; my girlfriend is the one that motivated me to create the website. I'm not trying to tell my life story, but I was in jail earlier this year. While I was in jail, I found GOD, and it made me a better person while I was in there. I developed a poetry club while in jail. It helped inspire a lot of people in there, so why not create a website that can inspire the whole world? Hopefully, you don't look at me differently after that." Steven wonders what the Mayor thinks about him as he is expressing his true honesty toward him. The Mayor responds, "I'm not going to lie; I do. For a person your age to go through that and inspire people while you are trying to find your way yourself speaks volumes to me. I want to stay in contact with you, Mr. Steven; you have a lot of potential. I have a golfing event coming up next Saturday. The event is for young entrepreneurs. I want to invite you to the event." Steven is ecstatic to hear that the Mayor wants to invite him to an event. Steven's intention was to make connections within the Augusta community. He did that and made a connection with the Mayor of Augusta. In Steven's mind, GOD is opening up doors for him. Proof that some people see the true value in people even when many people don't. Mayor Scofield says, "I guarantee you that by going to this event, you will make powerful connections, but not only that, it will be a great chance for the people in this city to get to know you. So, do you accept my invitation?" "Well, I have golfed once in my life, but I will definitely be at your event." "Sounds good; there will be plenty people that can help you with your business and with your own brand. First thing tomorrow, I will help endorse this clothing line." "Appreciated, Mr. Mayor, that means a lot; I have a request though?" "Name it." "Can my two business partners also come to the event?" "Bring them along; see you on Saturday, kid."

After talking to the Mayor, Steven goes back to the party and finds Lily. Lily asks, "You took a long time in the bathroom. Is everything ok?" Steven explains why he was in the bathroom for a long time. "Yes, you will never guess who I ran into in the bathroom." "Who?" "I ran into the Mayor, and he's going to endorse our clothing business and help me with my brand, too." "OMG, bae, that's huge; you are on your way to greatness." "They are not prepared for me, baby."

Lily says, "Hey, you remember Tom, the manager of the poetry club I took you to." Mr. Tom shakes Steven's hand and says, "Steve, Lily told me you started a clothing business, and you have plans on starting your own motivational website." Steven responds, "Yes, indeed, making big moves out here." "I see, and I want to help. Can you get 50 of your shirts to my club on Wednesday? If your website is launched by then, I can help with that also." "I might be able to do that, but in exchange for what?" "The Poet that was originally scheduled to speak canceled on me, so I need a poet for that day, and I want it to be you. I'm willing to pay you $500 and help you market your product. Your set would be from 15-30 minutes." Steven doesn't hesitate to answer. "Sounds good, man; I appreciate it. I will take that offer, and I will be in touch with you before Wednesday."  "Sounds good to me; you guys have a lovely evening."

After talking to Mr. Tom, Steven has a conversation with Lily. Steven says, "I owe you big time; you really are like a flower because you are helping me blossom right now." Lily smiles as she puts her hands on Steven's shoulders. "You welcome. I want to see you win, and I'm going to do everything in my power to help you do that." "I love you." Steven kisses Lily.

As Steven and Lily are leaving the party, a young man starts yelling out Lily's name. The man says, "Lily, what's going on? I haven't seen you in a while. Who's your friend?" Lily isn't excited to see this person and tries her best to avoid him, but he runs toward her and Steven. She responds sarcastically and introduces him to Steven. "Hey Dennis, this is my boyfriend, Steven. Steven, this is Dennis, my ex-boyfriend."

Steven and Dennis stare at one another for a brief moment. Steven isn't fazed by Dennis, and he keeps it cordially with him. Steven reaches out his hand and says, "What's going on, bro?" Dennis stares at Steven's hand and starts laughing. Dennis mocks Steven's voice, "What's going on, bro? I can tell you from the slums. I'm surprised by you, Lily. I thought somebody like you would be dating someone with more class and more proper grammar." Steven gets closer to Dennis. "If you want to take it there, I can show you class." "Don't hit me, dope boy; what school you go to anyway?" Lily steps in. "That's none of your business, and why won't you go somewhere."

Steven defends himself, "No, it's ok. Granted, I might not be the guy who has Mom and Dad spending their money on my education and have flashy jewelry. Though, at least, I'm not the guy that is hating on another man because he didn't value the precious jewel he had and is mad somebody else is cherishing that precious jewel the way it should be." Dennis laughs again, "Me jealous of you, crazy." "You not dumb; when you first saw me, you were probably thinking 'how the hell she is with that guy instead of me.' Now you here in my face trying to down me in my lady's face to make yourself look good. So, ask yourself this: if you weren't jealous of me or wanted what I had, then why in the hell are you in my face? See, look at you now; you tried to make me look like a fool, now you the fool. Now excuse us; my lady and I are going home. You have a nice night."

After the confrontation with Lily's ex-boyfriend, Steven and Lily head back to Lily's apartment. Lily is concerned that Steven might be upset. "Steve, I am so sorry about that. Dennis has always been super arrogant." Steven wonders about Lily's past with Dennis. Steven asks, "You and him dated?" "For a quick minute, but I dumped him; he stayed lying and cheating on me." "So, I'm guessing you lied to me when you told me I'm the first guy that ever made you feel special." "No, I was not lying. You are the first guy other than my Dad to make me feel like a queen. Dennis and I never had deep moments together like you and me. With me working at the mall, it's always guys trying to get with me. The reason why I chose you is you truly saw something special in me. You just saw the full version of me. When I'm around you, I feel protected and loved. I will never do anything to jeopardize that. I love you, Steve, and deep down, I know you love me too." "Even though I have only known you for a couple of months, I do love you. With all my heart, more than any girl I ever liked. The main reason is you give me hope; not a lot of people have done that for me." "You give me hope, too. I love you." "I actually got a surprise for you; give me one second."

Steven goes to his car and gets his laptop. Steven shows Lily something special on his laptop. "Now look at this and tell me what you think." Lily reads. "Steven's Inspirational Word website, yes, you finally created the website!" Lily hugs Steven, "Yes, I did, but I wanted to launch the website with you by my side." "Let's go ahead and launch this website, Bossman." Steven officially launches his motivation website with his lady by his side. And he also created social media accounts to help support the brand.

The next day, Steven, Lenny, and Jose meet at Lily's apartment to discuss their clothing business. Lenny asks, "Where's wifey at?" Steven says, "Diamond ain't up in here just playing; Lily is gone to spend time with her parents. After this conversation, I'm going back home." Jose says, "So, I see you have made us some connections. Our followers are going through the roof, and our sales are going up." "We got a feeling that by you going to that event, you probably made some major connections." "I did, especially with the Mayor." Jose says, "Wait, hold up the Mayor, that's a major connect." Lenny says, "Man, you are making moves out here like James St. Patrick." Steven says, "I showed him the clothes on the website, and he said he liked them and plans on promoting them for us." Jose is excited. "Yes, sir, we are about to be popping out here." Lenny asks, "Hold on, is there a catch to this?" Steven says, "Kind of; next weekend, the Mayor has a golfing event going on. There will be fellow business people and young people like us who desire to be business people who will also be out there. He said we're invited to the event." Lenny says, "I never golfed a day in my life." Jose says, "Facts, I hardly can't even play."

Steven tells the guys about another opportunity. "I also have another opportunity for us; I got an opportunity to spit some poetry at Tom's Poetry Club on Wednesday night. The manager told me we can sell 50 of our shirts, and I can promote the website I done launched." Jose says, "Well, first off, congrats on the website, and second, 50 shirts! That's a good amount, bro, but I can pull that off by Wednesday and get with me on the day before. So, how do you guys want the prices for that event?" Steven asks, "Lenny, what's your take on it?" Lenny says, "Well, if we sell it at $5, we would make $250 that night. We sell the shirts online at $10, so at the event, let's keep it the same, and we get two times that and make $500 instead." Steven says, "I'm with that; it sounds like a good plan to me."

Jose says, "Sounds like a good plan to me also, but what is this website you created?" Steven says, "The website is called "Steven Inspirational Word" It's a motivational website that can help inspire people in life; just launched last night. What I wanted to do with you guys' blessing is sell some of our shirts on my website." Lenny says, "I don't mind; that brings more promotion our way." Jose says, "I'm ok with it too. I'm proud of us; we out here making major moves." Lenny says, "Big facts; these people are not prepared for us." Steven says, "My fellow hustlers, we going to stay popping out here; nothing is stopping us."

After talking to the guys, he goes home. As he arrives, he is greeted by Darius's Mom and Darius's brother. Darius's Mom says, "Mr. Moneymaker, what's going on?" Steven says, "Everything going well, ma dukes; making big moves out here." Darius's Mom says, "That's what I love to hear. I'm going back inside; I'm helping your mother cook Sunday dinner. I will let you and Danny talk."

Steven and Danny talk to one another. "Alright, Danny, little homie, what's been going on with you?" Danny tells Steven what's been going on in his life. "I'm doing good; I'm a little bit nervous about this football game I got coming up. If we lose, we miss the playoffs." "Well, you been working on your game, have you?" "Yes, I have. I just don't want to disappoint my team and the city." "Your teammates support you, man; you the best quarterback in this town. I don't care what nobody says. It's like what Hoodrich Pablo says in one of his songs: I'm a diamond in the rough, I was made under pressure. Man, you are the perfect person to lead your team to victory. Us being from the projects, nobody don't believe in us, but what counts, bro, is that we believe in ourselves. You going to do your thing and stunt on them boys. When is the game?" "This Thursday, are you coming?" "Wouldn't miss it, bro; I know you going to pop off. Now let's play some video games while waiting for our mothers to get done with cooking this food."

The next day, Steven goes back to Augusta to retake the GED test. Before taking the test, he calls Diamond. Diamond answers, "Well, hello stranger, haven't heard from you in a minute. What you been up to?" Steven says, "About to retake this GED test. I hope I pass. I was wondering if we could hang for a quick minute after I get done." "Yes, we have a lot of catching up to; do text me when you get done. I hope and pray that you pass this test." "I hope I do, too, sis; I will text you once I get done."

Steven walks into the Brooks Tech campus and takes the GED test for the second time. Steven only needs to pass the science and math portion in order to obtain his GED. After two hours of testing, Steven comes outside and patiently waits for his test results. After a few minutes, Steven gets his test results and is stunned. "Damn, I thought I had passed the test. Just when I think everything is going right in my life, this happens. GOD, please guide me in the right direction." As Steven says that, a young man runs by and drops his paper. Steven says, "Hold on, bro, I will help you pick that up." Random dude says, "Appreciated; got to go to my job, that's why I'm in a hurry." Steven looks at the paper and reads it. "A loss isn't a loss; it's a lesson that can be turned into a blessing." "It's a motivational quote I wrote down; thanks for helping me out, bro, but I got to go; you be easy." "You too, bro." At first, Steven was feeling down, but after seeing the motivational quote, Steven gets more motivated.

After the encounter, Steven meets up with Diamond at Starbucks. Steven greets Diamond with a hug and says, "Well, hello. I'm surprised to see you with one of my shirts." Diamond says, "Lenny told me about the clothing business you guys started, and I wanted to support." "I appreciate the love, so you and Lenny back talking?" "We are taking things slow; I see that he is trying to change his ways. And that's probably thanks to you. He really looks up to you." "Lenny is like the little brother I always wanted to have. Don't give up on him; bro is going places, but other than that, what has been going on with your life?" "Been busy working in school and just got a new job." "Where you working at now?" "Working at this healthcare place right now; once I graduate, it will show that I have some experience in nursing. Though, the main thing I'm trying to do is being a positive role model for the young black girls in my neighborhood. Like you stated, we have to be the ones to influence the kids after us in the right direction." "I'm proud of you, sis; you doing big things out here, boss lady." "Well, thank you, boss man; one of these days, I'm going to see you pull up in a foreign." "Best believe that is going to happen." "I'm proud of you also; I forgot to ask; did you pass the GED test?"

Steven, with his head down, says. "No, I was one point away from passing the GED test, but I'm going to get it." Diamond gives Steven assurance that he will get his GED. "You will, but also, I will say take your time scheduling the test and studying for it. I know you are super anxious to get this GED so you can go to college. All I'm saying is take your time with everything, and everything will fall in place for you. You doing good. You inspiring the whole hood, in my opinion. I can tell your relationship with Lily is going well; every time she talks about you, her face glows up." Steven with a smile and shrugs his shoulders. "I just got that effect on women." "Boy, hush, I can tell you going in the right direction; just a couple of months ago, you was out here in these streets and didn't know where to go in life. Now you know your purpose, but GOD is blessing you in a big way. Not only that, Darius has a baby, and Rich is about to ball out at UGA; all of us are doing big things." "Big facts, it seems just like yesterday we used to be on the playground together; now we out here chasing our dreams. I forgot to tell you I created a Motivational website." "Oh, snap, you got to show me the website." "Here it is; it's called Steven's Inspirational Word, and it's mainly just giving inspiration to people. I launched it about two days ago, so I got a couple of views on the website." "Steve, you popping out here. Steve Harvey better watch out because it is a new Steve on the scene. Everybody better watch out; youngin on the scene, and he got no plans on leaving." "I know I got a letter from my Dad; he sent me a visitation paper to come see him. I decided to sign them, so I'm waiting to hear an approval for my request to see my father." "That's a big step for you. I know you held in a lot of anger toward your father for not being there for you." "I did, and I still do; if I'm being honest, that's why I'm going to go and try to see him. I got to make peace with this situation. Not for his sake, but for mine. Plus, talking to Darius about the situation helped me understand my father's point of view." "I think by doing this, you are one step closer to releasing all that anger in your heart. Hold on. I'm actually getting a call from Rich."

Diamond says, "Richard, what's going on? haven't heard from you since you left. I'm here with Steve." Rich says. "Well, the three amigos back together; I actually had plan on calling you Steve. Diamond, do you mind giving Steven the phone so I can talk to him really quick?" "Yeah, don't be going through my text messages, Steve." Steven says, "Nobody ain't trying to see your Moesha pick-up lines with Lenny."

Rich and Steven have a phone conversation. Steven asks, "What's been going on with you, bro?" Rich answers, "Busy, bro; I'm training almost every day out here. My first game will be in a couple of weeks. Have you been staying out of trouble?" "I am doing big things out here; started my own clothing line with a couple of friends of mine and started my own website." "I saw that on Facebook and Instagram. I'm proud of you. You are doing big things; seeing you winning is inspiring me, bro, for real." "Appreciated, man; that means a lot coming from you. I'm proud of you too, bro; you putting on for the city also." "They having homecoming up here in two weeks. If you trying to sell some shirts and make some good amount of money, you come up here and see your boy. You can come sleep in my dorm room with me and my roommate." Steven thinks about how much money he and the guys can make by going up there and agrees to visit Rich. "You mind if I bring my guys Jose and Lenny with me; they are my business partners, and I want them there with me to sell the shirts." "I don't mind; bring them along. We are going to have a great time up here, bro." "Yes, indeed, bro. I'm getting a phone call from my GED teacher; going to have to talk to you and Diamond later. Diamond, here's your phone; I will talk to you later."

Mr. Marcus calls Steven with great news. Steven answers, "Hey, Mr. Marcus, it's great to hear from you." Mr. Marcus responds, "I did call with some news, but first, did you pass the GED test?" "No, I failed again. I thought I was going to pass this time, but I didn't." "You are going to get it; I think you are too anxious to get it. Let's go back to the drawing board and figure out solutions to help you pass the GED test. So, let's wait a couple of weeks before you try to re-take the test. We will talk more about that on Wednesday, but I'm calling because I just got a call about the paragraph you wrote for the Rising Star Award. You have been accepted as one of the finalists for the Rising Star Award."

Steven is in disbelief and is shocked he is picked as a finalist. "Stop lying; for real, I got accepted?" "I'm not lying to you, man; you earned this. Congratulations." At first, Steven was feeling sad due to him failing the GED Test. Now, he is super happy with the news that has been brought to him. "Man, I'm so excited; so, when do I go down there?" "The speaking event will be on Friday next week at 11 am in Atlanta; if needed, a vehicle can come and pick you up. You just talk about being a GED student and talk about the impact you want to make on this earth. If you need some help preparing for it, I would be glad to help you out." "Thank you; we can talk about it on Wednesday. See you then." Steven jumps with joy and smiles brightly.

Steven calls his mother and tells her the exciting news. Steven says, "Mom, I got some exciting news." Steven's Mom asks, "What is it, son?" "I have been accepted as one of the finalists of the Rising Star Award. I got to go to Atlanta next week to give my speech." Steven's Mom yells in excitement. "That's my son. I'm proud of you, boy! You know I'm going to be up there to cheer you on. A lot of people thought you wasn't going to make it, but look at you, son. We going to stay moving in the right direction, with nobody stopping us. Love you, son; stay prospering in the right direction; see you later tonight." After the conversation, Steven texts everybody he knows about the good news.

The next day at work, Steven has a conversation with Jamal. Jamal says, "Little homie man, I'm proud of you. You are doing big things." Steven says, "Appreciated, big homie; this is like the first time in my life that everything is coming together for me at once." "That's GOD, bro; he has a plan for all of us; what he is doing with you right now, he's showing you off. One of the main things I learned in life is that in order for us to have blessings in life, we have to learn from our lessons. For example, with me, I didn't get any of my blessings until I learned from my mistakes. If I never learned from my mistakes in life, I wouldn't have the family I have. Wouldn't have the job I have and many more stuff. The main thing is that learning from our mistakes helps make us better people, but also it helps benefit the people around us." "Agreed; GOD has given me many blessings, bro; some of the stuff I envisioned for myself while I was in jail is actually happening for me. Most kids that have been through what I have been through don't make it out or become something, but I am going to be one of the ones that make it out." "You will, bro; when you get that mil, you better break me off with a piece." Steven starts laughing. "I got you, big homie."

After getting off work, Steven calls Jose to see if he has the shirts ready for tomorrow's event at the poetry club. Steven says, "Jose, I'm trying to see if we have enough shirts to sell for tomorrow's event at the poetry club." Jose says, "I got you, boss. I already got the shirts ready for the event tomorrow; all we need you to do is show out on the stage." "I am most definitely going to show out, and we are going to make some dough." "Yes, indeed, brother; see you tomorrow at school."

After talking to Jose, Steven calls Lily. Steven says, "Beautiful, how are you doing?" Lily says, "I'm doing great now that I'm hearing your voice." "I was wondering if you could help promote the poetry event tomorrow." "I already posted about it on my social media accounts; I got you, babe. I got a question for you: what are you going to talk about at the main event? You are the main headliner, so I know you are going to put on a show."

Steven says, "I'm going to talk about something that I feel will inspire and uplift the room. You know better than anybody that I'm great at uplifting and making people feel good." Lily says, "I most definitely do; in my opinion, that is one of your best talents and one of the reasons why I am in love with you." "Well, I hope I make your eyes sparkle like I did the first time I spoke at the poetry club." "I'm going to hold you to that. I have some special guests coming, too." "That sounds good to me; bring them along so they can enjoy the show." "Sounds great. I can't wait to see you do your thing tomorrow." "I'm going to shine like the star I am. I love you, babe; I will see you tomorrow." "Love you too; you are going to do great."

The next day, Steven returns to class and talks to Mr. Marcus before class starts. Mr. Marcus says, "Young scholar, so glad to see you; let's talk. So again, congrats on being nominated for the Rising Star award; I'm going to announce to the class about your big accomplishment today, but what I wanted to talk to you about was the GED test. I know you done failed the science and math two times. If you fail both again, you will have to wait two months before you will be able to take the test." Steven puts his hand over his head. "I'm doing my best. I thought it was going to be a piece of cake, but I'm going to pass it." "You are one of the hardest working students I have ever had. Not only that, I love the way you are helping the other students. You have made a great impact on them. I feel the best thing to do is just give it a couple of weeks before you go back and take the test. Plus, I heard you are making boss moves out here, having your own clothing line with Jose and Lenny. And having your own motivational website, I must say I love the daily quotes on the website."

Steven smiles. "You been following my social media accounts." "I keep my ears to the streets; I'm proud of you, Steven. You are doing big things." "I appreciate; that means a lot coming from you. Just know I'm just getting started."

After their conversation, all of the GED students walk into the room, and Mr. Marcus announces to the class that Steven is being nominated for the Rising Star Award. Mr. Marcus says, "Class, I have a very special announcement: Our very own Steven Anderson has been nominated for the Rising Star award; he will be representing us next Friday at Spellman College. The whole class gives Steven a round of applause. Mr. Marcus says, "Again, Steven, congratulations, let's do some math problems. Steven, can you come up here and work out some math problems for the class?" "Yes, sir, I sure can."

After class ends, Steven gets approached by Will. Will says, "Little homie, I been following the steps you been doing for the math problems; that stuff been helping me out, bro." Steven says. "I'm glad I'm able to help you out; it's all about looking at the problem and knowing how to break it down." "You smart as hell, bro; you don't meet too many young brothers from the hood like you. I know I won't be in Atlanta for your event, but represent your hood and your people. Show them what a boy from the dirt can do and be about. I'm about to go stay pushing forward, little homie."

After talking to Will, Steven talks to Jose and Lenny about the poetry event that is happening later on in the evening. Steven says, "Whatsup guys, are we straight for tonight's event?" Lenny says, "Me and Jose got everything covered. We got the shirts at his house and your business card with your motivation website." Jose says, "This is going to be a great day for the gang. Though the part I'm wondering about is what are you going to talk about." Steven says, "You just got to watch and see all I got to say; it's going to be an inspirational piece that's going to make a great impact on people." "I can't wait. I will see you guys later tonight."

After Jose leaves, Steven and Lenny talk to one another. Lenny reflects on how far he and Steven have come. Lenny says, "It's funny. I was just thinking: me and you was just on a block a couple of months ago selling drugs. Now we selling clothes; we are on a different path." Steven says, "That's one of the beautiful things about life: we write our own story, and it's up to us how we want the story to be. I'm proud of you, bro. I see the way you moving out here. Your hard work is going to pay off; just do what you do and stay envisioning yourself being where you want to be in life. Because sooner or later, if we envision that and work hard on that, eventually, we will be living in the vision or dream we see for ourselves. That's why I'm not giving up on my GED. Granted, I might fail, but I shall not give up." "I'm not going to lie; I'm scared to take it; I'm scared to fail if I'm being honest." "It's going to be obstacles in our way on our path to greatness. We might get knocked down, but we have to stay getting back up." "I needed that, big homie; you really are like a big brother to me; thank you for everything." "You do not got to thank me for nothing, bro. Like I said before, you remind me of myself. I want to see all my brothers win. I'm going to do my best to help us all win. We are going to make it to the top together. I'm going to head out; see you tonight, bro."

Steven goes home and writes the poems for the poetry event. After writing, Steven gets dressed and heads straight to Lily's apartment. Lily looks at Steven in awe as he is wearing a red suit and tie. Lily says, "You look amazing as always, bae." Steven says, "Thank you, baby; you look amazing also." "Tonight is going to be a great night for us. So, you have everything setup for me at the Poetry Club for the event tonight?" "I do; everything is setup perfectly for you. I also invited some friends to the event. I hope you don't mind." "I don't mind; any friend of yours is a friend of mine. I can't wait to move the crowd with all of my poems, especially my last piece." "What's the name of it?" "On My Way to the Top," that's the name of the poem. The poem is all about the journey to the top." "Well, I am glad to accompany you on your journey to the top." "We going to rise high; we going to show out on these people. It's almost that time; let's go ahead and head to the club."

Steven and Lily leave to go to the poetry club. When Steven and Lily arrive at the poetry club, it is a packed house. The room is filled with many people who are already buying the shirts Steven helped create. Steven sees Lenny and Jose selling shirts. Steven says, "I see you guys are handling business." Lenny says, "When you're a hustler, you always got to make a profit." Jose says, "We holding it down for you, bro. Do your thing on the stage."

While passing through the crowd, Steven sees an unexpected guest. Steven yells out, "Hector!" Hector says, "My boy, what's going on." Steven and Hector hug one another. Steven asks, "How did you find out about the event?" "Your girl told me; she said I would not want to miss you speak true greatness. I remember when we were behind them walls, you used to do poetry; it was amazing and beautiful. I can't wait to see these people's faces be amazed by your words like me and the other homies were amazed by you in jail." Officer Brown also is there to support Steven. Officer Brown says, "Yes, indeed, hello Steven." Steven says, "Mr. Brown, oh my god, I'm so happy to see you here." "Hector told me about the event, so I told myself I'm not going to miss Mr. Steven speak poetry. Can't wait to see what you do." "It's going to be wonderful, but you guys know how I get down with my spoken word."

Steven and Mr. Tom have a one-on-one conversation before he goes on stage. Mr. Tom says, "Steven, I'm so happy to see you. Can I talk to you really quickly?" Steven says, "Sure, guys, thank you for coming out. I will talk to you after the show." "So, we have everything set up for you. I'm going to have you go in the back, and you will wait your turn. Again, thank you for doing this for me. I can't wait to see you blow the crowd away."

Steven goes backstage and patiently waits his turn. Steven is not nervous about being on stage; he's showing full confidence while preparing for his set. After waiting for his turn for an hour and a half, Steven finally hears his name called. Mr. Tom says, "This young brother who's coming up next is a very special talent. He's going to wow you guys with his Beautiful Poetry. He and his friends are also selling some shirts right in the front, so if you want some merch, definitely check them out. I'm not going to hold you guys any longer; give a warm welcome to the intelligent, sophisticated Steven Anderson."

Steven walks on the stage and is greeted with a standing ovation. Steven, with a smile on his face, says, "Thank you guys for having me here and showing up. I hope the poetry that I will be speaking upon you uplifts somebody's soul tonight."

Steven wows the crowd with his first four poems. The last poem he's performing is the most personal one for him. "The poem's name is "On My Way To the Top". Just another young brother trying to make it in this world, I see the vision of sunshine, but darkness is trying to take me away from the great light. I have to remind myself I'm a great knight; I have to use all of my might to make it past the obstacles that are coming in my pathway. In a hard place right now in my life, but I'm not going to stay in it forever. I might fall, but at the end of the journey, I will stand tall. Before I can become the man GOD wants me to be, he had to do a makeover in order for me to be one of the ones to take over. I'm just a rising king that is floating like a butterfly and stinging like a bumble bee. I might stumble, but forever going to stay humble. The obstacles are getting harder, but they don't know the hard times is making the brain smarter; young brother is growing wiser each and every day. He's going harder because he is closer to the great vision in his mind. This little light of mine, I shall make it shine. Told his momma 'you know your son is going to shine. Momma, just stay looking up because your son is on his way to the top.'"

Steven finishes his poem and gets a standing ovation. The crowd is amazed by Steven's poem. Mr. Tom comes on the stage and says, "I told your this was one deep brother. Your give it up for Mr. Steven Anderson."

As Steven walks off the stage, he is greeted with a hug from Lily. Lily says, "You were amazing, baby; I'm so proud of you." Steven is greeted by more people at the club who loved his poem.

After talking to some of the people in the crowd, he goes to the back to talk to Mr. Tom. Steven says, "Mr. Tom, thank you for this opportunity; I can tell the crowd loved my poem." Mr. Tom says, "I loved it myself. You were phenomenal; you are a talented kid; always remember that. Here's your payment tonight. Thank you for your services." Steven is surprised at how much money he just received. "This is a whole band; I thought it was going to be $500." "For your performance, you deserved way more than $500. Enjoy that, man; just know you are welcome here anytime. I will talk to you later."

After talking to Mr. Tom, Steven talks to Hector and Officer Brown. Hector says, "Dude, you were amazing; your words touched a lot of people today." Officer Brown says, "It sure was something special; I'm glad the people got to hear you speak. I recorded this for the inmates in the jail. Do you mind if I let them listen to this?" Steven says, "I don't mind. I would definitely love them to hear this." Officer Brown says, "Great. Also, if you not doing anything on Sunday, I want you to come to the Sunday Service at the jail and be a guest speaker." Hector says, "The guys will be happy to see you." Steven says, "Say less, I will definitely be there; can't wait to see the homies, but I will talk to you guys later."

After talking to Hector and Officer Brown, Steven talks to Jose and Lenny. Lenny says, "Big homie you did your thing up there." Jose says, "You made us proud, and while you were on that stage, we were making that paper." Lenny says, "We met our goal, made $500 off the merchandise, and lot of people got your card for your website." Steven says, "I'm proud of us; we are doing big things and just getting started." Jose says, "I think this calls for a group hug." Steven, Jose, and Lenny hug one another. Steven says, "Well, guys, I will talk to you later; I got to find my lady." Jose says, "We will talk to you later, but Steven, you better wife her, bro. If it wasn't for her, this event might have never would have happened." Steven responds as he looks at Lily, "Hopefully, one day I will."

As Steven approaches Lily, he sees a man and a woman right next to her smiling and laughing. Steven says, "Hey babe, who are these fine people you are talking to," Lily says, "Steven, these are my parents." Steven gets nervous when Lily announces that the two people she is standing next to are her parents. "It's so nice to meet you guys; Lily always talks about you guys all the time. It's so great to meet you." Lily's Mom hugs Steven and says, "It's so great to meet you; we have been wanting to meet the guy that has made my daughter's life joyful." Lily's Dad gives Steven a stern handshake and says, "Yes, indeed, I must say we definitely enjoyed your poem; you seem like a very intelligent young man. I do want to talk to you just to get to know you. We are having Sunday dinner at 3:00 on Sunday; would love for you to join us." "I would be delighted to join you guys for Sunday dinner; I can't wait. I will talk to you guys later; love you, babe." "I love you too; drive home safe."

Before going home, Steven drives to the Riverwalk in Augusta and walks around, reminiscing about tonight's event. Steven says, "GOD, you are amazing; thank you for guiding me in the right direction. Those people loved me there. I never experienced anything like that before in my life. It's crazy that for almost my whole life, I felt villainized by people judging me for where I am from and for my past street life. This is like the first time in my life I've felt a lot of love from people. I got this beautiful lady who loves me for me. It's like everything is coming together. GOD, we are just beginning; people are not ready for what we got in store. I'm just like a lion in a jungle that is making his presence known."

The next day, after getting off work, Steven heads to Danny's football game. As Steven gets to the game, he is welcomed by his Mom, Darius's Mom, Destiny, the mother of Darius's baby, and Darius's Son DJ. Steven says, "What's going on, family?" Steven's Mom says, "Well, hello, son." Darius's Mom says, "That's my boy; how you doing, baby?" "I'm doing good. I can't wait to see our boy Danny do his thing. Destiny, how are you doing? You looking great; how's my nephew doing?" "I'm doing great. It's great seeing you; say hello to your uncle D.J." "What's going on, youngin? I got something for you." Steven pulls out a toy he bought for D.J. Destiny says, "Steven, you didn't have to do this; thank you." Destiny hugs Steven. "We are family; I been told you I got you. I'm going to talk to Danny before the game starts."

Steven walks onto the field to talk to Danny. Danny yells, "Steve, you came!" Danny goes running toward Steven and hugs him. Steven says, "I told you I wasn't going to miss it. So, are you going to show off today or what?" "I got to put on for the city and the family; I'm going to make your proud." "Show these people who you are." Steven goes back to the stand with his family to watch the game.

As halftime ends, Danny's team is down 3 to 17 in the football game. Danny has only thrown 69 yards and two interceptions. People are yelling out that the team and Danny suck. Steven sees Danny walking back to the bench, crying. Darius's and Danny's Moms are upset. "My baby is crying; I got to go talk to him." Steven says, "Let me go talk to him."

Steven goes down to the lowest bleach in the stands to talk to Danny. Steven yells, "Danny!" Danny walks over to Steven with the tears in his eyes. Danny says, "I suck, bro. I'm letting my team down. Man, if we lose this game, we miss the playoffs." "Get that out of your head; don't ever say if when it comes to accomplishing your goals. In your head right now, I don't want you to think about the possibility of you losing this game. Believe in your mind and heart that you will win this game and make the playoffs. Tom Brady and the Patriots were down 3 to 28 in the Super Bowl and came back to beat the Falcons. Everybody counted them out, but one thing about Tom Brady and his team was that they never gave up on themselves, stayed believing in themselves, and got a Super Bowl Ring because of it. Danny, you are great at what you do, so don't let the mistakes you made impact how you see yourself. You are a powerful and impactful person for your team. Deep down inside, you know you are that person, too. Don't let what anybody says get you down; instead of worrying about the negativity, stay focused on the positive." Steven's words motivate Danny to believe in his abilities. Danny's Coach yells for him to get back in the game. Steven says, "You got this; remember who you are. We from the Harmony Projects, we soldiers, we don't fold!"

Steven goes back up in the stands and watches the game with his family. On Danny's first play back in the game, he throws an 85-yard touchdown. On his next drive, the other team turns over the ball. Danny throws another touchdown. Danny throws three more touchdowns to win the game for his team. Everybody in the crowd starts cheering for Danny and his team. Darius's Mom says, "Yes, that's my baby!" Steven's Mom looks at Steven and says, "Son, I don't know what you said to Danny, but it definitely motivated him." Steven smiles as he looks at Danny. "It wasn't really nothing I said; it was all about Danny just believing in himself, and that's what he did." As Danny celebrates with his team, he smiles at Steven and whispers thank you to him.

It's Saturday Morning; Steven, Lenny, and Jose arrive at the Golfing event that the Mayor invited Steven to. The guys are amazed by the Golf Course. Jose says, "This is one big Golf Course." Lenny says, "This is like something you see in the movies." Steven says, "Today is a beautiful day; we are going to have a fun time and make some connections today, fellas."

As Steven and the guys walk on the course, they are greeted by Garrett. Garrett yells, "Steven!" Lenny says, "Who's the White boy yelling out your name?" Steven says, "That's Garrett; if it wasn't for him, we probably wouldn't be at this event. My boy Garrett, it's good to see you, bro." "It's good to see you too, bro; I see you brought some friends with you." "Yes, these are my homeboys, but also my business partners. This is Jose and Lenny; guys, this is Garrett." Garrett says, "It's great meeting you guys;

your boy Steve helped me out with an essay I was working on for class. If it wasn't for him, I probably would be failing my English class right now. This dude is one of the most intelligent people I have ever met." "Thank you, bro; it was my honor to help you out. So, is this your first time at this event?" "This is my second straight year being at this event; it's a great way to connect with fellow young people like ourselves who are trying to be powerful figures in the world." Jose says, "I'm not going to lie; I was thinking some of these people were going to be acting preppy, but I'm glad you're not one of those people." Garrett laughs, "Appreciated, but hold your horses; we got a cocky person coming our way right now."

The cocky person that Garrett is talking about is Dennis. Dennis is Lily's ex-boyfriend. Steven shakes his head and turns away as he sees Dennis. Steven says, "Not this dude." Lenny asks, "You know bro?" "Yeah, that's Dennis. Him and Lily used to date; dude is arrogant as hell." Dennis starts talking to the guys. "Garrett, my guy, it is so great to see you. Well, well, well, look who it is, Mr. Boyz n da hood. I'm surprised to see you here." Steven says, "My guys and I are here just like everybody else; we are just trying to have a good time." Dennis says, "Well, around here, gang on this course, we hit on the green; we don't smoke it. Just in case you guys might have got confused when you got the invite." Lenny says, "I don't know you, homie, but you're out of pocket." Jose says, "Facts, we don't even know you, and you are trying to look down at us." Dennis says, "What is there to look down on? Also, I see is nobodies." Garrett says, "Dennis, you're tripping." Dennis says, "I'm not tripping; thugs like these people shouldn't be on this course or at an event like this. I don't know what Lily sees in you." Steven smiles, "Well, that has to make you feel a way because me, the thug, is cherishing your ex every chance I get. And you, on the outside looking in, it's sad to live a life as a hater; remember that."

After that, Steven walks away from Dennis. Jose says, "That was badass, bro." Garrett says, "It sure was a lot of people would have punched him in the face." Steven says, "You can't let no negativity and hating energy affect your spirit. You got to stay keeping it pushing." Lenny says, "On everything, fam." Garrett says, "I got to talk to some people; I will catch up with you guys later."

After Garrett leaves, the guys run into Kurt, Rich's friend. Kurt says, "Steve, what's going on, bro?" Steven says, "I'm doing good, bro; Rich told me you would be here."  "I wasn't going to miss this. Something I learned from my father is that you got to stay networking. I didn't introduce myself to you guys. I'm Kurt." Jose says, "What's going on, bro? I'm Jose, and this is Lenny. Take one of our shirts. We have our own clothing brand. With our clothing brand, we are just trying to inspire people with it." Kurt says, "The Boy That Comes From Nothing: I love the motivational quote on the back of the shirt." Lenny says, "That's how we roll; it's all about uplifting one another." Steven says, "Yes, indeed, our mindset with our clothing brand is having our customers look fresh and inspired at the same time." Kurt says, "Man, you're doing your thing out here. I'm proud of you, Steve. I'm going to tell my Dad you are here so you can speak to him."

After talking to Kurt, Steven and the guys walk to the stand to get something to drink. While getting something to drink, Steven sees a surprised guest. Steven asks, "Hey, could I have the Body Armor Strawberry Banana?" As the person gives him a drink, he notices who the person is. Steven says, "Dani!" Dani is shocked to see Steven. Dani says, "Steven, what are you doing here?" "I was invited here. What are you doing here?" "I'm working at the concessions stands; my Mom hooked me up with this job. I'm totally surprised to see you here." "Well, when you're a business man, you got to promote your brand. Plus, it's a golfing event, so I got to show these people how good my game is. You know how great my strokes are." "What business do you have?" "I have my own clothing brand with my homies; we up and coming, but sooner or later, we going to take over. And thanks to my loving girlfriend, I have my own motivational website that helps inspire people around the globe." Dani looks stunned as Steven tells her all about the good news that is happening in his life.

Before Dani could respond to Steven, her Mom approaches them. Dani's Mom asks, "Dani, do you need anything dear?" Dani says, "No, I'm good, mom." Dani's Mom asks, "Who is this handsome gentlemen you are talking to?" Steven turns around with a smile on his face. Steven says, "Hello, Ms. Martinez, it's great seeing you again." Ms. Martinez says in a stern voice. "Dani, what did I tell you about talking to this hoodlum? Forget him. I see the Mayor. Mr. Mayor! Mr. Mayor!"

The Mayor walks over to where Steven, Dani, and her mother are. Mayor Scofield says, "Hey, ma'am, how are you doing?" Dani's Mom says, "I'm doing great. I don't know if you remember me, but we met a couple of weeks ago at a town hall meeting. I wanted to introduce you to my daughter Dani. She has actually applied for an internship with you guys." "I'm not going to lie; I meet a lot of people every day. I don't recall meeting you, but I do wish the best for you and your daughter. Mr. Steven Anderson, it's so great to see you. I have been waiting to see you here." Dani and her Mom are surprised that the Mayor knows Steven. Dani's Mom asks, "You know him?" Mayor Scofield brags about Steven. "Absolutely, this young, intelligent man is gifted and is going to be a powerful figure in this world. Don't forget the name Steven Anderson. Steven, come with me. I want to introduce you to some people." Steven smiles and says, "Sure, you ladies have a nice day." Dani and her mother's faces are left stunned when Steven and the Mayor walk away together.

Steven introduces the Mayor to Jose and Lenny. "Mr. Scofield, I would like to introduce you to my business partners, Jose and Lenny. All of us are in GED class together." Mayor Scofield says, "It's so great meeting you guys; it's awesome to see young men do big things. Can I have one of those shirts you're holding, young man?" Jose says, "Sure, we hope you enjoy our product." Mayor Scofield says, "You guys come with me. I want to introduce you to some people."

The Mayor walks the guys to a tent. When the guys enter, they are around local entrepreneurs in the community. Some of those entrepreneurs include Kirk's Dad and Mr. Tom, the manager of the Poetry Club. Mayor Scofield says, "Gentlemen, I want to introduce you to these young men; this is Mr. Steven Anderson and his business partners Jose and Lenny." Kirk's Dad says, "Steve, it's so great to see you." Mr. Tom says, "The same here, guys; this is the kid I was telling you about who did the awesome poem at my club; this kid is phenomenal. I got to play you guys the video of him speaking. It's very inspirational."

Mr. Tom plays the video of Steven speaking his poem at the Poetry Club last Wednesday. After playing the video, everybody in the tent gives Steven a round of applause. Kirk's Dad says, "Powerful, this kid is a special talent." Mayor Scofield says, "You have a bright future, and you have the potential to be something special in this life. You all do. Love the poetry, but what is the business breakdown of you guy's clothing business?" Steven explains, "Well, we all work as a team. Jose designs the clothes; I create the slogans, and Lenny sets the prices for the clothes." Lenny says, "Our main aim with our clothing brand is to have our customers look fresh and be inspired at the same time." Jose says, "When people wear our clothes, we want them to feel confident and powerful." Steven says, "Exactly, just like the great Deion Sanders says: when you dress good, you play good. Basically, stating when you wear something fresh, it will make you feel empowered." Mayor Scofield says, "You guys are something else; you all are intelligent and have special gifts. Steven, let me talk to you privately really quickly."

Mayor Scofield and Steven walk away to talk to one another. Mayor Scofield says, "You know Steven, I did some research on you; I see that you were in jail a couple of months ago. I'm amazed how somebody at your age turned negativity into positivity. If you keep on going in the direction you are headed, you can inspire so many people. In life, it doesn't matter where you came from; what counts is where you are going. Let me ask you this: This is a business question. Why should people invest in somebody who used to be a drug dealer and is a high school dropout?"

Steven takes a step back and gives a great answer to the Mayor's question. "Well, first, that former drug dealer will have to re-invest in himself before somebody can invest in him. This means he has to believe and trust in his abilities before anybody else can. Then, eventually, somebody will come along and invest in his abilities as a person. It's just like that old saying that for somebody to love you, you must love yourself first. Granted, with me, it doesn't matter who's with me; as long as I believe in myself and Jesus Christ, I will be alright." Mayor Scofield starts smiling. "I was expecting a great response, but not one like that. The words you just spoke to me prove to me that you are not just a great leader, but you are a person somebody should definitely invest in. I'm glad you're here; now, let's go and play some golf."

Steven plays golf with the Mayor and other participants at the golf tournament. The winner of the tournament comes down between Steven and Dennis. Dennis says, "Well, homeboy, get ready to lose because I'm about to take this win." Steven says, "We shall see, shoot your shot." Dennis hits the ball and misses the hole by an inch. Dennis yells, "What!" The crowd starts cheering for Steven to hit the winning shot. Lenny says, "Knock it in, bro." Kurt's Dad says, "Do your thing, Steve." Steven slowly hits the ball, and the ball rolls slowly into the hole. The crowd goes crazy. Jose yells out, "That's my boy!" Kurt's Dad says, "Put some respect on Mr. Steven's name." Dennis accepts his defeat from Steven. "Well, I guess the better man won?" Steven responds, "I guess he did." Dennis and Steven shake hands and go their separate ways.

Kurt's Dad talks to Steven. "You were spectacular out there. I also loved getting to know your friends. I love the clothing business, and with what you are doing with your website, here's my business card. Get your business name's trademark, an LLC, and then call me. See you later, future entrepreneur." Mayor Scofield speaks to Steven, Jose, and Lenny. "Steven, Jose, and Lenny, thank you guys for coming out. Me and the other businessmen who were here today were deeply impressed by you guys. You guys have a great future and stay moving forward. I will stay in touch with you guys."

After the Mayor leaves, the guys talk about everything that transpired today. Steven says, "Guys, was today great or what?" Jose says, "It was excellent; the snow bunnies were all over your boy. And we made great connections out here." Lenny says, "I didn't know what to expect when I came here today, but I had a good time. Thanks for inviting us; you could have just come here by yourself and sold yourself as your own businessman, but instead, you brought us along to make connections; that's love." Steven says, "We are more than business partners; we are brothers, and I will always look out for my brothers. Together, we shall be successful."

As Steven is talking to the guys, Dani's Mother goes to talk to him. Dani's Mother asks, "Can I speak with you for a minute, Steven?" Steven says, "Sure, I will talk to you guys later. What can I help you with, Ms. Martinez?" Dani's Mother, with sincerity in her voice, says, "I wanted to apologize for calling you a hoodlum. I learned today that you are more than that." Steven understands why Dani's mother didn't want her with him and accepts her apology. "Ms. Martinez, I honestly don't blame you for calling me a hoodlum or for not wanting me to be around your daughter. At the time I was seeing your daughter, I was selling drugs, and I lied about being somebody I wasn't to you. While I was in jail, I decided to change my ways for the better. I accept myself for the man I used to be and the man I am today. I don't let other people's words validate me as a person. I do accept your apology, though." "I'm glad you accept my apologies; here's Dani now. I will leave you two to talk."

Steven and Dani have a one-on-one conversation. Dani says, "You looked great out there today, Steven. You still are great at your strokes." Steven and Dani start laughing. Steven says, "I appreciate it; I'm just good when it comes to performing under pressure." Dani says in a soft manner, "I apologize for not being there for you while you were in jail. You needed support during that time, and I left you stranded. When you got locked up, I thought you were going to be in jail for a good while. Then I thought when you got out, you were more than likely going back to the streets, but I was wrong." Steven looks into Dani's eyes and holds her hands. "You broke my heart when you dumped me while I was in jail. I was already down and out before, but you made it ten times worse. Though, just like a boxer in a ring, when I get knocked down, I shall get back up. You thought I would just be another nobody, but look at me now. If you had just believed in me, you would be my leading lady, but now you're on the outside looking in. I hope it was worth it; you have a nice day, Dani." Steven hugs and kisses Dani on the cheek and walks away. Dani's face is filled with regret as Steven leaves.

After leaving the golf tournament, Steven goes home and calls Lily. Lily says, "Hey babe, how was the event?" Steven says, "Baby, it was amazing; your man was doing his thing out there today. They know about Tiger Woods, but they found out who Mr. Tiger Hoods is today. Me and the guys made so many connections out there. Baby, we are about to be doing big things." "You're already doing big things, baby; you guys are already stars. Everybody just haven't seen you guys shine yet. I wish I didn't have to work today so I could have seen you work your magic today. Are you ready for dinner with my parents tomorrow?"

Steven is nervous about having dinner with Lily's parents. Steven says, "I'm not going to lie; I'm a bit nervous, especially with all the questions your parents are probably going to ask me." "Don't be nervous. I accept and love you for you; that's what truly counts. We're going to have an amazing time tomorrow. You get some rest; love you." "Love you too."

It's Sunday Morning, and Steven gets ready to go to Sunday Service at the county jail. This will be Steven's first time returning to the jail since being released. Steven arrives at the jail wearing a suit and tie and is greeted by Officer Brown. Officer Brown says, "Well, hello there, pastor." Steven starts laughing. "First off, thank you for doing this; most people who get out of jail want to just stay away from it completely, but I believe you preaching the word to the inmates today can help a lot of them out." Steven says, "Well, I guess it will be just like old times, except I'm a free man this time. Does anybody know I'm going to be here today?" "No, I wanted it to be a surprise; a lot of the guys are going to be happy to see you. Sunday service is about to get started, so come inside." Once was a broken man who was inside the jail; now is a reformed man trying to live his purpose. How will he be perceived by the inmates in the jail?

333

# Chapter 12: Living In My Truth

Steven walks into the county jail and starts reminiscing about his time in jail. As Steven walks by, some guards and inmates speak to him and shout out his name as if he were a wrestler. Finally, Officer Brown and Steven arrive at Sunday Service. Officer Brown says, "Steve, stand outside of the doorway. I'm about to introduce you."

Steven stands outside the doorway so none of the inmates in Sunday Service is unable to see him. Officer Brown stands in front of the inmates and introduces Steven to the inmates. "Gentlemen, I have a special speaker for you guys today. This young brother also used to be an inmate just like you; his time in here made him a better man, and he is now living in a positive direction in his life. Some of you already know who he is, but for those of you who don't, let me introduce you to the one and only Steven Anderson."

As Steven walks toward the podium, the inmates start cheering his name. This also brings a smile to Michael and Robert's faces. Steven says, "I thought I would never say this, but it is good to be back in jail." All the inmates start laughing.

Steven says, "The reason why I came back was to speak inspiration to you guys like I did when I was doing the poetry club. As all of you know, I was once an inmate. Just a couple of months ago, I was out here on these blocks selling all types of drugs without taking time to think about my future. I was making bands out here, but one day, I realized that the street life wasn't for me. So, I decided to quit the game, but the same day I planned on quitting was the same day I got arrested. It was two things that made me want to change my life while I was in jail. One was looking at my Momma's face when she saw me behind these walls. My Mom looked so disappointed in me, but in my mind, I felt like she thought she had failed as a mother. My Mom didn't fail as a Mom; I let her down by going against the principles and guidance she gave me in life. I told myself that when I get out of jail, I'm going to make my Momma proud and turn the tears of sorrow in her eyes into tears of joy. I'm grateful that I am doing that for my Momma now. The second and main reason why I decided to change my life was thinking about my future. Being in the streets, I was wasting my true potential and the plans GOD had planned for me in my life. Granted, I was in the streets for survival, but I was wasting my GOD-given abilities being out there. So, when I was here, I envisioned a better life for myself. I have accomplished some of the goals I envisioned for myself, some of which I am close to accomplishing. All I'm saying is this: during your time in here, think about your life and ask yourself who you want to be and what you want your life to be, and do everything in your power to be the person you want to be and achieve your goals and dreams. That's all I got to say you guys; be blessed."

After Steven is done speaking, the inmates give him a round of applause, with Robert whispering My boy. Steven stays to listen to Officer Brown preach Sunday Service. After the Sunday Service,

Steven is greeted by the inmates, including Robert and Michael. Robert says, "How are you living, youngin?" Steven responds, "What's going on, bro?" Robert and Steven hug one another. Robert says, "Been praying for you, little homie; how's life going?" "Life has been going great for me since I got out. I'm close to getting my GED. I got two more tests to pass, then I will be done." "You going to pass it, bro; you're smart as hell, bro; just study hard and believe in your abilities and skills." "Best Believe, I also got nominated for the Rising Star award, an award for GED students striving for greatness. I'm facing 4 more people for the award; whoever gives the best speech at Spellman College wins. I also started my own clothing company with a couple of homies of mine and a motivational website. And I went golfing with the mayor of Augusta yesterday." Robert smiles as he hears the great things Steven has been doing. "Man, hearing you speak about all that is going on in your life is uplifting your brother. Bro, playing golf with the mayor and shit. You out here balling like you in the NBA. What about the love life? How's that going?"

"Well, the girl I went out on a date with that I was telling you about; I'm dating her. She is one of a kind. Bro, I had tried to hide from her that I used to be a drug dealer, but the truth came out." "How did she take the news?" "She was mad that I lied to her, but she accepted me for the man I was and the man I am today. I'm actually going to go to Sunday dinner at her parents' house after I leave here." "Bro, I know you're eighteen and all, but you need to wife her; she's a keeper. You have a woman that rides for you and accepts you for your past, supports you in the present, and believes in your dreams for your future; that woman needs to be your wife." "I'm going to make that happen one day, best believe.

Enough about me, how about you? How's the poetry class going?" "I'm not going to lie; when you left, I got scared. I thought the guys wouldn't accept me like they did with you, but they did. It's been great. I believe a lot of people's lives have been changed because of the poetry class. And that's all thanks to you. Michael teaches the class alongside me. I know I can't wait to get out of here. I got four months left, and like you, I will go for my dreams and goals in life and be reunited with my son. Speaking of which, let me ask you this: have you talked to your father since you got out?" "Just once; I actually got plan on seeing him. It's time to speak my peace and release all of the anger I got against him." "You need to, bro, not for him, but for you. In order for us to find peace in life, we have to release any anger or hatred in our hearts. Because if you keep holding it in, it will hold you back. Not only that, with you being in jail yourself, I believe you understand your father's perspective on why he did what he did. The Bible in Mark 11:25 says, And when you stand praying, if you hold anything against anyone, forgive them, so that your Father in heaven may forgive you for your sins. Remember that verse, bro. There goes that boy, Michael."

Michael says, "You know I was going to speak to the chess king. Michael and Steven hug one another. Steven says, "Man, you're looking great. I can tell you been working out." "Yes, indeed, I have, but mainly focus on positivity. Just know all of us in here love you, bro; you impacted a lot of lives in here, including mine. I'm more socially active in here, thanks to you. I've even been inspired to get back my medical license when I get out of here." "For real." "Yes, I'm going do it; ever since a kid, all I wanted was to be a doctor. Granted, even though I made some costly mistakes, I want to go back to that. I can go helping and assisting people with the right mindset this time. I got a few more months left in this place; I'm using my time wisely in here so it can help me become the successful man I dream of being." "I'm happy for you, Mike. I know my girlfriend; she got plan on being a nurse. Her Dad is also a doctor; I might put in a good word to help you out." "I would greatly appreciate that; there might be something I can do to help your girlfriend out. I have a good friend named Michelle. She's a head doctor at the Main Hospital in Augusta. She does internships and has young nurses work alongside her to teach them the ropes of the medical field. I could put in a good word for your lady."

Robert says, "Michael also got a crush on Michelle; they got chemistry, though you should see how they talk when she visits him here." Steven says, "Look at you, Michael, macking in jail." The guys start laughing. Michael smiles. "Me and her actually got our medical licenses at the same time; she's a good person. To be real with you, I don't think I'm good enough for her. Look at me; I'm in jail; she is an educated, beautiful lady. She can do way better than me." Steven says, "Don't you dare down yourself like that; I was the same way when I got with my girl, but you know something, she accepted me for me. That's what truly counts. Mike, you are an intelligent guy, and she recognizes that; if she didn't, she wouldn't be visiting you. For me, what I learned is that you have to love yourself first and accept yourself before anybody else will." Michael responds, "You know something, Steve; you should be a pastor someday." The guys start laughing. "Although on the real, I needed that. You are wise beyond your years, and you stay on the positive road. I love you, and I'm proud of you. You're really like a little brother; I got somebody waiting for me in the visiting room. When you get your GED, send me some pictures in the mail." "Will do, brother."

Robert says, "I'm about to go myself. My son is actually visiting me today. I want you to remember something, Steve. You inspire all of us in here; we're proud of you. Always hustle hard for yourself, but also do it for us behind these walls."  Steven says, "Best believe, I will, big homie. I owe you; you inspired me to become the man that I am today. Just now, I'm forever grateful for that." "GOD put us together for a reason; being around you made me gain more knowledge and more belief in myself." Robert hugs Steven, "Got nothing but love for you, young nigga; stay popping out here, and don't let nothing stop you."

As Steven gets ready to leave, he is stopped by Officer Brown and a fellow inmate. Officer Brown says, "Steven, I want to introduce you to Antwan; he was the one that sent you that letter that said you inspired him." Antwan says, "You inspired me in so many ways, bro. I thank you for the poems you created in here and the poetry club you created. It changed my life, and I got a new vision about life now; I'm trying to do the same thing as you get my GED, just like you. What I wanted to ask you is what I need to do to be successful once I get out of here?" Steven says, "First off, I appreciate the love, fam; secondly, the main thing you need to do is believe in yourself and believe in GOD. Believe in the vision you see for yourself. Even when obstacles come in your path, stay pushing. Then, eventually, you will be living in the vision you set for yourself. Take my word for it; I'm living proof." "Appreciate you, big homie." Antwan and Steven dap up one another. "You're an inspiration, big homie; you stay pushing forward also."

After Antwan walks away, Officer Brown says, "That kid wanted to meet you, so I told myself I had to make that happen. You're making everybody here proud of you, and you are inspiring everybody. Keep going hard; you are living proof that it doesn't matter what circumstances or hard times happen in a person's life. You can still be successful. I'm proud of you, young brother." "Thank you; that means a lot coming from you. One thing about me is that I'm going to stay going hard; I'm never going to stop. I need your advice on something. I'm about to meet my girl's parents for Sunday dinner."

"And let me guess, you scared of how they might perceive you, correct?" Steven responds, "In a way, I am." "Just be you and be honest; your lady already accepts you for who you are; that's what truly counts. If they accept you, they accept you; if they don't accept you, it is what it is. As long as you accept yourself for who you are, and your girl accepts you for who you are, forget what anybody else got to say." "You are one hundred percent right. I appreciate you, Officer Brown; thank you for everything. If you ever need anything from me, just hit me up." "Same thing with me, too; you have a great day and a great dinner with your girlfriend's family."

After leaving the jail, Steven heads straight to Lily's apartment to pick her up and go to her parents' house. On the way there, Steven talks to Lily about her parents. "So, how do you think this dinner is going to go?" "My parents are good people. If I accept you for you, they will accept you also. Either way, just know I'm not going nowhere." Steven and Lily arrive at Lily's parents' house. As Steven knocks on the door, he wonders if Lily's parents will accept him. Will they judge him for his past mistakes? What shall happen?

As Steven waits patiently for Lily's parents to open the door, Steven becomes nervous. Steven starts thinking about whether Lily's parents find him good enough to date their daughter. Finally, Lily's parents open the door. Lily's Mom says, "My sweet baby, I'm glad to see you here. Steven, I'm glad that you're here; we are grateful to have you as a guest." Lily's Mom gives Steven and Lily a hug. Steven says, "I'm grateful to be here in your home." Lily's Dad gives Lily a hug, shakes Steven's hand, and says, "Baby girl, glad you came. I see you brought the leading man of your life. Steven, it's great to have you here. I can't wait to get to know you. Please come inside and enjoy this lovely food we cooked for you guys today." Lily's Mom sarcastically says, "You mean me because you know dang well you don't cook." Everybody starts laughing.

Steven walks inside the house and is introduced to Lily's brother. Lily says, "Steven, this is my obnoxious brother Braxton; Braxton, this is Steven." Braxton says, "Glad to meet the dude that be kissing my sister on Snapchat." Steven starts laughing. Braxton says, "On the real, bro; I been checking out your content on your website. You be speaking on real stuff; it's very uplifting." Lily's Mom says, "Yes, we loved your spoken word and the motivational words you put on your website. I think it shows what type of person you are."

As Lily's Mom and brother speak, praising Steven for the motivation he gives to others, Lily's Dad doesn't say anything. Lily's Dad says, "Well, the food is getting cold; let's sit down and eat." Everybody sits at the table and starts eating.

While eating, Lily's family gets to know more about Steven. Lily's Mom asks, "So, Steven tells us about your life. Where are you from?" Steven says, "I'm from Thomson, Georgia; I was raised by my mother and had a tough childhood. We went through a lot of stuff, but me and my Mom always found a way to overcome it. I was an A honor roll student all my years during school, and I was even captain of my high school debate team." Lily's Mom says, "Got us a scholar in the building." Lily says, "Yes, Steven is very intelligent and a unique individual." Lily's Father says very sternly, "That all sounds wonderful, but why did you drop out of school, Steven?"

Everybody looks at Steven for an answer. Steven doesn't hesitate to answer. "My Mom got diagnosed with breast cancer when I was 15. She ended up losing her job, and bills had to be paid, so I dropped out to help her out. Granted, the way I was getting money was illegal, but I have paid my debts to society for my past life." Lily's Brother says, "So basically, you were like Franklin Saint out here in these streets?" Steven smiles, "I wasn't that big of a drug dealer, but I was making money though."

Lily's Dad says, "You have been through a lot for a person your age; with all this going on in your life, where was your father, if you don't mind me asking?" Steven says, "My father has been in prison since I was two years old. Other than letters and phone calls, he hasn't been involved in my life." Lily's Mom asks. "What did your father do to get locked up?" "He and a friend of his killed somebody they were trying to rob." Lily's Brother says, "Dang bro, you done had a tough life; it's like something out of a movie." Lily yells, "Braxton!" Lily's Brother says, "I'm just speaking facts." Steven starts laughing. "It's cool. My life is like a movie, and God's my director. And I'm the co-director and the actor in it." Lily's Dad is astounded by Steven's life story and says, "Amen, Steven, I like that response." This puts a smile on Steven's face. Lily's Dad says, "The main thing about hard times in life is you never let it keep you down; you let it humble you into being a better person. Learn from your mistakes in life, so you learn from your lessons, and in return, you will live in your blessings. Remember that Steven and you will go far in life."

After eating dinner, Lily's Father invites Steven to his man cave to talk one-on-one. Lily's Father asks, "Steven, do you mind joining me for a drink in my man cave?" Steven asks, "Is it safe to go in there?" Everybody starts laughing. Lily's Dad moves his hand toward the door and says, "There's only one way to find out."

Steven steps into the man cave to talk to Lily's father. Lily's Dad says, "You know when Lily told me she was dating you, I did a background check on you. I found out a lot of stuff about you, including you being locked up in jail for selling drugs. I'm not going to lie; you aren't the type of person I envisioned my daughter being with. Though, I believe you are the one for her. Lily's ex-boyfriend was a jerk to her and treated her like a dog, in my opinion. I've never seen her be joyful and happy as she is with you. In your mind, you might think she only uplifted you into being a better person, but you have given my daughter joy and happiness and help uplifted her into a better person. And for that, I'm forever grateful. Here's my question for you, Steven: what is your true intention with my daughter?"

When Lily's Dad asks Steven that question, Steven doesn't hesitate to answer the question. "My true intention is for her to be my lifetime partner. I know that's crazy for an 18-year-old to say that. Lily has shown me the true definition of love. The first time I saw your daughter; in my mind, I was like, I got to know this beautiful lady. Looking at her was like looking at a butterfly in springtime. I hid my past lifestyle away from her because I thought she would leave me, but when she found out about my past, she was mad that I lied to her, but she accepted me for the man I was and for the man I am now. I'm in love with your daughter, and when I'm with her, I know everything is going to be ok because I am around a true angel. I don't know how you view me, sir, but I'm a changed man. All I ask from you, sir, is don't judge me for my past; judge me for the man I am today." "Those were well-spoken words you spoke Steven. With that being said, I think you are the perfect person for my daughter. Just know that if you hurt her, it's me and you." "Understood, sir."

"I got one last question for you: Steven, are you a man of GOD? We all need to have GOD in our lives." "I most definitely am a man of GOD; if it wasn't for him, I wouldn't be where I am today in life. With GOD on our side, who could be against us." "I'm glad to hear that; we are having revival two Sundays from now at our church. I would love for you to join us and your mother." "I will be there; plus, it's been a long time since I been in God's house." "You have great potential, Steven, and I want to see you win not because you're dating my daughter, but because I can tell you have a great heart and are doing everything in your power to better your life. Do you mind if I say a prayer with you?" "I don't mind."

Lily's Father prays with Steven. "Dear Heavenly Father, please watch over this young man, give him wisdom, give him strength so he can become the man you designed him to be, bring positivity toward his way and drift away all negativity in his presence, stay pushing him forward and stay showing him great visions. I believe this young brother is going to be a powerful figure. In Jesus' name, we pray. Amen." Steven and Lily's Dad says, "Amen." "I honestly believe you are something special, not only from the way my daughter talks about you but also from meeting you. You are on the right track; don't let nothing stop you from your destiny." "I won't, sir. I'm forever going to believe in myself and GOD."

"My wife wanted to give you something, so let me invite her in. Lily's Mom walks into the room with a Jesus Christ necklace and a Bible. Lily's Mom says, "You have brought a great light to our daughter's life; every time me and her talk, she always talks about you. I was listening to your conversation with my husband. We believe you are the perfect guy for our daughter. And we want you to have this necklace." Lily's Dad says, "The Jesus Christ necklace symbolizes that Jesus Christ is with you everywhere you go." Steven is in awe of Lily's parents. "Y'all got me feeling like Kanye West up in here." Lily's parents start laughing. "I appreciate; it means a lot to me." Lily's Mom says, "We are here for you, Steven." Lily's Dad says, "Since you are dating our daughter, that makes us family." Steven hugs Lily's parents and her brother. "I promise you, Mr. and Mrs. Henderson, and you too, Braxton, I will keep our Lily safe." Lily's Mom says, "We have faith and believe that you will do that."

After leaving Lily's parents' house, Steven and Lily talk about her parents. Lily asks, "So, what do you think about dinner with my parents?" Steven says, "It wasn't what I expected. I thought your parents and brother were going to be judgmental, but they were loving and supportive. Just like their loving daughter." "Well, they see what I see: somebody that is really special." Steven and Lily hug one another.

Over the next week, Steven studies for his GED test and prepares for the speaking event he has at Spellman College on Friday.

It's Wednesday afternoon; as Steven leaves GED class, he gets a phone call from Mr. Dixson, Rich's father. Mr. Dixson says, "Steve, it's been a good while since we last talked. How you been doing?" Steven says, "I been doing good, mainly focusing on the positive and preparing for this event on Friday. I'm sure Rich told you about it." "Yes, he did. I'm proud of you; you are moving in the right direction. Listen, the debate team has an important match tomorrow, and I was wondering if you could speak to them and give them inspiration." "Most definitely, I will head to the school right now."

Steven heads to his old high school as he can't wait to give great advice to the debate team. As Steven walks through the halls of the school, he starts reminiscing about his time in High School. As Steven gets close to going to the auditorium where Mr. Dixon and the Debate team are, he notices the Debate team trophy he had won a couple of years back when he was the team captain. As Steven looks at the picture of him and his team winning the Debate

Team trophy, he starts smiling. Steven says to himself, you came a long way.

Steven walks into the auditorium, and Mr. Dixson introduces him to the debate team. Mr. Dixson says, "Steven, so glad to have you here. Ladies and gentlemen, I would love to introduce you to our former debate captain, who led this team to a championship a couple of years ago, the one and only Steven Anderson."

As Mr. Dixson introduces Steven to the Debate team, one of the team members recognizes him from his days of being in the streets. Jake, one of the members of the Debate Team, says, "Hold up, I know you; I do remember when you were captain of the team, but also, don't you sell drugs? I don't mean no offense; I'm not trying to learn how to sell dime bags. I'm trying to learn how to win the Championship." Steven is not offended by the comment; instead, he laughs about it. Steven says, "Well, you are about to learn that from the guy who brought this school a championship and who used to sell dime bags for a living. If you don't want to learn that from me, by all means, that's the door; you won't hurt my feelings." "My bad, big homie, that was wrong for me to say that to you." "It's cool; one lesson in life to learn is never to let somebody's judgment of you validate you. Now, let's get started. For my team and me, the way we won the championship was by always being prepared. You always have to stay prepared for any question that comes your way. For example, let's say you get asked if college helps make a person successful. How would you answer that question?" Jake says, "Well, I would say it does because, with that, a person with a degree or a certification can get the job they want in their desired field. And they would be recognized by jobs more due to having a college degree vs. somebody with just a High School Diploma." Steven responds, "That's a great answer, but I will have to disagree. In my opinion, a degree or a certificate doesn't define a person's full abilities. Not only that, graduating from College doesn't guarantee success. You have a lot of people that graduate from college and never reach their full potential. College or any educational system doesn't define a person's success. What defines a person's success is believing in themselves, having the right abilities in what they're trying to do, and staying working hard on their goals and dreams."

The whole debate team and Mr. Dixson start clapping. One kid tells Jake he told you. Jake says, "That's a great answer, but how can we win the championship like you and your team did?" Steven responds, "It's simple, by being a team, being there for one another, uplifting one another while the other one is down. All of you guys got to do your part to be successful. I believe in you; Mr. Dixson believes in you guys, also. The main thing is to believe in yourselves and in each other. That's all I got to say. Thank you guys for having me."

After watching the Debate team practice, Mr. Dixson introduces Steven to the captain of the team, Jake. "Steve, let me properly introduce you to our team captain, Jake." Steven gets up and shakes Jake's hands. "I must say, bro, you have a good choice of words when you speak to people." Jake says, "My apologies for saying what I said to you. I admire you; I remember when you led this team to a championship a few years ago. When I saw you holding the trophy, I told myself that one day, that's going to be me. I'm from Harmony Projects also; just like you, I'm just another brother trying to make it out. I'm not going to lie; it gets hard, but I stay going for mines." "That's the mentality you got to have. Me and you from the hood. Most people don't see guys like us making it. What we have to do with that is show people what we are made of and who we are. That's what I want you to do when you have your debate matches. Like Boosie says, you don't know my struggle, so you can't feel my hustle. Stay on the right path; don't do what I did in getting in these streets. Granted, I am rebuilding my life and going in the right direction, but stay living in positivity; don't let nothing negative get in your way." "That's love, bro. I appreciate that I'm going to rep for the hood just like you're doing, Steve." "Likewise, fam." "Your be easy." Mr. Dixson says, "You too, Jake."

After Jake leaves, Steven and Mr. Dixson have a one-on-one conversation. Steven says, "That kid is something else, but in my opinion, he is very intelligent. And he does make a great debate captain." Mr. Dixson says, "I wanted to introduce you to him because he reminded me of you. You both are intelligent and smart. And you both come from the same neighborhood. With you, I saw you as my second son Steve, no lie, but I didn't try to get super close to you and help you with your issues. I made a mistake on my end when it comes to that, and I'm sorry about that. With Jake, I'm not going to make that mistake as an educator and a man of GOD. I got to be there for my students all the way.


Now, with you, let me just say you are balling out here. I just saw you in the newspaper playing golf with the Mayor of Augusta. Congrats on the nomination for the Rising Star award. I'm proud of you, kid; many people counted you out, but you didn't count yourself out. The future is bright, young man; stay pushing, and bigger things will come your way. I'm going to be there on Friday to support you." "I appreciate you for everything. You were the first teacher I ever had that believed in me; just know I'm going to make you and everybody else proud of me when I get on that stage on Friday." "I know you will; just remember you are a star that shall shine. And on Friday, everybody at Spellman is going to see your light."


The next day, Steven calls Lenny and Jose to make sure they have a good amount of clothes to sell at Rich's College during the weekend. Steven says, "Guys, I'm calling to make sure we got our clothes set up to sell at the University of Georgia." Jose says, "Yep, we straight; we got a whole bunch of merchandise to sell." Lenny says, "We're going to make a lot of money out there this weekend." Steven says, "Yes, indeed we are; a lot of these kids have a lot of money, which means we will make a lot of money on our side. I'm going to talk to Rich about where we are going to be staying on campus and spots on campus where we can go to sell our clothes." Jose says, "That's sound good to me." Lenny says, "Me too." Steven says, "Alright. Well, I will see you guys tomorrow."

Later in the day, Steven gets an unexpected phone call. Steven answers, "Hello." Steven's Dad says, "Hey, Son, how are you doing?" Steven responds, "I'm doing good. I've got a lot of stuff going on." "I bet you are; your Mom told me all of the stuff that you have been doing. I'm proud of you; I'm glad you staying on the right path. Are you prepared for your event tomorrow?" "I'm a bit nervous, but I believe I will be okay." "I was the same way when I gave my valedictorian speech in High School; the main thing is to speak from your heart, but speak what you believe in. Like your grandmother used to tell me when I was younger, if you open your mouth, GOD will speak for you.

Listen, the real reason why I called is that I got some good news. The warden approved your request to come see me. We usually are allowed visitors every Saturday and Sunday, so if you're able to come on one of those days, that would be great. I would love to see you." "I'm glad it got approved; it's about time we see each other face to face." "Yes, indeed, son, I'm not going to hold you any longer. I love you and can't wait to see you in person. And remember to always believe in yourself and GOD. And speak what you believe in."

After talking to his father, Steven decides he's going to speak from his heart at the event tomorrow. It's Friday Morning, and Steven wakes up and prepares for the Rising Star award at Spellman College. Steven puts on his suit and tie, looks in his mirror, and recites Philippians 4:13 from the Bible. "I can do all things through Christ which strengthens me." Steven's Mom looks at Steven and says, "Baby boy, you are looking good; I can't wait to see you lay down your wisdom upon everybody today. Just know that whatever happens, your Momma is going to always be proud of you. Remember, son, you have GOD on your side. You will prevail against anything that's in your way and achieve anything you want in this world." Steven says, "I'm going to make you proud, Mom; them people aren't going to be prepared for me. They going to see a young kid from the hood do his thing today."

Steven and his Mom head to Atlanta to go to the event. While on the way to Atlanta, Steven starts reminiscing about his time in the streets, thinking about all his homies on the block, especially Darius, and thinking about what his father said to him about speaking on what he believes in. Steven is not only just representing himself, but he's representing the whole Harmony Neighborhood. Steven and his mother arrive at Spellman College.

As Steven and his mother get out of their vehicle, he is greeted by a lot of supporters. Lily sees Steven and hugs him. "Babe, you are looking good." Steven says, "Thanks, beautiful; I can't believe all of you came. Steven had a good number of supporters come out and support him. Hector daps up Steven. "My brother, can't wait to see you do your thing." Officer Brown says, "We already know you are a special talent. Now everybody in this building is going to know how special you are." Dee says, "I already know you going to represent Harmony Street in a good way." Mr. Dixson says, "Let your light shine." Diamond says, "You got this, bro; we all believe in you." Mr. David says, "Knock them dead,

Steve." Steven says, "Mr. Joe, you took the day off to come see me?" Mr. Joe says, "You are one of my best workers. I want to see you win, so I'm here to support you." Rich says, "You already got this award in the bag." Jose says, "You got this, bro." Lenny says, "Pop your stuff, my guy." Steven says, "It means a lot that all of you guys came to see me."

Steven starts tearing up as he is not used to a lot of people supporting him. Rich says, "Don't cry, thug." Steven says, "I never experienced this amount of support before; it means so much to me." Mr. Marcus says, "You're going to do great. Come with me; I'm going to walk you into the building and show you where you got to go, too." Lily stops Steven before he goes. "Before you go, Steve, I would like all of us to pray for you." "I'm down for that, so let's pray." Lily prays, "Dear Heavenly Father, thank you for letting us see another day. We pray that you give Steven strength and wisdom and that the people he speaks to today gain knowledge and wisdom from him. Either way, we know you're going to be by his side. In Jesus' name, we pray. Amen. The only thing you got to be is the star I already know you are. I love you, and I will see you inside."

Steven walks inside Spellman College with Mr. Marcus. Mr. Marcus shows him around the campus. After showing Steven around the campus, Mr. Marcus takes Steven to where the other Rising Star Award participants are hanging out. Mr. Marcus says, "Well, this is where all the other participants are; they're going to be calling you guys on stage in about 30 minutes. See you in a few minutes; can't wait to see you bless the stage."

While waiting to get on stage to give his speech, Steven interacts with the participants. One participant leaves a great impression on him. The participant says, "Excuse me, young brother; what's your name?" Steven says, "My name is Steven, and I'm one of the participants in the Rising Star award." "My name is Kim, and I'm also one of the participants in the Rising Star Award." "I'm not going to lie; I didn't expect you to be a participant; no offense when I say that." Kim laughs. "None taken. I know I'm the oldest participant here. I'm 40 years old; I had my son at 17, and due to that, I had to drop out of school. I had three more kids after my first son; I worked multiple jobs to support them. I went through a lot of tough times, but I never let it defeat me. Last year, I decided to go back to school to get my GED; it's something that I always wanted, and it was something that was missing from my life." "Salute to you. I'm happy that you're on the right track in life. How close are you to getting your GED?"

Kim says, "I have one more test to take, then I will be done." Steven says, "I got to pass two, then I will be done." "I'm going to give you some advice: before you ever think about giving up, think about why you started. My motivation is my kids. I want them to be proud of their mother. All of us in this room dropped out of school, so we know how it is getting knocked down. We just got to stay getting back up; it's like driving on the street; there are going to be bumps en route to your destination. Though, eventually, we reach our destination. Always keep that in mind, and you will do well. And good luck on the Rising Star Award; let the best person win." "Yes, indeed, I appreciate you, and I wish you well."

The conversation Steven had with Kim inspires him in a big way. Steven patiently waits for his name to be called. While waiting, Steven thinks about what his Dad told him to speak from the heart. Finally, Steven's name is called to get on stage. Steven says to himself. "It's showtime, baby."

As Steven walks on the stage, he sees his family and friends in the crowd. He also sees four people sitting in front of him at a table, who are going to be asking him questions on why he is deserving of the Rising Star award. Moderator says, "Mr. Anderson, welcome to Spellman College me and my colleagues will be asking you questions on what makes you a Rising Star. First, tell us about your time in GED class; how has your time in there benefited you?" "It has benefited me in a great way; due to my time in GED class, I have gained more skills and abilities. And I have met great people along my journey while getting my GED. It has also made me into a better person and helped me understand that in life, we all take an L. Most consider that a loss, but I consider it a lesson. For example, I failed the GED test two times. I don't consider my failure a loss; I consider it a lesson because I look back at my mistakes and learn from them. It's the same way in life; a wise man once told me that for us to get blessings in life, we have to learn from our lessons first. The GED class has benefited me in a great way, but I will say the lessons I have learned there are what have benefited me the most." The moderator asks a few more questions.

Moderator says, "Ok, and one final question, Mr. Anderson, what is the impact you want to make on this earth?" Before giving an answer, Steven starts thinking about the impact and legacy he wants to leave on this earth. Steven speaks from the heart, "The impact that I want to make and will make is going to be something powerful. I want people to look at me and be like, 'If he can make it, so can I.' Most people from my neighborhood don't make it out. A lot of people I know have become victims of the environment in our neighborhood, including myself. Just a couple of months ago, I was in a county jail trying to figure out what I want to be in life. I decided I wanted to be somebody that young kids in my neighborhood can look up to. I want to be an inspiration to the streets and to the world and show them that it doesn't matter where you are from or what you've been through; you can still be successful in life. The impact that I'm going to make on this earth is going to be powerful and inspirational."

As Steven finishes his speech, everybody in the auditorium applauds Steven. After giving his speech, Steven goes backstage and waits for everybody to get done with their speech.

After everybody gets done, Steven and the rest of the participants are called back on the stage. The Moderator says, "Participants, we thank you for coming here today; we loved all of the statements and speeches you all gave. Unfortunately, only one person wins the Rising Star Award. And the person that is the recipient of this year's Rising Star Award is Steven Anderson."

Everybody in the room gives Steven a standing ovation. He jumps in the air with tears of joy in his eyes. Just a couple of months ago, Steven was selling dope, and now he is bringing hope to people. Steven's Mom yells, "That's my Son!" Kim shakes Steven's hand as she stands next to him. "Congrats, Steven; remember what I said; the future is bright for you, young brother."

All of Steven's friends and family who came to see him congratulate him on winning the Rising Star Award. Steven's Mom hugs him. "Son, I am so proud of you; GOD is letting your light shine." Lily hugs Steven and says, "You did your thing up there. I'm glad I'm by your side to witness greatness whenever I'm around you." Steven says, "I feel the same way about you." Mr. Marcus says, "I knew you could do it, Steven; proud of you. The only thing that's left now is getting that GED." Steven says, "You already know I'm going to get it." Hector says, "Congrats, my brother; it's my honor to witness your greatness." Officer Brown says, "Yes, indeed, you motivated a lot of people today with your speech, including myself." Diamond says, "Proud of you, my brother, but they haven't seen nothing yet." Jose says, "You did great, bro; congratulations." Lenny says, "You did your thing, big homie." Rich says, "Proud of you, bro." Mr. Dixson says, "Proud of you, my boy. The Rising Star is definitely shining right now." Mr. Dave says, "Steven, you are a prime example. It doesn't matter what you've been through; you can be successful." Mr. Joe says, "I'm proud of you; me and the team are going to get you something when you come back to work on Tuesday, so expect a present."

360

# Chapter 13: Marketing Genius

After talking and saying goodbye to friends and family, Steven, Jose, and Lenny go with Rich to the University of Georgia. As the guys arrive on campus, Rich says, "Welcome to my campus. Where would you guys like me to show you first? Steven says, "The best places we can sell our clothes to set up a shop." "I got four locations around here where you can sell at. The first is going to be the cafeteria; there's always somebody up in there. The second is Study Hall, which is a lowkey hangout spot. You will definitely make a lot of connections up there. The third will be where we are now. When most people got something to sell, they come here at the front of the campus. And the fourth is at the parties we throw here; we have one tonight and a frat party tomorrow. So, you guys can definitely make a lot of money this weekend." Steven says, "Best believe we will; take us where we will be staying so we can plan everything out." "Sure thing; follow me."

Rich shows him his dorm room, which the guys will be staying in during their time on campus. Rich says, "This is my palace, also where all the magic happens. This is my roommate, Nate. Nate, this is my homies; they're going to be staying with us until Sunday. Nate introduces himself to the guys and says, "What's good, guys? Rich told me you guys got plan on selling clothes out here." Jose says, "Yep, here's some of our merch; tell us what you think."

Nate looks at the shirt and is impressed. "This is some fresh gear I will definitely buy from you guys. How much does it cost?" Steven says, "Since you're Rich's friend, $15." Nate pays Steven $15 for the clothes. Nate asks, "So, who's doing what for the company?" Lenny says, "Jose does the designs; Steven comes up with what would be on the clothes, and I come up with the prices. Our guy Steven also has a motivating website, so if you're looking for some motivation, go to his website." Nate says, "Y'all some hustlers for real." Steven says, "If you are not trying to hustle, then what are you doing." Nate says, "Rich told me you're a go-getter. I can tell you a Boss. I got to go. I will catch up with you guys later. You're going to the party tonight?" Jose says, "Hell, yeah, your boy is trying to get with some ladies." The guys start laughing. Steven says, "Do we have to worry about anybody pressing us up here or any security?" Rich says, "No, people know me, so you're straight, plus security hardly is ever on campus." Steven says, "Sounds good to me; let's get to work."

Steven and the rest of the guys plan on how they will sell their clothes. When it comes to business, Steven uses the same business mindset he had in the streets. Steven says, "Alright, guys, so this is how we're going to sell the clothes. Jose, you are going to go to the cafeteria to sell some of the merchandise there. Lenny, I was thinking you'd go to the front of the campus where we were previously to sell the clothes there. Rich, the way you can help us out is to wear some of our clothes, promote us, and take a pic for us and put it on Instagram. We can gain a lot of social media and notoriety from that. Rich, are there a lot of kids in the study hall right now?" Rich says, "It always is." Steven says, "Alright, me and you will head there." Lenny says, "What do you think is the best way to sell the clothes?" Steven breaks down his plan. "It's a lot of kids here, and we aren't going to sell the clothes to them like we are at the Lenox Mall. We will sell it for $20. I can see all of us making a band or even more this weekend. Your ready to make some money?" Jose says, "Let's get this guwop."

Steven and his squad set up a shop and start selling clothes. Within three hours, the guys all make about $500. Steven and Rich are selling some of the merchandise in the study hall. After getting done selling, Steven is approached by a beautiful, sophisticated girl. Rich says, "Bro, we made a killing; you a motherfucking genius, man." Steven smiles, "I'm just a man with a vision who is doing his best to turn his dreams into reality." A young lady walks up and says, "Hey Rich, who's your friend?" Rich says, "Sophie, this is Steven, Steven, this is Sophie. Steven shakes Sophie's hands and says, "Hey, nice to meet you." Sophie says, "It's nice to meet you too; I've never seen you around campus before. Did you just transfer here?" "No, me and a couple of friends came down to sell our clothes and visit the homie, Rich. Rich is like a brother of mine, so I had to check to see how he was doing. Tell me about yourself since you're asking me questions like you're Olivia Benson." Sophie starts laughing. "Ok, you got jokes; well, I'm a freshman just like Rich. I took up Business Management; I also got my own clothing business, Boss Lady Enterprises. I really respect the way you do your business, and I would like to also support your business. Do you got clothes for a boss woman?"

Steven says, "If you're a boss, we always got some gear for you. Here you go; right here, it will be $20." "Thank you, sir. Are you guys going to the party tonight?" Rich says, "Yes, we are; we are trying to get lit." Sophie says, "Great. Well, I will see you guys there, and Steven, will you save me a dance?" "It depends; if you got the right step, I will save you a dance." "Alright, bet; see you guys later."

Rich is surprised that Sophie talked to Steven. "All of the guys been trying to get with her, and she's stepping to you. Bro, you got skills; you don't even have to say nothing, and girls step to you." Steven smiles with his hands up. "I guess it's my charisma; you have some people that when they see somebody, they automatically recognize greatness. But I'm not trying to get with shawty; I already have a great lady by my side. I do want to know about her clothing business. Is it a big business around campus?" "It's the main thing the girls on campus wear. That's why I'm trying to make her my wife. She's the whole package: beauty, brains, and she's a hustler." Steven starts laughing. "You never know; she might be your wife. I would like to do business with her; you don't find too many young black people out here owning our own stuff."

After talking in Study Hall, Steven and Rich meet with the rest of the guys in Rich's dorm room. Steven says, "So, guys, how much we made? Me and Rich made $500 combined." Jose says, "I made $300 selling in the cafeteria." Lenny says, "I made $500 also; you wasn't lying. Being in front of the campus, a lot of money was made, and people wanted our merchandise." Steven says, "We are all hustlers; I know we are going to make a great profit while being here. And we are just getting started.

Also, did anybody give you guys any trouble?" Jose answers, "Yes, the girls; they was on your boy. They want me to put the beef in the taco." Everybody starts laughing. Lenny says, "The girls have been stepping to us, but no issue with security." Steven says, "Good, we will do the same thing tomorrow, but for now, let's get prepared for this party."

The guys prepare for the party that is happening on campus tonight. Rich says, "So, your got plan on selling at the party?" Steven says, "No, but we're going to forever promote our brand. We're going to have some fun tonight." Steven and the guys head into the party dressed fly from head to toe. Jose says, "It's lit as a motherfucker up in here." Rich says, "This is what we do at UGA; we stay getting lit. You only live once; you got to have fun every chance you get. And that's what we going to do tonight." The guys start partying and making connections.

As the party slows down, the DJ starts playing slow jams. And Steven gets approached by Sophie. Sophie says, "Excuse me, boss man,; may I have this dance?" Steven smiles and says, "You again, if you know how to step, let's dance." Steven dances with Sophie for about 20 minutes.

After dancing, Steven and Sophie sit down in a corner and talk to one another. Steven says, "I will say, you do got some moves on you." Sophie says, "I told you I can move around, but I wanted to talk to you about your business and your views on ownership." "Ok, but first, go ahead and tell me what you know about me. I know after meeting me, you probably did some research on me." Sophie starts laughing. "I'm not going to lie; after meeting you, I found you on Instagram and other social media profiles. I was a little bit disappointed when I saw you got a girlfriend because I was definitely going to try to get with you. However, I want to collaborate with you and be friends. I know that sounds crazy coming for a woman, but I'm trying to make my business grow. And I look at how you're doing your thing. I'm trying to take notes." "I'm flattered, and I'm thankful for my girlfriend. If it wasn't for her, my business wouldn't be as successful as it is now. I would also like to collaborate with you; there are not a lot of young black owners out here. So, I would definitely love to partner with you." "I'm glad to hear that, so first, tell me, what is your mindset when it comes to selling clothes?"

Steven explains his approach. "Well, I used to be a drug dealer, so the way I used to do my dealing in the streets is the way I do my dealings with the clothes. I get somebody I know who is well-known and loves the type of product I'm selling, and I get them to promote it for me. I don't ask them to do it for me. They are in love with my product so much they're going to tell their friends and people about my product. Which in return brings profit my way and my team's way." "So, you were like Big Meech out here in these streets?"

Steven starts laughing. "I made a good amount of money in the streets, but it wasn't that big. I did pay for my mistakes in the streets and paid my debts to society. I wounded it up doing a few months in jail due to my time on the streets. During my time in jail, I wanted to be an inspiration to my people in the projects. That's what made me change my ways and create all I have created so far." "That's powerful; I salute you. Most young brothers fall victim to the system. Granted, you did fall victim, but you bounced back and are becoming a leader in your community. Let me ask you this: what does it mean for you to be your own boss?" "It means everything. I want to leave a legacy on this world. Something my kids and grandkids can live off of. Especially with us being black people, most of us were never taught how to be our own boss. It's important for us to learn about ownership so the young black people after us can know about ownership. I have answered all of your questions, so answer mine. What made you want to become a boss?"

Sophie explains the reason why she wants to be a boss. "Kind of the same reason you want to be a boss, but my main reason to be a boss is to be an inspiration to young black queens. Like you said, it's not a lot of black bosses out here, especially black women. And I want to represent the black queens in America and show them we also can be bosses. Like what Kimora Lee Simmons did with Baby Phat and the impact she made in the 2000s. And April Walker with what she did with Walker Wear. I'm trying to make that same impact." Steven says, "Respect, we're both hustlers and have a boss mindset, so we will definitely make it." "Yes, indeed, let me ask you this: what do you think is the best way for me to sell clothes?" "Just look around; you have a lot of beautiful women around here. Have them help support your brand. Because when you have a fine woman wearing your product, it will attract a lot of people to your brand." "You're smart as hell. Listen, I'm going to this event tomorrow. You know Young Kwan?" "Hell yeah, bro is the hottest rapper out right now." "Well, I'm going to his concert tomorrow. I got plan on marketing my product there, and I was wondering if you would like to come with me. It might be a great way for you to get your business out there." Steven thinks about what Lily would think about him going to a concert with another woman. Although Sophie is a beautiful lady, Steven sees Sophie as a great friend and someone who can be a great business connection for him. "I'm down; let's have a great time and make some money." Sophie, with her drink in her hands, says, "Cheers to young black people being bosses; now let's get back dancing." Steven and the rest of the gang party the whole night.

The next morning, Steven gets a phone call from Darius. Darius asks, "How you living, homie? Congrats on winning your award." Steven says, "Appreciated and getting to that skrilla you already know, but mainly doing big things out here. I'm actually out here hanging out at UGA with Rich, marketing my clothes and website out here." "You're doing it big out here. I'm proud of you; seeing what you're doing is inspiring me. Speaking of which, your boy got his GED."

Steven is excited to hear Darius got his GED. "My boy, I'm proud of you; we always tell one another the only way is up." "I appreciate. I got to be a positive role model for my son and my little brother. Thank you for what you did for my brother; my Mom told me about that. I'm just like you, bro. Every day I wake up, I'm going to stay becoming a better person. I can't wait to get out of here and show the world the new and improved Darius." "You're going to be great when you get out; me and you are going to put on for the hood in a legit way.

I know; I'm going to the Young Kwan concert tonight with this girl I met yesterday. Me and her are going to promote both of our clothing lines." "Man, you got another one, bro flipping girls like he's Hugh Hefner." Steven starts laughing. "It's not like that; I'm still with Lily. Me and her still going strong." "Glad to hear, bro. Don't mess that up."

"I won't. I'm going to visit my pops also; everything is going well in my life, but I feel like that's the one thing that is holding me back." "You need to do that as soon as possible, bro. One thing I learned from being here is that the quicker you let go of the pain and hurt, you will become a better person in life. Being here made me forgive my own father. On some real stuff, hearing all the things you're doing here is inspiring me, bro. You showing me and other people in the projects that we can be somebody. Stay pushing and stay going forward. Like we always used to tell one another when we were on the block together. We are soldiers and survivors out here. Brother, stay marching in the right direction, and you know if I got my GED, you can get yours too. One love thug, I'm going to be home soon." "You know I'm going to stay pushing; when you get out, you know I got you for anything. One love, bro. Stay keeping your head up."

Later on in the day, Steven and the guys go and sell clothes in the same spots again. While selling clothes, Steven and Rich have a deep conversation. Steven says, "Bro, thank you for letting me and the homies come up here and sell our merchandise." Rich says, "No problem; like I always tell you, I got your back no matter what. I'm glad you're up here because I got somebody I can confide in."

Steven is concerned about what might be going on with Rich. "Talk to me, big dawg." "I'm lowkey scared about how my college career will play out. I feel like this is a win-or-lose opportunity for me. If I mess up, I will never make it to the NBA. I do have a backup plan, but I'm trying to live in the dream I envisioned for myself. A part of me feels like if I don't achieve or get a chance to live in the dream I envisioned for myself, I have failed in life." "Don't you ever think that way. All you can do on your end is do your best and work hard to achieve your goals. And let's say if you don't achieve that goal, that's not necessarily a failure. It would be a failure if you gave up on that dream. However, I honestly believe you will achieve your goal and dream. Man, you are a beast on the court; nobody can mess with you. I believe you will make it to the NBA. I'm not just saying that because I'm your homeboy, but because I believe in your talent and skills. And when you ever think about giving up, always remember who you are." "I needed that, bro; sometimes, I guess doubts be creeping in my mind, but I'm going to do everything in my power to be the person I envisioned for myself." "That's the right spirit to have, my brother. I talked to Darius earlier today; he just got his GED. Bro has a positive mindset. All three of us are going to be successful. "You are not lying, bro; we are going to be successful and make our town proud. Speaking of which, I know you're helping out with his kid, but for the money I'm making with you this week, I want it to be given to him once he gets out." "I can do the same on my end, so when he gets out, he will be straight." "We're going to make sure he's straight once he gets out, but back to you what's going on with you and Sophie?"

Steven starts laughing. "Nothing is going on; she and I are friends. Plus, she's a future entrepreneur, just like I am. She can help me out with my business; I can help her out with her business. A guy and a girl can be friends without it escalating to anything else. Me and her are actually going to the Young Kwan concert tonight." "I didn't even know that it was tonight. Have you told Lily about your new friend?" "You got jokes; not yet. I'm going to talk to her about that. I'm not going to do anything to jeopardize my relationship with her. Every time I'm with her or speak to her, I always get a true vision of what beauty and love really is." "I can see the impact she made on you. As long as I have known you, I have never seen you this happy before." "That's why I'm not going to do anything to mess this up. Speaking of which, I'm getting a call from wifey right now."

Steven gets a phone call from Lily. Lily says, "Hello, Mr. Entrepreneur, had you on my mind. How's everything going?" Steven responds, "I'm doing well, hanging with the fellows and making a good amount out of money. How about you? I hope you're doing well. Even though I know you missing me." "I'm not going to lie. I am missing you, and I'm glad you getting to the money. I wish I didn't have to work this weekend so I could be up there with you. I know you are making connections up there." "I most definitely am. I actually met this girl named Sophie; she has a clothing line. And she's going to the Young Kwan concert and invited me to go with her. She knows about you. I'm not trying to get with her or anything like that. I wanted to let you know that I'm not trying to keep any secrets in our lives. I'm mainly going because it will be a great investment for my business and our future. Tell me, what do you think?"

Steven is hesitant about what Lily might say to him. He doesn't want to do anything to mess up their relationship and not to do anything to hurt Lily's feelings. "I trust you, Steven. I believe you wouldn't do anything to hurt me. Do what you feel is best and right for you; either way, I know you will do the right thing. I have to go. I love you, and I will talk to you tomorrow." "Love you too." Steven decides in his mind that he will go to the concert to promote his brand. Rich asks, "How was the phone call?" Steven says, "It went well; honestly, better than I expected. Let's hang around town for a bit."

After riding around town with Rich, Steven meets up with the rest of the guys to discuss their strategy for selling clothes for the rest of the day. Steven asks, "Alright, guys, how much money have we been making?" Jose says, "I done made about $700." Lenny says, "I made almost a band here. What are we going to do for the party?" Steven says, "I want you guys to have fun and have a blast. You guys deserve it; you've been working hard all weekend. Enjoy the party tonight." Jose asks, "What about you? If it wasn't for you, we wouldn't have no money in our pockets?" Steven says, "I got a huge opportunity. One of the students here invited me to the Young Kwan concert tonight to promote our brand. I'm going to put on for us and help people recognize our talent, so these people know what a great clothing line is." Lenny says, "Man, you the smartest person I know; you can make something happen at that concert." Jose says, "Make us proud. Do your thing, bro." Rich says, "Go handle your business, Bossman."

Steven gets dressed and gets clothes for the clothing line to promote and sell at the concert. Steven says, "Alright, guys, about to head out. Rich, thank you for letting me use your Mustang." Rich says, "No problem; don't do no Fast and Furious type stuff with my car." Steven picks up Sophie from her dorm room. As Sophie enters Steven's vehicle, Steven says, "Boss lady, how are you doing today?" Sophie responds, "I'm doing great. Can't wait to promote our brands; I must say, you dripping out here." "When you're a boss, you got to dress like one." "Big facts; this is going to be a big concert and a big opportunity for us." "Tonight, both of our lives can change for the better. Let's have a fun time tonight."

Steven and Sophie arrive at the Young Kwan concert. This is Steven's first time attending a concert, and he is amazed by the atmosphere. "Dang, it's super lit up in here. You know, this is actually my first time going to a concert." "Well, let's show you how us city people party, country boy." Steven starts laughing. "Alright, but where do we go to sell our clothes?" "The concert hasn't started yet, so we're going to sell our clothes at the entrance." "Alright, let's get this money."

Steven and Sophie sell both of their merchandise in front of the arena. Steven and Sophie both struggle to sell their clothes. Steven says to a concertgoer, "Aye, bro, got some fresh merch; it's $20." Random dude says, "Nobody don't want that shit." Steven doesn't let the negativity get him down. He stays pushing to sell his clothes. Sophie says, "I hardly haven't made a whole bunch out here tonight. What about you?" "I only made $60 out here. I'm not going to lie; the old me would be mad as hell right now, but you know what? We got to stay pushing." "Yep, we got to stay pushing, but the concert is about to start, so let's go in and enjoy."

Steven and Sophie go inside for the Young Kwan concert. This is Steven's first time going to a concert. The enjoyment on Steven's face is like a little kid at the fair. While at the concert, Steven and Sophie interact with some of the people in the crowd and sell some of their clothes.

After the concert ends, Steven and Sophie head back to the entrance to try to sell more clothes. While heading to the entrance,

Steven bumps into a random dude who knocks the shirts on Steven's back. Steven says, "Yo, my guy, you knocked down all of my clothes." The random dude helps Steven pick up the clothes and says, "My bad, young homie. Is this your own merchandise?" "Yeah, I came up with what appears on the shirt. Then I got a homeboy that does the designs for the clothes. And then I have another homeboy who comes up with the prices for the clothes. Me and a homegirl of mine mainly came here to promote our clothing lines."  "I respect that; it reminds me of when I was younger and hustling out here. This is some nice merch, too. Not no knockoffs, either. What's your name, kid?"  "My name is Steven." "Steven, my name is Jamie. Do me a favor and get your friend. I want to introduce you guys to somebody."

Steven gets Sophie, and they go with Jamie to meet his friend. Jamie takes Steven and Sophie to the backstage area, and they are surprised who they meet. Sophie, with a shocked look on her face, says, "Ain't no way, Young Kwan, that's you?" Young Kwan turns around and says, "In the flesh, baby. Who are your friends, Jamie?" Jamie says, "This is Steven and Sophie; they both came to the concert to sell their clothes." Young Kwan says, "Ok, your some hustlers; let me see your clothes." Sophie says., "I only got one shirt left." Young Kwan says, "I will buy it. How much is it?" "20 dollars." "There you go, shawty. Homeboy, you still got a lot of shirts on you; how many you got left?" Steven says, "I got 10." Young Kwan says, "I'm going to help both of you guys, but my guy, I'm going to help you make some quick money super-fast." Steven asks, "How?" Young Kwan says, "Just watch."

Young Kwan pulls out his phone, puts on one of Steven's shirts, and goes live on his Instagram page. Young Kwan says, "Yo, what's going on everybody? I got two fellow hustlers with me: Steven and Sophie. I want you to support their clothing lines, The Boy That Comes From Nothing, is Steven's clothing line. I'm wearing Steven's merch right now, and your support Sophie's clothing line, Bossy Lady. If your looking for some fresh merch, my boy Steven got some shirts he's selling in front of the State Farm Arena. You see, I'm looking fresh in the merch; your come and get you some."

Steven and Sophie are stunned to see Young Kwan promote them on his platform. They just came to the concert to sell their clothes; instead, they got a huge shoutout from a famous rapper. If Steven and Sophie weren't well known, there are now. Steven says, "Big homie, I appreciate that; what you just did probably just changed my life and Sophie's." Young Kwan smiles and says, "It's no problem; your remind me how I was when I first started. I was selling my mixtapes at gas stations. It wasn't until my boy Jamie here took a chance on me that's when I started to blow up. Let's go outside and help you make some money, bro; remember, yesterday's price ain't today's price. When we go out here, sell your shirts way more than $20, bro. That goes for you too, Sophie; now let's go out here and make you some dough, bro."

Steven, Sophie, and Young Kwan's crew go to the front of the arena to help Steven sell his clothes. With Young Kwan promoting his brand on Instagram, Steven increased his price from

$20 to $40. Within 20 minutes, Steven sells 9 out of 10 of his shirts. The last person that shows up to buy one of Steven's shirts is the guy who told Steven nobody didn't want to buy his clothes. Random Dude asks, "Hey, can I buy one of your shirts?" Steven remembers the guy right away. Steven says, "Well, a lot of people want to buy this; the shirt will be $50." The guy gives Steven $50 and apologizes for earlier. "My apologies for earlier. I'm used to buying naming brand clothes. I didn't know nothing about you or your clothing business. Though after seeing Young Kwan promote your gear, I knew you had to be official." Steven says, "Well, I will say this: never judge a person. Because you will never know how much value that person has to offer." Young Kwan says, "Remember what my boy said. This dude right here is going to be a star; just watch and see."

After the guys leave, Steven and Young Kwan talk to one another. Steven says, "Man, I owe you big time. I had planned on making about $200 out here, but thanks to you, I made almost two times that." Young Kwan says, "It's no problem; you remind me of myself. One thing about me is that I'm a hustler, which is the main reason why I respect other hustlers. Like I say in my song "Coming Up," just a young nigga from the bando trying to make it to the condo. Just stay grinding and hustling; the hard work is going to pay off soon. I got a feeling the next time I see you, you going to be bossed up. I got to go to the studio; you be blessed, little homie."

And just like that, Steven got the biggest endorsement he could have asked for and wasn't even looking for it. Steven says, "OMG! Sophie, we are superstars." Steven and Sophie hug one another. Sophie says, "I only hung out with you for a day, and I got the biggest endorsement I ever had for my clothing line. Thank you, bro." Steven says, "It's not me. It's just GOD giving us our blessings in life. It's crazy a person like me doing big stuff like this."

Steven starts crying and remembering all he's been through. Steven, with tears in his eyes, says, "I was in a jail cell a few months back, and now I got a famous entertainer endorsing my clothing line on the internet." "It is just proof that you are a diamond from the rough that was born to shine. My brother, this is just the beginning; they haven't seen nothing yet." Steven and Sophie hug one another.

Steven takes Sophie back to her dorm room. Steven says, "It was great hanging out with you. I'm leaving tomorrow morning, but I have a homeboy of mine I want to introduce you to. I believe he can help you out with the designs on your clothes." Sophie says, "That sounds like a deal. I must say, Steven, it's been an honor hanging out with you over these past two days. You're going to be huge out here in these streets. I'm glad that I met you. I hope that we will be friends for a long time." "We are bosses; we are most definitely going to stay connected. You're going to blow up to you. Have a nice night. I will talk to you in the morning."

After dropping off Sophie, Steven returns to Rich's dorm room. Seeing there is a sock on the door, Steven decides to sleep in the Study Hall for the night. When Steven wakes up in the morning, he wakes up to a bunch of notifications on his phone. Steven yells. "Holy Shit!" Steven runs to Rich's dorm room; all the guys are asleep except for Jose. Steven says, "Yo Jose, you see the notifications about the clothes?" Jose says, "Hell Yeah, we done already sold out, and I saw Young Kwan's IG story too." Steven and Jose both yell out, "We're going to be rich!"

This wakes up everybody else in the dorm room. Rich asks, "What the hell is going on?" Nate says, "For real, I still got a hangover from yesterday." Lenny says, "What's going on, guys." Steven says, "Our clothing line gained major recognition, mainly thanks to Young Kwan shouting us out. Look at the phone." Lenny says, "We up big time, us dropouts doing big things; fuck what a hater says." Rich says, "Man, if it wasn't a Sunday, we would get super lit tonight. I know you guys got to go back home today, but we celebrating today." Lenny asks, "Hold up real quick, Steve. I'm curious; how did you pull this off?" Steven says, "I accidentally bumped into Young Kwan's manager on my way out of the concert. And he liked our clothes and introduced me to Young Kwan. Me and Sophie talked to him for a good while and he decided to endorse our clothes and hers. Speaking of which, she's calling me right now."

Sophie calls Steven. Sophie says, "Bro, all my clothes sold out since last night, and my followers grew a whole lot on social media. I know your stuff popping off right now also." Steven says, "It is in a big way; me and my crew are talking about it right now. Rich might have plan on us celebrating our accomplishments for our clothing lines. So, I will text you the location where we will be at." "Sounds good; see you then."

After getting off the phone, Rich plans a celebration for the guys. Rich asks, "What's Sophie talking about?' Steven says, "Her clothes sold out and her social media platforms grew overnight also. I told her we might be celebrating our accomplishments. How do you got plan on celebrating us, Rich?" Rich says, "Steven, you know me better than anybody. I'm the king when it comes to parties. Nate, post on Snap and Instagram that we're throwing a cookout on the beach. Guys, be prepared; we are going get super lit today, and Lenard, like I told you last night, mustard on the hot dog, sir." Lenny says, "Your boy wild, Steve." Steven says, "I got to call Lily and tell her the good news."

Steven calls Lily and tells her the exciting news. Steven says, "Bae, have you seen the great success me and the guys have achieved overnight." Lily says, "I have. I don't know how you got a megastar to endorse you guys, but that proves how special you are. The clothing line is doing numbers, and so is your website; you are finally getting recognized for your greatness." "This is just the beginning; the light is going to stay getting more brighter." "That's on everything. I have a surprise for you and the guys once you guys return." "I can't wait to see what it is. Well, me and guys are going to celebrate. I will see you once I get back; love you." "Love you too."

After Steven's conversation with Lily, Rich takes the guys to the beach and throws a party on the beach. While on the beach, Steven and the guys are being celebrated like they won a championship. As Sophie arrives at the beach, Steven takes a break from the party to talk to her. Steven hugs Sophie and says, "Sis, cheers to our success." Sophie says, "Bro, we came up overnight. I got to get more shirts shipped in to sell due to me being sold out. I owe you, bro. If you ever need anything, you hit me up." "Most definitely." Steven and Sophie hug one another. Steven says, "I want to introduce you to somebody; this guy is the best designer I know. Jose!"

Steven introduces Jose to Sophie. "Jose, this is Sophie; Sophie, this is Jose. He does the designs for my clothes and is also co-owner of the company. He can hook you up with major designs for your company if needed." Sophie says, "Steven didn't tell me how cute you were, Jose." A connection starts developing between Sophie and Jose. Jose says, "You mean sexy baby? Let's talk business." Steven says, "Talk to you guys later."

After hanging out on the beach, Steven and Rich talk to one another. Steven asks, "Who would have ever thought this would happen to me?" Rich says, "Me, bro, you are a genius; that is something I noticed about you since we were in school together. GOD gives us all great opportunities and abilities in life; it's up to us to use them for our benefit and success. And my brother, you are doing a good job at it. I'm proud of you; this is only just the beginning. One day, we are going to have the whole town of Thomson looking up to us." "That's on everything. I'm proud of you, too. I love you, my brother." Steven and Rich hug one another. Steven says, "Well, I got to head back to the city, bro. I will see you later." Rich says, "Glad to have had you up here; stay popping your shit, and you already know I'm one call away."

Steven, Jose, and Lenny head back home; on their way back home, they stop by Lily's Apartment." Lily says, "You back!" Lily jumps in Steven's arms. Steven says, "Yes, I am beautiful. I'm glad to see your beautiful face. So, what is the big surprise you have for me and the guys." Lily pulls out two pieces of paper and shows them to Steven and the guys. Jose says, "I know that ain't what I think it is." Lenny says, "It's an LLC for our business." Steven says, "An LLC business for our clothing line and one for my website. And papers of the trademark of The Boy That Comes From Nothing. You are the best girlfriend of all time." Lily says, "I paid for the LLCs and trademark registration a couple of weeks back. They finally came in the mail yesterday. I support you guys and love each and every one of you, and I want to see you all succeed." Jose says, "Steven's our brother, but just know we see you as our sister." Lenny says, "I love all of you. I never experienced this much positivity in my life before." Steven says, "We're family, bro; we forever got each other back. We're just getting started. We are destined for greatness, so you better be prepared for more blessings coming our way." All of the guys and Lily hug one another. Lily says, "Cheers to our success and to what is in store."

After leaving Lily's house, Steven returns home. Steven says, "Mom, I'm back; where you at?" Steven's Mom runs and hugs Steven. "Baby, you are back. How was the trip to UGA?" "It was great. Had a fun time; me and the boys made a good amount of money and made some connections." "I'm glad you had a fun time, and again, congrats on the Rising Star Award." "Now it's all about focusing on getting my GED; it's time for your son to get that diploma." "You going to get it, baby. Since you are back, give this pie I baked to Ms. Arlene." "Did you bake me one, too?" "You know dang well I made you one too. Now take Ms. Arlene the pie, boy." Steven takes the sweet potato pie to Ms. Arlene.

Ms. Arlene is like everybody's grandma in the neighborhood; everybody loves her because she always shows them love. Steven knocks on Ms. Arlene's door. Ms. Arlene asks, "Who is it?" Steven says, "It's me, Ms. Arlene, little Stevie down the street." "OMG, boy, come on in this house. I haven't seen you in a good while. You done got big." Ms. Arlene hugs Steven. "I appreciate; my Mom wanted me to give you this pie she made for you." "Well, tell your Momma I said thank you. Please have a seat with the ole lady; your Momma been telling me all of the great things you been doing. I'm proud of you, baby.

Steven and Ms. Arlene have a deep conversation. Ms. Arlene says, "I was praying for you while you were in jail, hoping that GOD put you on the right path in your life, and it looks like he has." Steven says, "I'm doing my best every day to be the man he designed to be, but I'm not going to lie. It gets hard sometimes." "That's life, baby, but the hard times in our lives are what humble us into the human beings we are. You remind me a lot of your Father; before he got locked up, he used to always make sure I was good. He used to say the same thing you saying. Sadly, with him, he let the pressure and the wrong people around influence him in the wrong direction. The main thing I would ask him is if he's at peace." "What would be his answer to the question?" "He always used to tell me the day he would be at peace is when he don't have to sell drugs no more and be the man he truly wanted to be. And he used to say the day my son don't have to struggle for nothing. Your Father is a smart young man, but just like other young black men in our neighborhood and other hoods in America, he became a victim of his environment. When you find peace in life, it's going to help you grow in life. So, I want to ask you this: are you truly at peace in your life? If not, what's holding you back?"

Steven takes a minute, thinks, and gives an answer. Steven says, "Honestly, it's forgiving my father and seeing him face to face and speaking my truth. I been holding anger against him since I was a kid. It's time I let it go; I need to go see my father so I can release the pain in my heart against him so I can grow in life. That's the only thing in my life that I feel like is holding me back." "Well, baby, go and see your father so you can make peace with him and within yourself. And when you do that, I promise you it will help grow you into a better person. Let me know how it goes; I want to see you win, young man. Stay rising."

After talking to Ms. Arlene, Steven decides he's going to visit his father this weekend. Steven realizes that for him to be the man GOD designed him to be, he has to let go of all the anger and hatred in his heart.

386

# Chapter 14: Finding Peace

Steven goes back to his house and reveals to his mother that he has decided to go and see his father. As Steven enters his house, his Mom says, "You gave Ms. Arlene her pie?" Steven says, "I did; talking to Ms. Arlene helped me realize that we as people have to find peace in life. I've decided I'm going to see my Dad this weekend mainly so I can be at peace in life." Steven's Mom hugs him and says, "Son, I'm so proud of you making that decision. When you do go see him, speak from your mind and your heart." "I will, Mom; well, let me prepare for class tomorrow."

The next day, Steven returns to GED class and is treated like a celebrity due to Young Kwan promoting him. As Steven walks into class, everybody in the room gives him a round of applause. Mr. Marcus says, "Let's give it up for the Rising Star winner, Mr. Steven Anderson!" Everybody in the classroom gives Steven a round of applause.

After class ends, Mr. Marcus talks to Steven about getting his GED. Mr. Marcus says, "Mr. Superstar, man, you're becoming a big name out here; first, winning the Rising Star Award and then getting shouted out by a famous rapper." Steven says, "I'm just out here striving and hustling to achieve my goals." "That's one of the reasons why I wanted to meet up with you. I want to work with you more closely so you can get your GED. What I want to do is, starting today, I'll spend two hours with you every Monday and Wednesday and help you study so you will be able to get your

GED." "Mr. Marcus, I'm grateful, and I will definitely accept your request. Getting my GED is my most important goal in life right now." "Since that's the case, let's go ahead and get started."

For the next two hours, Mr. Marcus helps Steven study and practice for his GED. Mr. Marcus says, "Well, sir, our two hours is up; how do you think it went?" Steven says, "It went well; this has helped me out big time. A lot of teachers don't do this for their students." "I just do me. I will always do my part to make sure my students are straight when it comes to gaining knowledge and being more educated. You have great potential. I'm going to do everything on my end to make sure you succeed. We are going to stay doing this until you get your GED." "I appreciate. Best believe I'm going to get it, too."

Before leaving for the day, Steven runs into Garrett. Garrett says, "Steve, I seen Young Kwan's IG story; man, you done blew up." Steven says, "I'm just getting started; I owe you in a big way. Thank you for allowing me to go to your party. I made a lot of connections, thanks to you." "It was my honor, bro; plus, everybody has loved you ever since the Golf Tournament. Everybody talks and asks about you. What's crazy about you is you have a different background and more setbacks than any of the people who were at the tournament. Yet you shined the brightest out of everybody." "I was born to be a star, so I'm always going to shine." "Facts, I see you owning your own business one day. When you make it, just don't forget about me." "You did me a solid; trust and believe I don't forget the people that do for me. I got to go. I will talk to you later."

The next day at work, Steven talks to Jamal about the good things going on in his life. Jamal says, "Young buck, what's been going on with you? Been walking around here like you got a million bucks." Steven says, "Man, just been blessed; GOD is out here making way for your boy. My clothing line and website are popping off in a big way. I'm mainly trying to get full peace in life. That and getting my GED are my life's main priorities right now." Jamal looks proudly at Steven. "Proud of you, Steve; we all are. You're like a little brother to us around here. It took me years to find full peace in my life; when you find it, you will feel like a brand new person." "How did you find peace in your life?" "I drifted away from all of the negativity in my life; see, we all have our own way of finding peace in life. Once you figure out the way to find peace, your life is going to grow in a big way." "I believe I'm close to doing that, big homie."

Before Steven leaves for the day, he is stopped by Mr. Joe. Mr. Joe says, "Steven, wait one second; me and Dave got a present for you." Mr. Joe hands Steven a box. When Steven opens up the box, he is stunned. Steven, with tears in his eyes, says, "$500! Why are you giving me this?" Mr. Joe says, "Me and my brother see your greatness; plus, I know you have a business you're developing. I believe that money can help you out in a big way." "Thank You." Steven gives Mr. Joe a hug. "You put that money to good use and just watch how that money is going to repay you. I'm blessed to have you on my crew, and I can't wait for the world to see you shine." After getting off work, Steven calls Jose and Lenny to go to the bank to create a business account for their business. Steven also creates a separate account for himself.

The next day, before class starts, Steven, Jose, and Lenny talk about their clothing business. Steven says, "All right, guys, so now that we got more clothes in Inventory do you guys still want to sell the clothes the same way as before." Jose says, "I will say we do it the same way, but I got an idea. When I was talking to Sophie at the party, an idea grew on me. Why won't we get some college kids to endorse our clothing line? I mean, with Young Kwan endorsing us, we are making a lot more money, but if we get some kids in College to endorse us, we're going to pop off in a big way because our clothing line is streetwear, which represents inspiration. Like our clothes could be in a retail store." Lenny says, "That's a good plan, Steven; what do you think about it?" Steven says, "I think it's an excellent plan. I can call Rich to arrange for you guys to go back to UGA. To have some people model for our clothing line this weekend." Lenny asks, "You're not going to come with us?" Steven says, "I got to meet up with my father this weekend; haven't seen him in a long time. It is something I have to do to make peace in my life." Jose says, "You do what you got to do; we got your back. If you need anything, just know we got you." Lenny says, "That's on everything; we're going to hold it down for you at UGA." Steven says, "That's why I love your boys. Let's head to class."

After GED class ends, Steven stays with Mr. Marcus and studies for the GED test and also helps tutor Ashley and Will for their GED tests. After getting done tutoring and studying for the GED test, Steven comes to a decision pertaining to his GED. Steven says, "Mr. Marcus, I came to a decision regarding getting my GED. I decided I'm going to go back to the main campus at Brooks Tech next Wednesday and get this GED." Mr. Marcus asks, "Do you think you're fully prepared for it?" "I honestly am. Plus, I got a great teacher who is doing his part to make sure I'm fully prepared for it." Mr. Marcus smiles. "Since that's the case, I say go for it. I believe in you and know you can do it. We will come back Monday and study again; have a nice weekend and get some rest."

After leaving class, Steven meets up with Lily in the School's parking lot to talk to her about him making amends with his father. Lily says, "Babe, I got your text; you said you needed to talk. Is everything ok?" Steven says, "Yeah, everything is ok. I need to talk to you about a big decision I'm about to make in my life. In my life right now, I'm trying to be at full peace. To do so, I have to release all the anger and hatred that is still in my heart. All of that negative energy I still have in me is toward my father. I decided to finally see my father this Saturday face-to-face so I can speak my peace, and I want you to come with me to see him." Lily doesn't hesitate to answer. "Like I told you before, I'm always by your side. If you want me to be there to support you, I'm there. I'm glad you made this decision. I believe this will help you find true healing. I also believe this will help your father find peace. So where is the prison located?" "It's about three hours away, so it's going to be a long drive." "You will have a lot of time to think on your way up there. Just always remember, Steve, you are loved by many people, including me, and I will always support and love you." Steven and Lily hug one another.

After meeting up with Lily, Steven goes home and is greeted by Darius's little brother, Danny. Steven says, "Little D, what's going on with you?" Danny says, "I've been doing great. I have got to show you something." Danny pulls out his phone and shows Steven the state championship and MVP he won. "Me and my team won the championship, and I won the MVP. This would not have happened if it wasn't for you; thank you." Steven says, "It didn't have nothing to do with me, bro; you just had to believe in yourself, and that's what you did. I'm proud of you, bro; you're repping the city in a big way. I'm going to give you some money."

Steven gives Danny $200. Danny has a very big smile on his face. "YO! Appreciated, you didn't have to." Danny gives Steven a hug. "When you do good, you should always be rewarded; take that money and do what you want with it. Come in the house and play some video games. Plus, I got some clothes to give you also."

Over the next two days, Steven studies for his GED test and prepares to see his father on Saturday. It's Friday evening; Steven goes to visit Dee. Dee says, "Youngin, you are looking fresh to death. Congrats again on winning that award in Atlanta. Seeing you up on that stage was something powerful. I have never seen nobody from this neighborhood do something like that before. You are about to take off big time. Just don't forget your people once you pop off in a big way, but tell me, what's been going on with you." Steven says, "Big things, my clothing line and website are going up big time, and I'm going to see my father tomorrow. It's time for me to make peace with him in order for me to find full peace in life."

"First off, I'm proud of you for doing your thing, and you're doing it legit, too. Second, I'm happy that you are making amends with your father. That's something I wish I had the chance to do; I was mad at my father for years for not being there. Then, when I had wanted to make amends with him, it was too late. He had passed away. That's something I got to live with forever. I had a chance to make peace with my father, but I didn't. Speak what you feel in your heart and mind when you talk to your father. Don't hold back, but knowing you and him, I believe it's going to work out fine for you. I do believe it will help you grow as a person. Don't do like me and live with regret for not making peace. Trust me, you don't want to live with that on your mind. My beautiful wife is cooking a delicious dinner, so come inside and get a bite."

After returning home and hanging out with Dee, Steven starts thinking about visiting his father the next day. Before the night is over, Steven says a prayer: "Dear Heavenly Father, I thank you for what you have done for me in my life. I pray that this visit with my father goes well tomorrow. I hope it helps me find peace, but it also helps him find peace. In Jesus name, I pray. Amen."

It's Saturday morning; Steven gets dressed and talks to his Mom before going to see his father. Steven's Mom asks, "How are you feeling, son?" Steven says, "I'm not going to lie; I'm a bit nervous. I just hope everything goes well." "Son, it will be alright. Going up to that prison today is going to help you and your father out. I'm so glad you're making this decision, so you can let go of all the anger built in you. I'm proud of you; you are no longer a little boy; you're becoming a man. Remember, son, speak from your heart, and all will be well." "Thank you, Mom, not just for the advice, but for being my Mom and Dad when you shouldn't have had to do that. I forever appreciate you, Mom; please don't never forget that." "I love you, son." "I love you too, Mom."

Steven hugs his Mom. As Steven hugs his mother, Lily arrives to take him to see his father. Lily sees Steven and his Mom hugging one another and asks, "Everything's ok?" Steven's Mom answers, "Yes, it is, baby; just having a mother and son Moment. And thank you for going with Steven to see his father. I'm glad that you are supporting him." "It's no problem. I know if the shoe was on the other foot, Steven would do the same for me. He's got my back, and I got his." "And that's on everything. Well, Mom, we are going to head out." "Have a nice trip."

Lily takes Steven to see his father. On his way to visit his father, Steven thinks heavily about what he will say to his father. After driving for three hours, Steven and Lily arrive at the prison. Steven looks at the prison and says, "Well, we're finally here; I believe it will go well." Lily says, "I believe it will; I want to say a prayer with you before you walk into the facility."

Lily prays with Steven before he walks into the facility. "Dear Heavenly Father, as we call upon you today, I pray that Steven finds peace with his father. I also hope they build a strong relationship with one another today and that they both start healing after their conversation today. In Jesus' name, we pray. Amen. You got this; everything is going to work itself out." Steven says, "I believe so; thank you for taking this journey with me." Lily says, "I'm with you through the good and bad. Steven and Lily hug one another, and Steven walks into the prison.

As Steven walks into the prison, he is searched by a correctional officer. Correctional Officer asks, "What's your name, young man?" Steven says, "Steven Markel Anderson Jr." The Correctional Officer starts smiling. The Officer says, "Let me guess, you are coming to see your father?" "Yes, sir." "We love your father; we call him Big Steve. He has helped out a lot of people in here. He's always talking about you, and he's going to be so happy to see you. Have a seat in the visiting room; I will tell him he has a visitor."

Steven waits to see his father in the visiting room. While waiting for his father, he hears somebody call his name. Steven looks up and sees who it is. Steven says, "Big Mike!" Steven is stunned to see Big Mike in person in prison. Big Mike was one of the guys Steven looked up to on the block due to the way he hustles and the jewelry and cars he had. Big Mike was also Steven's plug when Steven was a drug dealer. Big Mike was once the guy everybody looked up to on the block. Now, he's just another inmate in prison. Big Mike says, "Lil Steve, aka young hustler, how are you doing, fam?" Steven says, "I've been doing good, making moves out here trying to represent for our community." "I been hearing. I keep my ear to the streets. Man, you're doing your thing in a big way and doing it legit. I wish I had done like you when I was younger, but I probably wouldn't be here." "It's not too late to turn it around. I thought the same thing when I got locked up. How much time did they give you?" "I'm doing 5-10 years up in here. I'm going to be in here for a good while. I'm not sad or mad at myself for being here. It's all a part of the game; when you're in the streets, you got to accept the good with the bad. I knew what I was getting myself into. While I'm in here, I'm going to try my best to better myself and be a better man for my kids. I love what you are doing, though, young blood; don't never stop doing your thing. You give all of us from the bottom hope; I got to go. You be easy."

After talking to Big Mike, Steven sees his father walking down the stairs to come see him. As Steven's Dad walks down the stairs, he notices Steven, and he stops walking. Correctional Officer asks, "Big Steve, you know who this young man is?" Tears start falling down from Steven's Father's face. Steven's Dad stares at his son and says, "That's my son." This is Steven's first time seeing his father since he was a little kid. Tears also start flowing down Steven's face. Steven says. "Hey, Dad." Steven's Dad says, "OMG, you have gotten so big. Officer, I haven't seen my son in 14 years.

Can I hug him?" Correctional Officer says, "Go ahead." Steven and his father hug one another, tears falling down from both of their faces. Both have yearned for each other hugs for a long time. "I have missed out on so many years of your life. I'm so proud of the man you have become. Have a seat; let's talk. How you been doing?"

Steven and his father have a deep conversation. Steven says, "I'm doing good. I actually won the Rising Star Award. I feel like I owe it to you. This is mainly due to the advice you gave me about speaking from the heart; it truly resonated with me." Steven's Dad smiles and says, "I'm glad you won. I prayed for you. And don't thank me. When something is stored in the heart, it shall come to light pretty soon. I know the real reason you came here is to ask me why I wasn't there for you?" Steven expresses himself. "Yes, I want to know your story and why you chose the streets over me. I went through a lot of shit because you weren't there. I went through a lot of stuff a kid shouldn't have had to go through."

Steven's Dad starts tearing up and reveals his reason for not being there. "I'm sorry, son; I'm sorry that you and your Mom had to go through all of that pain and torment. A lot of it is due to the poor choices I made. I wasn't always a street dude, so let me explain how I got caught up. I was an A honor roll student through all my years in school. I was the smartest person in all of my classes. Even though I was valedictorian in my graduating class, and I excelled in school, my home life was very different.

When I was 15, your grandmother was struggling to pay bills, working two jobs to make sure I was straight. I got tired of seeing her struggle, so I got with my friend Rico. Rico was making a lot of money in these streets, so I got with him to do the same for my family. I only had plan on doing it until I graduated, but I got addicted to the money. I had plans on being a doctor, but with the amount of money I was making out here I didn't think I needed to be a doctor. And the money I was making benefited my family in great ways.

Then, when I was 19, I found out you were going to be born, and that changed my whole life. I told myself I would not have you struggle like I did. I hustled seven days a week in these streets to make sure you and your Mom were straight. When you was born, you brought a light to my life. I was so happy I used to bring you around everybody. At the same time, as I was a well-known drug dealer in the city, I wasn't proud of the man I became. I knew in my heart that I was meant for more than what I was doing.

When you were two, I decided I wanted to get out of the game, but I made a costly mistake. One day, my guy Rico was telling me about this plug, who nobody didn't like, who had all of this money and drugs. I saw it as a great opportunity to bring wealth to our family. And he wanted me to help him go get it. Your Mom begged me not to go, but I allowed the greed of money to take over my mind and heart. So, we went to the plug's house, held him at gunpoint, and got all of the money and drugs. In my mind, I thought we were straight; he would never know it was us because we had masks on. So, as we were about to bounce, the plug reached for his gun, and Rico shot him. Just like that, I became an accessory to murder, and my whole life changed forever. I went home and tried my best to forget it, but you can never forget when somebody gets killed in front of you. That is something you will live with forever; plus, I could have prevented the killing. At first, nobody didn't know who did it, but within ten days, thanks to DNA evidence, the police found out it was Rico and me that had something to do with the killing.

When you are deep in these streets, you get hypnotized by the money, the girls, and the attention you get. All that stuff brought up in our path is the devil's plan to keep us down. Especially for young black men. Because, at the end of the day, there are no happy endings in these streets. Streets don't have love for nobody out here." "Let me ask you this: why didn't you think of me before everything happened?" "Son, I was young and dumb. I was trying to take the easy way out to make a living, and it ended up costing me. To be honest, I was thinking of a way to make big money for us, but I was selfish, and I let the devil control my path instead of GOD, which led to a path of destruction. Every night I go to sleep I think about all of the stuff I missed out of my life, but the main thing I think about was not being there for you. My Dad wasn't there for me; I wasn't there for you. I hate that I haven't been there for you. When your Mom told me you got locked up, I was mad at myself because, in my opinion, it was my fault. If I had been there for you, you wouldn't have had to be in these streets selling drugs.

About five years ago, I started a program here called Help a Brother Out; it's all about us motivating fellow inmates in here to go on the right path in life. Something I wish I had participated in before I got locked up. In a way, I started the program because I didn't want none of these guys to deal with the consequences in life like I have. I hope and pray I make it out of here one day, and we can bond together."

Steven hears the remorse in his father's voice and comes to a decision pertaining to their relationship. "For years, I was mad at you and angry at you. It wasn't until I got locked up myself that I fully understood why you turned to the streets. I forgive you for not being there for me. I have let go of all anger against you. Seeing you has brought me peace and relief, and I want to build a father-and-son relationship with you also."

Tears start falling down Steven's father's face as he smiles. "That's all I have ever wanted all of these years. I might not be deserving of your love, but I promise you I'm going to do everything in my power to be there for you. Hopefully, I will come up for parole in two years. If so, we can spend time together outside of these walls. Your Mom told me you also got a girlfriend."

"I do her name is Lily. I thank GOD for her; she's something special. She actually came with me on the trip here; I can tell her to come in if you would like to meet her." "I would love that; I know it would be ok with the officers for her to come in. Please let me meet my future daughter-in-law." Steven brings Lily inside of the prison and introduces her to his father. "Dad, this is Lily; Lily, this is my father." Lily says, "It's an honor to meet you, sir." Steven's Father says, "It's an honor to meet you as well; manners and beauty, son, this is a keeper right here. Please have a seat. I would love to get to know the lady who is bringing happiness into my son's life."

Steven's Father bonds with Steven and Lily. After two hours of bonding and making peace with his father, visitation hours were over." Correctional Officer says, "Time's up, Big Steve." Steven's Father says, "Well, guys, that's my time. Lily, it was an honor meeting you. I'm grateful that my son has someone like you in his life. Stay being you; you are an angel." Steven's Father hugs Lily. "And my son, I'm glad you came to see me. I know this visit has brought peace to your life, but I also know this visit has made my day and has brought me peace. I love you, and I'm always here for you. And before I go, never forget who you are, son; always stay true to yourself. And always remember to know your worth and value. You are a powerful king who is going to be an inspiration to a lot of people." Steven and his father hug one another. "Love you, son," Steven says, "Love you too, pops."

After his visit with his father, Steven and Lily talk about the visit with his father. Lily says, "Your father seems like a nice man, but how do you feel after the visit?" Steven says, "I feel at peace now; that's something I have been waiting to do since I was a kid. I'm glad I made amends with my father. A lot of people don't get this opportunity, but the visit has uplifted me in a way that I have never experienced before. And again, thank you for coming with me; I know you probably aren't used to this type of environment." "I love you; I wanted to come and support you, and I want to keep getting to know every part of you, no matter what environment I have to enter."

On his way back home, Steven thinks about seeing his father and Big Mike in prison and seeing the true realities the street life brings to a person's life. Steven thinks to himself; him and his Dad lowkey lived the same life. He knows in his heart and mind that it is something he has to change in his family and his hood.

Lily drops Steven back to his house. Steven says, "Home sweet home; after being in that prison today, I'm going to try to do everything in my power to bring positivity toward my brothers and sisters in this neighborhood. We all have these unique abilities and talents, but it's sad some of us never discover it. And you have some that discover their skills and talents, but it's already too late." Lily says, "That's why it's great you dealt with all the stuff you dealt with. With all the stuff you've been through, you are living proof that it doesn't matter where a person starts in life; it's where they're headed that counts. I believe you can help influence a lot of young kids in the right direction, and I can't wait to help you with that." "Lily, this journey we are about to take will be something special." "It already is; I can't wait to see you and your Mom in church tomorrow." "I can't wait either; it's about time I get back into GOD's house. Well, I will see you and your family tomorrow." "Have a goodnight."

As Steven walks into the house, his mother is sitting on the couch waiting for him. Steven's Mom says, "Son, I've been waiting for you. How was the visit with your father?" Steven says, "It went better than I expected. I was able to get to know him. I can tell he was sincere about the mistakes he made in his life, mainly because he was not there for me. Me and him both found peace today." "I'm happy mainly for you; I can tell the way you are looking now your spirits are uplifted." "I'm grateful to have had that visit. I'm going to go to sleep and prepare for church in the morning."

Before going to sleep, Steven says a prayer to GOD. "Dear GOD, I want to thank you for reuniting me and my father today. I've been waiting to do that for a long time; I feel at peace now. I no longer feel anger and pain in my heart. I feel like a brand new person. I pray that you stay having me soar like an eagle. Just know I will follow where you lead me, GOD. In Jesus name, I pray. Amen."

The next morning, Steven wakes up to go to church with his Mom, Lily, and her parents. As Steven finishes getting dressed, he yells, "Ma dukes, you ready to go?" Steven's Mom says, "Yes, baby." Steven's Mom is dressed fancy for church. "Look at you looking like Shirley Ceaser out here." "Well, son, like you young people like to say, I got to stunt. Are you nervous about church?" "I am kind of scared about how I would be perceived by the people at the church, but I just want to have a good time with the family today." "Baby boy don't care about what anybody has to say about you. You go in there to worship GOD because he is the only person that can truly judge you. Now come on, let's go."

Steven and his mother arrive at the church before Lily and her parents arrive. This is Steven's first time going to church since he was a little kid. He's a bit nervous but is grateful to be in GOD's house. The nervousness went away as soon as Steven walked through the church and was greeted by a good number of pleasant people.

While waiting for Lily to show up, Steven runs into a former enemy. The former enemy taps him on the shoulder. Steven turns around and says, "Nikolas, hey bro, how you been doing?" The former enemies, now friends, hug one another in church. Nikolas says, "I been doing good. As you can see, I'm no longer wearing a boot or wearing crutches. I thank you so much for saving my life. If it wasn't for you, I probably would be dead. Also, when you prayed for me in the hospital, that gave me hope. I recently started working for the Norris High School Football Team as an Assistant Football Coach. Granted, I can't play football no more, but my heart will forever be in Football. Going through my situation showed me there is a lot to live for, and every day I wake up, I'm going to do something impactful each day." "I'm so glad to hear that; one thing I learned in life so far is that when we are given a second chance, we have to take advantage of it. So how long you been going to church here?"

"My family has been coming here for a few years; I just started coming to get closer to GOD. What about you?" "My first time being here; my girlfriend and her parents goes here, and they invited me to come. Speaking of which, here comes my beautiful angel right now." Lily hugs Steven and says, "Well, hello, sir, I must say you looking super sharp today." Steven says, "Appreciated, my lady, Nikolas, this is my girl Lily; Lily, this is a good friend of mine from High School." Nikolas says, "Nice to meet you, Lily. You are lucky. Steven here is one of the smartest and most gifted people I know. I got to wait for my parents to come; nice seeing you again, Steven, and thanks for everything. Nice meeting you, Lily."

Lily says, "Nice meeting you too, Nikolas; what did he mean by thanks for everything?" Steven smiles as he thinks about his past with Nikolas. "Me and Nikolas hated each other in High School, but a couple of months back Nikolas was involved in a hard situation. GOD brought me toward his way to help him out. Due to that, GOD made us brothers in Christ." "That just shows how powerful GOD is. Here comes my parents." "Let me get my Mom. I know she's talking somebody's ear off somewhere."

Steven introduces his Mom to Lily parents. Steven says, "Mr. and Mrs. Henderson, it is so great to see you again; I would like to introduce you to my Mom. Ma dukes, this is Mr. and Mrs. Henderson." Lily's Mom says. "It is such an honor to meet you; you did a fine job raising this young man." Lily's Dad says, "You sure did; this young man has God-given talents and is going to be a force to be awakened with. Well, it looks like church is about to start so let's get our praise on."

Steven and the rest of his and Lily's family sit down for church. After the praise team perform, the pastor preach the Book of David. The same story in the Bible that Steven learned about while he was in jail. Pastor Terry says, "Today, we are going to talk about the Book of David. I believe there are some souls in here today that need to hear the message that I'm going to say today."

Pastor Terry starts by telling the beginning of David's story. The part that touches Steven's soul is in the middle of the storytelling. Pastor Terry says, "Nobody believed in David, not even his own father, but God saw the potential and greatness in him. He chose David to be the chosen King of Israel. David beat the biggest person on the earth; his name was Goliath. Nobody didn't believe David would beat Goliath. David was a short guy, while Goliath was this big giant. With Jesus Christ on our side, we can defeat any obstacle that comes in our pathway. That is what David did; he defeated the biggest obstacle before him, with all the odds against him. You see, David was downed by many people that he couldn't defeat Goliath, but he believed in GOD, and when you believe in GOD great things will come your way.

One of the main things we have to do in life is not allow other people's opinions and judgment to validate who we are as people. In life, we have people who judge us about our past or the difficult circumstances we have dealt with in our lives, but that doesn't define us as people. That's not what makes a person who they are. You can come from nothing when you arrive in this life but have a fortune of everything that people said you would not have during your lifetime. In this life, it doesn't matter what type of life you were born in or the past struggles you deal with; it's where you are going in life that counts. I do not know who I am talking to, but do not let the circumstances from your life stop you from God's great pathway in your life." The Pastor's message deeply touches Steven's soul. The message motivates Steven more than ever.

After church is over, Steven goes to speak to Pastor Terry. Steven says, "Hey, Pastor, I just had to say your preaching deeply moved my soul; you have a lot of wisdom." Pastor Terry says, "Appreciated Brother Steven, it's about motivating people, but helping people see their true potential." Steven is surprised that the pastor knows him. "How do you know my name?" Pastor Terry says, "Little sweet Lily always talks about you in our prayer meetings. Plus, I'm a huge fan of your website and clothing line; I actually bought one of your shirts. What you're doing in your life right now is something beautiful. Just always remember you are defined by GOD, but also defined by yourself." "Appreciated, Pastor. I'm going to use your great words of wisdom."

After talking to the pastor, Steven talks to Lily. Lily asks, "How did you enjoy service today?" Steven says, "I loved the service today; the preaching was great. I definitely got to come back. Ma dukes, what do you think about everything? I saw you getting down up in there." Steven's Mom says, "It was great; thank you, guys, for inviting us. My son and I needed this." Lily's Mom says, "It was our honor." Lily's Dad says, "Let's get something to eat, guys."

While eating lunch, Lily's Mom ask Steven's Mom an important question. Lily's Mom says, "Ms. Anderson, in your opinion, what inspires you the most about your son?" Steven's Mom says, "His strength; my son has been through a lot in his life. A lot of people counted him out. I'm not going to lie; I counted my son out myself, but through all the odds, he made it through. I'm proud of my son; he is going to leave a lasting legacy on this earth." Steven's Mom smiles as she watches her son. After returning home from church, Steven stays thinking about what the pastor said in church and uses it as motivation to get his GED.

The next day, after GED class ends, Steven talks to Mr. Marcus. Mr. Marcus says, "Well, I guess this will be the last time I will see you in here as a student." Steven says, "I believe it will be. I thank you for all the teachings and wisdom you have laid upon me. In my heart, I feel like this is going to be it. I'm going to finish the job. A part of me is thinking about what I will do next after getting my diploma, but you know what they say: one step at a time." "I'm here for you; in all honesty, you are the best student I've ever had. You're going to do great things. Just always remember to stay believing in yourself." "Thank you for teaching me everything." Steven and Mr. Marcus hug one another. The next day, Steven studies all day for his GED test after getting off work.

It's Wednesday Morning, birds chirping outside, and the Sun is rising high. Steven wakes up with confidence and feels very motivated, like a lion walking in a jungle. He goes downstairs and sees breakfast is made for him. He sees a note that was left for him by his mother. Steven reads the letter his mother wrote for him. Steven reads, "Dear Son, I wish I could be there with you as you take your test today. Just know I'm there with you in spirit, but GOD is with you also. I pray to GOD that you get your GED today. I know how much getting it means to you. Just remember, son, believe in yourself and have faith in Jesus Christ. Enjoy the breakfast I made for you. Love, Mom."

After eating breakfast, Steven goes to his car to drive to Augusta. Steven runs into car trouble. He's unable to start his car and is frustrated. "Come on, turn on, dammit! Jeez, on all days, why is this got to happen to me. I got one hour to be there; I got to hurry up and think."

Steven thinks about what to do and runs straight to Dee's house. Steven bangs on Dee's door. Dee says as he answers the door, "Woah, young blood, calm down, knocking like the police. What's going on?" Steven says, "I got to take my GED test in one hour, and my car won't start up; I don't know what to do." "Give me one moment, and I will be right back." Dee heads back inside and gives Steven one of the keys to his vehicle. Dee says, "Don't crash my vehicle; take the key. I know you will do good today. Go ahead and get that GED, fam." Steven says, "I most definitely will thank you so much for this." Steven takes one of Dee's vehicles and heads straight to Augusta.

As Steven arrives at Brooks Tech to take his GED test, he says a prayer. Steven says, "Dear Heavenly Father, today is a big day for me. I have faith and believe in myself that I will pass this test. I ask that you stay guiding me in the right steps so I can live to my full potential. As I can do all things through Christ which strengthens me, in Jesus' name, I pray. Amen.

Steven walks into the building with full confidence and takes the GED test. If Steven fails, he will have to wait two months before he can take the GED test again. In Steven's mind, though, failure isn't an option.

After two hours of taking the GED test, Steven waits for the results of the test. Steven says, "Here we go; let's see what we got." Steven drops to his knees and starts crying. Steven passed the GED test and finally got his GED. Steven starts thinking about all he went through to get to this point: from dropping out of school, becoming a drug dealer, then getting locked up, and now is a GED graduate. Steven falls to his knees and starts praising GOD. Steven says, "I wasn't supposed to make it, man, but you brought me through GOD." Tears of joy drop from Steven's face as he calls all his friends and family and tells them he got his GED. The key question now is, since Steven got his GED, what is his next step?

411

# Chapter 15: A Rose in a Concrete World

After getting his GED, Steven goes straight to Lily's Apartment. Lily hugs Steven as she is super proud of him. Lily says, "I'm so happy for you, babe! I knew you could do it. We have to celebrate; let me call everybody for you, and I can arrange for everybody to meet tomorrow at a restaurant. Now that you got your GED, what's the next step?" Steven says, "I really don't know. I'm going to take some time and think about it, but in the meantime, let's celebrate."

After celebrating with Lily, Steven arrives home and is greeted by his mother. Steven's Mom hugs him and says, "Baby boy, I'm so proud of you." Steven's Mom hugs Steven, tears of joy falling down her face. Steven's Mom says, "I have been waiting for this moment for a long time. Just a couple of months ago, I was scared I was going to lose you, and you would end up like your father. GOD redeemed you in the right path. I'm so happy. I prayed so hard for you, son. You not only made me proud, but you made the whole neighborhood proud. You are giving hope to a lot of lost boys out here in these streets. Son, this is only just the beginning; you have a heart like a lion. Stay rising above any obstacle and always stay true to who you are. Love you, Son."

The next morning, Steven calls Judge Brown, who told Steven to call him after he gets his GED. Steven says, "Hey, Judge Brown, this is Steven Anderson. You told me to call you once I get my GED." Judge Brown says, "Mr. Steven, first of all, congrats on getting your GED. I'm very proud of you. And I still do have a proposition for you; come by my office at 12 o clock so we can talk. Bring your lawyer Dave with you also." "Sounds like a plan; see you then."

Steven and Mr. Dave arrive at Judge Brown's office to meet up with him. Judge Brown says, "Gentlemen, thank you for coming today; have a seat. One thing about me is I'm a man of my word, and Steven, I have a proposition for you. And Dave, I invited you because you saw the potential in this young man at his lowest moment. Steven, I want you to be the Youth Leader for the Mcduffie Youth Council down here in Thomson. I believe somebody like you can lead kids in the right direction. I believe you can make a great impact. So, Steven, do you accept my offer?"

Steven is amazed by the Judge's proposition but wonders why he chose him. "I'm honored, but I got to ask, why me?" "Because you're somebody that's been through obstacles in your life, and you didn't let those obstacles defeat you. That's the type of person we need for this position. You have the power to inspire many people with your story and your great words of wisdom." Mr. Dave says, "You are deserving of this, Steve; cherish the gift that has been brought your way." Steven is surprised that him, of all people, has been offered this position. But when you correct your wrongs and do good deeds, good things shall come your way. Steven responds with a smile on his face. "With all that being said, I accept your offer, Judge Brown. Let's help the youth."

After Steven returns home, a young kid who's a drug dealer who looked up to Steven when he was selling drugs says to him. Young Kid says, "Aye, Steve, I heard you got your GED. Congrats, that inspired me to go back to school and get my diploma. You give me hope that a lot of us can make it out here." Steven says, "We can, little homie; it's all about believing in ourselves and seeing greatness for ourselves in the future."

Later on in the day, Steven's family and friends meet up at a restaurant to celebrate his accomplishments. Lenny stands up with his drink in his hand and says, "Cheers to my boy Steve on getting his GED and becoming the youth leader in his hometown. Bro is a showstopper; he is just getting started out here." Steven stands up and says, "I want to thank you guys for showing up and helping me celebrate; this means a lot to me, but just know this is only just the beginning."

As Steven gets done with his speech, a waitress comes to the table to take the order. And Steven knows the waitress pretty well. The waitress says, "Well, it looks like we have a big crowd here. What are you guys celebrating? Lily says, "Celebrating my boyfriend getting his GED and becoming the Youth leader in his hometown." Steven says, "That lucky guy would be me; Dani, I didn't know you worked here." Dani is shocked to see Steven; as she looks at him, she sees the growth in him. Everything he told her he was going to do, he did it. She's proud of him as she knows all of the things he has been through to get here, but she is disappointed in herself as she wishes she had stayed believing in him. Dani smiles and says, "I just started a couple of weeks ago, and I must say I'm proud to see how successful you have become. Even when you had people who didn't see your true potential, you kept going. I'm proud of you, Steve." "I appreciate; that means a lot." "Let me get you guys' food; nice to see you, Lenny, and you too, Steven; again, congratulations." As Dani walks away, Lily asks, "How do you guys know her?" Steven says, "She's an old friend of mine who was a great supporter of mine. Sadly me and her had a falling out. I do wish her the best in life, though." Dani looks at Steven and Lily and regrets the decision she made on giving up on Steven as she could have been the lady right by Steven's side.

As everybody celebrates Steven's accomplishments, Darius's Mother walks in with a surprise guest. Darius's Mom hugs Steven. "Steven, I'm so happy for you and for what you have all accomplished. And I have somebody with me that wants to congratulate you also." A young man comes through the door and says, "Congrats, my fellow hustler." Steven yells out, "My boy!" Darius is the surprise guest and has been released from prison. Darius and Steven hug one another. Steven asks, "When did you get out?" "I just got out a couple of hours ago; I just got done spending time with my son. I had to come see you and celebrate with you, fam." All of Steven's family and friends greet Darius.

After the greeting, Steven and Darius head outside to talk to one another. Steven says, "Man, I'm so happy to see you; you look different." Darius says, "Prison will do that to you. I can't wait to start putting my plans to fruition. When I first got locked up, I just wanted to hurry and get out, but when I found out I had a son on the way, that changed everything for me. I told myself I wouldn't want him to be like me, and that's what made me want to change my life. When my son sees me, I want him to be proud of me.

As you know, I also got my GED just like you did. I'm going to be working for Dee and his landscaping company and try to go to college. I'm going to be a great father to my son and also be a great role model for my brother and the other young homies in the neighborhood. Looking at you, though, and hearing everything you accomplished while I was locked up. A lot of people didn't see greatness in you, but you saw it in yourself, and that's powerful. I'm sorry for what I contributed to your mishaps in life. I'm glad to see you on the right path. Seeing you doing what you're doing gives me hope that all of us can make it out of the projects." "My brother, GOD gave us one mind, and with that mind, we can dream and envision who we want to be. We are stars that shall shine bright; as long we stay believing in ourselves and GOD, everything will be alright. We aren't going to be in the hood forever. We're going to show the world how a person from the projects can be powerful." "That's on everything; we're going to put on for our people in a big way."

As Steven and Darius get done talking, Lily comes out to introduce herself to Darius. Steven says, "Bro, I got to introduce you to my lady: Lily, this is Darius. Darius, this is Lily." Darius smiles, "The one and only Lily; this man right here stays talking about you. He truly adores you; stay by his side; he's going to big places." Lily says, "Trust me, I know; I'm glad that me and him are connected. He's a wonderful man. He always talks about you, too. Just know we are here for you always and want to see you succeed." "That means a lot to me; all of us will shine brightly, but for right now, let's eat; your boy hungry." Steven, Lily, and Darius go back into the restaurant.

The next day, Steven gets a call from Kurt's Dad pertaining to "The Boy That Comes From Nothing clothing brand." Kurt's Dad says, "Hey, Steven, this is Mr. Vince, Kurt's Dad. I want you and your guys to meet me at a property of mine. I believe you will like what I have in store. I will send you the address." Steven says, "Sounds like a plan. I will get the guys, and we will meet you there."

Steven, Jose, and Lenny meet Kurt's Dad at one of his properties. Kurt's Dad says, "Guys, what's going on? Glad to have you here. The property I have you guys standing in is an old convenience store that I recently bought. I thought to myself, who can I sell this property to? Then I was reminded there are young kids that have an amazing clothing business that could use this property to their benefit." Steven looks around the property and says, 'I know this property probably cost at least $40,000, and I know we can't afford it." Kurt's Dad says, "Well, I actually have somebody who wants to buy this property and invest in your company because he sees potential in all three of you. Mr. Mayor, can you come inside and join us."

Mayor Scofield walks into the building, and the guys are surprised. Jose says, "Man, this is like an episode of Undercover Boss." Lenny says, "For real." Mayor Scofield says, "Well, thank you guys for joining us. I am the person that has plan on buying this property for you guys. I know you guys got your LLC, plus all of you guys made a great impression on me and on a lot of business entrepreneurs at the Golf Tournament. With this being a clothing store and a clothing line, I believe you guys can inspire a generation. Like how Kurt Cobain and Nirvana inspired their generation with their grunge style, I feel like you guys could do the same with your clothes. In my opinion, you can impact your generation with your personality, but mainly with your realness because that's what The Boy That Comes From Nothing clothing line is all about." Steven says, "You are correct about everything you just said, but I'm wondering, is there a catch?"

Mayor Scofield says, "I do want to invest 10 percent in the company because I purchased the property for you guys, and that's all I want." Lenny says, "That's not a big margin. It sounds like a good deal to me. Jose, what do you think?" Jose says, "Sounds good to me. Steven, what do you decide? Whatever decision you make, we're down with you." Steven says, "I will take you for your word. I know you guys got a contract written up, so I will take a look at it." Steven takes a look at the contract and documents for him and the guys to own the property. Steven and the guys decide to sign the papers so they can own the property. Kurt's Dad says, "Well guys, it looks like we are in business." Mayor Scofield says, "I'm happy for you guys; you all deserve it. Steven, do you mind if I talk to you outside." Steven says, "Of course."

Mayor Scofield and Steven talk to one another outside. Mayor Scofield says, "How do you feel about everything that has transpired?" Steven says, "It's like I'm in a movie, first getting my GED, then becoming the Youth Leader of the Mcduffie Youth Council in Thomson; now me and my guys own our own store at 18. It's like I'm living in a dream." "Something I learned in life is this: when you ask for something, it can be given to you. It's just like ordering a meal at McDonalds; granted, you're probably going to wait a few minutes to get the order, but eventually, you will receive your order. That's the same thing with our dreams and goals in life. You are wise beyond your years; you are already a great leader. Who knows, one day, you might be mayor. Since you're done with getting your GED, have you decided what you're going to do?"

"I decided I'm going to Brooks Tech to take up Business Management to learn more about the aspects of owning and operating a business. My ultimate goal in life is just to be an inspiration to my people." "That's what I like about you the most: your passion for inspiring people. I know for a fact you will inspire many. Stay rising, young king; the future is going to stay getting brighter."

After leaving his new property, Steven returns to his neighborhood and runs into Ms. Arlene as she is walking down the street. Steven asks, "Ms. Arlene, how are you doing?" Ms. Arlene says, "I have been doing good, baby, but not like you. Your Mom told me you got your GED." "Yes, ma'am, a lot of great things have happened: I got my GED, made amends with my father, just became the Youth leader of the Youth Council down here, and me and some friends of mine are opening a clothing store down here for our clothing business."

Tears of joy start falling from Ms. Arlene's face. Ms. Arlene hugs Steven. "You are one of a kind. Ephesians 6:10 in the Bible says, "Be strong in the Lord and his mighty power. Put on all of God's armor so that you will be able to stand firmly against all strategies of the devil, put on salvation as your helmet and take the sword of the spirit, which is the word of God, pray in the spirit at all times and on every occasion. You are the definition of putting salvation as your helmet and taking the sword of the spirit. GOD is using you as an example that it doesn't matter what hardships or struggles you go through; you can still make it. Here's my main question for you, though, Steve, are you at peace?"

Steven starts reflecting on his life and thinks about everything he has been through and where he is today. With a small tear coming out of his eye, Steven gives Ms. Arlene an answer, "I am at peace; all I can say is the future shall be bright."

Five years later, in the present time, there is an event going on in the Harmony Projects congratulating the Business Man of the Year. Judge Brown, who is now the Mayor of Thomson, is presenting the Business Man of the Year award. Judge Brown says, "Ladies and gentlemen, thank you for coming today; I am proud to present the Business Man of the Year award to Mr. Steven Anderson. I met this young man when he was a defendant in my courtroom a couple of years ago. Now, he is a businessman and a pillar of his community. He is living proof that it doesn't matter where you come from in life, but you can be anybody you want to be if you just believe. I would like to present the 2023 Businessman of the Year Award to Mr. Steven Anderson.

Right after getting his GED, Steven went to College and got an associate degree in Business Management. Steven is now a successful businessman who owns several businesses and is a great role model in his community. He stays giving back to the youth and his neighborhood—everything he envisioned for himself he has accomplished. Judge Brown says, "Welcome Mr. Steven Anderson, to the stage." The crowd claps for Steven.

Steven says, "Mayor Brown, thank you for presenting me with this award; it's an honor and privilege to be honored with this award. First I got to thank the Lord up above for the blessings he has brought my way. I would like to thank my Mom for always being there and never giving up on me. I would like to thank my father. Ever since you got out of prison, you have inspired me and helped me a lot with my business. And I am proud of everything you have accomplished since you got out. To my wife, Lily, thank you for always being there and supporting me. You were one of the first people that saw greatness in me and I'm glad that GOD brought you by my side. And to everybody who is from the Harmony Projects, we might come from the bottom, but always remember that we are strong and will never fold. Greatness is upon all of you; just believe in the vision. To all my friends and family who are in the crowd today, thank you for all the love and support you have given me. Again, guys, thank you for this award."

After giving his speech, Steven is greeted by family and friends. Steven's Mom hugs him and says, "Proud of you, baby; you're living in your purpose, and I love it. I knew you would be something special." Steven's Mom is now retired and helps Steven with his businesses as she is his assistant. She lives in a beautiful house in a gated community that her son bought for her, and she started a foundation for single mothers.

Steven's Dad hugs Steven and says, "Son, you are one of a kind; you're inspiring a lot of people with what you're doing. I'm proud of the man you are. Steven says, "I'm proud of the man you are to Dad." After getting out of prison, Steven's father continued with his mentorship program, Help a Young Brother Out, where he helps mentor young kids. He works for his son's real estate company. Steven hugs his parents.

Lily hugs Steven and says, "Baby, you were amazing up there, and we're just getting started. We are going to stay rising." Steven and Lily are now happily married and have started a foundation to help Young Adults. Steven says, "That's on everything, my sweet lady." Lily is now a nurse at a hospital in

Augusta, but also part owner of a clothing company called The Girl From the Dirt with Steven.

Steven is congratulated by Nikolas. Nikolas says, "Great job, Steve; proud of you." Steven says, "Proud of you too, coach." Nikolas is now the football coach of Norris High School Football. Danny, Darius's little brother, daps up Steven. Danny says, "Congrats, big homie, and thank you. If it wasn't for you, I probably wouldn't have been the quarterback of the high school and one of the most scouted athletes in the nation." Danny, Darius's little brother, is now one of the highest-scouted athletes in the United States.

Darius hugs Steven. Darius says, "My boy, look at you; it's good to see where we came from, first slinging on blocks, and now doing our thing in the corporate world." "A lot of people thought we wouldn't be nothing, but we turned nothing into something. Project Boyz going to stay going up." Darius is now a Cyber Security Analyst and is happily married to Destiny with a second kid on the way."

Steven is also congratulated by some of the friends he met while in jail. Hector says, "Amigo, happy for you. you're popping your stuff out here." Hector now owns his own flower company."

Michael says, "Congrats, Mr. Chess King, because you definitely know how to make moves." After getting out of jail, Michael got his medical license back and is now a doctor again.

Robert says, "Proud of you, little homie; it's crazy that all of the things we envision for ourselves in jail, we're living in it right now." Steven says, "Yes, indeed, brother, thank you for everything." Robert now owns his own trucking company.

Steven is congratulated by Officer Brown, Mr. Dave, Mr. Joe, and his former teachers."

Steven sees Rich at the event. Steven says, "Mr. Ballplayer, I saw you last night on TV; you balled out." Rich says, "Well, you know I had to show them who the boss on the court is. We envisioned this just five years ago, and now we're living in it. I'm proud of you; we made it, fam. With tears coming out of both their eyes, Steven and Rich hug one another." Rich is now a professional basketball player who plays for the Atlanta Hawks.

Sophie and Jose greet Steven. Jose says, "My brother, aka Steven the Don, I love you, man, and I'm proud of you." Sophie says, "We are proud of you; you are a true inspiration." Jose now owns his own designer business and is still a co-owner with Steven and Lenny for The Boy That Comes From Nothing clothing line. He is also engaged to Sophie. And Sophie is still running her Boss Lady fashion line.

Lenny and Diamond greet Steven. Lenny says, "Big homie, you stunting on these folks, showing these people how somebody from the trenches can be powerful." Diamond says, "Brother, I'm so happy for you; I knew since we were kids you would be something special." Lenny says, "Thank you for everything, my brother. I owe you everything. If it wasn't for you, there's no telling where I would be." Steven says, "Thank you, bro, and I'm proud of what the both of you have accomplished also." Lenny and Diamond are now both married to one another. Lenny still owns The Boy That Comes From Nothing clothing store with the guys. He just started his second business and is a youth pastor at his church. Diamond is now a nurse who works alongside Lily.

Dee greets Steven. Dee says, "You did it, little homie; seeing you up there brought tears to my eyes. Never seen nobody from our hood make an impact like you have. Your motivation to the streets keeps going." Dee still runs his landscaping company and is still happily married to his wife and kids.

As Steven is still talking to people, a young kid runs up to him. As Steven looks at the young kid, the young kid reminds him of a younger version of himself. The Young Kid says, "Excuse me, sir, I'm from the Harmony Projects, just like you, trying to make it out. I'm in High School trying my best to graduate. Can you tell me what made you successful?" Steven starts reflecting on his life as he looks at the sky and gives the kid an answer. "My belief in myself and Jesus Christ. Also, when you're from the gutter like us, it's hard for us, but the key thing is never letting hard times in life stop you from your destiny. And remember, we are Boys from the Dirt; we might stumble or fall down, but we stay getting back on our feet so that one day we can live in our vision. And my brother, I'm living proof that a boy that comes from nothing can make it."

426